(Slow Burn) PBK
FiC
BAN
BKS

5/17

JUST ONE TOUCH

JUST ONE TOUCH

A Slow Burn Novel

MAYA BANKS

AVON

An Imprint of HarperCollinsPublishers

JUST ONE TOUCH. Copyright © 2017 by Maya Banks. All rights reserved. Printed in the United States of America. No part of this book may be used or reproduced in any manner whatsoever without written permission except in the case of brief quotations embodied in critical articles and reviews. For information, address HarperCollins Publishers, 195 Broadway, New York, NY 10007.

HarperCollins books may be purchased for educational, business, or sales promotional use. For information, please email the Special Markets Department at SPsales@harpercollins.com.

FIRST EDITION

Library of Congress Cataloging-in-Publication Data has been applied for.

ISBN 978-0-06-241018-4 (trade paperback)
ISBN 978-0-06-246650-1 (hardcover library edition)

17 18 19 20 21   DIX/LSC   10 9 8 7 6 5 4 3 2 1

JUST ONE TOUCH

SHE ran through the gnarled forest, her breaths of fear spilling raggedly from her lips as she sought to suck in precious oxygen. Another tree limb slapped her painfully in the face and she brought up her hand in automatic protection. She flung it out to protect herself from other obstacles shielded from her in the inky night where overcast skies hid the half moon, rendering her blind as she continued to crash haphazardly through the woods.

It was only a matter of time before her absence was detected and they wouldn't wait until dawn, just an hour away, to set the dogs loose to track her. They had the advantage. She had none.

Her feet became entangled in exposed tree roots and she slammed face-first onto the ground, all the wind knocked brutally from her lungs. She lay there wheezing for breath as tears burned. Gritting her teeth in determination, she shoved herself upward and took off once more, ignoring the crippling pain that seized her entire body.

They would find her. They'd never rest until they had her

back. She couldn't stop. Couldn't give up. She'd die before going back.

A shiver went up her spine when she heard a distant coyote howl. She pulled up sharply when she heard another and then a third, much closer than the first. The sound of the entire pack yipping and barking only to end in long, haunting howls made goose bumps rise on her skin, which was already prickled from the cold.

They were in front of her. They were the only obstacle between her and the open land that represented her freedom. *Possible* freedom. But then she realized if the coyotes were near her, then perhaps the dogs sent to track her would be reluctant to follow her this closely to them.

Her chances with wild coyotes were infinitely better than— and preferable to—the fate she knew awaited her if they dragged her back to the compound. Already the sky was beginning to lighten in the east, but not enough to give her a clear sight path. Knowing she had to keep moving at all costs, she plunged recklessly ahead, shoving thick bramble away as she tried to gain passage through the dense vegetation.

Her bare feet had no feeling in them. Cold and the many scrapes and bruises had rendered them numb. For that she was grateful. The moment she regained sensation she knew she would be helpless.

How much farther? She'd studied the maps, snatching stolen moments, taking great risks to delve into the off-limits areas of the compound. She knew the path she'd chosen—north—was the shortest path out of the heavy forest that encompassed the compound. She'd committed every marker to memory and had taken a due-north route from the northern edge of the compound walls.

What if she hadn't taken a straight line? What if she was merely running in circles? A sob escaped her bloodied mouth but she bit it back, purposely injecting pain by sinking her teeth into her bottom lip.

And then another sound stopped her cold. Panic scuttled up her spine and she went rigid in terror. Dogs. Still a distance away, but the sound was unmistakable and one she was intimately acquainted with. Bloodhounds. And she'd certainly bled all over the woods, leaving a trail that would be child's play for the dogs to track.

With a sob, she pushed forward again, her flight more desperate than before. She hurdled stumps and downed branches, falling half a dozen times in her frenzied flight, fueled by desperation and a lifetime of despair.

A cramp knotted her thigh and she gasped but ignored the crippling pain. And then another seized her side. Oh God. Slapping her hand over her side, pushing, massaging the taut muscle, she turned her tear-streaked face upward to heaven.

Please help me, God. I refuse to believe I'm the abomination they named me. That I'm to be punished for what wasn't my choice. They don't do your work. I can't—won't—believe that. Please. Grant me mercy and grace.

The dogs seemed closer and she could no longer hear a single coyote. Perhaps they were frightened away by the loud baying and sheer number of the dogs hunting her. Another cramp nearly sent her to her knees, and she realized that soon she'd no longer be able to continue running.

"Why, God?" she whispered. "What is my sin?"

And then suddenly she burst from the last snarl of bramble and bushes and was so shocked to have no further obstacle that she tripped and went tumbling forward, landing flat on her face on a . . . gravel road?

She slapped her hands down on the ground, curling her fingers into the dirt and gravel. Droplets of blood soaked into the dirt, and she hastily wiped her mouth and nose with the arm of her tattered hoody.

Elation swirled. She'd made it!

Then she quickly got back to her feet, castigating herself. She hadn't made anything yet. She was merely free of the woods, and now she was more of an open target than before. But at least she would know where she was going.

She hoped.

She began sprinting down the road, quickly moving to the ditch when the rocks tore into her tender feet. The grassy area wasn't much better, but at least she wouldn't leave such an obvious blood trail on the roadway.

To her shock, just a hundred yards ahead was what looked to be a small filling station and fruit stand. She put on speed, her gaze darting back and forth as she neared it. She even glanced over her shoulder, terrified that she'd see the dogs behind her. And worse . . . the elders.

Seeing nothing and no one yet, she continued to run toward the gas station, not having the first clue what to do when she got there. She knew little of the modern world outside of the books she'd snuck, the magazines and newspapers. It seemed strange and scary, enormous beyond her wildest imagination. But she'd armed herself with as much knowledge as possible in preparation for this day.

Her freedom.

As she reached the station, she observed an old truck parked out front with a tarp completely covering the bed. She glanced side to side and toward the station, thinking quickly of her options. Then she heard voices.

She immediately squatted behind the truck, her heart thundering in her chest and her breath coming out in painful wheezes.

"Gonna run this produce to our Houston stand. Expect I'll be back 'round two this afternoon. You need anything from the city, Roy?"

"Not this time, Carl. But be careful. I heard traffic is a real bitch this morning. Something about a pileup on the 610 loop."

"Will do. You take care too. I'll see you later."

Making a quick decision, she eased the tarp upward to expose the open tailgate and to her delight, saw just enough room for her to huddle between the freight boxes containing fruit and vegetables. As quietly and as quickly as she could, she slithered over the tailgate, her body screaming its protest. She slipped the tarp back down, hoping she'd left it arranged as she'd found it, and then pushed her body forward as much as possible so she wouldn't fall out.

The older man was driving into the city. The thought terrified her. The very idea of being swallowed whole by a city as large as Houston was paralyzing. But it would also play to her advantage. Surely the elders would have much more trouble tracking her in a city teeming with life. Not to mention they couldn't very well abduct her in broad daylight. Both things they could readily do as long as she remained where she was in the rural, isolated area well north of Houston.

She held her breath as she felt the truck shake with the slam of the driver's door, and then the engine cranked and the vehicle began backing up. She put a fist to her swollen mouth and bit into her knuckle when the truck halted its backward motion, but a mere second later it began moving again and she could tell they'd pulled onto the gravel road.

Thank you, God. Thank you for not forgetting me. For letting me know I am not what they named me and that you aren't the vengeful God they named you.

TWO

ISAAC Washington collected the to-go cup of coffee and two bagels and headed out of the small shopping center a few blocks from the DSS offices. Due to the popularity of the locally owned coffee shop and bakery and the fact that it was the morning rush hour in Houston, he'd had to park all the way on the other side of the highway in the extended parking lot by the strip mall.

Good thing it was winter—or as close as Houston weather ever got to winter—so he didn't sweat his ass off by the time he'd made the long trek. As it was, there was a slight chill to the air—courtesy of last night's cold front—that was a nice change from the oppressive heat of summer and fall.

He was almost to his SUV when he noticed that his driver's side door was open. Son of a bitch! He was forever forgetting to lock his damn door and, well, he left his keys in the ignition more times than not when he was doing a quick in-and-out someplace.

He dropped his coffee and bagels, quickly drew his firearm

and then stepped between two cars before slowly advancing around the front, keeping low as he closed the distance between him and his vehicle.

He continued to do figure eights around the remaining cars until he had just one left to go. He crept around the back, wanting to come up behind whoever was trying to jack his fucking SUV, trapping the punk between the open door and a loaded pistol.

Cautiously he rose just enough to get a good sight line to the perpetrator and frowned when he saw a slight figure in a hoody with several holes in it. The jeans weren't in any better shape and the hood of the top was covering the guy's head. Judging by the size, it looked to be a teenager looking for a joyride.

Whoever it was sucked at stealing a vehicle. The guy wasn't even checking his six to make sure the owner—or anyone else— was coming up on him. When he started to slide behind the wheel, Isaac knew he had to act now and hope to hell the dude wasn't packing firepower.

"Hold it *right* there," Isaac said, coming into view, his gun trained at the back of the kid.

The body in front of Isaac went rigid and then the teenager slowly turned around to face Isaac. All the wind rushed from Isaac's lungs in one forceful exhale when he got his first good look at the "kid" trying to steal his ride.

A young woman stared back at him with huge, frightened eyes. She'd gone unnaturally pale, which made the blood and swelling around her mouth and nose even more evident. Even dressed as she was, in the condition she was in, the only thing that came to his mind was that he had to be staring back at an angel.

Strands of pale blond hair stuck out from the hood of her

top, framing marred but otherwise porcelain skin. The blood looked incongruous with the image she projected. As his gaze drifted down her poor attire, he noticed she wasn't even wearing any damn shoes. It wasn't freezing by any means, but it was too cold to be running around dressed as she was and barefooted.

"Please, don't hurt me," she whispered, her lips trembling.

Her entire body shook, her hands held upward in a gesture of surrender. His earlier anger over having his vehicle stolen fled and was replaced by a strong sense of protectiveness—and rage at anyone who would hurt such a tiny, innocent-looking woman.

"What's your name?" he asked gently as he lowered his gun before sliding it back into its holster.

Terror flared in her crystal-clear blue eyes. He'd never seen such an unusual shade of blue in someone's eyes before. That, paired with the blond silky hair and her delicate-looking, fair skin, further cemented the image of an angel in his mind.

"I-I c-can't tell y-you that," she stammered.

His face softened. "Are you in some kind of trouble? I can help you. My job involves helping people who are in trouble."

She shook her head emphatically. "Please just let me go. I'm so sorry about . . ." She broke off and her hand fluttered weakly toward his vehicle. "I just didn't know what else to do."

"Honey, I don't think you've taken a good look at yourself," he said gently. "You're bruised and bloodied up pretty bad and you're not dressed for the weather. You don't even have shoes on."

"I need to go," she whispered. "I *have* to go."

Isaac took a step forward, sensing her urgency and her impending flight. He didn't know why it was so important to him not to let her just leave, but hell, could he let anyone just walk away after seeing the condition this mystery woman was in?

She shrank back, drawing into herself, a protective measure that was likely instinctual and not at all conscious. He could feel his expression blacken at the thought of why she might assume she had so much to fear from a complete stranger. But then again, he could see her point. They hadn't exactly met on the best of terms. Certainly not when he'd been pointing a gun at her.

"Let me buy you something to eat. I just came from the coffee shop in the strip mall, but when I saw my door open, I ditched my coffee and bagels. I think you could use a little warming up too."

He could see the yearning in her eyes at his mention of food and hot coffee and his gaze automatically swept over her slight figure, noting her thinness. There were hollows under her eyes that suggested lack of sleep as well as lack of having anything to eat.

God damn it. She had all the hallmarks of a domestic abuse victim. Boyfriend? Husband? Hell, maybe it was her father. She looked young enough to be a teenager. Her eyes were the only thing that made her appear older. Eyes that had seen too much. Old beyond her years. Educated the hard way, at the University of Life Sucks.

"I swear to you I won't hurt you," he said in a soothing voice one might use with a wild animal. "I'm sure as hell not calling the police or turning you in for attempted auto theft."

Her face went even whiter at his mention of the police and he cursed his reckless words.

She opened her mouth to speak when Isaac heard the familiar whine of a bullet, and then the car next to him shuddered violently on its frame as the shot struck the tire, the echo of the shot reverberating loudly in the distance.

"Down!" he yelled, lunging for the woman.

As he circled his arms around her waist, he turned to thrust her to the ground so he could cover her with his body. He was simultaneously reaching for his own gun when more shots struck his SUV and the car beside it, and then pain exploded through his chest.

His mouth fell open in shock and for a moment he was rendered incapable of movement. Then the strength left his legs and he collapsed like a deflated balloon, hitting the ground with a thud right beside the woman, who was sprawled on the concrete a mere foot away.

"No. No!" the woman said hoarsely. "No, no, *no!*"

Her face appeared over his, concern and agony making her features starker than before. A sense of shock—and failure—assaulted him as he felt his body begin to shut down. After everything he'd encountered and fought against over the past few years, *this* was the way he was going out?

"Listen to me," he rasped, startled when his voice came out as the merest thread of a whisper. "Get in my SUV. The keys are in it. Haul ass out of here. Get yourself to safety. There's no helping me. I'm dying."

"No!" she denied. "I won't let you! I *won't!*"

She scrambled to him and suddenly her face hovered over his, her blue eyes flashing nearly silver as her hoody fell back, and a cascade of curly pale hair blew around her neck as wildly as her hands ran over his bloody chest.

"Go," he croaked, coughing and then choking as the metallic taste of blood coated his tongue.

Then she closed her eyes and her forehead creased in agony, and he gasped when her palms pressed deeply against his chest.

It was like being hit by lightning. An electrical charge. His heart stuttered, then paused and his vision went blurry, her delicate features growing dimmer.

He stopped fighting the inevitable—death. He relaxed, expecting the end to come at any moment as coldness reached the inner core of his body. But then the most amazing sensation jolted him to awareness. Warmth. The most beautiful warmth he'd ever felt in his life slowly seeped into his veins, carrying with it the whispers of hope, of a new beginning,

He tried to speak, to protest, to ask if this was the end, but all he could do was gasp as his vision cleared once more and he saw the unbearable strain etched into every facet of her face.

Never had he felt a more wonderful sensation. Being warmed from the inside out. His laboring heart and lungs seemed to relax and still, and there was no pain, only . . . a resurgence. As if a surgeon had his hands inside Isaac's chest, meticulously repairing the mortal damage done by the bullet.

He lifted his hand, shocked that he had the strength to do so. He greedily sucked in sweet, life-giving breath and marveled that not only was there no pain, but that what he felt couldn't be described. No drug, no narcotic or pain-relieving agent could ever produce such a wonderful feeling.

He reached for her wrist, shackling it with his fingers, unsure of what she was doing but knowing she had to stop. She was in danger. The shooters were still there. Could be coming for her even now.

Her eyes flickered open the instant he touched her and his own eyes widened when he saw the turbulent whirl of flashing colors that made the once pale-blue orbs undetectable.

"Don't," she gritted out between tightly clenched teeth. "I am not finished. You must let me finish. I will *not* let you die."

He let his hand fall away, numb with shock over what he was witnessing—no, experiencing. He'd thought by now nothing could shake him, catch him off guard, that nothing unbelievable was ever so in the world he lived and worked in. But never had he imagined such power, such an ability. Surely only God had the power over life and death?

But no, that wasn't true. Men and women killed one another every day. Humans decided death far more than they ever decided life, and yet this woman . . .

His entire body shuddered and the upper half jolted upward as if he'd been defibrillated. He felt the cold concrete through his blood-soaked jacket and realized that he was warm. Alive. Whole. And breathing.

He stared at her in awe, only to see utter despair wash through her soulful eyes. Her hands fell away and she pulled her knees to her chest, hugging them as she rocked back and forth, tears sliding down her cheeks.

Realization was swift. By saving him—*healing* him—she'd given up any opportunity to run, to escape. The resignation on her face broke his heart even as he lay gasping in wonder at being alive. He cautiously ran his hand over his chest and drew it away to see the smear of blood on his palm. But it came from his clothing. No longer was *he* bleeding. No longer was there a gaping wound in his chest. But there was residual weakness, or maybe he was just in shock—who wouldn't be? He was in no shape to haul himself *and* her into his vehicle and make a getaway. He'd just end up getting them both killed, or rather himself killed *again*. Her only shot was to get the hell away and leave him behind.

He reached over and snagged her ankle, shaking her gently to gain her attention. She glanced up at him with dull eyes and he gestured to his SUV.

"Hurry, before they come! The keys are there. Go!"

She shook her head even as more tears trickled down her face.

"God damn it, get out of here! I have backup coming and I still have my gun. Someone will be here for me in a few minutes. For God's sake *move!*"

For the first time, hope flickered on her face even as shock registered in her eyes. He started to shove himself upward when he found himself flattened by her entire body as the sound of more bullets punched a dozen holes into the side of his SUV.

Her eyes were wide, a swirling vortex of pain, grief and abject terror. He *felt* her intense stare to the bone, the weight of her stare drawing him straight into its turbulent depths. There wasn't a single part of her that wasn't pleading with him, and when she spoke, he flinched at the anguish so thick in her every word.

"You have to hide. They can't know of what I did. No one can. Never tell anyone about me. *Please*," she begged, wrapping her tiny hands around his, lifting them and pressing them to her chest. He felt the erratic beat of her heart against his knuckles and then registered the fact that she was shaking violently.

He didn't dare draw attention to the fact that the pool of blood he was still lying in would be a dead giveaway or she'd completely fall apart. As it was she was only holding on by the thinnest thread. Letting go of her hands, losing her touch left him feeling suddenly bereft and hollow, like a part of him had died. But he pushed her toward his vehicle anyway, his tone purposely harsh and commanding as he pinned her with his most forceful and authoritative stare.

"Go while you can, damn it. I said someone will be here for me any minute now. Don't you dare let those fuckers get their hands on you."

God, he hoped he wasn't lying to her about his back up. He'd managed to activate the "oh shit" button, as his teammate Eliza had named the transponder they all carried with them. He wasn't far from headquarters. Hell, someone should be on the scene already.

"For fuck's sake *listen* to me" he bellowed. "I don't know who the hell you are, lady, or what the hell you did, but I'm not about to let someone who just saved my life get her ass killed instead."

She scrambled up, keeping her head low, and slithered between the door and the interior. She turned and looked one last time at Isaac and he could swear she was pleading with him for forgiveness. The door slammed behind her and the engine cranked. He winced when the SUV lurched forward, stopping then going, the brakes screaming in protest.

Well, fuck. Maybe it hadn't been such a good idea to send her away. It didn't appear that she even knew how to drive. Hell, she didn't look old enough to be driving. He ground his teeth in frustration over his inability to provide her with the protection she so desperately needed and just prayed he'd made the right decision.

Testing his body's responses, he rolled to his stomach and then belly-crawled around the front of the remaining vehicle, his knuckles white from his fingers being wrapped so tightly around his gun. He leaned heavily against the grill of the car and waited, one hand still rubbing his chest in disbelief.

"Isaac," a low, distant voice called. "Sitrep."

Isaac blew out his breath in relief when Zeke, one of the newer DSS recruits, announced his arrival.

"You got backup?" Isaac said in a voice just loud enough to carry.

"Dex is with me. What's going on, man?"

"Shooters. Didn't get a bead on their location, but they weren't close when they first shot. No idea if they're still on scene or if they're closing in. Watch yourselves, and I hope to fuck you're packing some serious heat."

He heard Dex snort and took that as an affirmative.

"You take a hit?" Zeke demanded.

Isaac opened his mouth and them promptly shut it again. How the fuck did he answer that question? Yeah, he'd taken one hell of a hit. He should be on his way to the morgue to get a toe tag, but it was as if the wound had never happened. As if his heart and lungs hadn't taken a mortal blow. How to explain *that* to his partners?

"No time for questions. I'll explain later. Get me the fuck clear. Just don't get *your* asses shot."

"Not in the game plan, my man," Dex retorted. Then he paused a second. "You need a medic?"

"No. Just wheels."

"Shadow is on scene now and is scouting for the shooters. If they're still here, he'll take care of it," Dex said.

That much was true. Shadow came by his code name because he was just that. A shadow that no one could detect. No one would ever know he was on them until it was too late.

"Good idea," Isaac murmured. "But tell him to watch his six. There was more than one. Shots were fired from at least three different sources."

"He'll take care of it," Dex said confidently. "I'm more concerned about your condition."

"I'm fine," Isaac insisted. "Just don't like being a sitting duck."

"We'll have you out of here in no time. Just relax and keep your guard up. Zeke and I have you covered and Shadow will take care of any remaining threat."

But what worried Isaac was that he hadn't been the target. His thoughts froze. Or . . . Maybe he had been? The shots hadn't been aimed at the woman. Not a single bullet had hit the vehicle she was closest to, while he, on the other hand, was lucky he still had his balls. This hadn't been about him at all, nor was it a random shooting by rank amateurs. It had been an intended abduction resulting in collateral damage—almost. They wanted him dead and her alive. At least only one of the results they'd wanted had been accomplished.

Either way the mysterious angel was in serious trouble, and he'd be damned if he left her helpless and running from the assholes who'd made it clear they didn't play nice. He had no idea what they wanted with her, but even as he contemplated the reasons why, he rubbed a hand over his chest—his completely healed chest that showed no sign of the very real kill shot. His unmarred chest gave him a pretty damn good idea why a bunch of damn assassins had her on the run and terrified out of her mind.

If her abilities were known—and he'd bet his last dollar that someone knew about her miraculous gift—they wanted it. There were any number of factions that would stop at nothing to have her under their thumb.

Fuck that.

She'd saved his life. And even if she hadn't, after one look at the bruised and bloodied, fragile slip of a woman, there was no way in hell he wouldn't move heaven and earth to make *damn* sure she was protected at all times. This was personal. This wasn't a DSS mission where she'd be assigned to a team or another man. She was *his* to protect. And if Caleb, Beau or Dane had a problem with that, then they could go to hell. He'd hand in his resignation and take on the job himself.

"What the fuck?" Zeke roared as he and Dex appeared in front of Isaac. "You said you hadn't taken a hit. Jesus fuck, there's blood everywhere. You need an ambulance and to get to the hospital *now*."

Isaac sighed and then simply pulled away the blood-soaked shirt so they could see the unmarred flesh of his skin.

"Look, guys, I know what it looks like but if I told you what happened, even with the shit you've been exposed to working for DSS, you'd likely haul my ass to a psych ward."

"Try us," Dex said calmly.

Isaac blew out his breath and then related the entire story, from the time he saw his door open to when he took a mortal shot to the chest and was miraculously healed by the mystery woman.

To their credit, the only response they displayed was a rise in their brows.

"So you just let her go? Without protection? So those assholes get another shot at her?" Zeke asked in disbelief.

"I made her take my ride," Isaac snapped, glaring at Zeke. "I wasn't in a position to protect *myself*, much less her, and I couldn't justify such a huge risk to her when I knew my backup would be here within minutes."

Shadow appeared seemingly from nowhere, but his scowl indicated he'd been privy to the entire explanation. Which was just as well, since Isaac really didn't want to rehash it.

"And that helps her how?" Zeke asked in a persistent tone.

Isaac shook his head at how slow on the uptake Zeke was. And reinforced his glare, his nostrils flaring in irritation. "She took my *company* vehicle."

Realization flickered in his teammate's eyes.

"You going after her?" Shadow asked, drawing Isaac's ire from Zeke and right on himself.

"What the fuck kind of question is that?" Isaac snarled.

"Okay, so *when* do we go after her?" Dex questioned.

"Now," Isaac said impatiently. "Hell, it didn't even look like she knew how to drive, so it's not like it'll be that hard to tail her. While we're wasting time here rehashing shit that can wait, they could be on her even now."

Zeke gave him a concerned look. "Shouldn't you go to the ER or at least the private clinic used by DSS just to get you checked out?"

"And tell them what exactly," Isaac said his patience fraying precariously. "That I was shot in the chest, heart and lung hit? Bled like a stuck pig and I felt myself dying and oh, by the way, my mystery woman laid hands on me and healed me? I *felt* the damage being repaired from the inside out. Trust me. If a doctor examined me, he'd find no evidence of a gunshot wound."

Dex whistled. "That's some pretty crazy shit."

Isaac snorted. "After knowing what Ramie, Ari and Gracie can do, nothing should surprise you by now."

"Yeah, man, but this is different," Shadow said quietly. "She *heals* people. She pulled you back from the brink of death. You said it yourself. You felt yourself dying, shutting down, and yet now no one would ever know you'd even been injured at all. That goes beyond the psychic abilities our women possess."

"Yeah," Isaac said, blowing out his breath. "Now you're getting it. Which is why I have to find her as soon as possible before someone else nabs her. She's going to have a target on her back for the rest of her life. Probably always has. Makes sense to me now that I know the story and why she was trying to steal my ride, why her face was so battered and she wasn't dressed for shit. Hell, she didn't even have shoes, for fuck's sake."

Zeke's expression blackened to the point of being murderous. "You never said some asshole had beat her up."

Dex and Shadow's reactions were no less volatile.

"Help me up and let's get the fuck on the road. We'll need to activate the tracking system on my SUV so we know where she is and how far she got, or if she's still going."

Though it was left unsaid, the grim expressions on their faces reflected the knowledge that she could already be in her pursuers' hands.

THREE

"FUCK," Isaac ground out from the passenger seat as Zeke drove and Shadow and Dex rode in the backseat of the SUV.

The men came to attention, and Zeke cast him a sideways glance. "What's up?"

"There's been no movement on the tracking device ever since I first got a bead on it a few minutes ago."

Shadow shrugged. "Maybe she bedded down somewhere hiding."

Isaac shot a look at Shadow over his shoulder. "You didn't see her eyes, man. I've never seen eyes that were windows right into a person's soul until I looked into hers. I don't think for one minute she would stop running once she took off in my ride."

Zeke looked pensive. "And yet she stuck around to save your sorry ass."

Isaac sighed and rubbed a hand down the front of his face. "Yeah. She did. And why? I don't get it. Never seen a woman that terrified in my life and it pissed me off. And yet when I told her to go, that there was no hope for me because I was fading fast, she refused. And after . . . God. Once she healed me, she was shattered because she knew she'd given up any opportunity to escape because of me."

"Hell of a note," Dex muttered.

"Yeah, tell me about it," Isaac growled.

Why had she saved him?

People that desperate didn't normally think of anything but themselves and yet she risked everything, had seemed grief-stricken that he was dying.

He wanted an answer to his questions, but in order to do that, he had to find her.

"So where's your SUV?" Shadow asked. "If it hasn't moved then it should be easy to find, right?"

Isaac held up the transmitter but didn't volunteer the fear that gripped his chest over what they'd find. Or wouldn't find.

"Three miles out," Zeke said in a low voice. "Isolated area. She had enough sense to at least get to a secluded spot."

"Hell, I doubt she knew where the hell she was going," Isaac bit out. "She didn't even look like she knew how to drive, or was even old enough to drive for that matter."

"What did she look like?" Shadow asked curiously.

"Like an angel," Isaac murmured. "A bloodied, bruised, *beautiful* angel. Bluest eyes I've ever seen and long, pale blond curly hair. Hell, maybe I hallucinated the entire thing and I'm just crazy as fuck."

"You didn't imagine being shot or us finding you lying in a pool of your own blood," Dex growled.

"Just ahead," Zeke said in a grim voice.

At his statement, the men drew their weapons. Zeke came

to a halt a few moments later and they were out of the vehicle, guns drawn.

"Split off in pairs," Isaac said. "According to the tracker, it should be straight ahead, just off the road in the woods. Zeke, you're with me. Shadow, you and Dex circle around and come in from the front."

Shadow and Dex melted into the woods while Isaac and Zeke took the straight route to where the SUV should be located. They were barely into the woods when Isaac halted and held up his hand to Zeke, pointing to where the SUV was parked haphazardly in a large area of brush, as if she'd tried to drive straight through it. To hide.

Isaac swore, not forgetting for one moment the sheer enormity of her selflessness and her willingness to risk everything so he wasn't lying dead in his own blood right now. There was no way in hell he was going to let her fend for herself. Once he had her in his possession, he was going to do everything in his power to get her to open up to him and he damn sure wasn't ever going to let her take that kind of risk again.

He crept stealthily toward the vehicle, Zeke taking his six. When he peered into the front seat, his heart sank and his pulse ratcheted up. God damn it. Had they gotten to her? Then he peered into the backseat and his knees went weak with relief. Until he got a full view of her.

She was curled into a tight, protective ball and even in sleep—and she looked completely wiped—there were deep lines in her forehead and she twitched and made whimpering noises. Or was she unconscious?

Had he done this to her? Had saving his life made her so helpless that she was incapable of defending herself?

And then he softened in places he didn't think he had the capability to ever be soft in when he saw the tracks of silent tears sliding down her cheeks.

Zeke was no less affected and muttered a grim, "Fuck. What are we going to do, Isaac?"

"She goes with me," Isaac said in a tone that brooked no argument. "No way I'm leaving her to those assholes. God only knows what was done to her before she managed to escape."

Zeke's expression became thunderous. "We should put a team on her so she has twenty-four-hour protection."

"She goes with me," Isaac snarled.

"Dane's going to want a full report and a say in how this goes down."

"Fuck what Dane wants. She's mine. This has nothing to do with Dane. She isn't technically a client. Therefore, whatever is done will be done my way, my decision."

Zeke's eyebrows went up, but he wisely didn't push the point.

Isaac carefully opened the back door, not wanting to awaken her with a sudden noise. She'd already endured far too much fear and stress. He wanted to end that shit for her right now. But he also knew that she wasn't someone who was going to trust very easily. He would have to be patient and extremely gentle with this woman.

He hesitated, almost touching her, as he stared at the tiny ball she'd curled herself into. She looked so fragile he was *afraid* to touch her. Hell, his hands were enormous compared to her bones, her hands, her arms. What if he hurt her unintentionally? But no way in hell would anyone else be the one to carry her anywhere.

Holding his breath, he gently smoothed one hand up her

arm, testing her awareness. But he shouldn't have worried. She didn't so much as flinch. She was clearly beyond her limits, and guilt surged freshly through his veins.

She was a fucking miracle. He was still numb and in disbelief that he was here, whole, no evidence of having been shot, instead of in a morgue where his teammates would have the unfortunate task of identifying his body.

Knowing he needed to hurry, he slid his other hand beneath her soft body and then moved the hand resting against her arm so that he could put his arm underneath her legs. He lifted her effortlessly and began to back out of the vehicle, paying close attention to her every breath, movement or facial expression.

She still hadn't shown any sign of rousing. This both worried him and relieved him. Holding her close to his chest, close enough that he could feel both their heartbeats, he strode toward his vehicle even as he gave orders to his teammates.

"Get rid of my SUV and then disable the tracking device. I'd destroy it, but Beau would throw one hell of a fit. But make it disappear for a while. When it's safe . . . someone can retrieve it."

When it's safe. Now there was a leading statement. Knowing as little—which was nothing—about the situation he was now squarely in the middle of, having any idea when it would be over was the least of his concerns. Knowing what he needed to know in order to keep her safe and protected against harm? That was his number one priority. She'd saved his life without knowing a thing about him other than that he was dying a foot away from her. There was no way in hell he would allow her to suffer or be afraid a single day longer.

"What do you want to do, Isaac?" Shadow asked as Isaac carefully laid the woman in the backseat of their SUV.

When Isaac was satisfied she was as comfortable as he could make her, he turned back to see all three of his teammates gathered around him, their expressions concerned and questioning.

As much as he hated the idea of leaving the woman he considered his, as crazy as the idea of her belonging to him may be, his responsibility, to anyone's protection but his, he knew he couldn't simply disappear without giving Dane and Beau an explanation. He dragged a hand through his hair and muttered a curse. Then he pinned the three men with his intense stare.

"I have to go in and let Dane and Beau know what's going down and that I'm out of commission for a while. I need the three of you to take her to my place and lock it down. I don't want her out of your sight even for a second. I'm trusting you to ensure nothing happens to her. I'll make it quick and be back as soon as possible, but I need you to do this for me."

"You know we'll do whatever you need, man," Zeke said quietly. "Even after. This isn't something you should be doing alone. That's not the way we work and you know it."

"But this isn't an official assignment," Isaac began.

"Shut the fuck up," Dex said rudely. "Granted we haven't worked for DSS as long as the rest of you. We're the new recruits. But we've been here long enough to know that this isn't the way shit ever goes down. We're a team—family—and that means not leaving you on your own just because she isn't an official fucking assignment. So suck it up. Can't speak for the others, but you've got me as long as you need me. I'll have your back and whatever you need done. All you have to do is say the word."

Zeke and Shadow didn't say anything, but their expressions said it all. They weren't going anywhere either.

Isaac breathed out a sigh of relief. "Thanks. I really appreciate this. Let's move out. I need you to take her to my place. One of you stays on her every single minute. I don't want her waking up alone and terrified. The other two need to scout the entire perimeter and make damn sure no one's poking around. This won't take long at HQ, and I'll meet you back at my place as soon as possible."

"You got it," Zeke said. "No one will get close to her, Isaac. Swear it to you on my life."

Isaac gave him and the others a chin lift. "That was never in doubt. Dane only hires the best, so even if I didn't already know how steady y'all were, just the fact that he hired and put his stamp of approval on the three of you would be enough for me to trust you with my life—and hers."

Dex tossed him the keys to the other SUV and Isaac stole one last glance at the woman who'd miraculously healed him. He hated leaving her even for a short while, but he had no choice. Clenching the keys in his fist, he forced himself to turn and start walking to the other vehicle.

"Keep me posted," he said, turning back for a moment. "I want to know if she comes around, how she is." Then he sucked in a breath and stared at his teammates, not caring what they could read into his tone or expression. "Keep her safe for me," he whispered.

"You know we will," Dex said in a quiet voice. "Now go so you can get back to her."

FOUR

ISAAC parked in the garage where DSS was headquartered in downtown Houston and quickly got out. He needed to make this short and sweet and then deal with whatever the consequences were. He didn't give a shit whether he had Dane and Beau's stamp of approval or not. It wasn't even negotiable. If they wouldn't stand down, he'd simply walk away.

He jerked in surprise at that thought as he got out of the elevator on the floor of the DSS offices. Quit? Walk away? From a job that was his entire life? The job that consumed him to the exclusion of all else? Never would he have imagined *any* scenario where he'd choose something else over his job—his teammates—his . . . *family*. But he wouldn't even have to think twice in this situation.

She needed him and he owed her more than he could ever repay. It was also obvious she was in serious trouble, and if he didn't protect her, who would?

He walked into the offices and nearly ran into Eliza. He

hugged her fiercely and she didn't even threaten to cut his nuts off, instead hugging him back just as fiercely.

As he stepped away, his gaze inspected her, leaving no detail out. She looked relaxed. Happy. Healed. There was a soft light in her eyes that had never existed before. Isaac supposed that was what love and redemption did for a person.

Then he also realized something else and frowned. "What the hell are you doing here, Lizzie? You aren't due back at work for another . . ."

She scowled. "Three weeks. Yeah, yeah, I know. Not sure who the bigger asshole is—my *husband* for arranging three months off or Dane for agreeing to it. All without my knowledge or anyone asking *me* how much time I wanted off."

"You were shot, woman. You nearly died," he said gruffly. "Cut yourself—and us—some slack, okay? Especially that poor bastard you married. You damn near died in his arms. Hell, you did die."

Her eyes softened and then she frowned again. "I get it, but three months? It's not as if I hadn't already had time off before the wedding."

"Uh, do me a favor, Lizzie. Don't push to come back just yet. Not until I get a chance to talk to you, okay?"

Her eyes immediately became piercing, concern crowding her features as she took a step back. "What's going on, Isaac?"

He rubbed a hand through his hair. Lizzie not being back at work could be a huge help to him. It would mean he could enlist her help with his current problem. Hers and that of her husband, Wade Sterling. He had connections Isaac didn't.

"Look, I don't have time right now, Lizzie, swear. I have about thirty seconds to catch Beau and Dane while they're both still in the same office. But I'll fill you in later, okay? I may need your help. Yours and Sterling's."

Eliza frowned even harder, her concern sharpening as she took in his words. "You need me to stick around until you get done, then?"

Isaac sighed and shook his head. "I'll get in touch with you and Sterling later if that's okay. I have something to take care of after I talk to Beau and Dane."

"Why don't Wade and I just come by later. How about seven? I'll bring dinner," she said.

Relief made his head a little light. He'd been worried as hell about leaving his charge to speak to Lizzie and her husband and if they came over, not only would they see firsthand what he was dealing with, but he wouldn't have to leave her.

"That would be great. And thanks, Lizzie."

"Anytime, Isaac. You know that," she said softly. "Now go so I can go home and after giving my husband a piece of my mind, I'll inform him that our plans have changed for this evening."

Isaac grinned. "Sure that won't be a piece of your ass you give him?"

Eliza scowled and then flipped him off as she stalked from the office. Isaac laughed and held his grin until she left. Then he heaved in a deep breath and hurried toward Dane's office, where he knew Beau would be.

He knocked once and then stuck his head in. "You two have a minute?"

Dane looked surprised to see him, but Beau scowled.

"Where the fuck is my SUV?" Beau demanded. "And why the hell did it go offline earlier today?"

Isaac rolled his eyes as he took a seat in front of Dane's desk.

"It's fine and in one piece—mostly. Just had some technical difficulties."

Dane lifted one eyebrow. "Those difficulties have anything to do with you wanting to speak to us?"

"Yeah," Isaac said after a brief hesitation.

Beau's scowl transformed into a look of question and of concern. "Everything okay, Isaac?"

Isaac rubbed the back of his head, not sure of how the hell to explain the morning's events. They'd likely think he'd finally lost what was left of his marbles. So he just put it out there bluntly. It was the only way he knew how to be.

"This morning when I stopped to get coffee and bagels, someone tried to steal my ride. Then I got shot in the chest and damn near bled out all over the fucking parking lot."

Both men's eyebrows flew upward.

"What the fuck?" Dane asked in a low, scary voice. Then he blinked. "Wait. You said shot. In the chest. Then how the fuck are you sitting across from me calmly *telling* me you got shot, and why the fuck aren't you in a goddamn hospital, and furthermore, who is the asshole who tried to kill you? And why the hell are we just now hearing about this?"

His fury crackled through his office, but Dane was seriously protective of the men and women who worked for him.

"He didn't *try* to kill me," Isaac said softly. "He did. I was dying. Knew I was dying. I could *feel* myself dying. I knew it was the end, that my time was up. Scariest fucking thing I've ever experienced in my life and yet . . . I was calm. Accepting, I guess. Never really thought about death or dying, which is stupid, I know, with what we do and the close calls we've had. And after Lizzie . . ." He stopped when Dane flinched and went pale. Dane was still dealing with almost losing Lizzie when she'd damn near died the same way Isaac was sitting here calmly telling them he'd nearly gone down.

Beau and Dane exchanged puzzled, alarmed looks. Then both shook their heads as if trying to understand what the hell Isaac was saying to them.

"What the fuck?" Beau asked in a low voice. "Isaac, are you sure you're all right?"

Isaac sighed and rubbed his hands over his eyes. "Look, I know I sound crazy and you're wondering if you need to drag me to a psych ward. After I'm done explaining this entire day to you, if you still have any doubts, you can call Zeke, Dex and Shadow, because they were all there. I hit the 'oh shit' button and they got there a few minutes later."

"Then where the fuck are they now?" Dane asked, his eyes narrowing.

Isaac held up his hand. "I'll get to that. Just let me finish."

"One of us is losing his mind," Beau muttered. "I think it might be me. Finally. I need a fucking vacation. With my wife. If I could guarantee she'd stay out of trouble for more than a day, we'd take one. Right now."

"Let me back up to the part about someone trying to jack my ride."

"It wasn't the same person who shot you?" Dane asked.

Isaac shook his head. "As I was walking back to the truck, I noticed the driver's side door open and cursed because I'd left the keys in the car. I dropped everything, drew my gun and snuck up on the person. It was obvious it wasn't a professional, and equally obvious she had no idea what the hell she was doing."

"She?" Dane and Beau both demanded, latching on to his wording.

Isaac nodded before continuing. "She never even checked her six. Just as she was about to get in, I stepped around the back and pointed my gun at her and told her to hold it. It was only after she turned around that I even knew it was a woman and not some damn kid. And Jesus. She looked like an angel. Bluest eyes I've ever seen in my life. Pale porcelain-looking skin and long blond hair with crazy curls and twists in it. And she was barefooted. But worse than her not being dressed for the weather and her trying to steal my ride was the fact that some asshole worked her over and did a real number on her."

Dane's and Beau's expressions darkened. A growl rolled from Dane's throat and he gripped the edge of his desk.

"She was bloodied and bruised over most of her face, neck and what skin I could see. Who the hell knows how bad it was in places I couldn't see. She was terrified of me and begged me not to hurt her. And she apologized, for fuck's sake. For trying to steal my vehicle. She said she didn't know what else to do, that she had to get away.

"I was trying to talk her down when someone opened fire on us. Rifle shot and from a good distance away. I was trying to get her down and my gun out when I caught a bullet right in the heart and lungs. Fuck! Never felt anything like it in my life, and I'd just as soon never experience that shit again."

Dane and Beau were staring in bewilderment at his chest covered by a simple T-shirt, no evidence of any injury anywhere.

"This is where it gets weird, but well, you two are certainly accustomed to the weird and unexplained, so you shouldn't even blink an eye over this."

Dane's brow furrowed while Beau just stayed focused, his concentration on Isaac's story absolute.

"I knew I was dying and there was no helping me. I'd already activated the call for backup and knew someone was on their way. I told the woman to take my vehicle and go, to get out of there before whoever was shooting got close enough to either kill her or take her. And now I know they wouldn't have killed her, but they sure as hell would have taken her."

"What happened?" Dane asked calmly, sensing something huge.

"She was hysterical and kept screaming *no* over and over, and then said she wouldn't let me die. She wouldn't! And then ...Jesus. I don't even know how to say this, but she put her hands on me. Her entire body tightened and her expression was strained to the point of agony. She looked as though *she'd* been the one shot and that she was in horrific pain. And she fucking healed me. I felt her warmth from the inside out as it spread throughout my entire body. It was like ... a miracle. She's a fucking miracle. My miracle. Afterward it was as if it had never happened. And she was devastated, her arms wrapped around her knees, rocking back and forth in complete despair. I realized that she'd given up any chance of escaping by deciding to save me. I was still a little weak, probably from shock more than anything, and I knew backup would be arriving shortly but she might not have that much time, so once again I told her to take my vehicle and go. She finally did, and I regretted telling her to do it when I saw it didn't appear that she even knew how to drive."

Dane's brow crinkled again. "How old is this woman, Isaac?"

Isaac shrugged. "No clue. My guess is early twenties, but who the hell knows? I could see how someone could easily mistake her for a child or a teenager, but her eyes. Jesus, when you look into her eyes, you see someone a hell of a lot older."

"So you lost her? She's gone?" Beau asked incredulously.

Isaac scowled. "Fuck no! I waited until Dex, Zeke and Shadow got there. Explained everything to them because when they saw all the blood, they wanted to take me straight to the hospital. Using the tracking device on my vehicle, we followed her to where she'd pulled off into a wooded area several miles away, and I found her in the backseat, unconscious and crying in her fucking sleep."

"Jesus," Beau muttered.

"Tell me about it."

"So what exactly did you need to talk to us about?" Dane asked in puzzlement.

Isaac sucked in his breath as he stared at the two men he considered not just friends, but family. "She's not a DSS client, but there is no fucking way I'm turning my back on her. I left her with the others so I could come talk to you two, but then I'm going back and I'm going to do whatever's necessary to get her to confide in me, and then I'm going to protect her and figure out a way to take out any threat to her."

He paused again for a moment to let his statement sink in.

"And I need to ask for a leave of absence to do that," he said quietly.

Beau frowned and Dane's head came up, his eyes narrowing with anger.

"What the fuck?" Dane growled. "Leave of absence? What the hell, Isaac?"

"I can't give DSS my full time and concentration and do what I need to do for her at the same time," Isaac said in a low voice. "It wouldn't be fair to her or you. If that's a problem, then I'll resign and you can fill my position."

"You need to shut the fuck up now and quit talking before I lose what's left of my goddamn temper," Dane snapped.

Beau didn't look any happier.

"When did you get the idea that I or Beau or anyone at DSS would ever turn their back on someone who is not only in great danger and need but also saved someone very dear to us all, just because she isn't a paying client?" Dane asked through gritted teeth. "Jesus Christ, Isaac. We damn near lost you today and the woman you've sworn to protect is the only reason we still have you and aren't making fucking funeral arrangements instead. You'll protect her all right, but so will the rest of us. She gets my and DSS's full priority from now on."

"Means a lot," Isaac said around the knot in his throat.

"You don't get it, do you," Beau muttered. "You've risked your life for the most important person in my life. In Zack's life. In Wade Sterling's life for damn sure, and you've risked your life for us time and time again. Dane and I just had to sit through listening to you talk about damn near dying, and only because this woman risked her life to save yours are you able to sit here in front of us, whole, not dead. And you don't think that would mean something to us? That she wouldn't mean something to us, no matter who she is, what she's done or not done or what kind of baggage she brings to the table? Or that we wouldn't all take an active role in protecting her and eliminating the threat to her?"

The knot only grew larger in Isaac's throat.

"She's pretty goddamn special," Dane murmured. "I mean God, when I think of what Ramie, Ari, Tori and Gracie can do, it's mind-boggling enough. But this woman pulled you back from death. She performed a fucking miracle. I'd be more surprised if she wasn't in danger or if she didn't have assholes constantly trying to take her so they could take advantage of her powers. Because Isaac, she's always going to be in danger. No matter if we eliminate the current threat to her, with what she can do, she will never be safe."

"I know," Isaac said softly. "But she will never be without protection."

The room went silent while Dane and Beau digested Isaac's response, but they didn't comment on it.

"Where is she now?" Dane asked.

"For now, my place with Dex, Shadow and Zeke guarding her. I need to get back as quickly as possible. I don't plan to keep her there. It's too risky."

"You got a plan?" Beau asked.

"Yeah, or at least an idea. Just need to finish working it out when I get back and hopefully get some intel from her."

"Let us know if you need anything, and I mean anything, Isaac," Dane ordered. "If it's all the same, I'd rather not be making funeral arrangements for one of my own."

Isaac smiled faintly. "You always were a fucking mother hen."

"You've been talking too much to Lizzie," Dane muttered.

"No, but I did see her when she left and she wasn't very happy with you," Isaac said with a grin.

"She's just pissed because not only does she work for an overbearing, overprotective asshole but now she's married to one as well, so there's nowhere she can go to escape it."

Beau and Isaac laughed, but they also knew it was very true.

Isaac rose. "Hate to cut out so quickly, but I have to go. She was still unconscious when I left her, so I need to get back so I can figure this shit out."

"You going to report in later?" Dane asked.

"I'll call one way or another. Just can't promise what information I'll be able to give you."

"Good enough. And be careful, Isaac. I do not want you getting shot again."

"No shit," Isaac muttered as he walked out of Dane's office.

He paused at the doorway and turned back to the two men he not only worked for but considered his only family.

"I need you to be patient on this. I don't want to drag DSS into this yet. Not until I know the whole story and know what we're dealing with. It's too dangerous. If any connection is made between her, me and DSS, then you'll all be in danger. The wives will be in danger. It's obvious that this woman is highly sought after and that they'll stop at nothing until they have their hands on her. Knowing now what she can do, I understand why. This is bigger than anything we've ever come across and I don't want anyone in this organization to be collateral damage like I almost was. I know this slays the control freak in both of you, but I need you to stand down and wait for my move. I'm not going to do anything stupid. I'll absolutely call if and when I need help. But for now I have to keep all risks to a minimum and I have to keep her off the radar. But I'll report in. I won't keep you in the dark. And at any time if I sense we're in any danger, you'll be the first to know."

Dane nodded slowly. "Don't do what Eliza did, Isaac. I'll be pissed. No going it alone to protect the rest of us. We're big boys and we make our own choices. You're family and nothing is too much to ask of us. For now, I agree with your play, but I'm not going to sit around on my hands and do nothing for long. So find out what you need to know and find out fast so we can assess the situation and come up with a plan going forward. If she can do all you said she can and did do, then the people after her aren't just going to give up and walk away at the first sign of difficulty. They'll just go harder after her and they won't care what kind of mess they make in the process. And Isaac?"

Isaac's gaze lifted to his team leader and drifted over to Beau, who was staring every bit as intently at him. "Yeah?"

"You need to understand what you're taking on. This isn't a temporary assignment where we take out a threat and then the client walks away safe and able to resume their life. Someone with her abilities is always going to be sought after. Someone will always want to use her, control her, and it'll never go away. You need to think about that before you decide just how involved you want to be in this. You've already hit their radar and you damn near died. There's no shame in walking away and letting one of us take on her protection. Just say the word and I'll make it happen."

Rage boiled in Isaac's veins and he barely managed to hold on to his temper. Barely. Only the knowledge that these men and this organization would go to the wall for him just as he would for them every goddamn day prevented him from putting his fist right through Dane's face.

"She's mine, Dane. No one else's. I told you I'd ask if and when I need backup or help. Until then, it's better that none of you are associated with her or are seen anywhere near her. She risked everything to save me when I could have been no better than the assholes trying to get to her. She sealed her fate in that moment because I'm not going anywhere. I need time to hear her side and I have a feeling she's not just going to volunteer any information about herself, so I'm also going to need time to gain her trust and I'm going to prove to her that she can trust me. I appreciate the offer. More than you know. But she isn't a DSS client or assignment. She's mine, and I'll protect her with my life."

Dane sighed but nodded then held up a hand to stop Isaac before he left. "If you can get any information from her at all, call Quinn and put him to work on it. God knows he already spends twenty-four seven with his goddamn computers. Might as well give him some real work to do and let him wow us with his technical prowess. His pride is still smarting over the fact that Lizzie is very likely far more adept at hacking than he is, but she pretends to be dumber than she is to spare him the embarrassment."

Dane snorted at the very idea of Lizzie playing dumb, but she had a soft spot for the youngest Devereaux brother and it didn't surprise Isaac at all that she'd play down her abilities to make him look better.

"Good idea," Isaac said, as he turned to hurry out. "I'll give him a call if I have anything he can work with."

FIVE

ISAAC parked in his garage and then hurried in through the garage entrance. He was met by Dex, whose expression gave nothing away.

"How is she?" Isaac demanded.

Dex shrugged. "She's been out like a light. Never even stirred when we carried her in and put her in your bed."

In his bed. Something within Isaac settled at those words, as if everything had righted itself. Then concern took over his momentary inattention.

"She hasn't come to even once?"

Dex shook his head. "We've taken turns watching her. Didn't want her to wake up and freak out, so we've made sure someone has been in the room with her so we could calm her fears if she roused. But she hasn't so much as twitched. She looks like she's completely out of gas."

Isaac frowned and then pushed by Dex on his way to his bedroom. Zeke was in the living room watching television.

He paused at the door of his bedroom and turned back to the two men.

"Eliza and Sterling are coming over at seven with dinner. Since Lizzie is officially off for another three months and Sterling is a man of many talents, I've enlisted their help. If at all possible, I want to keep DSS off the radar with this. I don't want my actions to bring danger to everyone's doorstep. Our women have suffered enough, and I won't be the cause of more pain to any of them."

"You want us here for the sit-down?" Zeke asked carefully.

Isaac stared at him and then at Dex. "Yeah. But only if you want to be. This isn't official. It's off the books and you won't be paid for it."

Dex scowled. "Fuck that. You think our offer has anything to do with money?"

Isaac shook his head. "No, but you need to know what you're getting into and what getting into this means."

Zeke shook his head. "Just shut the fuck up before you piss me off even more than you already have. Go check in on your girl and give Shadow a break. We'll let him in on the plan."

Isaac acknowledged Zeke's words with a chin lift, and then he opened the door and slipped into his bedroom.

He sucked in his breath when his gaze lighted on his mystery angel. She was curled into a protective ball in the middle of his bed, her unruly curls spread out over his pillow. The bruises were still evident on her face, but it had been cleaned of the blood and she wasn't wearing what she'd worn when she'd been taken here.

Irrational jealousy crawled up his nape, seizing his chest as he turned to where Shadow sat.

"You undressed her?"

His words came out as a snarl before he could take the time to control his outburst.

Shadow blinked in surprise. "Not me personally. But shit, man, we couldn't put her to bed in those ragtag clothes and with blood all over her. And we needed to know the extent of her injuries. We had no way of knowing how badly she was hurt. I would think you would want her to rest comfortably and not wake up believing herself still in the nightmare of before."

Isaac closed his eyes, wishing he could recall his words and the fact that he'd practically bared his damn soul to his teammate.

"Sorry," he said gruffly. "Is she . . . is she okay?"

Shadow rose and walked to where Isaac stood, but his gaze never went to the woman but instead locked on to Isaac. "It doesn't look serious. Just looks like she was knocked around. She has some bruises on her abdomen and one hip in addition to the ones on her face, but the bleeding stopped a long time ago. Most of the fresh blood was . . . yours."

"Christ," Isaac muttered. "Who the fuck would rough up such a tiny angel?"

"Good question, but you aren't going to get your answers until she wakes up, and here's some advice, man. If you don't want to scare the fuck out of her, get rid of the scowl. She's going to be terrified enough when she wakes up in a stranger's bed after all she's gone through. You're going to need to be easy with her if you want her to trust you."

Isaac expelled a long breath and rubbed his neck wearily. "Yeah, I get it. And thanks, man. I appreciate the help. Dex and Zeke are waiting for you outside. They'll fill you in with what's going on or what will go on."

Shadow took it for the dismissal it was and with a nod, he exited the room, leaving Isaac alone with the woman who'd saved him. He moved quietly to the bed and slid into it beside her, staring down at her delicate, ravaged features. Rage consumed him all over again. Was this the price she'd paid for her miraculous gift? Were people hunting her so they could control her and her gift?

He knew the answer. Of course they were. He'd witnessed the hell that the other women of DSS had endured, each of them possessing an amazing psychic or supernatural talent. Even now, they were vulnerable. Targets. But they had the best protection possible. They had husbands who adored them and who would die for them. They had the rest of DSS, who'd die for them just as their husbands would.

But this angel had nothing. No one. Until now.

Unable to resist, Isaac gently traced his finger down the unbruised side of her cheek and then tenderly tucked a wayward lock of her hair behind her ear. Leaning down, he pressed his lips to her forehead.

"Never again will anyone hurt you," he whispered, a vow. "Never will you have to face the world alone. I will protect you with my life. A life you saved even though I was nothing to you."

She stirred restlessly and he froze, afraid he'd awakened her, and it was obvious she needed sleep. Healing sleep. Apart from whatever hell she'd endured before the parking lot incident, healing him had sapped her of any remaining energy. Thank God he'd found her before someone else did.

But she merely snuggled deeper into the covers, burrowing her head into the mound of pillows in his bed. Unable to resist the urge, he slid closer to her and carefully wrapped an arm around her slight body, pulling her into his much larger frame. She sighed as his body heat enveloped her, and she wiggled closer to him as if wanting or at least needing his warmth and the security and safety he'd promised her.

She moved her head from the pillow and nestled it against his chest, her hair tickling his nose as her scent washed over him. It was a gesture of trust even if she wasn't cognizant of it. Or maybe she'd just been devoid of any kind of human touch, tenderness and gentleness for so long that she was drawn to it.

He settled in, pulling her closer until they were skin to skin, and he closed his eyes thinking he was fucked. Well and truly fucked. He should be putting distance between them. There was too much he didn't know and he couldn't afford to make assumptions. That wasn't the man he was. He was a man who dealt with cold, hard facts. The truth. Not supposition or maybes. Assuming anything in his line of work could get him killed.

She felt right against him. So small and fragile, and it riled his protective instincts like nothing ever had. He couldn't resist touching and caressing her baby-fine skin even as he felt like an asshole for taking advantage of her when she was sleeping.

His fingers ran lightly up and down her arm and then up to stroke her long, curly hair. She brought him contentment, which was ridiculous considering the very real danger they were all in and the fact that he knew nothing about her. She could belong to someone else.

His mood immediately blackened. If she belonged to someone else, then they didn't deserve her and they damn sure weren't protecting her and taking care of her like they should. No matter what used to be, she was his now and even as he knew that was an arrogant, presumptuous statement, he also knew it was true.

He was interrupted from his thoughts by a light knock on his door.

"Eliza and Wade are here," Zeke called in a low tone.

Reluctantly, Isaac extricated himself, already missing her warmth and softness. Oh yeah, he was fucked in a big way. But his first priority was keeping her safe. Anything else was secondary to that. Even the way he felt about her.

Hopefully she'd remain asleep until he could hammer out a plan with Eliza and Sterling. Then and only then would he awaken her and lay it out. And hope to hell she wouldn't resist him becoming a very permanent fixture in her life.

He was a man who knew what he wanted and never hesitated to go after it, and he wasn't about to change the way he lived his life now. This woman was his and her future was linked with his. It wouldn't be easy. He didn't expect it to be, but nothing good ever came easy and he wasn't about to let her go without one hell of a fight, and he never lost.

SIX

ISAAC returned quietly into the bedroom to see that his girl was still asleep. Except she wasn't as deeply under as he'd left her. She was restless, tossing and turning, and when he saw the silent streams of tears sliding down her pale, bruised cheeks, his chest tightened to the point of pain.

With no hesitation and giving no thought as to whether he should, he pulled back the covers and slid into bed next to her. He wrapped his arms around her and tucked her head beneath his chin. She trembled even in sleep, and he'd give anything in the world to be able to prevent the fear he knew she felt every hour of every day.

It was instinctual. He didn't even consider what he was doing when he pressed his lips to her soft curls. He wanted to stay this way and simply enjoy holding her in his arms, but they didn't have time. She didn't have time.

Reluctantly he pulled away, putting distance between them. He slid his hand over her shoulder, gently shaking her.

"Baby, I need you to wake up. Can you do that for me?"

Her brow furrowed and her eyelids fluttered as though they were too heavy to open. Her mouth pursed and then fear chased across her features as she tensed beneath his touch.

"Hey," he said softly. "I won't hurt you. Nothing will ever hurt you again. I need you to believe that. Now can you open your eyes so we can talk?"

She went rigid and pulled away, her eyes slowly opening, but it gutted him when her gaze settled on him and panic swamped her entire face. She immediately began scrambling backward on the bed.

He shackled her wrist to prevent her from falling off the other side of the bed and swore when his action only seemed to alarm her more.

"Honey, listen to me. I'm never going to hurt you, and if you keep moving away you're going to wind up on the floor on the other side of the bed. We need to talk. Nothing more. Can you trust me enough to do that?"

She nibbled nervously on her bottom lip, and he'd never been more tempted to suck that lip between his and soothe the damage she was currently doing to it. And he still didn't even know her name, much less her story.

Patience was not one of his stronger virtues. Hell, it wasn't even in his vocabulary, but he knew he'd have to go slow and pull on every reserve he possessed not to overwhelm her and start demanding the answers he needed.

To his satisfaction, she scooted over a few inches so she wasn't about to take a fall, and she sat up against the pillows behind her. She looked nervously at him and he released her wrist. Not because he wanted to, but because he needed her to know she could trust him and that he wouldn't do a damn thing she was uncomfortable with.

"How did I get here?" she asked in a small voice. "Where am I?"

"You're safe," he said firmly. "As to how you got here, we found my SUV in a wooded area with you passed out in the backseat. You've been out for hours and you were an easy target there, parked in the open, unconscious. Anyone could have found you and taken you. I'm just thankful as hell that I found you first."

"Why?" she whispered.

Her response enraged him. It took everything he had not to explode on the spot. Jesus, but this woman evidently was so used to no one giving one fuck about her that she was genuinely perplexed as to why someone would actually want to help her. That someone would care.

"You saved me," he growled. "You put yourself at great risk to save someone you didn't even know, and there was no way in hell I was going to leave you to whatever those fuckers who are after you have planned for you."

Tears filled her eyes and she hastily looked away so he wouldn't see her distress. Taking a chance, he gently cupped her chin and turned her back to face him.

"What's wrong, honey? Why are you crying?"

"Because they'll never let me go," she said in a resigned voice. "They'll never stop looking for me, never give up, and anyone in their way they'll dispose of, just like they tried to do to you."

"Lucky for me, then, that I had my own little guardian angel to save me."

"You should get as far away from me as you can," she said with utter gravity. "No one who helps me is safe."

He growled and she jumped, eyeing him nervously. He moved closer to her and then cradled her cheeks with both his hands, his palms engulfing her small face.

"You aren't getting rid of me, baby. Now, there are other things we need to talk about and we don't have much time. I need some answers from you so I can keep you safe."

"The less you know about me, the safer you'll be," she said in a low voice.

"Fuck that. Let's get something straight right now. You aren't protecting me. I'm protecting *you*."

He could swear he saw relief flicker in her eyes just before it was replaced by fear. He'd remove it permanently if it was the last thing he did.

"What's your name, honey?" he asked gently.

She blinked in surprise.

"I can't keep calling you 'baby' or 'honey' forever."

She blushed, and he found it adorable.

"No one has ever called me anything sweet before," she said wistfully.

"I didn't say I'd stop calling you honey or baby or a number of other endearments, but I do need to know your name because no one else is going to call you those other things but me," he growled.

Surprise flashed in her eyes and then she blushed again, and it took all his restraint not to kiss her.

"J-Jenna," she stammered.

"Last name?"

To his surprise, shame crawled across her face and she turned away, tears sparkling on her lashes. What the fuck?

"I don't know," she whispered. "I was just Jenna. Not important enough to have a last name."

Again, what the fuck?

"Jenna is a pretty name. It suits you. Perfect name for a beautiful woman."

She turned back to meet his gaze, her expression hopeful. Jesus, was she so accustomed to rejection that she expected it at every turn? Did she not realize how sweet and heart-stoppingly beautiful she was? Stupid question. Of course she didn't. This was a woman who'd never been assured of her self-worth. A woman who felt she had no worth. He wanted to put his fist through the wall.

"What's *your* name?" she asked shyly.

"Isaac. Isaac Washington. At your service, ma'am," he said with a charming grin.

She smiled and holy fuck, what a smile she had. He made a vow then and there to coax them out of her as often as he could, because something told him she didn't smile a lot, nor did she have a whole hell of a lot *to* smile about.

Then he became serious. "Jenna, I need to ask you some questions and we don't have a lot of time, because I'm moving you to a safe house in the next hour. And I know you'll have some questions before you blindly trust me. I get that."

She stiffened, and apprehension once more sparked in her eyes.

"Please don't be afraid, honey. Not of me. Never of me."

"I'm afraid *for* you," she burst out.

Isaac sighed. "Okay, before we get into what I really wanted to discuss, I think it's a better idea to tell you who and what I am so that your fears will be eased."

She looked puzzled.

"I work for a security company. Personal protection. We're the best, Jenna, and that's not an idle boast. Our job is to protect people and we're damn good at it. So you don't need to be worried about me or any of the men who will take part in protecting you."

Her eyes widened at that statement.

"They will offer peripheral protection, but I am the one who will protect you. The only damn one," he said gruffly. "And listen to me, Jenna, because I don't make promises lightly. Anyone who tries to hurt you or take you away from me will have to come through me to do that."

"But you don't even know me," she said softly.

"You're right. But I will."

It came out as a vow. Matter of fact. Inevitable. She looked too stunned to respond to his promise.

"But why?" she choked out.

He touched her cheek, stroking it in the lightest of caresses. "You may not know why yet. But you will." Another promise.

"Now, tell me about the people after you. I assume they want you because of what you can do."

Her expression turned bitter, but before she could respond, a forceful knock sounded at the door. She jumped, her gaze jerking to the closed door and Isaac shouted, "Not right now! Whatever it is can wait. Just give me a goddamn minute," he bellowed in frustration.

Instead of going away as Isaac had ordered, someone knocked again. More forcefully than before, and this time, there was no waiting for Isaac's invitation to enter. Sterling burst inside holding some of Eliza's clothing, a grim expression on his face.

"We need to move. *Now*. We have company. My men just reported movement in the northern quadrant, which means Eliza and I need to get out now. You wait fifteen minutes and then head west. One of my men will pick you up and take you to a safe house. We don't have time to hash this out unless we want to engage, and there's no way in hell I'm going to do that when my wife's safety is at risk and she still hasn't fully recovered from the last time she was shot."

Isaac cursed the timing, but knew hers and the others' safety came first. He'd just have to get Jenna to talk whenever they got settled again. He turned to Jenna, all business now, and handed her the clothing Sterling had tossed him. "Get dressed and make it fast. There's a bathroom there," he said, pointing to another door in the room. "You need to hurry, Jenna. We don't have much time."

Jenna jumped off the bed and fled to the bathroom, already pulling the T-shirt one of his men had put on her over her head when she closed the door behind her.

"Three minutes, sweetheart. Then we have to roll," Isaac called loudly enough that she'd hear through the door.

Isaac turned to Sterling and then eyed him seriously. "I appreciate this more than you'll ever know. Keep Lizzie safe. I don't want her hurt because she's helping me."

"No one is going to so much as touch my wife," Sterling said in a rigid tone. Then he turned and stalked from the room.

SEVEN

ISAAC stood with Jenna in the back of the house where it was dark, and long shadows were cast over the rear entrance. A slight rustle was his only indication that they were no longer alone and then Shadow appeared, barely discernible, much like his name indicated.

"Dex, Zeke and Knight have scouted the perimeter, and it appears they took the bait and are following Sterling and Eliza."

"What the fuck is Knight doing here?" Isaac demanded.

Shadow sent him a look. "If you think this job is about money to him any more than it is for us, then fuck you."

"I never said that."

"Yeah? Then why would you expect *any* of us to stand down when one of our own is in danger and an innocent woman is being pursued by assholes who've already roughed her up once?"

"Gratitude," Isaac whispered.

"Fuck your gratitude," Shadow grumbled.

Isaac chuckled. "Anyone ever tell you how graciously you accept a thank you?"

"Even if she wasn't wearing bruises and her safety wasn't at stake, she saved you. That's enough for me—for us. She gets our protection whether you like it or not."

He almost said thanks again but just shook his head, grinning. "Nice to have the backup," he said instead. "Never said I'd turn it down."

Shadow checked his watch. "Time to roll. Sterling arranged for a pickup, but it's a bit of a hike, and we need to keep to the shadows and be as quiet as possible."

Isaac turned, twining his fingers with Jenna's. "You ready, sweetheart?"

She looked dazed and shell-shocked, as though she was still trying to process the day's events. Then she gave a short nod. But when she took a step forward, Isaac didn't miss her wince, though she tried hard to cover it up.

"Fuck this," he muttered.

He swung her slight form into his arms, cradling her close to his chest, and took off after Shadow.

"Isaac, what are you doing?" she asked in bewilderment.

"You're hurting, and there's no way in hell I'm making you walk through the woods in the dark."

"You can't carry me the entire way," she said, embarrassment clouding her words.

"Can't I?" he challenged. "Honey, you're a tiny slip of a thing. I barely notice the extra weight. Besides, we'll move faster this way, and the quicker we get to the rendezvous point the safer you'll be. And when we get there, I'm having you checked out by a doctor. I'm worried you may have broken some ribs and by the way, Jenna? You're going to tell me exactly how you got those bruises. Every single one."

His tone was fiercer than he intended, and she stiffened in his arms, whether in fear or embarrassment he didn't know.

"I will *never* hurt you, Jenna," he said softly. "And there is nothing for you to feel shame over. Ever. Do you understand me?"

She buried her face in his chest, avoiding both of his statements, but it didn't bother him because by burrowing closer into him, she'd displayed another gesture of trust, even if she wasn't aware of it.

A dark vehicle loomed ahead and Isaac quickened his step, wanting Jenna out of harm's way as quickly as possible. Then the unmistakable whine of a bullet striking metal sounded just as Shadow grunted beside him.

"Fuck. Fuck!" Isaac roared. He vaulted toward the open door and threw Jenna into the backseat, where Knight broke her fall and immediately pushed her down to the floor, out of the line of fire.

"Shadow, you hit?" Isaac demanded as his teammate threw himself into the front seat of the SUV.

"Doesn't matter," Shadow growled. "Let's get the fuck out of here."

The man Sterling had sent to drive them to the safe house wasted no time and floored it, roaring through the wooded area while Zeke, who was in the third row seat with Dex, lifted his head, staring toward the front seat.

"Shadow, man, *did you take a hit?*"

"I said it doesn't fucking matter. We have more important shit to worry about right now," Shadow snapped. "It's nothing."

Despite Knight's attempts to keep Jenna down between him and Isaac, she lifted her head, her face a mask of sorrow as she stared at Shadow. Tears gathered in her eyes and Shadow swore, but he didn't bite her head off or even raise his voice. Instead he gentled his tone into one Isaac had never heard his teammate use.

"I'm okay, sweetness. I've certainly had worse. Now you need to stay down until one of us tells you it's safe to come up."

Ignoring his soft command and shaking off both Knight's and Isaac's hands as they tried to pull her back, she leaned over the front seat and gently peeled Shadow's T-shirt up his side to reveal blood flowing downward from either a graze or a direct hit.

"I'm so sorry," she said in a devastated voice, tears welling in her beautiful eyes.

Before anyone could set her straight on the fact that she had nothing to be sorry for, she reached out and placed her hand over the bleeding wound, splaying her fingers wide. She closed her eyes and strain became evident on her face. The others watched her in fascination, but Isaac had already witnessed the miracle she was and he didn't like that she was going through it all over again. Even if it was necessary.

Shadow's grim expression eased, and then he relaxed and stared at Jenna in astonished disbelief. Then he closed his eyes, and Isaac could swear that the deep lines and grooves that were permanent fixtures on his face eased as peace overtook him. He looked caught up in the most beautiful experience. To Isaac's further amazement, when Shadow finally opened his eyes, there was a light sheen of tears, gone nearly before they'd registered.

Jenna's hand fell away and she slumped over the back of the seat she'd leaned over to get to Shadow, her strength seemingly sapped. Tentatively, Shadow feathered a hand over her hair, caressing the strands as if to offer her even a fraction of the comfort she'd just given him.

"That was the most incredible thing I've ever felt—experienced—in my life, Jenna," he said, every word laced with sincerity. "I don't know how to thank you. Not only for this, but for what you did for Isaac. I haven't felt peace since I was a child and you gave me that. I felt warmed from the very bottom of my soul, from the inside out. In places that have been cold longer than you've been alive. I don't pretend to understand your gift, but what you need to understand is that *you* are a gift. A very special gift. More special than you'll ever know, and if I had to guess more special than anyone has ever made the effort to make you feel. I don't lie, Jenna. I don't say smooth shit to make people feel better. I'm not one to spare feelings. I'm blunt and I say it like it is. Always. And I'm telling you that you are a beautiful person inside and out, and furthermore you have the most beautiful soul I've ever encountered in my entire life. That's twice you've saved someone you don't even know at great risk to yourself. I know you're scared and I know it's likely you don't trust anyone and that you can't afford to trust anyone. But I'm making you a promise right here and now. On my life, Jenna. On my *life*. Isaac will protect you. I will protect you. We will protect you. Isaac is a good man, one of the best, and you'll always have my gratitude for saving him instead of saving yourself. You can trust him. He'll never let you down. And the rest of us will have his back the whole way. You aren't alone in this. You can trust all of us because we're going to make sure those assholes never get their hands on you again. Do you understand what I'm saying?"

Jenna was trembling, both with extreme fatigue and with

emotion. Her eyes were glossy with unshed tears as she stared back and forth between Shadow and Isaac.

"I want to believe you," she whispered brokenly.

Isaac couldn't stand being a passive participant any longer. He curled his hands around her shoulders, turning her until she faced him, and then he pulled her against his chest, listening to her weary sigh as he guided her damp face into his neck.

"Then believe, honey," Isaac whispered against her ear. "Everyone has to believe in something. I want your something to believe in to be me."

"Everyone always leaves," she choked out. "They never stay. They never keep their promises. They lie. They never mean what they say. They hurt . . ."

She went utterly still, refusing to say anything more. Isaac bristled with rage. He knew damn well what she'd been about to say. They hurt her. God, she'd been hurt her entire life. Treated as a subhuman. Used for others' conveniences, no doubt. It enraged him and broke his heart at the same time.

"We're going to talk about the people who hurt you," he said firmly. "But for right now you're exhausted from healing Shadow and we still have an hour to drive, so I want you to try to relax and get some rest. Try not to think or worry about anything. We're going to protect you, baby. If you believe in nothing else, if you trust in nothing else, hold this one truth to your heart. We will protect you and I will take care of you, and I don't make promises lightly. Others may not mean what they say, but I do. We all do. Our word isn't given lightly, but it is given to you."

Not even caring that the others would see or that he didn't know anything about this woman in his arms other than she was in trouble and that she was an angel, he pressed his lips to her soft hair to seal his vow.

She stiffened for a moment and then finally relaxed in his hold. Within seconds she was completely under. Warm, limp and unconscious, her weight so very precious against his body.

For a long moment, no one said anything, though plenty of looks were cast her way and Shadow's. After half an hour, Shadow turned in his seat and looked first to see that Jenna was still sleeping before glancing up at Isaac, raw emotion simmering in his usually unreadable eyes.

"Jesus Christ, Isaac. You didn't tell me how . . ." He shook his head. "Hell, I don't even have the words to explain it, so how can I expect you to have had them?"

"I was too mind-fucked at the time and convinced I *had* died and that she was welcoming me to heaven," Isaac said grimly.

"That was the most . . ." Again he shook his head. "Jesus, I still don't have words. It was the most beautiful, peaceful thing I've ever experienced in my life. It felt like liquid sunshine had invaded my body and warmed me from the inside out, erasing any pain, worry or guilt. Removing a lifetime of pain and regret and replacing it with something more precious than I've ever possessed. She's a fucking miracle, man."

"I know," Isaac said quietly.

My miracle.

He couldn't help the possessive claim that bubbled from the depths of his heart. It was crazy, it was ten kinds of fucked up, it was something right out of a science fiction movie, but one simple truth prevailed. She was his, and she'd been his the moment she'd laid her hands on him and he'd felt her touch all the way to his soul. She'd saved him, and there was no way in hell he'd ever allow anyone to hurt her again.

Shadow's eyes were worried as they stared intently back at Isaac. "Do you even know what her life will be like? Will always be like? She'll always have assholes trying to take her and use her and even if she had a chance at a normal life, if it got out what she can do, she'd never have a moment's peace. People would never let her be. There'd always be someone wanting her to save a loved one, someone hurt, someone dying. And it takes a piece of her every time she does it. I could *feel* it. I could feel what it did to her even as what she gave me was the most fucking beautiful thing I've ever been given. It chips away at her, Isaac. And if it happens enough, there won't be anything left of her and she'll be left broken."

Isaac's chest tightened and his throat knotted as Shadow's words sank in. She was already so damaged. He was right. She had little left to give and yet she hadn't hesitated to give it to him and to Shadow, two men she didn't know and to whom she didn't owe a single thing.

"You said you'd protect her," Zeke said from behind him. "That we'd protect her. But can we, Isaac? Can we really? This is way bigger than what Ari, Ramie, Gracie and Tori can do. This is bigger than all of us. How the hell can we guarantee her any kind of safety? How can we make her promises we don't know for sure we can keep?"

"I *will* protect her," Isaac growled. "I will never leave her to the kind of life you described. I will never allow her to live the hell she's lived her entire life until now."

"Can you make that promise?" Dex challenged, speaking

up for the first time. "Even knowing nothing about her, who she is, who's after her or knowing what *she* wants? Are you sure you even want to? Do you fully understand what you're signing up for?"

"You get one pass and only one, but if you ever ask me that shit again you and I are going to have serious problems. No one is making you participate. This isn't even an official assignment, so if you want out, say the word. Go back to HQ and have Dane put you on a different case."

"Look, man, I'm just looking out for you. She comes with a lot of baggage and already two of you nearly became collateral damage. I just need to know that you have your head on straight and have fully thought this through," Dex said calmly.

"I carry her baggage and her burdens from now on," Isaac said, fire in his eyes and words. "Never said it would be easy. But there is no fucking way in hell I'm turning my back on this girl and throwing her to the wolves."

"Then I guess we better come up with a plan once we get to Sterling's hidey-hole," Dex said. "With the speed in which they found us at the last one, I'm worried as fuck as to just what we're up against. It's obvious they don't mess around, and equally obvious they don't give a fuck who gets in their way or about taking out anyone between them and the end goal."

"I'll know more when I talk to Jenna," Isaac said as he cradled her even closer to his body. "Once I hear all she has to say, we'll have a better idea of what we're dealing with and can act accordingly."

EIGHT

STERLING stepped from the shadows when they pulled up at a very out-of-the-way, very hard-to-find and likely not-on-any-map house that had been constructed to seamlessly blend with the hillside it had been carved into. It was in a forested area and it had been a very bumpy ride with no road or pathway to smooth the way, making it necessary for Isaac to hold tightly to Jenna so she wasn't jostled right out of his lap.

Instead of the heavy growth falling away as they approached the house, the trees and brush grew much denser. It was a perfect place to stash someone because it wasn't a place that could easily be found from the ground or air.

"You took fire when you left?" Sterling demanded.

Knight got out on his side to allow Dex and Zeke to crawl out of the back while Isaac got out on the other side and carefully helped Jenna down, not letting go of her waist until he was sure she was steady on her feet. She looked washed out. Completely exhausted.

Knight jerked his thumb over his back in Shadow's direction. "He took a hit, but he's fine now."

Sterling swore. "I'll have my doctor out to take a look."

"I'm fine," Shadow said as he walked around the front of the vehicle. "See?"

He pulled up the bloodied shirt to display perfectly unmarred skin with no evidence of any trauma.

"What the fuck?" Sterling demanded.

"Jenna," he said simply. "Now, we need to get inside. Jenna is wiped. We're wiped. And we have a lot of shit to go over."

Sterling's piercing stare moved over Jenna, a hint of concern in his usually unreadable gaze. "Come on in and make yourself comfortable," he said in a soft voice. "Eliza and I will have a meal ready for all of you in a few minutes. Until then, make yourself at home."

At that statement, Jenna sent Sterling a startled look and confusion was evident in her expression. Isaac honed in on her obvious befuddlement and wondered what about Sterling announcing the presence of food would cause her to react in such a way.

Then his jaw clenched as he realized that he had no way of knowing when the last time she'd eaten a decent meal was.

Jenna's expression suddenly eased. "Oh, I understand now. I misunderstood, sorry."

Sterling cocked his head but his words were still gentle, almost as if he were wary of spooking a wild animal. "Misunderstood what, sweetheart?"

"You were being a good host," she said, causing everyone to stare at her, wondering where on earth that statement came from or why she'd said it. "You meant that Eliza was preparing the meal and you were merely letting the men know they could eat soon."

Isaac ran his hand through his hair, picking up on the oddity of more than one part of her assessment.

Sterling looked no less perplexed. "No, that isn't what I meant at all," he said, careful to not sound as though he were reprimanding her. "I did most of the cooking. Eliza helped, but she mostly gave me a hard time and called my manhood into question," he added with a laugh.

Jenna's mouth dropped open in obvious shock and then nervousness crowded her features.

"You aren't angry with her, are you?" she asked anxiously.

What the fuck?

Isaac's mouth fell open and his teammates' reactions were much the same. Sterling looked surprised himself, but then his expression softened and he reached for Jenna's hand, squeezing in reassurance.

"Of course I'm not angry. I love Eliza dearly. She's my whole world."

Jenna seemed stunned that he would openly express his love for his wife. Then she blushed and looked downward once she realized everyone was staring at her.

"I'm sorry. It wasn't my place to question you."

Jesus, but this got weirder by the minute, and Isaac had a very bad feeling in the pit of his stomach.

"Come on, let's go inside or Eliza's going to wonder where we are," Sterling said, motioning for everyone to precede him into the house.

Isaac fell into step beside Jenna, making sure she was steady enough to make it on her own.

When they entered the house, Jenna stepped away from Isaac, a look of wonder on her face. She began examining the contents, stopping to run her fingers almost reverently over some of the pictures and knickknacks, allowing her hands to slide over the expensive furnishings.

At times, her lips pursed and her brow furrowed in confusion as if she had no idea what some of the items were. The others watched her odd behavior and exchanged puzzled glances.

"Is this where you live?" she asked Sterling in a soft voice.

"It's one of the many residences I own," he replied. "But this isn't where Eliza and I make our home."

"It's beautiful," she said wistfully. "Is this what all homes look like?"

Isaac's heart nearly shattered on the spot. What kind of hell had she endured in her life that she didn't even know what a normal home looked like?

"Where I was kept looked nothing like this," she said sadly. "I've never seen a real home. It must be nice."

Then, as if realizing she was revealing something she wasn't ready to share, she clamped her mouth shut and looked down at her hands, effectively ending any further outbursts. Instead she retreated to the far end of the living room and wrapped her arms protectively around herself and withdrew.

There wasn't a single man in the room whose expression didn't reflect absolute fury.

"Hey, isn't the game on?" Dex said, flopping onto one of the couches and pointing the remote at the television. It was obvious he was trying to take the focus off Jenna and alleviate the heavy tension filling the room.

As soon as it flashed on and the loud noise filled the room,

Jenna nearly jumped out of her skin and let out a startled cry. She looked in horror at the TV screen, rooted to the spot where she was standing.

"What is that?" she demanded in an almost hysterical tone. "What is that thing?"

By now, however odd Isaac's teammates considered her behavior before, now there was genuine concern, and it was obvious no one knew how to handle the situation.

Isaac tentatively put his hand on Jenna's shoulder, feeling the tension radiating from her in waves.

"It's a television, honey."

He didn't think it was possible for her to look more horrified.

"Turn it off!" she said in a shrill voice. "It's the devil's instrument. It's evil. It isn't allowed. It's *forbidden!*"

She was near tears, her hands curled into tight fists at her sides as Dex quickly turned off the TV.

Eliza poked her head into the living room. "Soup's on, guys. Come and get it while it's hot."

Isaac left Jenna staring at the television, shaking so hard that her teeth chattered. He murmured to Eliza so Jenna wouldn't hear.

"I think it best if Jenna and I eat out here and the rest of you eat in the kitchen. I need time. Something is very wrong here and she's beyond upset. This situation is so fucked up I can't wrap my head around it. I need to get her to talk to me and tell me everything fast, and she's not going to do that in front of a room full of people."

"If I can do anything to help, you know I will," Eliza said, compassion in her voice.

"I know, Lizzie, and I appreciate it. Jenna isn't like anyone

I've ever known. It's like she's a child in an adult's body and she has no knowledge of everyday things you and I take for granted. I have a very bad feeling about what her life has been like."

"You only have to look into her eyes to see that she is one very damaged woman, Isaac. You're going to have to take it slow and not push too hard."

"I just hope I can get her to trust me enough to open up because until she does, we're flying blind. We have no clue who's after her, though the reason is evident enough. We've already been through this with Ramie and Ari, but this is way beyond what we faced protecting them. I think she's been held captive and forced to use her gift for a very long time. That she managed to escape tells me more than I can handle without losing my shit.

"Whoever is after her means business and they aren't going to give up. They shot me and they shot Shadow. If it weren't for Jenna, I would have bled out and died within minutes."

Something dark and feral flashed in Eliza's eyes.

"Don't even think about it, Lizzie," Isaac warned. "You're still on leave whether you like it or not and you're not fully healed from your own brush with death. If I think, even for a minute, that you're plotting anything, I won't hesitate to rat you out not only to Sterling but to Dane as well."

Annoyance shone in her expression. Scowling at him, she walked back to the island and prepared two plates, gathered utensils for him and Jenna, and then shoved them at him.

"I'll make sure y'all get the privacy you need," she said, despite her irritation. "Wade and I will be shoving off after dinner anyway, but he's leaving several of his men around the perimeter of the property to keep an eye on things."

Isaac grinned. "You know you love me, Lizzie."

She rolled her eyes and then made a shooing motion with her hand.

Isaac walked back into the living room, where Jenna still stood rigidly in the same spot he'd left her. He sighed and then sat down on the couch, setting the plates on the coffee table.

"Come eat with me, sweetheart. I don't even want to think about when the last time was that you had a decent meal."

Jenna moved forward, eyeing the plates. As she sat down, she sniffed appreciatively. Her eyes were wide when she took in the steak, baked potato with all the fixings and grilled asparagus.

Her gaze was hesitant when it lifted to Isaac's. "You mean I can have all this?"

He frowned. "Why the hell couldn't you? As you can see, I have my own plate."

She twisted her fingers nervously together until she was wringing her hands. "It's just that I was never allowed to have . . ."

She broke off, immediately closing herself off once more, and then picked up the fork and knife, looking down as if she didn't know which part of the meal she wanted to try first.

Just like that she became distant, the shields going up, and he knew he wasn't going to be able to get any of the answers to the questions burning his tongue tonight. Damn it, but the parts she'd inadvertently disclosed frustrated and angered him and had him thinking that wherever she'd come from, whoever she was running from hadn't treated her any better than an animal.

There was something unworldly about her, a cloud of innocence and ignorance of the most basic things that made him believe she'd been kept tightly under wraps. A prisoner never allowed out of whatever hellhole she'd been sequestered in. And the fact that she knew so little of the modern world also told him she hadn't been there a short time, either.

He sighed, seeing that she was tense and wary, probably expecting him to start demanding answers at any time. After all, he'd told her as much on their way here. That she was going to tell him everything.

Wanting to give her one night when she wasn't so burdened down that she staggered under the weight of so much worry, he reached over and brushed his fingertip down the line of her cheek.

"Just eat, Jenna. We'll talk when you trust me enough to let me in and share what you were running from. Until then, I'm just going to have to prove to you that I'll never hurt you, I'll always protect you and that I'm willing to wait until you're ready to tell me your secrets."

He nearly groaned because when she lifted her gaze to his, she looked at him like he was the only man in the world. Like he was some kind of damn hero. *Her* hero. Her eyes went shiny with tears and her smile . . . Jesus, her smile. It had the effect of a sledgehammer to his gut.

"No one has ever been nice to me," she said, almost whispering. "I had given up hope that kindness existed in the world, but you—all of you—have shown me that it does. You'll never know how much this has meant to me."

He wanted to weep at the sincerity in her words. The calm, matter-of-fact way she'd said that no one had ever shown her kindness. And yet she was an angel in a world that had shown her no mercy. His damaged angel. An angel with broken wings just dying to fly. He made a vow that she would fly again, no matter what he had to do in order to make that happen.

"Eat," he ordered in a gruff voice laced with emotion. It was all he could say without risking breaking down in front of her. He wanted to put his fist through the wall, but what he most wanted was to get his hands on the bastards who'd made her suffer, who'd made her life a living hell for so long.

She excitedly dug into the steak first and he watched her expression as the first bite hit her tongue. She chewed reverently and then closed her eyes, sighing deeply as she savored the taste of the perfectly cooked meat.

"Good?" he teased.

"Amazing," she breathed.

He noticed she dug into the steak and the baked potato with enthusiasm, delighting in every single bite. In fact he'd never seen anyone take such pleasure in such a simple meal, but then he had to remember it was doubtful she found much satisfaction at all in the food she'd eaten before. Yet despite her obvious enjoyment of the steak and potato, she didn't so much as touch the asparagus.

"Not a vegetable eater?" he teased.

But then he cursed his words and his attempt to lighten the mood when her face fell and once again she became fidgety.

"Vegetables were all I was ever allowed to eat," she said, her head low in embarrassment. "Sometimes bread as a reward when I . . ."

Once more she broke off before revealing further information.

Isaac ignored the anger simmering in his veins, determined to make the meal as enjoyable for his angel as possible.

"Then I'll make sure you never have to eat anything you don't want again," he said, solemnly.

Her smile was small, but at least she lifted her head again and most of the shame shadowing her eyes had disappeared. Just to make her smile again, he leaned over and forked her asparagus, moving the stalks to his plate.

"Now their offending presence is gone from your plate and won't interfere with your steak and potato," he said with an exaggerated grin.

Her smile broadened and once more he felt like he'd been punched in the stomach, momentarily robbed of air. Even bruised and fragile looking, she was the most beautiful, tiny angel he'd ever seen in his life.

"There. That's better. I like it when my girl smiles."

She blinked in surprise and he wondered if he'd gone too far in his teasing. There was sadness in her eyes, but also what looked like a flash of hope and yearning, as if she wanted more than anything to belong to anyone.

Fuck that. She might not know it yet, but she did belong to someone. She belonged to him.

NINE

ALL too soon the others began filtering back into the living room and Jenna retreated into observation mode, shrinking against the couch as if to make herself invisible as she watched the others interact.

Isaac had used the need for more seating room as an excuse to move closer to Jenna until they sat side by side, their thighs touching. Eliza walked out ahead of Sterling to collect Jenna and Isaac's plates, but before she could return them to the kitchen, Sterling was there, taking them from her, and then he leaned in and kissed her deeply.

"We need to be going," Sterling said to Isaac and his men. "But my guys will be staying to guard the perimeter and if you need anything at all, don't hesitate to call me."

Jenna had watched Eliza and Sterling, her eyes glazed with shock, but she waited until they'd left the room before she whispered to Isaac.

"Why did he *kiss* her?"

He could tell she was deeply confused and hell, so was he.

"He loves her," he said simply. "She's his wife. Hell, he can barely keep his hands off her most of the time," he added with a chuckle.

There was no change in her expression.

"The men never kissed their wives," she said in a low voice. "I was told I was unworthy of being kissed, of being held in such high regard, but none of the women were kissed. They were just possessions, married or not. I guess I don't understand the point of kissing."

Isaac swore under his breath. Just how old was Jenna? Was she even legal? He knew she looked young and there was definitely an air of innocence and naïveté about her that he'd never encountered even in very young girls. Jesus, if she wasn't even of legal age, that meant he was almost twenty years older than her and he had no business having the thoughts he'd had of her.

"There are many reasons to kiss someone," he said in a near whisper so the others wouldn't hear. He knew she'd be deeply embarrassed if they were overheard. "Kisses can be a gesture of affection. Friendship. They can be an indication of passion. Of love. Of wanting someone. Or they can show a person that they are deeply cared about."

Her sad expression of longing told him that she'd never felt any of those things, or at least that no one had ever felt those things about her.

He leaned forward, sliding his hand behind her neck to pull her toward him, and pressed a kiss to her forehead.

"See?" he said huskily. "It's not so bad, is it?"

She stared strangely at him, color tinging her cheeks, her eyes glazed and her respirations speeding up as she emitted shallow breaths. Then she raised a shaking hand to touch the exact spot he'd kissed, almost as if committing it to memory.

"And, honey, if anyone is worthy of being kissed, of being held, of being given the utmost regard, it's you. I don't know what kind of bullshit you've been told and I know you've been told it often enough and long enough that you believe it, but if it's the last thing I do, I'm going to prove you wrong."

She turned away, but not before he saw the betraying glimmer of tears in her eyes and the sadness that seemed to swamp her entire expression. God damn it, he hated fighting a faceless, unknown enemy. Worse, he hated fighting against her own deeply ingrained belief that she had no worth.

He knew he should be pressuring her to answer his questions and provide the information he needed, not only to keep her safe and protected, but also his teammates, who were in more imminent danger. Her pursuers wanted her at all costs. Alive. But he and his teammates were expendable, mere obstacles in the way of the ultimate prize.

He doubted he knew even a fraction of the horror Jenna had been subjected to, but what little he did know instilled a fury unlike any he'd ever felt in his life. Not even hearing of Ramie's gruesome ordeal and experiencing firsthand Ari, Gracie and Eliza being taken, tormented and tortured or learning of Ramie's horrific ordeal before DSS was created and Isaac had come to work for the Devereaux brothers had made him feel this murderous.

How would he react when he finally knew it all? When the time came that Jenna trusted him enough to confide in him, he needed to be strong and in control for her. A rock for her to lean on. Her shelter and shield against anything or anyone that could ever hurt her again.

But he also knew that it would be the most difficult thing he'd ever have to do. To sit there and stoically listen as Jenna outlined what she'd been made to endure without losing his everloving mind. He wanted to lash out and destroy everything in his path, anything to unleash the terrible rage that bubbled within him even now *before* he knew everything, but he couldn't afford to lose control, scare the fuck out of her and have her shut down and worse, shut *him* out.

Zeke spoke up, breaking the silence. "I know Sterling has men posted, but I think we should alternate taking watch through the night. Doesn't hurt to double down."

Dex and Knight nodded their agreement.

"I'll take first watch," Shadow said, standing up. "I'd like to see how close I can get to Sterling's men without them noticing. Doesn't do us any good to have them if they don't do their jobs worth a shit."

Jenna's worried eyes found Shadow's. "Please be careful," she begged. "I've already caused so much harm to come to you all. I couldn't bear it if anyone else was hurt or even killed this time because of me."

Shadow immediately softened and then merely dropped a kiss atop her head as he walked by her. Not a single man in the room was unaffected by her statement or the guilt that lay so heavy in her voice. They looked as though they wanted to go to fucking battle, and they weren't alone. Isaac wanted to lead the goddamn war and punish every last bastard who'd made her life a living hell.

"The rest of you get some sleep. I'll wake Dex in three hours. Isaac, your only watch is to make sure Jenna is safe at all times."

Jenna's brow furrowed as Shadow disappeared and then she

turned to Isaac, question and confusion in her beautiful blue eyes.

"So what kind of kiss was *that*?" she whispered. "I never realized there were so many reasons to kiss or reasons *for* kisses," she amended.

"It was an affectionate kiss and one meant to reassure you," Isaac said. At least that had better be all it was. It had taken everything not to growl when Shadow's lips had touched her, even if it was just a light touch to her hair.

Isaac showed Jenna to the room at the end of the hall so she'd be flanked by two rooms, one he'd take and Dex, the other. When he flipped on the light and they entered, her eyes widened and she looked captivated.

"This is where I'm sleeping?" she asked in a hushed tone.

"Do you like it?" he asked, prepared to switch with her if it wasn't to her liking.

"It's the most beautiful room I've ever seen," she said, her voice escaping in a sigh. Then she looked anxiously up at him and he was immediately desperate to do whatever necessary to ease her anxiety.

"What is it, Jenna?" he asked softly.

She bit her lip and then glanced between him and the bed. "Do I . . . do I get to sleep in the bed?"

He had to take a moment before responding, as rage mottled his vision and he had to bite back vicious curses. Unfortunately, she took his momentary silence as his response and her shoulders sagged, disappointment making her face droop with sadness.

"Of course you'll sleep in the bed. Jenna honey . . . where did you think I meant for you to sleep?"

She flushed. "I was never allowed to sleep on a bed or even

one of the cots. Only on a pallet on the floor, and sometimes it was taken away if I was being punished."

Her eyes widened in horror and she clamped her mouth shut, turning away. It was just as well, because the expression on Isaac's face would have scared the hell out of her. Someday, and he didn't care how long it took, he was going to make every single one of the assholes who'd abused his angel pay dearly. It wouldn't be quick and it wouldn't be merciful. But it would be righteous.

Thank goodness her attention was drawn to the bed so she didn't see the blackness in Isaac's features. Her fingers ran reverently over the bedspread and then caressed the soft down pillows, so much longing in her eyes.

He couldn't stay a minute longer without losing his composure. He wanted to smash something. He wanted blood. The blood of every person responsible for Jenna's imprisonment.

"Why don't I leave you to get dressed for bed and turn in for the night. You're exhausted and you need your rest," he said gruffly.

At her questioning look, he pointed out the large T-shirt and pajama shorts Eliza had left for her on the end of the bed.

"I'll be next door if you need anything at all, okay?"

"Okay," she whispered. "Good night, Isaac."

"Good night, sweetheart."

She looked so vulnerable standing there in the middle of the room that it took all of Isaac's strength to leave.

At the door, he turned back one last time. "Remember, I'm right next door. Nothing can hurt you here, okay? You need *anything*, you come get me."

She gave a small smile and nodded and then he left, closing the door behind him.

TEN

ISAAC lay quietly in the dark, staring up at the ceiling, his thoughts consumed by the blue-eyed angel in the next room. Would she be able to sleep? And if she was, did nightmares plague her dreams?

What was it about her that called to a part of his heart and soul that had never been breached before? He could come up with plenty of reasonable explanations, like the fact that she'd saved his life. Or that he'd made it his life's work to protect the innocent. Or the fact that she was lost in a world of which she had little understanding or knowledge. Or the fact that she needed him.

But the simple truth was that he needed her every bit as much as she needed him, and he couldn't come up with a reason that made any sense to him.

He'd come across plenty of victimized women who'd desperately needed help, his protection, DSS's protection, but never had he been even remotely possessive of them. He'd done his job, and it never failed to enrage him and rile his protective instincts. It was who and what he was; he'd never been a man to stand idly by while a woman was in danger or being abused.

But his angel wasn't just any victim. She wasn't just any woman in trouble and in need of protecting. And he had no idea what to do with that realization. He couldn't even call it a realization, as if he'd just been struck by an epiphany as he lay there with no hope of sleeping. He'd known it from the moment she'd touched him, laid her hands on him, and he'd felt her in the very depths of his soul.

It wasn't sexual—wholly—because he'd be a damn liar if he didn't want her with every breath in his body. It was spiritual, and he felt like some hokey fool mooning over things like destiny and fate, but how could he call it anything else when from the moment she'd touched him he'd felt a connection that transcended any physical want or need?

And he was consumed with guilt for having sexual thoughts, lustful, needful thoughts, about a woman child whom he didn't even know if she was of an age for him to be having such thoughts about her. She had the innocence of a girl with the body of a desirable woman. Hell, it was obvious that no matter how many years she'd lived in this world, she'd spent the majority of them sheltered, sequestered from the real world. She was either enraptured with or terrified of things that he and others took for granted.

She'd been conditioned.

He frowned. It appeared that at a very early age she'd been indoctrinated. Brainwashed. Taught an alternate reality that was twisted to fit the agenda of the people who'd kept her under lock and key, and they'd proven they would go to extreme measures to retrieve her. She was a valuable asset to them. Irreplaceable. He wondered when her powers had manifested themselves and as he pondered that question, he wondered if it was what had saved her from a far worse fate. Even the dumbest fucks would realize the enormity of what they possessed in Jenna.

He rolled over to retrieve his cell and punched in Eliza's number, knowing it was late and that Sterling likely wouldn't be pleased, but Eliza of all people would understand his suspicions. He needed to bounce some ideas off her.

"This better be damn good," Eliza growled into the phone. "Because I was about to be the recipient of the mother of all orgasms, and Wade is just pissed enough to throw my phone in the pool and withhold sex for a week."

Isaac burst out laughing when he heard Sterling in the background.

"Jesus fuck, woman, can we keep our sex life and your goddamn job separate?"

"Apparently not," Eliza said acidly. "Since one of my esteemed coworkers just called me right in the middle of your best move."

"You haven't seen my best moves, baby. *Yet*," Sterling said in a silky voice. "I'm saving those for when you've been a *very* good girl. It'll give you something to look forward to."

"Lizzie, stop. Please. I'm begging you. I'm going to need to bleach my eyes *and* my ears. I wouldn't have called if it wasn't important. Give me a few minutes and then I'll let you get back to your, uh, nighttime activities. And my advice, for what it's worth: work on being a very good girl."

She snorted, but then all humor left her tone. "Hit me with it."

"I was lying here thinking about Jenna and the weirdness of her situation. It's almost like she's been conditioned and indoctrinated over a period of years to accept an alternative reality and to reject any semblance of the modern world."

"Yeah, I could see that."

"What if she came from one of those survivalist groups. Living off the grid. Government and the modern world are the enemy. It would explain her unfamiliarity with the most basic essentials of what's everyday normal life to you and me."

Eliza paused for a moment. "Could be, but that's not what my gut tells me. Survivalist groups are very aware of the world around them. They have to be, in their minds. How else will they know how to survive, how to resist invasion, being taken over, et cetera. And Isaac, that shit about how the women were treated in whatever fucked-up place she lived? That's not how most, and I say most because there's always the one exception, of these groups operate. They have wives, families, children, and they're very protective of them. They don't treat them like cattle or breeding stock or starve them of love and affection. I'd say you've got yourself one fucked-up situation where a person or persons only play by the rules they themselves make. Those are the most dangerous kind because in their mind, they aren't doing anything wrong. But they've been wronged. First by Jenna by her leaving the fold, and then by the people aiding her. They're all about control and if they lose that control, they become dangerous and unstable. More so than they already are."

"Don't mean to drag up bad memories for you, Lizzie," Isaac said quietly.

He could almost hear Eliza's smile through the phone. "He's dead now, Isaac. He has no hold on me. He can only hurt me if

I let him and he can only do that through memories or dreams, and Wade is very good at keeping him out of my head."

Isaac laughed. "I can well imagine. Thanks, Lizzie. I just needed another perspective. This is driving me crazy. I know we need answers, but I won't push her. I won't force her to do anything. I want her to trust me enough to tell me on her own."

"Understandable," Eliza said quietly. "And smart on your part. Good luck, and I know I don't have to say this, but handle her gently. She looks to be very close to her breaking point."

"You're right. You don't need to say it, but thanks anyway."

"Anytime, Isaac. And be careful, okay? I'd rather not hear about someone I care about having another brush with death."

"Now you know how I felt when it was you, Lizzie."

"Good night," she whispered.

Isaac slid his phone back over onto the nightstand and then went stock-still, his hand automatically reaching for his gun when his door slowly cracked open the barest of inches. But when the door opened wider to reveal Jenna illuminated by the dim hall light, her hair tousled like she'd been restless and unable to sleep, his hand eased away from the gun.

"Isaac?" she softly called.

"Yes, honey, I'm here."

She took a hesitant step forward, her nervousness evident in her stance and demeanor.

"I'm sorry. I didn't mean to wake you."

"You didn't," he reassured her. "Is something wrong?"

She bit into her bottom lip and glanced downward, and he knew if the light were better he'd be able to see the blush that was surely adorning her cheeks.

"Hey, come here," he said.

She walked forward, stopping at the foot of the bed. She continued to avoid his gaze, finding anything else to focus on.

"Jenna, look at me," he commanded gently.

Finally she lifted her gaze, and he was gutted by the unease reflected in her eyes.

"What's wrong, sweetheart?"

"I wanted to ask...I mean if you didn't mind...I wanted...well, it's stupid, but I couldn't sleep because I'm afraid," she whispered. "Would you mind if I stayed in here with you?"

His heart damn near stopped. It was the very last thing he'd expected her to ask, but there was no way in hell he was telling her no. The idea that she'd been lying in the room next to his unable to sleep because she was afraid damn near broke his heart.

"Of course I don't mind. Get the door, okay? And then come here."

She turned and retraced the few steps to close the door and then walked to the side of the bed and to his utter bewilderment, she settled down on the floor, curling her knees into her chest, obviously planning to sleep there.

"Jenna, no," he said, more harshly than he intended.

His tone startled her and then she looked crushed, tears of mortification welling in her eyes.

"I'm sorry," she choked out. "I shouldn't have come. It wasn't my place. Don't be angry, please. I couldn't bear it if you were angry with me."

He was momentarily speechless as she hurried to get up, but then he was out of the bed and in front of her before he even realized he was there. He placed gentle hands on her shoulders, forcing her to look at him.

"Honey, I'm not angry with you. I'm pissed that you thought you had to sleep on the floor. You will never sleep on the goddamn floor again, is that clear?"

The shocked look on her face only intensified when he simply lifted her slight figure into his arms and then leaned over the bed, depositing her on the opposite side so her head was nestled on the pillows. Then he crawled up on his side, pulling the covers over both of them.

"Come here," he said again, his voice soft and full of apology.

She awkwardly moved toward him a few inches, so he reached for her and hauled her against his chest, wrapping his arms tightly around her so her cheek was pressed right over his heart and his chin rested atop her head.

She was stiff as a board and he could barely feel her breathe as she processed the situation. He could feel the panic coursing through her veins and her rapid pulse and increased respirations.

"Relax, Jenna," he ordered. "Nothing can hurt you here. Now what were you afraid of? Did you see something? Hear something?"

Gradually she began to relax, though it seemed an eternity before she finally capitulated and her soft curves melded to his much harder frame.

"It's stupid," she muttered, obviously embarrassed now that she was over her initial fright.

"There aren't rules when it comes to fear, honey. Everyone fears something and it can strike at any time with no warning, and even the simplest, unassuming thing can trigger it. What was it that scared you?"

"The window," she blurted. "Since my room is in the middle, the only window is at the back of the house and faces . . . nothing. It's just dark, and the window is so big and it's so close to my bed, and all I could think was how easy it would be for someone to take me out of that window before anyone even realized I was gone. I used to long for windows. I hated the room where I was kept because there was never any sunshine. Nothing to see but four walls. But now I hate them, because now I know what's out there just waiting and how easy having a window makes it for people to get in."

"That's not stupid, sweetheart," Isaac soothed. "It's smart, and it means you're aware of your surroundings and the possible dangers associated. But I promise you that nothing will hurt you in this room when you're with me. And there is no way I'll let anyone take you from me. Can you trust me that much, Jenna?"

She snuggled even closer to his chest, their legs sliding and bumping together until finally he trapped hers between his and held her close, lending her his warmth and comfort.

"I do trust you," she whispered. "I know it seems like I don't because I haven't told you anything, or at least much. It's just that I'm so ashamed."

Tears were thick in her voice and he threaded one hand through her hair and then pressed his lips to the top of her head, inhaling the scent of her honeyed tresses.

"You have nothing to be ashamed of, Jenna. I wish I could make you see that, believe that. God, I can't think of a person more worthy and undeserving of shame than you. Do you even realize how good you are? How brightly you shine? It's all there for the world to see. Your gentleness, your compassion, your goodness. And your beauty," he whispered. "Never have I seen a more beautiful woman than you."

Her small fingertips dug into his chest and he felt her slight tremble, the effect his words had on her. Then she lifted her head so that she could look him in the eye.

It was obvious she was nervous, and she had the most adorably shy look as her gaze traveled over his entire face.

"Can I ask you something?" she asked in a hushed whisper he had to strain to hear.

His fingers, still tangled in her hair, gently pulled through the strands as he caressed their length and then the tips, wrapping them around his knuckles.

"You can always ask me anything," he vowed.

"Can I . . . Can I kiss you?"

Heat traveled to the center of his being. His blood blazed a trail of fire through his veins until he was certain his entire core was molten lava. He stared at her with hungry, hooded eyes, nearly groaning with the dilemma before him. The moment her request had registered, he'd gone rock hard, and the last thing he wanted was to scare the hell out of her with a monster erection.

When she started to say something, likely to recant or apologize, he pressed one finger to her lips.

"I have to ask you one question first," he said huskily.

She looked at him in confusion but nodded her agreement.

Praying the entire time, he drew in a breath and said, "How old are you, sweetheart?"

Her brow furrowed and he cursed himself, because once more shame made her features sad and distant.

"I don't know," she murmured.

"I don't understand," he said with genuine confusion.

"I only have a few memories of my life before . . . them."

She shuddered with distaste when she said "them," and chill bumps erupted over her skin. He drew her in closer and rubbed his palms up and down in an effort to warm her.

"Mostly they're like random, brief snatches of time, gone before I can grab on to them and hold on long enough to make sense of them. I know I was at least a few years old when I went to live with them and I've been with them for almost twenty years, but they're all a blur, you know? In the beginning I would mark the passing of each day until I realized that no one was coming for me and that time meant nothing. I stopped counting because it didn't seem to matter anymore. I didn't matter," she said painfully.

Isaac cupped her chin, forcing her gaze upward, wanting her to see the sincerity in his expression and words.

"You matter, Jenna. Don't ever think differently. *You matter.*"

She swallowed back a sob and then buried her face in his neck, grasping his shoulders with both hands. Then she finally pulled back and looked pleadingly up at him.

"I want to kiss you, Isaac, but I don't know how. I want it to be all the things you said it could be. I want to pretend just for a moment. Will you help me?"

He wiped the twin trails of tears from her cheeks with his thumb. "It would be my pleasure, angel."

ELEVEN

JENNA'S teeth were chattering as she questioned for the sixth time coming into Isaac's bedroom. She knew it was wrong. Forbidden. That she'd be branded a harlot and worse. But she wanted this even if she wasn't sure what this was.

All her life she'd viewed kissing as nothing. No example of caring or regard because no one ever kissed anyone. The men treated the women in the group coldly, callously. Like they were possessions, there for the men's pleasure and nothing more. It had never occurred to her that a man would kiss a woman for reasons of affection, caring or even love.

Why had Isaac kissed her? He'd kissed her twice. Not on the lips, but she could still feel the warm imprint of his lips in the places he had kissed, and she never wanted to lose that sensation.

Did she have the courage to be so forthright and bold? So brazen as to kiss *him*? He didn't seem to mind the idea at all, but then he'd been nice to her and maybe that's all it was.

Shyly she moved her lips closer to his until she could feel his soft, even breaths against her chin. She wanted to kiss his lips but lacked the courage to be that bold, so she moved just to the side and feathered a soft brush of her lips right at the corner of his mouth.

He let out a soft groan and his arms tightened around her, holding her still and firmly captured against his body. Then he lowered his mouth and took her lips just as she'd wanted to do to him. He was so gentle, it brought tears to her eyes.

He took his time, the warm, gentle pressure of his lips against hers eliciting sensations in the rest of her body that she didn't understand. Then he softly laved his tongue over the seam of her mouth, making her gasp in response. His tongue probed inward, licking the tip of hers before withdrawing, and he kissed his way out of her mouth again, finishing by sealing her mouth completely with his, leaving her entire body flushed and aching with awareness.

As he drew away, his gaze was focused on her, piercing, studying her response.

"What kind of kiss was that?" she whispered, dazed and shaken by the experience.

"One that says I care a great deal about you and one that says you're a very special woman."

"You do? I am?" she asked in bewilderment.

Isaac sighed. "I don't know who made you feel like you were unworthy, like you were nothing, because you don't trust me enough to share that with me yet, but Jenna, it's bullshit. It's complete bullshit. You're a fucking miracle, honey, and I don't mean because of your gift."

"I do trust you, Isaac," she said, staring earnestly into his eyes. "I'm sorry if I made you feel as if I don't. I'm just worried. I don't want you or any of your men to be hurt or killed because of me. I couldn't live with myself if anything happened to you—any of you."

Isaac cupped her cheek tenderly, luring her further into his embrace.

"Jenna, I want you to listen to me. Really listen to me, okay? Nothing is going to happen to me or any of my men. Our job is to protect you. It is not your job to protect us. Do you understand?"

"You have no idea how ruthless they are," she said tearfully. "Or what their plans are."

"No, I don't," he said calmly. "Because you won't confide in me. If you want to protect me and the others, the best thing you can do is to trust me and tell me everything. We can't prepare for the worst if we don't know what the worst is."

She ducked her head, guilt overwhelming her. He was right. What was her shame compared to their lives? She was being selfish, choosing her pride over their safety.

"I'm so sorry," she choked out. "I know you're right. You need to know everything. You've been nothing but kind when I've been nothing but ashamed, and my pride could get all of you killed."

Isaac squeezed her in a gesture of comfort. "No one blames you, baby. But I won't lie. It's driving me crazy not knowing what those bastards have done to you. I want to kill every last one of them so you'll feel safe, so you can stop running and constantly looking over your shoulder. And honey, you can trust me to take care of you. If you let me in I'll make sure nothing ever hurts or frightens you again."

"I do trust you," she said softly, reaching up to palm his stubbly jaw.

Never before had she met a man like Isaac. So formidable, a warrior, and yet so gentle and patient with her that she wanted to weep.

"Then will you tell me everything?" he asked, stroking a hand through her hair. "And I mean everything. I want to know everything about you, Jenna. What makes you happy, what makes you sad, what makes you smile, and especially what hurts you and frightens you."

She didn't realize she was shaking or that her alarm was evident until Isaac sat up and pulled her across his lap, cradling her in his arms. He rubbed his hand up and down her back and pressed his lips to the top of her head.

"You're trembling, honey, and panic is all over your face. You're safe with me. Nothing can touch you while you're in my arms. I need you to relax and take some deep breaths, try to calm down. We don't have to talk about this right now. I'll wait as long as necessary until you're ready to tell me, okay? I will never pressure you."

She was silent for a long moment, grappling with painful and humiliating memories. Isaac didn't break the silence. He continued to hold her, rocking her in a soothing motion, hand rubbing lightly up and down her spine as he waited patiently, almost as if he sensed the intense battle waging inside her.

"I belong to a cult," she said boldly, her gaze immediately shooting to Isaac for any sign of judgment or condemnation. But he didn't react, nor did he stop the gentle caresses up and down her back.

"I say 'belong,' but belonging indicates a conscious choice," she said bitterly. "I was a prisoner and treated as such."

At that, Isaac's expression darkened but he remained silent, waiting for her to continue.

"I wasn't always with them," she said wistfully. "Or at least I don't think I was. I have memories of when I was young. I think they were of my parents. I remember a man—my father? Tossing me in the air and then kissing me on the nose."

Tears burned her eyelids as she strained to assemble those memories in her mind, desperately wanting to hold on to them and for them to be true. That at one time, someone had loved her and had wanted her.

"He always smiled at me. And the woman . . . I don't have as many memories of her, but I remember her making a birthday cake for me and me blowing out the candles."

"How many candles?" Isaac asked, interrupting her for the first time. "Think hard, baby. How many candles were on your cake?"

She frowned, concentrating on the fleeting image of the cake, the man singing "Happy Birthday" in an off-key voice, but one that was filled with love. She closed her eyes, focusing on the cake. It had been pink. Pink frosting with lots of flowers in different colors. The candles stood in a straight line, thin wisps of smoke rapidly dissipating when she'd blown them out.

"Four!" she exclaimed excitedly. She turned to stare at Isaac. "There were four candles on the cake. I was four years old," she said in a hushed voice. Then her expression became sad and she dropped her gaze from Isaac's. "That's the last memory I have of my parents."

"You must have been abducted soon after your fourth birthday," Isaac said gently. "How many years were you with the cult?"

Shame coursed through her all over again. "I don't know," she whispered sadly. "They seem like such a blur to me. The cult never celebrated birthdays. I mean, not for me."

Isaac tensed against her and she could feel the anger rolling off him in waves.

"I tried to use other people's birthdays to mark time, but people came and went."

She shivered. "It was forbidden for anyone to leave once joining the cult, but people disappeared over the years and nothing was ever said about them. No one questioned their absence. It was as if they'd never existed."

Isaac's hold around her tightened and he pressed a kiss to her temple. "Don't think about them right now, baby. Stay right here with me in the present where nothing can hurt you. Not ever again."

She leaned into his comfort and remained there in silence a long moment.

"My best guess for how long I was with them is nineteen or twenty years. Wouldn't that make me twenty-three or twenty-four years old now?"

Isaac squeezed her to him and he seemed relieved. "Yes, baby. You'd be twenty-three or twenty-four. It's hard to believe, though. You look and seem so much younger. So innocent for someone your age."

His reaction puzzled her but she didn't question him. She was lost in the past. After maintaining strict silence for so long, it was as if a dam had burst and the memories came tumbling out.

"I think I was targeted because of my ability to heal, but how had they known? I've never understood how they could have known when I was so young. But from the very beginning I was held separate from the others and I was routinely called upon to heal injuries. They convinced me that I was God's instrument and it was my duty to help those in need, and yet I was kept in complete isolation. I was never allowed to heal anyone except the elders or those who were high ranking in the cult."

"Elders?" Isaac asked, his brow wrinkled in confusion.

"They were the leaders. They held absolute authority over everyone. There were five of them. Older. Everyone feared them and were subservient to them. Their word was law, and they said that they were God's direct messengers and we should take their word and judgment as being from God himself."

"Nice way to ensure absolute obedience and for no one to question your actions," Isaac muttered.

Jenna nodded adamantly. "Questioning an elder was the greatest sin a member could commit and punishments were harsh. Those that questioned or disagreed with the elders went missing and were never seen or heard from again."

"Son of a bitch," Isaac snarled.

She glanced down at her hands, struggling with long pent-up emotion.

"What is it, sweetheart?" Isaac asked, hugging her a little tighter.

"In the beginning when I was so young, they treated me like I was special. As I said, they told me I was God's instrument, chosen by him, you know, like I was worthy in some way. But later I realized it was their way of brainwashing me and of gaining my compliance.

"As I got older, I began to question things like why a woman in the cult was allowed to die in childbirth when I could have saved her. I was told that it was God's will and I wasn't to interfere. Foolishly, I told them that every time I healed someone I was interfering, so why was I given a gift from God if I was only supposed to use it selectively and only at the behest of the elders, and why were only some in the cult deserving of mercy and healing while others weren't? I was beaten severely and then branded an abomination. Satan's tool, and that the cult's duty was to drive the demons from me."

Isaac swore violently, his arms loosening around her as his fingers flexed and curled into tight fists.

"I was told to renounce Satan and to admit that my gift was evil and not in accordance with God's will. I refused and I was beaten again. I was locked in a sublevel room with no light, no food or water, and left there until I was so weak that I didn't have the strength to feed myself or drink when it was finally offered to me. I couldn't even hold myself up, much less walk, when they came for me. They dragged me from the room after I had spent so many days there that in the end I lost count."

Isaac's rage was a terrible tangible thing in the air surrounding them. His entire body was taut, his muscles rippling, as he sought to control his reaction to the retelling of her treatment at the cult's hands.

Thinking only to soothe him in some way, she tentatively placed her hand on his chest and looked at him with pleading in her eyes. Begging him silently for calm and perhaps a warning that her story would only get worse. He placed his hand over hers where it rested against his heart and he gently squeezed, not only acknowledging her silent request, but also offering her the reassurance, comfort and encouragement she so desperately needed in order to continue.

Before she could go on, he gathered her hand carefully in his and lifted it to his mouth and pressed his lips softly over her palm. Then, cradling her hand as if it were something precious and infinitely fragile, he slid it from his lips to his jaw so that her fingers were splayed out over the stubble on his face. He left it there for a long moment, his hand covering hers as he stared intently into her eyes. There was more than just sympathy, comfort or even encouragement reflected in his dark gaze, but what exactly she couldn't interpret. The way it made her feel was something entirely unfamiliar. It was something she had never experienced before. And she liked it. Perhaps too much.

His gaze and his touch infused an intimate warmth into the very heart of her. Parts of her soul that had been cold for so very long felt as though the sun was shining on them for the first time ever. Perhaps more confusing for her wasn't just her emotional response to this man or the fact that trusting him had been so automatic, so easy. She who had never been safe in her entire life, who'd never been made to feel safe with anyone, felt as though nothing and no one could ever harm her so long as he was with her.

No, as confused as she should be by the faith she had in this warrior, her physical reaction perplexed her far more. Whenever he touched her, whenever he even looked at her in that soul-searching way he did so often, she was mystified and shamed by the fact that her breasts swelled and became tender. Her nipples tingled and tightened into hard buds, thrusting forward as if begging for his touch. More embarrassing was that her most private parts became moist and hypersensitive and she had to resist the sudden urge to touch herself . . . down *there*.

Sucking in a steadying breath, ashamed of the direction her thoughts had gone, she mentally shook herself and prepared to continue with all she had to tell Isaac.

As she opened her mouth to proceed with her story, Isaac moved her hand back over his mouth and once again pressed a tender kiss into her palm before lowering it to his lap, but he didn't release it, instead tangling his fingers with hers, lacing them together as they rested between them.

"A gathering was called, one that every cult member was forced to attend. They dragged me into the meeting room and then threw me on the floor in front of the entire assembly. I was again told to admit that evil lives within me and that only God decided life or death. I was ordered to renounce Satan, to renounce my gift and to beg the elders for mercy and forgiveness."

Tears of rage streamed down her cheeks as she relived the incident as if it were only yesterday. She lifted her chin so that she could look Isaac in the eye.

"They demanded that I beg the *elders* for mercy and forgiveness," she said bitterly. "Not God. *Them.* They believed themselves to be gods and here they were accusing me of being evil. Saying that Satan lived within me, when they were the ones guilty of all they accused me of.

"I defied them. I spoke out. I shouldn't have, but God, I couldn't do what they demanded. I don't know how I found the strength to stand up on my own, but I did, and I faced them down, staring them directly in the eyes. I told them they were wrong. That it was *they* who were evil. Not me. That God wasn't imperfect and that he created me, and it was he who gave me the gift to help others. I told them that Satan was evil and he would never, nor did he have the power to, grant someone the power to heal, to do *good*. They tied me to a whipping post and said that they'd drive the demons from me if it was the last thing they did."

"Jesus," Isaac muttered, reaching for her and holding her tightly. "Baby, stop. You don't have to relive this."

"But I do," she said tearfully. "You have to know everything, Isaac. So that you understand what you're dealing with and why I had to escape the hell I'd lived in for so long."

He tucked her head underneath his chin and wrapped his strong arms around her, creating a haven, a safe place where it felt like nothing could ever hurt her again.

"I held out for as long as I could. I swear I did," she said brokenly.

"Baby, stop," Isaac pleaded. "Do you think you have to defend yourself to me? You did nothing wrong and god damn it, I won't have you think it. I won't have you feel shame that you gave in when they damn near beat you to death."

"But that's just it. I was so stupid. They never intended to kill me. They would have never killed me. They were simply punishing me and setting the stage. It was all an act. A pretense. They needed me for their own selfish purposes and had no thought for anyone else in the cult who may have need of my healing power. They made me a pariah. It was all a carefully staged way to alienate me from the rest of the cult so the elders could be sure no one would ever help me. So I would be completely isolated and on my own so they could do with me as they liked."

A growl sounded low and fierce in Isaac's throat, startling her from the pain of reliving such terrifying memories.

"They didn't just try to isolate you, Jenna. They tried to break you."

"They succeeded," she said dully, looking away from him, not wanting him to see her shame and weakness.

"The hell they did!" Isaac barked, causing her to jump, nearly sliding off his lap and out of his grasp.

He immediately calmed, though rage was still blazing from his eyes, and he gathered her back up in his arms, repositioning her on his lap. He shifted so he could frame her face with his hands. His touch was exquisitely tender. His thumbs feathered over her cheekbones, his caresses as soft as a butterfly's wings.

"Look at me, Jenna."

Reluctantly she lifted her eyes to meet his and felt tears well up all over again when she saw so much emotion reflected in his gaze. There was tenderness, understanding. Compassion, but not pity. To her shock, she also saw pride, but there was something else staring back at her. Something she couldn't name because it wasn't something she'd ever seen. But it warmed her from the inside out and gave her peace at a moment when her thoughts were anything but peaceful.

"The woman sitting here in my arms is not broken," he said fiercely. "You may be down and they may have damaged you—hell, they did damage you—but honey, they did *not* break you."

His words only made her want to cry even more.

"Then why do I feel so broken, so shattered on the inside?" she asked in a small voice that stuttered as sobs knotted her throat. "Why does it feel like I have no idea who I am? That I'm nothing and that I don't even exist? And that even if I'm someone, I'll never be able to put the pieces back together of that person and I'll always be what they made me?"

Isaac gazed at her with a look filled with so much caring

and respect that she wanted to turn away from him and curl into a ball so small that no one would ever see her. What she really was and not this person Isaac thought he saw. The pitiful, weak woman who hadn't had the will or the strength to defy what she knew in her heart was wrong.

He looked at her like she mattered. With admiration she didn't deserve, but God how she wanted to be a woman worthy of having a good man, a man like Isaac who stood against evil every single day. Looking at her just like he was gazing at her right now. Like she was worth it. But she wasn't. She'd brought him and the people in his life—people he obviously cared about—nothing but pain, danger and deception. How could he even stand to look at her at all, much less with such warm understanding and kindness?

"You are not what they tried to bend you and shape you into, Jenna," he insisted. "Baby, everyone bends, but not everyone breaks. If they had broken you, if they had succeeded in making you what they wanted, would you be here with me right now? Would you have found the courage to stand up to them even after they beat you down time after time? Would you have found a way to escape them and run despite your fears of the unknown world you were escaping into? You can think and say what you want about what a failure you are, how weak you are and how unworthy you are of anything good in this world, but baby? I'm going to call bullshit every single time that fucked-up shit comes out of your pretty mouth. If it takes forever, I'll get you to see the woman I see every time I look at you."

She flushed, heat invading her cheeks until her face felt as though it were on fire.

"And I'll tell you something else," he said, his expression growing more somber and an edge to his voice that indicated he was deadly serious. "I will never let them take you back."

He stroked her cheek, letting the backs of his knuckles graze lightly over her skin, leaving a peculiar tingling sensation in their wake.

"I will never let them touch you or put their hands on you again. And furthermore, should we ever be so fortunate as for them to get injured or even better, killed, you will not lift a single finger to heal their sorry asses.

"I intend to hunt every single one of those assholes down and make them pay for every mark, every blow, every beating, every bruise and every single word they ever said to make you feel like you were nothing."

Terror exploded in Jenna's heart, nearly paralyzing her with its intensity.

"No!" she burst out.

Isaac looked at her in surprise, but before he could say anything else, she pushed his hands away from her cheeks and buried her face in her hands. She moaned in despair, because she knew she would have to confide her last shameful secret. The thing that had forced her to speed up her plan of escape.

"Baby, what is it?" Isaac asked in concern.

She lifted her head and saw him flinch at the rawness in her expression.

"You can't go after them, Isaac," she said hysterically. "The elders aren't the ones who are after me now."

TWELVE

ISAAC stared at Jenna in shock even as his mind burned with anger. Fury like he'd never known was about to force him right over the edge, and now to find out there was more? A bigger threat to his angel than he thought? He didn't even stop to have a "what the fuck" moment with himself over thinking of her as his angel—his anything. She'd been his from the very start, from the moment she'd shared the beautiful light of her soul with him. Now she was inside him, a part of him attached so deep that there was no hope or thought of ever digging her out. There were only two things he knew at this moment. She belonged to him and he would protect her from whatever the fuck threat she faced.

He reached out to touch her, but she flinched away, fear and self-condemnation clouding her beautiful eyes. Fuck that. He wrapped himself around her, holding her tightly against him until finally she stopped fighting him and went still, sobs wracking her tiny frame, and he swore to make those bastards pay for those tears. For every tear she ever shed because they'd made her life hell.

"Jenna, honey, calm down and quit crying," he soothed, holding and rocking her back and forth as months—hell, years—of pent-up pain and misery worked their way from her system.

"I need you to tell me everything, baby," he said softly. "I have to know how to keep you safe, and that means you tell me everything. There is nothing you can't tell me. Do you understand? There is nothing that will ever make me feel badly about you and there is damn sure nothing that will ever make me let you go."

She went completely still, her sobs halting. She went so quiet that it worried him. Then she turned, staring up at him with her heart in her eyes. She looked so innocent and utterly guileless, but then how could she be anything else having lived her life sequestered from the world, her only knowledge coming from fucked-up, twisted, sadistic minds?

"Do you mean that?" she asked, a note of anxiety in her voice.

His heart went completely soft, the hard steel around it splintering wide open.

"I never say things I don't mean and I don't make promises that I don't keep," he said, staring back at her intently, barriers down so she could see as easily into him as he could her.

She hung her head again and drew her hands between their bodies, twisting her fingers anxiously together.

"Baby, don't look like that," he said. "Tell me what has you so afraid so I can take care of it."

"I don't want anything to happen to you or your men because of me," she whispered.

"Jenna, look at me," he said, beginning to sound like a broken record. "Do you forget that if not for you I'd be dead, and Shadow would be in the hospital getting stitches and raising hell about being forced to receive medical attention?"

Her expression only grew sadder. "If it wasn't for me trying to steal your vehicle, neither of you would've been hurt in the first place."

"But then I wouldn't have you. Here right now in my arms. I'd say it was worth nearly dying," he said softly.

She stared at him, shocked, swallowing multiple times as she tried to get her emotions under control.

"No one has ever cared what happened to me," she said quietly. "Only so much as to make sure I was capable of doing what the elders wanted."

Isaac put a lid on the red haze of fury that billowed up inside him and focused on the woman he held, waiting for her to confide the last of her secrets. He lifted her from his lap and laid her next to him, and then he stretched out his long length and turned so they were on their sides facing one another.

She blinked and then flushed, discomfort evident on her face. "This isn't appropriate," she whispered. "It's a sin for me to be in your bed. I'm sorry. I didn't even think when I came in here."

"Jenna, I want you to listen to me and listen to me very closely. First, I'm very glad you came to me when you were scared. I want you to always come to me when something—anything—frightens you. Secondly, I want you to forget every fucked-up thing you were taught in that goddamn cult. They're wrong. You know they're wrong. It's why you wanted to escape so badly. Not just because of the shitty way they treated you and the fact they abused you and then used you for their selfish purposes. Aside from all of that, their teachings are wrong. Not just wrong but so fucked up I can't even wrap my mind around it. I get that what they taught you, what's been instilled in you for most of your life, is hard to just discard in a few minutes, days or even weeks, but this is where I need you to trust me, baby. You being in my bed isn't wrong, and not just because we aren't doing anything but talking. It won't be wrong when I make love to you either."

A horrified look crossed her face. "No! I don't want that. I *never* want that." She shuddered. "It's *horrible*."

A dull roar began in his ears and he had to clench his jaw to prevent the angry roar from escaping. "Did they rape you, Jenna? Did they put their goddamn hands on you? Did they force themselves on you? Did they ever force you to have sex with *anyone*?"

She shuddered again. "No, but I saw . . ." She shook her head. "I don't want to talk about it. Please don't make me talk about it right now," she pleaded.

"I just want to know one thing and then no, sweetheart, you don't have to talk about it right now."

He purposely injected *right now* because they *would* discuss it later. It was obviously a traumatic subject for her and he had to know why. Even if the very thought of having to listen to his angel tell him that someone had violated her was enough to send him spiraling out of control.

"Did one of those bastards ever touch you or hurt you sexually?" he ground out.

She flushed but shook her head. *Thank God*. He took in

several deep breaths to rein in the rage that had threatened to consume him.

"I was a pariah. It was forbidden. But not for the reasons you might think. It wasn't because they were protecting me or cared whether I was hurt. The elders had a stupid superstition that if I ever lost my virginity I would lose my power to heal. I was grateful," she whispered. "Their stupidity and ignorance is the only thing I was ever grateful to them for."

Finally he could breathe again, until she said her next words.

"But it was coming to an end," she said, fear flooding her features once more. But more pronounced, more raw than any fear she'd shown until now.

Before he could demand to know what she meant, she went on, her voice trembling as much as her body was.

"I had always planned to escape," she admitted. "It was the only thing that kept me sane. The idea of one day escaping. But they were so careful and they kept me under lock and key most of the time. The only times I was ever able to sneak from my room were after a healing session. Because I'm always so weak and exhausted afterward, they were more lax about watching me. They'd dump me in my room, but no one bothered to guard me. I played up my weakness, making it seem as though I was utterly helpless after healing someone. Then I would sneak into one of the elders' quarters, where they had information that was supposedly forbidden. It's how I learned of the outside world, what little I had time to learn. It was also the confusing and contradictory teachings of the cult. I knew it would take me time, years, to learn enough and plan my escape, but I didn't care. It became my obsession and the way I've dealt with the punishments I received.

I would imagine being free somewhere far away where I was just another face in the crowd and no one knew who I was or what I could do. I just wanted to be normal and to have a normal life," she said, tears welling in her eyes.

Her sadness made Isaac's chest ache, but more than that he wanted her happy, for him to be the one who made her happy.

"You can have that now, baby," he said gently, palming her cheek and caressing away the tiny damp trails.

"But I can't," she said sadly. "They'll never stop looking for me."

"Tell me about *they*. Who is *they*, and if you lived in such seclusion, how would anyone outside the cult know anything about you or that you even existed?"

"Because the elders sold me to them," she said bitterly.

"What the fuck? Who did they sell you to, Jenna, and is that why you ran?"

She nodded miserably, biting into her lip to keep from crying again. "I knew I had to take a chance and escape or I'd never have another opportunity."

"Who did they sell you to?" he repeated patiently. "And are they the ones after you now? The ones who shot me and Shadow?"

She flinched, flushing with guilt. "I don't know exactly who they are, but they're dangerous," she whispered. "They had guns. They always had guns. They offered the elders a lot of money for me but the elders had conditions. One was that I be made available anytime they needed my services and another was that I had to remain untouched."

She flushed deeply. "Their leader wanted to speak to me alone and he told me I was his property now, and then he laughed and said, 'Those crazy assholes believe that if you lose your virginity your powers will be gone, but you and I both know that isn't true, don't we?'"

She shivered and curled her body inward, pressing herself closer to Isaac, though he doubted she was conscious of it.

"He told me that he was going to enjoy fucking a virgin, that he would be the one to break me in, and then his men could have me as often as they wanted. He laughed more and told me that the elders would never have use of my powers again no matter what he'd agreed upon. He planned to kill them all when they came for me."

Isaac swore viciously, his fingers curling into tight fists as the urge to kill returned. And he would. He'd kill every last one of those fuckers before ever allowing them to touch what was his.

"The exchange was set up for a few days later and I knew I had to escape. I had to take the chance because even if I died, it would be preferable to being sold to those men."

Isaac closed his eyes, hurting for someone so innocent to have been exposed to so much evil in her young life. The knowledge that she'd embraced death so calmly as an alternative to being used and degraded by the men who'd bought her like a possession nearly broke him.

"God was with me," she said softly, surprising Isaac with her mention of God. He would have thought that with the twisted aberration the cult presented God as, she would have lost any and all faith in a higher being.

"One of the elders had a heart attack. He was dying and I was called to heal him. Everyone knew how grave his condition was, and until him and then . . . you . . . I had never healed someone so close to death. So I did just enough that he wouldn't die and pretended to be completely incapacitated, drained and exhausted. I told them I had to rest and then I would need to do a second session to completely heal him, but that he wouldn't die. And that after the second time it would be as if the heart attack had never happened and he hadn't been at death's door."

She looked down in shame and his brow furrowed as he looked at her in question, waiting for her to continue.

"I wanted to kill him, to let him die," she whispered. "It was only because I knew this would be my only opportunity to finally escape that I helped him."

"He deserved to die," Isaac bit out. "Don't waste one minute feeling shame for wanting him to die, baby. After all they put you through, it's only human to feel the way you did. Not even God could blame you if you had let him die."

His reassurance seemed to mollify her and she sucked in a deep breath.

"They dragged me to my room and tossed me in, and then they all went back to pray for the elder. To pray," she said scornfully. "How does one pray to God to save the very face of evil? They didn't spare a single thought to my escaping because they'd witnessed how weak I was so many times before after I'd healed. And though I had greatly exaggerated my condition, I *was* very weak, and it took me a while to gain the strength to crawl to the door and drag myself up so I could escape.

"I had found maps in one of the elders' offices before, so I knew the layout of the compound and which direction was the shortest route through the dense woods surrounding the place. I managed to slip out quietly and then I ran. It was so dark and I was terrified. I couldn't see where I was going, and just prayed that I was running a straight line through the woods and not going in circles."

Isaac's stomach churned, imagining how helpless she was running through God only knew what in the woods, still weak from the forced healing session. He'd never craved someone's blood more than he craved the blood of those bastards for all they'd done to his angel. Never had he entertained killing anyone in cold blood, but in this minute, he knew if he ever caught any of them he'd take them apart with his bare hands.

"Not long after I entered the woods, I knew my escape had been discovered, because I heard them turn out the dogs."

She shivered, her small body quaking as she moved even closer into his body, almost as if trying to crawl right inside of him where she could feel warm and safe.

"I knew I had very little time before they caught up to me, so I ran faster and prayed for mercy. And for help. Just when I thought I had no hope, I stumbled out of the woods and fell flat on my face onto a gravel road. It was just beginning to get light enough that I could see into the distance and there was an old gas station down the road. I fled, praying the entire way to find a way into the city. I knew it was the last place they'd expect me to go because I'd never even seen the outside of the compound, so what were my odds of surviving five minutes in a city the size of Houston? I snuck into the bed of a truck that was hauling produce into the city and when the driver stopped after what seemed like forever, I slipped out and ran."

Her mouth twisted against his chest, her next words muffled by his skin.

"I guess it was fate that I was so close to the parking lot where your vehicle was parked unlocked."

"Yes," he said quietly. "Thank God I'm forever leaving my keys in the ignition."

She pulled slightly away, and he could see her frown and the fact that her eyes had turned fearful once more.

"What's wrong, Jenna?" he asked sharply.

"Isaac, the elders don't have guns, and certainly nothing that could have shot you from such a long range."

She grabbed his hand, clutching it to her chest, and he felt her heart racing wildly beneath his palm.

"How could they have known?" she whispered. "How could they have possibly found me so quickly? They weren't supposed to come for me for two more days."

Isaac's brow furrowed as he considered her words.

"They had to have been watching the compound the entire time just in case you did exactly what you did. Then they followed you, tracking your every move. If I hadn't found you and interrupted you stealing my vehicle, they would have either taken you right there in the parking lot or followed you and either forced you off the road or abducted you as soon as you stopped."

"Then how was it that you and your men found me before they did after I'd pulled off the road?"

Isaac sighed. "They were distracted and forced to defend themselves when my backup arrived and began shooting back. I doubt they were expecting any resistance. They likely thought taking you would be effortless. I have a tracking device on my SUV that led us right to you. Unfortunately, I also led *them* right to you, which is how they found my house and shot Shadow as we were leaving to come here."

She shot upward in the bed, the T-shirt she was wearing stretching tightly over the lush ripeness of her breasts.

"Then we aren't safe here either," she said, panicked.

"Shhh, baby, I need you to calm down," he soothed. "We would know if they were anywhere close to this house, but you're right. We can't stay here. I'll have to make some phone calls while we figure out our next move."

She licked her lips nervously and Isaac nearly groaned at the innocent, sexy gesture.

"Will you be safe?" she asked hesitantly. "Will your men be safe?"

His expression went dark and anger was a fierce battle within him. She was only concerned about him and his team. Not one word about her own safety or whether they could keep *her* safe. Did she think she had so little value?

Of course she thought just that. When had she ever been shown anything to the contrary? Disgust filled him. She'd spent a lifetime being beaten down, devalued, told time and time again that she was nothing, not important, when in the space of a day she'd become his entire world.

Unable to resist and passing only a moment's worry over spooking her, he wrapped his arms around her body and pulled her to him, delving one hand into the silky pale curls of her hair as he lowered his mouth to hers.

He pressed his lips tentatively to hers at first, judging her reaction, but to his surprise she melted into his body, molding herself tightly to his as if they were meant to fit together. Then he deepened his kiss, sweeping his tongue over her lips, coaxing them gently to open under his persistent demand. With a breathy sigh, she parted her lips just enough that he could slip his tongue inside her mouth and entwine it with hers, absorbing the sweetness of her taste.

Never had anything felt so right in his life. So *perfect*. She was made for him just as he was made for her and he'd be damned if anything ever separated them again. He'd go to the wall for her time and time again, placing his body between her and any danger posed to her. And he knew one truth above all others. She belonged to him. Nothing that felt this right could possibly be not meant to be.

"I will never let anyone hurt you again, Jenna," he whispered against her lips. "You'll have me and my entire organization devoted to your safety just as soon as I sound the alarm and we call a meeting to plot our next move."

Her look of sadness was enough to break his heart into a million pieces.

"I'm nobody, Isaac," she said in a tone that told him she believed every word of it. "You can't risk everything for me. Do you think I could ever live with myself knowing that you—any of you—were hurt or killed because of me?"

"That's where you're wrong, honey," he said in his most loving voice, a voice he'd never imagined using on another woman. On anyone. "You are everything to me. My entire world. And if you think after finally finding you after so many years of missing a piece of myself that I'm just going to let you go, then you're quickly going to find out how very wrong you are. You're mine, Jenna. Do you understand that? You are *mine*. And I am responsible for every part of your well-being, your protection, your happiness, making you smile, making you laugh and making every dream you've ever dreamed come true. If you'll just trust me, I swear to you that I'll make every one of those things happen."

She looked shell-shocked. Tears crowded her beautiful eyes as she stared at Isaac in stunned confusion.

"Do you mean that?" she barely managed to choke out, asking him the same words she'd voiced earlier.

"I've never been more serious about anything in my life. But this can't be one-sided, Jenna. I have to know that you feel at least something for me. I need you to give me hope that I'm not operating solo here and that you feel even a fraction of what I feel when I look into your eyes, when I touch you and when I kiss you."

She flushed, dropping her gaze, but not before he saw such longing in her eyes that it made him want to cry for all she'd never had and all she'd ever dreamed of.

"Trust in me, Jenna," he said, huskily, nearly begging when he'd never begged for anything in his life. "Give me the chance to prove myself to you. It's all I'll ever ask of you. Just a chance. And for you to place your trust and your heart in my hand. I'll treat them like the most precious things I've ever been given."

"I'm broken, Isaac. How can you want that—me?" she asked tearfully. "How can I be worthy of a man like you?"

He scowled despite his best efforts not to. "That's the biggest line of bullshit I've ever heard in my life and I will not hear it come out of your pretty mouth again. Are we clear?"

She was shaking but she nodded her head, color tinging her cheeks as she stared at his lips, the lips that had just kissed her.

"I never knew," she said in wonder.

He cocked his head to the side, cupping her cheek in his hand. "What are you talking about, honey?"

"That kissing was so beautiful," she admitted hesitantly. "So intimate. It's like nothing I've ever felt before and I don't understand what it's doing to me."

He smiled tenderly at her and then kissed her softly once

more. "You'll understand this and a whole lot more very soon, baby. I promise you that."

Then he sighed and drew away. "I want you to lie down and try to get some sleep. You're exhausted and I need you rested for what comes next. I need to make some calls and plot our next move. I'll wake you in a few hours and I swear to you that I'll keep nothing from you. Deal?"

Slowly she nodded, glancing back at the bed longingly. Not waiting for her to move, he swept her into his arms and placed her on the bed with her head resting on the soft pillows. Then he pulled the covers up to her chin and kissed her one last time.

"Good night, sweet Jenna. Sleep well for me, okay? I need you strong for what comes next, so promise me you'll rest and let me worry about the details."

"I promise," she said in a somber voice.

"That's my girl," he said affectionately. "Lamp on or off?"

"On," she said anxiously. "I don't like the dark."

Unable to resist, he leaned over to give her one last, deep kiss, lingering for several long moments.

"Good night, love," he whispered. "Dream of me."

THIRTEEN

ISAAC punched in a series of encrypted codes that would signal every single DSS member that bad shit was going down and that everyone needed to get to one of the few safe houses that hadn't been breached over the years. As much as Isaac didn't want to involve DSS, he knew he didn't have a choice after all that Jenna had confided in him.

This was much bigger than a one-man operation or even for a small crew of teammates. Isaac needed every single person available in on this mission. It could mean the difference between life and death, and between Jenna being saved and her being kidnapped and subjected to a life in hell for as long as the men pursuing her had use of her.

Isaac knew that Caleb and Beau's younger sister, Tori, along with their wives and Zack's wife would accompany their husbands for two reasons. One, their husbands would never let them out of their sight when there was potential danger to any of them. And two, and Isaac nearly grinned, they would have insisted on coming no matter how fiercely their husbands argued differently, particularly Ari, because that woman could kick some serious ass without even having a weapon other than her devious, vengeful mind when it came to people she loved being hurt or threatened.

It was obvious that Dane, Beau and Caleb weren't happy with the fact that Isaac and the four newest recruits were holed up in a safe house provided by Eliza's husband, Sterling.

"I appreciate you all coming," Isaac said solemnly.

"What's going on, Isaac? Cut the crap. Does this happen to have anything to do with Jenna?" Dane demanded.

Isaac held up his hands as Dex, Zeke, Knight and Shadow stood from the couch, their arms folded over their chests, their expressions inscrutable.

"We're here because we want to be," Shadow said quietly, though his every word was heard. "This had nothing to do with DSS or our jobs there and it sure as hell doesn't have a goddamn thing to do about money, so take your paychecks and shove them up your ass."

Dane chuckled, but Beau's face looked like an angry storm cloud.

"You'd do well to remember who signs your paychecks," Beau snapped.

"Last time I checked, Dane hired us, Dane trained us and Dane signs our checks," Dex drawled. "As far as I'm concerned if he doesn't have a problem, and he hasn't voiced one yet, then my only job is to report to him and take orders from him and Isaac since Isaac is lead on this."

Three of the four women Jenna had been looking curiously at rolled their eyes and made faces at the men before turning and hurrying over to where Jenna stood. The other woman remained where she was and Jenna noted that she looked sad—and frightened. Did she resent Jenna for causing so much upheaval to all their lives?

"We're so happy to meet you, Jenna," Ari said warmly, after she'd introduced herself as well as the other two, Ramie and Gracie and explaining who their husbands were. "I think after hearing about the three of us, you'll find you aren't as alone as you think and you're most definitely *not* a freak."

Jenna lifted both eyebrows in question and then Ari launched into what power each of the women possessed, how different they all were and yet how helpful they were when they came together to save their men's asses.

Jenna's mouth fell open, and Ramie and Gracie laughed. "Now, don't go telling *them* that even if it's the God's honest truth. They like to think they keep us wrapped in bubble wrap and at home where nothing can ever touch us." She rolled her eyes again. "Never mind that we've gotten them out of more than one scrape by combining our talents and using them to bring down the bad guys."

Jenna looked beyond the group of women to the lone woman who was still standing alone across the room, her arms wrapped protectively around herself, her head down so that no one could catch her gaze.

"Who is she?" Jenna asked quietly. "She looks so . . . vulnerable." Much like Jenna felt, but in this moment, something about the other woman called to her, making her forget the danger to her. She was more concerned about exposing the other woman to the fanatics who were after Jenna.

Ramie's eyes darkened and she sighed. "That's Tori. She's

Caleb and Beau's baby sister. She's been through so much. She also has a gift, but it frustrates and hurts her more than it helps her."

Jenna's brow furrowed with confusion.

"She was abducted a few years ago by a sadistic serial killer who did unspeakable things to her before she was rescued. Just hours before he was going to kill her," Ari said in a low voice. "She dreams of the future. Of things that will happen, but she often can't make sense of the dream. Either she won't know who the people are in her dream which prevents her from warning them, or if she dreams of people she does know, the dreams aren't clear and succinct. She sees images and situations but not the events leading up to whatever happened. It makes her feel helpless. Between her dreams of the future and her nightmares of the past, she is never at peace, never feels safe, and who can blame her? I can't imagine having to deal with what she does. Just one of those things is enough to break a person, but the two combined? She thinks she's weak and unfixable, but what she doesn't realize is how much strength a person has to have to endure what she did and still does and hold up under the strain. She's far stronger than she gives herself credit for."

Jenna glanced at Tori again, her heart filling with sorrow. She agreed with Ari's assessment. This was no weak or irrevocably damaged woman. If she was, she wouldn't still be holding strong and making it through each day.

Even as she thought it, Isaac's impassioned words came back to her, so similar to her thoughts about Tori. Him telling her that she wasn't broken, that she wasn't weak. That a weaker person would have never endured as long as Jenna had and wouldn't have been able to escape.

It was a stunning revelation and it provided a view of herself she'd never imagined before. Could he be right? If it was true about Tori, could it be true about herself? She didn't like to think of herself as a weak, helpless and broken woman. She wanted to be strong. Wanted to be worthy of the way Isaac and the rest of his team seemed to view her. Perhaps she needed to reevaluate her assessment of herself and stop wallowing in self-pity and acting like a helpless twit. If she wasn't even capable of helping herself, then how could she expect anyone else to be able to help her?

"You look like you're about to collapse," Gracie said in her quiet, sweet voice. "Why don't you sit down. This will likely take a while and I promise and cross my heart that if Isaac withholds anything from you, the girls and I will fill you in on everything."

Jenna smiled and stifled a yawn. "Now that you mention it, I am pretty tired."

But when the women turned away to return to their husbands, Jenna retreated to the far side of the room and sank down the wall with her back against it, grasping her knees and pulling them to her chin.

She stared in envy and also felt keenly bereft of something she couldn't even put a name to when she saw how obvious it was that their husbands loved them. They didn't go a minute without touching them. Pressing little kisses to their heads, noses, necks and even lifting their hands occasionally to nibble on their fingers. There was no discomfort. The unmarried men took it all good-naturedly and judging by the rosy glows on the women's cheeks, they enjoyed their husbands' touches very much. As much as their kisses.

It was like nothing she'd ever witnessed. None of the men in the cult had kissed their wives, acted affectionate toward them, held them simply for the sake of touching them or teased them with soft laughter. God, the love that blazed in the eyes of these men for their wives was enough to make Jenna run from the room in shame.

Would anyone ever look at her like that? She was a product of what the cult had created. Conditioned to believe that the things she'd been taught were the same everywhere in the world. Except . . . Isaac had looked at her very much like these men looked at their wives, and when he kissed her, any previous notions about kissing being distasteful vanished and she became immersed, lost in a world she'd never known existed. What did it all mean? Surely Isaac couldn't profess to feel deeply for her so soon. They barely knew one another. But he was so convincing. Or perhaps she saw and felt what she wanted to and reality was a far cry from the fantasy she'd created.

How was she supposed to know what to think? To believe? How was she, with her ignorance of life beyond the boundaries of the compound that had been her prison, supposed to know what was real and what wasn't? Her mind was in absolute chaos and she couldn't process the bombardment of behavior that was completely alien to her any more than she could possibly believe that any of it was normal. What if they were the freaks and she was the only normal one?

She nearly choked as a harsh laugh burned her throat and she swallowed it back. If anyone was the freak, it was her. She viewed the obvious love between these husbands and wives with skepticism because deep down it hurt her to know that these women had something she would give anything for.

And, well, she had to be honest with herself because it was

the only thing left to her when everything else in her life was a lie. The truth of the matter was that she was bitterly envious of Ramie, Ari and Gracie. Her envy sliced deeper than any shame or any wound ever bestowed upon her by her captors ever had. The cut wasn't smooth or shallow. It was ripped open, scarring her and bleeding all the way to her soul.

Was it a sin to covet what most other young girls who grew into women wished for? All she'd ever fantasized about was the outside world being nothing like the relationships of the people within the cult. She dreamed of a normal life with a man, a husband who loved her, who would give her children and who didn't care about her powers nor was threatened by them. But she'd never known if the rest of the world was any different. Now that she knew the truth, it only made her yearning that much more pronounced. What if it was too late for her? She was too marked, the scars too deep and pronounced by her time with the cult to ever have anyone look at her with anything but pity or disgust. Or downright disbelief.

After what seemed an eternity, the women and even Isaac along with some of his men finally stopped glancing over at her in concern, and they began to make plans and discuss necessary precautions.

Jenna buried her face in her knees, rocking back and forth, making herself the smallest ball she could manage and as unnoticeable as she could so no attention was drawn to her. She simply couldn't bear the pity or even anger in their eyes, their expressions. She knew that they'd been dragged into a problem that wasn't theirs to solve, much less become involved in.

She needed to get away as fast as possible. She needed to run so that these people who represented everything good in the world weren't tainted by her and never had to suffer because they interfered on her behalf.

As much as she wanted to believe that Isaac cared for her and as much as she wanted to be to him what the other women were to their husbands, she knew it wasn't a realistic dream. She'd get him killed. Maybe even the husbands of the other women and then, God, how could she face any of them? How could she face herself or ever look in the mirror again knowing she was the reason for so much pain and death? She had to let go of her ridiculous dreams and embrace what was real. And what was real was the fact that she and anyone close to her would never be safe. No man could be expected to live his life having to look over his shoulder constantly and dodge death at every turn. And it would kill her to see Isaac walk away after having experienced, even for a little while, what life would be like with a man like him. It hurt her deeply to leave him now, but it would completely break her if he left after he'd been hers for even a short period of time.

It had to be this way. Not just for her own self-preservation but also for Isaac's safety and the safety of everyone in this room. She closed her eyes and took a moment to harden her resolve, knowing in her heart that this was her only option. She had no other choice.

The second she lifted her head just enough to peek at the others from underneath her eyelashes she froze. She was a complete idiot, because if Gracie truly did have the ability to read minds, Jenna's plan was likely already in shreds.

The more her gaze followed the women in the group, the more bitter envy swelled deep in her gut. She didn't hate them or bear them ill will, but she was so jealous of what they had and all that she didn't.

Jenna dropped her head back to her knees in case anyone caught her staring, and especially if Gracie had a mental pathway into her mind. She huddled as far from the others as possible, trying to make herself invisible, all the while slowly scanning the room with eyes that were hidden from the people standing several feet away. She took in every detail, trying desperately to find some way of escaping. A hysterical laugh nearly spilled from her lips before she slammed them shut and sucked in deep, steadying breaths through her nose, willing herself to be calm.

How exactly did she think she'd ever manage to escape these men? Anger at herself surged hotly through her body. She'd already escaped the impossible and if she'd done it once, then she could do it again. She just had to believe in herself. But first she had to find a way out and secondly, she had to make her move when everyone's attention was drawn away from her and focused on charting their course of action.

She softly blew out her breath over her knees in a nearly silent gesture of frustration. Who was she kidding? Only a few seconds ago she'd been all about being honest with herself and here she was contemplating that her odds of slipping away unnoticed were actually good. But she couldn't decide which was worse. Being dishonest with herself or being a pessimist. Neither was going to help her out in her current situation.

Refusing to give in to defeat, no matter how inevitable it seemed, she resolved to stop sulking, wallowing in self-pity and acting like a pathetic, useless twit. There was always a way. She just had to find it.

Being extremely careful not to be obvious, she resumed the search she'd so quickly abandoned only moments after beginning. She'd learned infinite patience while imprisoned in the cult, knowing that if she ever grew impatient and tried to escape before she had a flawless plan in place, she'd never get another chance. Luck certainly never hurt, though, and she'd take all the luck available to her.

Remaining completely silent, not even the puffy exchange of air from her lungs able to be heard, she lifted her head so gradually it would be undetectable and peeked from beneath her arms to survey the room, looking for a way out that wasn't barred by one or more of the DSS men. Ugh, the size that these men were, it would only take one to create an insurmountable obstacle to her.

Her breath caught when her gaze finally lighted on what looked to be an opening to a cellar in the floor. It was small, scarcely big enough for the large, muscled men to ever fit through. It would certainly be a tight squeeze for any one of them. But her slim figure could easily slip through the opening. The cellar door didn't look as if it had been used in years. Since she knew this to be one of the DSS strongholds and the most secure of their safe houses, the cellar door was likely an escape route in case the house came under siege.

It wasn't far from where she sat against the wall and if she could slowly, but most of all quietly, move the few feet between her and the cellar opening, she could quickly slip downward before she would even be detected.

There had to be a way out once she reached the sublevel of the safe house. These men would have planned for every eventuality, and in all likelihood had multiple escape routes in case the safe house was breached and any of the other exits had been compromised or blocked off by the enemy.

She mentally gave herself a pep talk even as panic threatened to overwhelm her to the point of breaking down into hysteria. *Get it together, Jenna!* All she had to do was drop down the cellar opening, slide the door back shut, hopefully not making the slightest sound, and then find the exit that led to the outside of the building and run as if her life depended on it.

Not her life. Isaac's life. The lives of the men and women of DSS. People's blood she refused to have on her hands when she was the sole reason they were all in danger.

She'd found her way around the city the first time, even if she hadn't gone far before running into Isaac—and trouble. But that wasn't the point. She'd done it once and she could do it again. She just couldn't let terror paralyze her and she needed to realize that this wasn't a game of hide-and-seek. Failure meant her capture, and it could also mean death for every single person in this room. Success meant she would continue to breathe and could disappear to where she'd never be a danger to anyone again.

That thought immediately sobered her and she vowed to take extreme care this time and not to trust anyone. She'd gotten lucky that Isaac *had* been someone she could trust, but what if she'd attempted to steal someone else's vehicle? If not for Isaac she'd now be in the hands of brutal monsters. Not everyone was good like Isaac and his men, and from now on, she'd take no chances, thus not giving herself any opportunity to trust only to then be betrayed.

Fear had lent her strength before when she'd fled. It had given her the adrenaline necessary to go through with her plan.

But this time she couldn't count on those things to save her again. She had to be smart and use her head if she had any hope of getting out of this place and staying alive.

It little mattered where in the city she went, only that she kept away from darkened alleys and dimly lit streets. Neighborhoods that were suspect. Anything that fired the sixth sense for danger she'd always possessed. This time she'd damn well listen instead of plunging recklessly through the streets looking frantically for something, anything, to aid her in her escape.

She needed to make it a point to keep to crowded areas where she could blend in. Stick to busy parts of town. Shopping meccas. Places where there were plenty of stores, maybe a large mall. It would be so easy to blend in with the thousands of people who scurried along like ants in and out of an anthill.

But before she got too carried away with her plan, she had to make some very important changes or nothing she'd planned up to now would make a darn bit of difference. Her looks were simply too distinctive, too memorable. So she needed to change her appearance, and not by just a little bit.

Her hair and features weren't forgettable. Isaac had called her an angel—his angel—in a tone of awe that made her think he truly did see her as an angel with her long, pale, almost white hair, her startlingly blue eyes and her nearly translucent skin.

She needed to dye her hair. She knew it made her sound not only vain but incredibly stupid, but she couldn't bring herself to cut the long tresses. It was her one rebellion. The elders had threatened her time and time again with shearing every bit of her hair off as a way to humiliate her and bend her to their will, but each time she vowed that she'd kill herself before ever agreeing to heal another person in the cult if they carried out their promise.

The fear in their eyes told her they knew she wasn't bluffing, and she wasn't. She'd lost so much already. Why was she even hanging on anyway? It was a question she'd asked herself dozens of times over the years, only to cry herself to sleep because she didn't have an answer.

Perhaps it was the sheer desperation etched into her features that convinced them, or the fact that she looked dully at them, like death was the ultimate freedom for her, one she wanted very badly. Though they hadn't followed through on their hollow threat, security on her had been doubled, and she was forced to eat whether she wanted to or not.

Often they forced a feeding tube down her and held her down while they inserted an IV so they could administer fluids intravenously in addition to the nutrients administered via the feeding tube. It was as though they feared she would make good on her threat to go through with it and end all her pain, humiliation and misery.

It should shame her that she allowed them to think that of her. That she was so weak that she would end her own life rather than fight with every breath for her freedom no matter how long it took. But it bought her precious time, time she needed if she was ever going to make good on the vow she'd made herself when she was but a young girl trapped in an environment where she could smell the stench of evil, so much so that it sickened her and many a night, she threw up every single bite of food or liquids forced on her during the day.

So while she refused to cut so much as an inch off her hair, and it could very well end up the worst mistake of her life, she could alter her appearance in other ways. She could dye her hair a color so different from her own that no one would ever recognize her. Red was out. She simply couldn't see herself as a redhead. But she could do dark brown or even black.

After consideration, she decided that coloring her hair black, like the sky at midnight when no moon or stars were visible through the inky darkness, was her best shot at being able to move through the shadows undetected. If luck and God were on her side, the sky would remain overcast so the moon and the stars couldn't cast their light to penetrate even the best disguise. Then the odds of her remaining undetected would greatly increase. But even better was the fact that visibility would be limited to feet instead of much greater distances.

She'd need new clothing, and nothing like the ragtag clothes she'd fled the compound in but at the same time, nothing that would draw unnecessary attention to herself. No, she wanted to be . . . normal. Blue jeans. Nice ones without rips or holes in the denim. Ones that fit her and weren't several sizes too big, making her look like she'd dug them out of a Dumpster and had to settle for whatever she was lucky enough to find.

Her tops needed to be oversized, at least two sizes too large so they showed nothing of her curves. She'd long cursed her ample breasts, curved hips and plump ass that men seemed to like staring after with a look in their eyes that scared her almost as much as the elders did.

Sweaters would be perfect and it was wintertime, though the temperature never got that cold stretching from southeast Texas to well on the other side of Houston. And sweaters were bulky enough that she wouldn't have to worry with a bra.

She winced because she'd forgotten all about shoes, and shoes were expensive. But maybe she could find some for a decent price at the Goodwill store or the Salvation Army when she went to look for the other items needed to complete her disguise.

And then another thought caused her to cringe. As Isaac had so patiently explained to her, it wasn't realistic for her to simply disregard ideas that had been part of her life since before she could remember. Only in time would she be able to see how the real world worked and allow herself to play by society's rules and not the twisted, disgusting teachings the elders impressed upon young, impressionable people. In time, and by time he didn't mean an immediate turnaround. He'd said it could take weeks, months or even longer to recondition herself and be able to admit not only to herself but to others that the people who'd imprisoned her had shoved lie after lie down her throat.

Shaking off that worry and the guilt over the next part of her plan, she knew she needed to either buy makeup and experiment with it or go to a professional and learn how to use it to alter her facial features.

She'd always worn her hair down, not by choice, but by dictate of the elders, and now she was dying to put it up in the number of ways she'd seen other women wear their hair. She thought it looked pretty. Carefree even. As if they didn't give a single care as to what others thought of them and wore their hair however they were most comfortable. What Jenna wouldn't do to have that kind of confidence and assertiveness.

As she went over the list in her head again to ensure she hadn't forgotten anything, her chest fell and foolish tears burned the edges of her eyes for even allowing herself the dream of being normal, of not having dangerous, maniacal people after her who would stop at nothing, even killing anyone who tried to help her. It was an impossible dream and she wiped her wet cheeks with the back of her hand, furious that she was sitting here feeling sorry for herself when she should be working on a way to get out of here *now*.

She had no money and when the idea hit her, her stomach revolted and she shook her head against her knees. It was obvious that Eliza's husband had plenty of money. For that matter, none of Isaac's men or even Isaac himself seemed hard up for money in the least. Would they even miss a few hundred dollars? She would take only enough to make the needed changes to her appearance and then she could begin looking for a job. But that thought only dug the knife deeper and heightened her despair.

She had no birth certificate. No ID. No idea exactly how old she was. No clue what her last name was and no job experience, save being a veritable slave to megalomaniacs, and she hardly thought that kind of experience on an application would get her very far.

Besides, she didn't want the kind of job that would only remind her of past shame and humiliation. Beggars shouldn't be choosers. She knew that well. She recognized on one level that she should be grateful for any job given to her, but every single part of her rebelled at ever being treated like she was so much less than everyone else. Like she was *nothing*.

She closed her eyes and began to rock harder, her tears soaking the knees of her jeans. Then she frowned, recalling a distant memory. It was a few years back, one of the few times she'd been able to sneak into one of the elders' offices undetected. She'd studied the layout and schematics of the compound, her best route of escape, but then she'd seen a recent newspaper and unable to contain her curiosity, she'd quietly and carefully thumbed through the pages, stopping on an article about more and more businesses opting to pay employees under the counter without requiring references, ID, work experience or even age. Who in their right mind would consider hiring her without knowing anything about her even if the pay was under the table?

Still, the idea was too tempting. It would be a dream come true. She could work until she had enough money saved up and then she could leave town and go anywhere in the country she wanted and start over where no one knew who she was or what she could do. She would simply be another nameless, faceless person in the crowd. The excitement that washed over her couldn't be controlled or called back no matter how hard she tried. It was stupid to get her hopes up only to have them dashed, but she had to try. She wasn't a quitter. If she had been, she would have done what the elders had wanted her to do years ago.

FOURTEEN

ISAAC had been so caught up in planning strategy and plotting their next move that he hadn't checked on Jenna in the last half hour. As soon as the realization struck him he turned around frantically, seeking her out. But when he saw her huddled against the wall on the far side of the room, her legs drawn to her chest in a protective posture, his pulse sped up. And when he saw the betraying quiver of her shoulders, he cursed long and loud under his breath.

Her face was buried against her knees, her hair providing an effective barrier so her facial expressions were completely shielded, but he didn't need to see her to know she was weeping silently, doing her best to hide her distress from the others. In that moment, she looked so alone and fragile, his heart ached and he vowed to alleviate the pain in any way possible. She was hurting, but so was he, because he couldn't bear for this beautiful, selfless woman to suffer so much pain. It made him feel helpless and inept, two emotions he was not accustomed to experiencing in his line of work.

But she wasn't work and she wasn't a goddamn job. She was fucking *everything*.

"We're done here," Isaac said sharply, his gaze never leaving Jenna's defeated posture, hating with every breath that she was silently crying and trying not to be a burden—a fucking burden! When in such a short time, she'd become his entire world.

When his teammates followed the direction of his stare, there was a mixture of softening and hardening of their expressions. None of them were happy that while they had been deciding their next move, Jenna had been ignored, sitting alone, frightened and vulnerable.

He strode over to her and simply bent and slipped his arms around her and lifted her, ignoring her startled gasp. He tucked her damp face into his neck so she would be saved the discomfort of the others' concerned scrutiny.

"Shhh, baby," he murmured as he carried her toward the bedroom. "Just let me take care of you. I don't want you to worry about anything. You never have to be afraid or uncertain when you're in my arms," he said in a whispered vow.

She relaxed against him, her body melting into his as he entered the bedroom and pushed the door shut behind him. He didn't release his hold on her until he eased her down on the bed and then he stood above her for a moment, hating to separate himself from her even for the few seconds it would take to collect one of his oversized T-shirts for her to sleep in.

He returned and slowly, so as not to alarm her, began undressing her. She swallowed, a small gasp escaping her sweet, puffy lips, and color stained her cheeks as she quickly wrapped her arms around her chest to cover her breasts.

"You never have to be shy with me, Jenna. You're so fucking perfect. So beautiful you make me ache. I need to get you in something more comfortable to sleep in. The girls brought over clothes and shoes for you, but tonight you'll sleep in my shirt so you know who you belong to."

Her cheeks flushed again, this time pleasure making her eyes shine, and her earlier sadness evaporated as she stared at him as though he were a goddamn hero. Like he was the only man in the world, and as long as he was the only man in *her* world he could manage to breathe without the ever-present panic of losing her, of her disappearing from his world and taking every shred of goodness and light with her.

He knew she was his entire world, that no one else existed for him, but he had to ensure himself an equal place in her world and future. There was nothing he wouldn't do to make her his, to bind her so tightly to him that there was no hope of escape for either of them.

With shaking hands, he pulled the shirt over her head and slowly dragged it down her body, his knuckles softly grazing the swells of her breasts. They both exhaled sharply and her pupils suddenly covered nearly all of the pale blue, leaving only a thin ring around the dark orbs.

Her chest heaved as though she struggled to breathe, but then he hadn't taken a single breath since he'd bared her delectable curves in order to dress her for bed. His chest burned with the need for oxygen, and only when she was fully covered once more did he find it possible to suck air into his starved lungs.

"You need to rest, sweetheart," he said as he tucked her beneath the covers. "Tomorrow's going to be a long day and this might be your last chance to get a good night's sleep for a while."

Her expression suddenly became anxious, her eyes troubled, and she looked like she was about to ask him something but hesitated.

"What is it, honey?"

"Where will you be?" she asked in a low voice, her gaze skittering toward the windows on the opposite wall.

"I'll be wherever you want me to be," he said simply. "Do you want me to stay? Do you want me to sleep in the bed with you?"

She licked her lips nervously, sadness flaring in her eyes for one brief second. "I want you to hold me," she said, her lips quivering. What was going on in her head? What could she possibly be thinking? It made him crazy that he couldn't just make everything all right for her and wipe away every worry, fear or sad thought just by willing it to be gone.

"There's nothing I'd love more than for you to sleep in my arms," he said, tucking a finger beneath her chin and nudging it upward so he could claim her mouth in the way he truly wanted. He wanted her taste permanently burned on his tongue and her scent to fill his nostrils until all he could smell was her every minute of the day.

It took every ounce of restraint he possessed to break the seal of their fused lips. He wanted to make love to her so badly he ached with need. But she deserved to be worshipped and taken slowly, with care and reverence, when they had all the time in the world and not when they could be interrupted at any minute because their security had been breached.

Soon, though. As soon as they moved her to a safe place tomorrow, a safe haven so isolated and fortified that no one would be able to get within a mile of the veritable fortress without hell being unleashed on them from all directions. Once again he had Sterling to thank, and not for the first time Isaac reminded himself that Sterling was not at all what he appeared to be. He was a wild card who played by no rules except his own, and he took his wife's protection *very* seriously and now had extended that offer of protection to Jenna. Isaac wasn't too proud to accept all the help he could get as long as his angel wasn't touched by danger or violence. And once they were safely ensconced in Sterling's impenetrable compound, Isaac would claim what was his and he'd bind Jenna so tightly to him that she'd never be free of him.

He stripped down to his boxers, nearly smiling at Jenna's shy gaze, full of curiosity and feminine appreciation. Her innocence enchanted him. He'd never put much stock in virginity. He didn't have a double standard when it came to women having as much sexual experience as men. But knowing he would be Jenna's first—and last—lover, the only man to ever possess her and be given such a precious gift, instilled in him a fierce surge of possessiveness.

His inner caveman came grunting and snarling to the surface, and he felt the urge to beat his chest and mark his territory. Repeatedly. He didn't even want another man's eyes on her, much less any other part of him. He'd never considered himself a possessive man but when it came to Jenna, the idea of anyone but him *ever* touching her nearly made him insane. And he didn't give a fuck how it looked to others or what anyone thought. The only person he was concerned with accepting his complete takeover of Jenna's well-being, protection, care and happiness was the woman nestled tightly in his arms, his much larger body dwarfing and completely encompassing her tiny frame.

"Go to sleep, baby," he whispered against the shell of her ear, watching as tiny chill bumps erupted over her skin and danced down her neck. "Dream the good and dream of me."

"They're one and the same," she whispered back, her breath sliding like silk against his neck. He gripped her tightly—too tightly—overcome by the sweetly spoken words. Words that gave him hope that one day she would feel the same savage need for him that had taken over him, heart, body and soul. But, until then, until she came to accept all that she was and would be to him, he had enough love, desire and determination for both of them and nothing in the world would ever make him let go of this precious gift he'd waited a lifetime to cherish.

"Kiss me one last time," she said in an aching voice that unsettled him and immediately put him on edge. Something about the way she said it nagged at him and his gut clenched, a sure sign that something wasn't right. But what?

Unable to resist her request despite the voice in the back of his mind telling him something was wrong, he wrapped himself around her so that no part of her skin was untouched by him and claimed her lips, more forcefully than he had until now. He absorbed and savored her taste and satiny sweetness like he was starving and she was his first meal in weeks. She whimpered into his mouth, moving restlessly against him, her movements almost desperate as she burrowed more deeply into his embrace. In that one sensual moment they were one person, not two separate entities. Nothing divided them, not so much as a centimeter of space existed between their flesh. Never had anything felt so fucking perfect. So beautiful and so very right.

"You're mine, Jenna." He whispered the words so quietly that they were swallowed up by her inhalation and were only audible to him. "I'll never let you go. There's nothing I wouldn't do to get you back if you were ever taken from me."

Jenna called upon the patience that had been so key to her survival during her years in the cult as she lay limply in Isaac's arms waiting for him to drift off into a deep slumber, and even then she waited until she was certain he had succumbed to his own need for rest and rejuvenation before she began the agonizingly slow process of inching her way from his hold, holding her breath and going completely still whenever his breathing changed the slightest bit. When she was finally free and had gotten soundlessly out of bed, she hurriedly surveyed the clothes hanging in the closet, searching for what suited her purposes best.

After donning warm socks and a sturdy pair of hiking boots she exited the closet, and though she knew she should leave immediately, she stood at the end of the bed greedily drinking in Isaac's appearance as he lay so still on the bed they'd shared for a few precious stolen hours. Guilt and so much regret overwhelmed her at the betrayal she was handing the man who'd been willing to risk everything to keep her safe. She wanted nothing more than to shut reality out and escape into a fantasy world where only the two of them existed and she could sleep in his arms, cherished and protected every night, but now she had to protect him and everyone else who were risking their lives to keep her safe from an unknown, powerful enemy who'd already proven the lengths they'd go to in order to capture her. She swallowed back her grief and steeled herself for what was to come and the pain that not only she would feel. She knew Isaac would suffer the pain of her betrayal every bit as keenly.

"Goodbye, Isaac," she whispered soundlessly. "You were the best and only good that ever came into my life. I'll never forget you and I'll never stop loving you, but I can't let you sacrifice your life for mine."

Choking back tears, she turned and crept from the room on silent feet, making her way back to the large room where the opening to the sublevel was located. She held her breath while she slowly eased the hatch sideways to uncover the opening below it. Leaning down through the exit, she felt around until her hand bumped against the rungs of a wooden ladder that descended beneath the structure. Hastily she backed down the ladder, feeling for each step with her feet until she was far enough down to reach up and slide the hatch closed once more.

The darkness was eerie, and she had to rely solely on her hands and feet to guide her farther down. Finally she stepped onto firm ground and she could smell dirt. She stretched her arms out first in front of her and then extended them from her sides until her hands came in contact with a firmly packed dirt wall. She was in a tunnel. All she had to do was follow it to wherever it led and she would be free, her escape a success. And yet with each step she took farther away from Isaac, the more she was consumed with grief.

After what seemed an eternity, she stumbled out of the tunnel and into a grove of trees. She sped up, putting as much distance between the others and her as possible. She had no idea where she was or where she was going. All she knew was that she couldn't stop even for a minute. She hurried into the dense forest surrounding the house, reminding her of her escape from the compound. After what seemed an interminable amount of time, the forest opened up into a clearing. She paused for a moment, frozen. While the dense vegetation was scary, the prospect of being in the open was even more terrifying. She needed to hurry and seek cover.

She'd taken only a half dozen steps when suddenly a large man stepped in front of her, halting her in her tracks. She let out a sound of fright and quickly turned to run, only to find herself surrounded.

"Well, well, well," the man who'd been in front of her said with an obvious smirk. "This was like taking candy from a baby. You fell right into our hands, Jenna. I have to wonder why you're out here alone and unprotected, but as it makes my job so much easier I'm not complaining."

Before Jenna could process his statement, fire exploded through her body and she was completely paralyzed. Finally she folded like a puppet, her muscles jerking spasmodically as she collapsed. Tears of pain and shock slid soundlessly down her cheeks while she lay twitching on the ground, completely helpless as she stared up in horror into the very face of evil.

FIFTEEN

ISAAC woke with the immediate sensation something was wrong. He instantly reached for Jenna, needing the reassurance of her soft, sweet body. When his hand met with cool sheets he shot up in bed, his gaze darting around the room in search of her. The house was too fucking silent and Jenna not being where she should be immediately tripped his "oh fuck" button. He broke from the bed in a dead run, bellowing her name as the first strains of dawn began to lighten the house.

He charged into the common room and swore when he found it empty. He ran to the kitchen, a knot so big in his stomach he nearly threw up. Finding the kitchen dark, he roared her name again, and the sounds of movement all over the house could be heard as the other DSS members and their wives scrambled in Isaac's direction.

"Has anyone seen Jenna?" Isaac barked as everyone spilled into the living room. Looks of dread filled their faces, giving Isaac all the information he needed to know. She wasn't with any of them, and no one could have goddamn well snuck into the bedroom and stolen her right out of his arms. Which meant only one thing, and it was retold on every single one of his teammates' faces.

"Fuck!" Shadow swore.

Isaac stood there in shock, not understanding what he knew had to be true. He was numb to his toes and he couldn't form a single word to save his life. Dear God, why had she run? Had he been completely and willingly played? Had he been so wrong about her?

No way. He couldn't—he wouldn't—believe that she'd been one big lie, using him until she no longer needed his protection. He refused to accept that. There had to be another explanation.

He watched the others as a slow realization crept into their expressions and he wanted to punch something, wanted to tell them they were fucking wrong, until Knight quietly called his name.

He numbly turned to see Knight standing over the escape hatch in the common room, a grim expression on his face. "You need to see this, brother. The hatch isn't fully closed, meaning someone used it since last night after we did a lockdown of the house."

Isaac lost it. He slammed his fist into the wall, sheetrock shattering as a sizeable hole formed where his hand struck.

"Isaac, stop." Eliza's soothing voice sounded close to him, but he didn't want to be soothed. He'd just had his fucking heart ripped out of his chest. Nothing was going to ease his pain or the tearing sense of betrayal that was like a knife to his chest.

But it was Ramie's words he latched on to, turning to her the moment she spoke.

"I can find her, Isaac," she said in her soft way, with eyes too old for her face. Eyes haunted by the grisly murders of the vicious predators she'd been victim to and played an instrumental part in bringing to justice.

"Ramie, no!" Caleb's pained protest sounded. "Baby, please don't do this to yourself, for God's sake. You have no idea what you'd be walking into."

Despite the brief hope that had beat in his chest when Ramie had first spoken, Isaac didn't want her risking herself for a woman who'd betrayed them all.

"Caleb, if she left on her own, then what could I personally experience that would be so horrible?" Ramie asked, with the mild exasperation in her voice that often accompanied her responses to her husband's concerns. "But at least I'll know where she is, if she's safe and why she left," she said, directing the last at Isaac as if knowing all too well that he wanted answers.

Oh hell yes he wanted to know why, god damn it.

"I want to know even if he doesn't," Shadow said, irritation evident in his tone. "Not only do I owe her, but I don't believe for one fucking moment that she played any of us. If she left, then she had a damn good reason in her mind to leave. I'd like to know what it is before we play fucking judge and jury on a woman we don't have any business judging until we have all the facts."

Knight shifted from his position in the doorway. "I agree. Not for a second do I believe she was playing us. We need to figure out what the hell scared her so badly that she ran, and we need to do it now. Where does the escape hatch lead to? For all we know, that's where she could be now while we stand around wasting time."

Isaac blinked, mentally kicking his own ass. While he was wallowing in fear, grief and disbelief, his teammates were demonstrating more faith in Jenna than he was. What kind of a fuck-up did that make him? It was his own damn fault she'd managed to sneak out of bed in the first place. She should never have been able to so much as get out of his sight.

Dane spoke as Isaac started moving toward the hatch. "The tunnel leads through a section of dense forestation and then into an opening about half a mile from the house. Shadow, you're with me. We'll check the tunnel and see if there's any sign she went that way. The rest of you fan out and cover every possible escape route."

His face softened slightly as he looked in Ramie's direction. "A decision needs to be made quickly. The choice should be Ramie's alone, and it's worth saying, if we'd wrapped the ladies in cotton in the past like we keep trying to do now, Lizzie wouldn't be with us today."

There was grim acceptance on the faces of everyone gathered as Dane's words settled over them. Caleb turned away, resignation clearly etched on his features, but pain and fear haunted his eyes. Beau and Zack exchanged uncomfortable glances, knowing Dane was right. Without the girls, Lizzie would have died in that fucking warehouse where she'd been tortured by the men who'd made Ari's and Gracie's lives a living hell. Isaac knew the sacrifice Ramie was making, and he hated it, but what other choice did they have? Would he ever forbid Jenna from using her gift to save a single one of his teammates—his family? Even knowing what it did to her? No. He wouldn't, and now he understood Caleb's terror and his fierce protectiveness toward Ramie much more than he had before.

"Zack and I will take the east exit," Beau said, glancing at his wife, his stare a silent command for her to remain without argument. Ari rolled her eyes while Gracie followed suit when she received the same pointed look from Zack.

"You stay too, Tori," Caleb said in a gentler tone to his younger sister.

Ari and Gracie immediately flanked Tori, each wrapping an arm around her slim waist, sending a silent message to Caleb and Beau that they would take care of the men's younger sister. Caleb sent them both grateful looks before he turned back to his wife, pulling her into his arms and holding her tightly, as if he already knew that she would do what she must to find Jenna.

Everyone quickly headed out in their search, leaving Isaac alone with Ramie, Caleb, Ari, Gracie and Tori.

Isaac waited, chest tight and heart hammering, as he watched the silent interaction between husband and wife. Then his attention focused solely on Ramie, knowing how selflessly she'd offered her talents time and time again, but also knowing the tension it caused between her and Caleb. She was watching her husband, determination in every line of her body, while understanding and love for Caleb's concern clearly shone in her eyes.

"Caleb, I can do this. I'll be okay. I can't live with knowing I didn't help Jenna. I have to do this and I need you to understand," Ramie whispered.

Caleb drew in a deep breath, but he looked at his wife with so much love and worry that it made Isaac's chest ache. He watched Ramie with every single emotion that Isaac was feeling for Jenna.

"I know you do, baby. I know."

There was a hint of helpless frustration in Caleb's voice even as he conceded that Ramie had no choice.

"But if anything goes wrong, anything at all, I'm pulling the plug immediately," he said with steely determination. "I won't risk you. Don't ever ask me to risk losing you. I won't even hesitate."

He sent Isaac a look of apology, though his words were directed at Ramie, and Isaac got it. He did. He had no right to ask another man to risk his wife's life for the woman Isaac loved, no matter how badly he feared Caleb's interference and Ramie being unable to locate Jenna.

"Do you want us to step away?" Ari asked, nodding toward Gracie and Tori as well.

"No."

The response came simultaneously from Caleb and Ramie.

"Just the usual instructions," Ramie said wanly. "Don't interfere and remain quiet. Listen to everything I say and for any useful information."

Left unsaid was that if it was bad, Ramie not only would have little recollection of specific details, but she would be completely incapacitated. She could even die, and that was what scared Caleb to death every time she called upon her talents.

The women moved toward Isaac, their intention not lost on him. Gracie looped her arm through his while Ari wrapped her arm around his waist in a hug.

"We'll get her back, Isaac," Ari whispered. "You can't give up hope. Ramie will find her."

But at what cost? And the million-dollar question, what would she see? Would she be too late to save Jenna's life if the worst had happened? He shook his head because he knew it did no good to entertain such hopeless thoughts. But hope was a vicious bitch as it clawed at his chest, warring with the worst-case scenarios that haunted his every thought.

This might not even work. Ramie might not be able to connect with her at all because it was too late. Or Ramie might connect with her only to find out Jenna really had betrayed him. Isaac slammed his mind shut to that possibility and fought for control. Once he'd found a shred of it and was reasonably sure he could speak without his voice breaking, he asked Ramie, "What do you need?"

"Whatever the last item was she touched that you know of," she replied, her eyes hopeful.

Isaac hurried to the bedroom he'd given Jenna, frantically trying to think. What could Ramie use? Jenna had come to him with only the clothes on her back. And those were with Lizzie. *Fuck.* He spun slowly, trying to find anything that might work. His gaze fell on the shirt she'd worn last night—his shirt. A night she'd spent in his arms before she'd disappeared. He snatched it up. It would have to do. If it didn't . . . He couldn't go there. It had to work or his only option would be to hunt down a cult in an unknown location, break in, and try to find something that belonged to Jenna and steal it. Jesus, this was a total clusterfuck.

He strode into the living room and dropped into a crouch in front of the armchair where Ramie was now sitting. "Thank you for this," he whispered, his voice rough. "I know I shouldn't ask this of you, that it's too much, but—"

"Stop," Ramie said softly. "You didn't ask. I volunteered. And it's not too much if we can make sure she's safe. I've been where she is, terrified and believing I had no one to turn to. I was proven wrong." She shot a loving look at her brooding husband. "Let's show Jenna she's wrong too."

Isaac swallowed the lump in his throat, hoping like hell Ramie understood the depth of his gratitude. He nodded, stood, then stepped away to give her space.

Ramie tentatively reached for the shirt, dread mirrored in her eyes despite her attempts to mask her expression. Then she sucked in a deep breath and closed her hands around the shirt, gripping it tightly as she closed her eyes. Long moments passed, Isaac's fear and sense of dread building with every second that ticked past. Then he saw her eyes start to move behind her closed lids as her fingers clenched the fabric tighter.

The color drained from Ramie's face, and it took everything Isaac had not to lunge across the room and start demanding answers. Only his previous experiences with Ramie's process kept him restrained, because he knew it could take time before she was able to provide any useful information.

Adrenaline coursed through his body, his hands trembling, muscles coiling into tight knots as he forced himself to stand still and quiet. He *couldn't* interrupt. It might break her connection to Jenna. Their *only* connection to Jenna.

Ramie's eyes suddenly flew open, and fear unlike any he'd ever seen was reflected there. Caleb moved even closer as she gasped. Then she spoke, the speech pattern familiar but not Ramie's. "Please, don't hurt me. Please. I'll do what you ask. Please." The last was a whimper, and Isaac fought not to drop to his knees as he realized he was hearing Jenna's words.

"Where are you, baby?" Isaac begged, no longer able to hold it in. "Just tell me where you are."

But Ramie's face remained strangely blank and he knew that

his words were useless. Jenna wasn't here. She was someplace where she had to beg people not to hurt her and he couldn't stop it. He could only stand helplessly in the house where she should have been safe and pray that it wasn't too late.

Then Ramie fell back, slamming against the back of the sofa with astonishing force. A cry of pain split the air and to the equal horror of both Isaac and Caleb, a large handprint appeared, bright red against the alarming pallor of Ramie's face. She staggered to the side, tilting precariously as Caleb lunged forward to catch her, hauling her into his arms to cradle her against his chest. He began softly running his hands through her hair, telling her he was there and begging her to come back to him.

Isaac stood paralyzed in fear and rage. What the *fuck* had just happened? He stared in shock at the vivid mark on Ramie's cheek. Was this what Jenna—his angel—was enduring while he stood here helpless to do anything but watch through the eyes of another? Tears burned like acid and for a moment, he had to look away from Ramie as she huddled, looking so fragile, in her husband's arms, or he feared losing the tenuous grip on his sanity.

He forced his gaze back to her, so choked up he wasn't sure he could even speak. He attempted to open his mouth to ask where the fuck Jenna was, but Caleb's sharp glare cut him off.

"Not now," he hissed, clearly incensed at the abuse his wife had suffered, even secondhand. His hands ran over her body as if checking for any hidden injury or evidence of pain and then he buried his face in her hair, tears glistening in his own eyes as he rocked her gently back and forth in his arms. "Just give her a goddamn minute!"

"No, we need to hurry," Ramie said urgently, the fear in her voice sending shards of panic down Isaac's spine. "She's so scared. And she should be. I know exactly where she is." She lifted eyes swimming with tears to implore Isaac. "It's not far, but they plan to move her soon. We have to go *now!*"

SIXTEEN

JENNA lay limply on the cold, hard floor in the room where she'd been carelessly tossed an hour ago, her hands and feet bound so tightly that she'd long lost feeling in them. She drew her knees up, her movements stiff and awkward as she tried to infuse any warmth possible into her numb body.

Her head ached from the harsh blow she'd received, but thankfully they'd been more concerned with ensuring her captivity so they could plan to move to a more remote location. One not very far from where she'd been with Isaac and the other DSS members.

Tears stung her eyelids but she refused to give in to the urge to cry. She wouldn't give them the satisfaction of knowing they had the power to make her crumble. She was just grateful that for the time being, at least, they were leaving her alone as they made their preparations to move out. They were expecting retaliation from Isaac and the other DSS members, but she wasn't about to tell them that Isaac had no idea where she was. If they were focused on a nonexistent threat, then that meant they wouldn't be as focused on her. Yet.

Even as grief consumed her at what she'd done, that she'd left Isaac to think the worst of her, she knew she'd done the right thing the moment she'd caught sight of her temporary prison. What appeared to be dozens of armed men patrolled the grounds and inside the building. This was nothing like the cult. This property had barbed wire along the gated wall, there were multiple televisions in every room they'd passed showing other areas, and all the men spoke into tiny devices that appeared to go to speakers in their ears. And this was only a temporary holding place! Wherever they were taking her was even more heavily fortified, according to the maniac who'd informed her that she was his property now and that the sooner she accepted it, the better things would go for her.

Even as grief stricken as she felt for the things she'd so briefly enjoyed that were now forever gone, she knew she'd done the right thing. Isaac and his men were no match for the heavily armed guards who patrolled her temporary prison. They were outnumbered, and the only result if they attempted a rescue would be their slaughter. Jenna would never survive if people who'd been nothing but kind and protective toward her had been repaid by death.

It had taken her years to escape the elders, and these men were far better prepared to keep her a prisoner. She knew she would never be free again, but at least she had the memory of a few stolen days to lose herself in when before, she'd known nothing but what the cult had chosen her to know.

Even now she closed her eyes and sought the solace of the

beautiful memories she'd made. The new and amazing world she'd discovered. The kindness shown to her by the wives of the DSS members and how by watching them she'd realized that what she'd shared, albeit briefly, with Isaac had been so very special.

Kissing. Different kinds of kisses. Lips pressed to her head by someone who actually cared about what happened to her. And then the kisses to her lips by someone who *wanted* her. *Her.*

Remembering Isaac's kisses, how very many different kinds he'd shown her in such a short time, was simply too much, and she finally lost control over her battle to keep her tears at bay. They trailed down her bruised cheek, and she realized that not all men were like the elders and the evil men who dealt in drugs and death who'd bought her from the cult like she was nothing more than an object.

Men like Isaac, like the men he worked with, had revealed a whole new understanding of men and relationships and how very wrong all of the examples were that she'd been witness to in the past. Her heart ached for the loss of something as beautiful as what she'd been given during those days. For the briefest of moments, regret stole over her, but she shoved it forcefully away, knowing it had no room in her mind or her heart. The men hunting her had been so very close to the safe house. If she hadn't left when she did, they would have come for her and the result would have been a massacre.

No, she'd never be free again and she'd never again experience the love Isaac had so selflessly shown her, but she would survive the loss because as long as she wasn't free, Isaac and all those associated with him would be alive and safe. For that, she could take whatever her captor had planned.

Isaac waited impatiently, cloaked in darkness outside the heavily fortified old factory that looked as though it had been renovated on the inside while keeping the run-down vacant look on the exterior. He and the others were waiting for Shadow to do what he did best and do recon so they could see exactly what they were up against and hopefully get a bead on Jenna's exact location.

From the moment Ramie had roused enough to give them more specific information, Isaac had been paralyzed with fear. The fucking bastard who'd purchased Jenna from the cult had quite the history of buying and selling things. Namely drugs. He'd eluded conviction for years because anyone agreeing to testify against him mysteriously disappeared or turned up murdered in a gruesome manner, a clear message to anyone else who thought to try to take down the vicious drug lord.

He'd nicknamed himself Jesus, spouting that he was the son of God. How appropriate that he'd gone shopping at a fucking cult for immortality and lucked on to the real thing. Someone who could keep him alive indefinitely. Until the day Jenna died. Knowing that only heartened Isaac a little. Jesus, or Jaysus as he was called by law enforcement and the numerous special tasks forces that had spent years trying to put him behind bars, would protect Jenna as fiercely as he would kill anyone who tried to take her away from him. Because if Jenna died—or managed to escape—then Jaysus was well and truly fucked, and right now Isaac was in a mood to fuck up every single man who had anything to do with his angel's capture.

Unfortunately, DSS didn't have the time or the manpower

to mount a full assault on the factory and finally mete out the justice Jaysus deserved. A mission like that would take days—not hours—to plan, not to mention they'd need to pull in a fuck of a lot more manpower and coordinate with local law enforcement. Hell, bringing in the military wouldn't be uncalled for because the drug lord ruled over an army of insanely loyal men all willing to die for their leader.

So this had to be a mission of stealth, and no one could know they'd even been there until they were long gone with Jenna. Standing here waiting for the go signal was eating a hole in Isaac's gut the size of the Grand Canyon.

Every single man employed by DSS had volunteered for the mission, even those who hadn't even met Jenna and didn't know anything about her circumstances. Isaac was damn grateful for the loyalty and sense of honor ingrained in every single one of his teammates, because even with every agent moving silently into position, they were still outnumbered at least four to one. And while Isaac stood here with his thumb up his ass, God only knew what Jenna was enduring. No, Jaysus wouldn't kill her, but he'd make her life a living hell to ensure her absolute obedience. Just like the fucking cult all over again—a different name and a different agenda, but crazy as fuck just the same.

For a brief moment, Isaac allowed himself to stop obsessing over the single most important thing in his life, and he turned his head upward, closing his eyes in prayer.

I know you and I haven't really had much of a relationship, God. I haven't spoken to you since I was a kid and I was angry—so very bitter—because you didn't answer my prayer to save my family and you left me alone for so very long. But Jenna hasn't lost her faith in you despite being shown a twisted, perverted representation of you.

She humbles me and if she can still find belief and trust in you in her heart, then how can I do any less? She's teaching me. By seeing you through her eyes, I'm learning and I'm trying to be a better man. I'm starting to understand that everything happens for a reason, even if those reasons are not understood at the time, and that prayers aren't always answered the way you want, but it doesn't mean they aren't one day answered. Please keep her safe for me. She's all that's good in this world, God. She's truly one of yours and I vow to you that I'll protect her with my life and that I'll never do anything to cast doubt in her belief in you and your mercy and grace. I'm not worthy, but she is, and it's for her I ask that she be spared, not for me, even though I'm selfish and want her with my every breath, with all my heart and all my soul. I don't know if you can hear me or if you stopped listening when I turned my back on you so many years ago, but I'm begging you to save one of your angels and I ask only one more thing. That you trust her to me, that you save me by saving her, because without her I am lost. And I finally realize that you did hear my plea not to be left alone and with no one who loved me, because you gave me Jenna. I'm trying to learn patience, God, and it's hard, but if Jenna is my reward for that patience then I'll never ask for another single thing of you. Only her.

Isaac lowered his head, shocked at the dampness on his face and the heavy ache in his heart. But he was suddenly buoyed by a ray of hope shining down on him and warming him as surely as if the sun's rays were beaming down on him in mid-afternoon.

"Thank you," he whispered.

It was all he could manage through shaking lips and a heart suddenly full of so much love and relief that he was dizzy with it. They were going to pull this off. He knew it as surely as he knew that Jenna was the only woman he'd ever love. He'd have her back in his arms where she belonged before the night was over, and if he had to make good on his promise to tie her to his bed, he'd feel no guilt whatsoever, because she was never getting away from him again.

Life, a sense of purpose, sizzled through him, replacing his earlier fear and dread and the horrible sense of doom that had settled into his very bones as he'd stared bleakly at Jenna's prison. Now he waited with anticipation for Shadow to give the all clear so his men could converge, slip in and out undetected with Jenna, and then haul ass to a safe, private place where he could make a few things clear to her, such as his insistence that she never come up with another harebrained scheme designed to protect him and the others.

He nearly snorted over that notion and he knew his men would love to have a few words with his angel as well, but they'd just have to wait until he let her out of his bed, and well, they might be waiting a damn long time.

Though they hadn't had the time to plan a full-scale assault, what they did have were some of the most brilliant minds and strategists, not to mention Quinn Devereaux, the youngest Devereaux brother and resident tech geek extraordinaire, who'd been able to access the schematics of the factory and even provide infrared satellite imagery that gave them an inside look at the renovated skeleton so they knew exactly how many rooms, escape routes and, most importantly, the most likely area where Jenna was being held.

They had it planned down to the nth degree. A cargo van large enough to hold them all and provide swift getaway was parked in a holding area a mile away, with Brent, a former race car driver who'd worked for DSS since its inception, waiting to either move to a closer spot or sit tight and be ready to haul ass.

Isaac allowed smugness to grip him when before he hadn't dared allowed himself even hope that they might succeed, because the possibility of failure had been so crushing that it had damn near brought him to his knees.

The warrior and protector in him chafed at the idea of not immediately taking apart the son of a bitch who'd hurt Jenna, but he'd wait, because her safety was paramount. And he'd get another opportunity. Oh yes, and he looked forward to it. He knew the crazy bastard wasn't simply going to give up his obsession with Jenna just because of one failed attempt to have her completely under his control. Then Isaac would avenge what was his and he'd make the drug lord sorry he'd ever so much as *thought* Jenna's name, much less the abuse he'd meted out on her.

A click sounded in his earpiece, the arranged signal that Shadow was in. More clicks sounded in rapid succession as one by one, the men moved into position, trusting Shadow not to lead them right into trouble. Isaac shook his head as he slipped through the piece of the fence Shadow had cut out. When the new recruits had signed on, they'd chuckled at Shadow's chosen nickname, but the man had quickly silenced them all with his eerie ability to move at will, invisible to anyone he didn't wish to be seen by.

Dane and Capshaw joined Isaac at one of the back entrances that they knew led into what had formerly been the kitchen area. The old laundry facility was adjacent to the kitchen, but it had no exit to the outside, and they needed inside that room. Dex had grinned when Quinn came through with the original blueprints in addition to the updated schematics, and when he'd pointed out multiple laundry chutes, all originating from upstairs rooms, the others had realized the reason for his smile.

The rest of Isaac's teammates converged from different directions, but their common goal was to access the room with the laundry chutes. Quinn had deduced that the only possible rooms Jenna would be held that had one of the old chutes were two windowless chambers right smack in the middle of the rectangular shaped factory building.

Isaac, Dane and Capshaw were the last to arrive at the rendezvous point and Knight sent them a look of relief.

"We need to move out fast," Zeke whispered. "Got three guards moving in our direction at a rapid clip."

Dane turned to Eric. "Radio Brent and have him bring the van to the south quadrant where we cut into the fence. There's enough cover that he won't be seen if he stays to the trees and shadows, but there's a drivable road that leads out to the highway from there and we can save a hell of a lot of time once we grab Jenna."

The others nodded their agreement and then quickly arranged their weapons so they wouldn't make noise as they climbed into the two chutes, but they left them within easy reach in case they chose wrong and surprised an unsuspecting victim.

Isaac used the palms of his hands to reach upward and provide traction against the narrow walls of the chute and heaved himself up, repeating the process until he reached the hatch that led into the room. He held up his hand for the men behind him to halt and then signaled them to be ready on his go. He counted down by folding one finger at a time and when he got to three, he busted out the boards closing up the entrance to the hatch and dove through, rolling even as he brought his gun up, his gaze scanning the room for a target.

When his stare finally lighted on the huddled form in a fetal position on the floor several feet away, his heart nearly exploded out of his chest.

Jenna!

"Cover me," he whispered to the others as he scrambled to his feet and dove toward her, reaching immediately for his knife to cut the ropes at her hands and feet.

Anger boiled in his veins as he unwrapped the tightly bound rope to reveal raw, bloody circles around each of her wrists and ankles. He yanked her up and into his arms, holding her tightly enough that he could feel her heart racing wildly against his chest. Then he pulled her away to inspect her for injuries, ignoring the fact that she was staring agape at him, eyes wide with shock.

Her blond hair was disheveled and as he took in the dark bruise to her cheek and the dried blood where her skin had been split, his nostrils flared in fury. But oh God, she was breathing. She was here. She was alive and he'd held her in his arms. For the first time since waking up alone, knowing she was gone, he felt himself relaxing and he could finally, finally breathe without Herculean effort.

Her lips curved into a surprised *O* and her gaze went from shocked to perplexed.

"What are you doing here?" she whispered. Her face lost some of its dazed look and her voice grew more urgent as she took in the other DSS members spilling into the room.

"You can't be here!" she said in agitation. "Oh God, they'll kill you. You have to go. Hurry! I'm begging you, Isaac. *Go!*"

She wrung her hands, drawing even more attention to the ragged, torn flesh. Every man's eyes were locked on the bruise on her face and the abused flesh of her arms and legs. Their expressions were murderous, and Jenna begging them all to leave only pissed them off more.

"If you think I'm going anywhere without you then you're crazy," Isaac bit out as he herded her resisting body toward the laundry chute.

She sent Dane a pleading look. "They'll hunt every single one of you down. They'll find you," she said brokenly.

"Good," Dane said savagely. "I'm looking forward to it."

"Fuckin' A," Zeke growled.

Jenna stared at them all in bewilderment, her shoulders slumping in defeat.

"No man left behind, darlin'," Shadow said, curling his arm around her waist to give her a one-armed hug. "That's the way we operate. Now come on before our presence is discovered."

Fear made her go rigid, her eyes wild as she frantically glanced back at the door to the room. A round of curses went up and the moods of the men were savage. They were all practically snarling, pissed off that not only was Jenna scared out of her mind, and they had no way of knowing just how much she'd endured *after* Ramie had broken the pathway to her. Knowing what had been done to her for the short span of time Ramie had been able to connect with her was already more than they could stand. But they were also pissed that even now, she begged for them to go and save themselves like a bunch of fucking pussies and actually leave a defenseless woman to a life of degradation and pain.

The men surrounded her, forming a tight circle of protection. When she tore her gaze from the door and saw what they'd done, her eyes became bright and red-rimmed and she gave a nearly silent sniffle.

"Time to go," Dane said tersely. "Brent's in position, so we have five minutes to make it to the rendezvous point. Let's load and go."

Unwilling to stand there while Jenna argued for them to save themselves and leave her in this godforsaken hellhole, Isaac scooped her up and hustled to the opening of the chute.

Shadow pushed in front of him. "I'll go first so I can catch her at the bottom and make sure no one is there."

"I'm going behind you," Dane said grimly. "If you hear *anything* at all except my okay to proceed with Jenna, find another way out immediately."

Not waiting further, Shadow tucked his feet downward and hoisted his big body through the narrow passageway, barely managing to fit his broad shoulders. Dane slid after him with no hesitation. Isaac carried Jenna to the opening and turned her sideways so her legs went down first.

She gripped him tightly, her fingers curling around his shirt as her frantic gaze found his. "Where does this go?"

"It's a laundry chute and don't worry, baby. Shadow and Dane will catch you. They won't let anything happen to you. I'll be right behind you. I swear."

She reluctantly let go of his shirt, but her hands shook as she inched farther downward.

"Use your hands to control your descent," Isaac said soothingly. "Press them against the sides and inch your way down."

She looked back sorrowfully at the men still standing behind Isaac, all alert, guns in raised positions as they monitored the doorway and listened for any sounds from the hallway.

"I'm sorry," she choked out. "You should have never come."

As the others let out growls of disagreement and Isaac felt his blood pressure rise to the point of exploding, she simply let go and disappeared from view. Isaac lurched forward, holding on to the edge of the opening, his ears straining for any sound.

"Got her," Shadow softly called up. "Move out. We're on the clock."

One by one, the men rapidly shot out of the chute and into the laundry room. The room was musty and neglected, its age evident in the crumbling sheetrock and the cracks in the ceiling and foundation.

"How often did they check on you, sweetheart?" Dane asked Jenna gently as they moved as a unit toward the kitchen where they'd gained access to the building.

"They left me alone after the first time when..." she trailed off, her gaze dropping and her cheeks turning pink with embarrassment.

The others exchanged grim expressions. They knew well about that first time and as angry as Isaac was about the son of a bitch who'd put his hands on Jenna, he was relieved that from that point no one had bothered her.

"They tied me up and left me on the floor," she said, her chin coming up, defiance glinting in her eyes. Almost as if she'd admonished herself for feeling shame for something she had no control over. Now if he could only get her to see reason in other areas..."I don't think they were overly concerned about me going anywhere. They were busy planning their move to a more secure location."

She dropped her head once more, but Isaac saw fury burning in her ice-blue eyes. It was a stunning contradiction. Fire and ice.

"I didn't exactly prove a challenge to them. He laughed at me and said I'd made it far too easy and that he was disappointed. Then he told me that I may have been able to waltz right out of protective custody but that where he was taking me I'd never see outside the walls of my prison. He seemed to think he was very amusing. He told me that he might consider torturing those who defied him, just so he could send them to me so I'd have company every once in a while."

Her voice dropped to a whisper and became tearful.

"But he also said he'd never allow me to heal them. He planned only to taunt them with my presence and the knowledge of what I could do so they'd know healing and life was so very close, just a touch away, and he wanted me to watch them die because he knew exactly what that would do to a person like me."

She shuddered, and Isaac put his arm around her to squeeze comfortingly.

Knight eased his head forward to get a sight line down the hallway in both directions, to and from the kitchen, their objective. He gave a simple nod and Isaac urged Jenna forward, wanting her out of this place as quickly as possible.

Just as he and Jenna were about to step into the hall, where they'd be visible to anyone present there, apprehension rolled down his spine. Without confirming his gut feeling, he slammed Jenna back, inserting his body in front of her. She stumbled, but Shadow caught her against his body and quickly covered her mouth with his huge hand to silence her.

The remaining group of men slid down the wall from the doorway so they wouldn't be readily visible. Only if the person walking rapidly down the hall chose to enter the laundry room.

Shit. Isaac hoped the others had already left the kitchen and were outside waiting because if not, they were all fucked. Isaac watched the outline of a large man pass by the laundry room and pause at the kitchen door. He peered in and then let out a grumble. Then he checked his watch and swore before lifting a radio to the side of his head.

"When the fuck is Chopper going to cook some goddamn food?"

"He's not, fool," the reply crackled over the two-way radio.

"Why the fuck not? I'm starving, and I'm sure everyone else is too."

"Perhaps you should worry more about doing as you were told and carrying out those orders instead of planning the next time to stuff more food into your lard ass," a silky, taunting voice sounded low over the radio.

Jenna went rigid, her hand flying to her mouth as if she were going to be sick. Her eyes were sorrowful and she bit down on her knotted fist just as an involuntary dry heave wracked her body.

Shadow's arm went around her for support and then he gently extricated her curled fingers from her mouth, rubbing the teeth marks left by her agitation.

"I think those hands have suffered enough abuse already," he whispered next to her ear. "He can't hurt you, Jenna. We'd never let that happen."

Her eyes flew to his, her misery so pronounced that it made Isaac's own gut clench.

"What is it, little angel?" Shadow asked, frowning at her extreme reaction.

"He'll kill him," she said, barely managing to form the words.

Her stomach heaved again, but this time she swallowed it back and balled her fists at her sides.

"We have to hurry. He's one of those people I told you about. One of the ones he'll torture for pissing him off. Then he'll bring him to me, just like he promised, and he'll let him die while I have to watch."

Tears trickled down her cheeks as everyone else exchanged looks of shock. She spoke with too much conviction for someone who hadn't seen it happen.

A noise in the hallway distracted Isaac from Jenna, and he focused on the man who'd been standing there a moment ago. Now two men flanked him, and the man who'd complained about being hungry had gone white as a sheet and was begging. Oh Jesus. What the fuck? He glanced sharply back at Jenna, knowing a hell of a lot more had happened than what Ramie had seen and what they'd assumed when Jenna had said no one had been back.

"We have to go now!" Jenna hissed with urgency. "We only have a few minutes before they'll know I'm gone."

Bile rose in Isaac's throat and Shadow didn't look any better as realization sank in. As soon as the hallway was clear, Isaac yanked Jenna to him and grabbed her hand. Shadow hovered on her other side while the rest took positions in front of and behind Isaac, Jenna and Shadow.

They rushed into the kitchen and out the back door, knowing they would have been alerted by Dane if the exit had been compromised. Dane looked up in relief from his lookout position when they barged into the night. The others were in similar guarded positions, but now they all turned in the direction of the section of fence that had been cut through.

"Situation upgraded to 'get the fuck out as fast as possible,'" Isaac barked to Dane.

Choosing speed over stealth, the men took off at a dead run while Isaac simply plucked Jenna from her feet and tossed her over his shoulder in a fireman's carry and then he too ran, keeping pace with them while bearing Jenna's slight weight.

"What the fuck did that sick bastard do to her?" Shadow whispered as he ran next to Isaac.

Isaac closed his eyes. He responded in a whispered voice to make sure Jenna didn't hear their exchange. "I think it's pretty obvious and I don't want to make her relive that now. I wanted to fucking throw up myself when I realized and Jesus, Shadow, did you see her eyes?"

Shadow's features became glacial, his expression icy. "I'm going to find that bastard if it's the last thing I do."

Alarm registered at Shadow's quiet vow.

"Need you to stick with me, man. You aren't going to have to find Jaysus. He'll be coming for us, and I'm going to need all the protection for Jenna that I can get."

Shadow briefly glanced over at Jenna. She was slung over Isaac's opposite shoulder, but held with extreme care so she was jostled as little as possible as they closed the distance between where she'd been kept prisoner and where Brent waited to drive them to safety.

"You got it, brother," Shadow said, his words a quiet vow.

SEVENTEEN

ISAAC glanced at Jenna, who sat huddled amid the group of grim-faced DSS operatives in the back of the cargo van, her face pale, eyes wide and swamped with a myriad of emotions, all of which made him seethe. Guilt, fear and sadness. He wanted to pull her into his arms and never let go, but he couldn't until he knew why she took off like she did and what the hell was going on in her mind before her flight—and now, he had to keep it under control. Which was pretty hard to do when he was on the verge of losing his fucking mind.

Silence lay heavy in the interior of the van and avoidance seemed to be the choice of everyone. Except Shadow, who'd apparently become Jenna's champion. Another thing that he had mixed feelings about. On one hand, he was glad she had Shadow's protection, but on the other it just pissed Isaac the fuck off. Anything—everything—having to do with Jenna was Isaac's job and his job only, and his teammate had better not cross the line or they were going to have serious problems.

Shadow turned to look at Jenna. Her gaze was fixed on a distant spot out the windows of the back door of the large cargo area, her mind obviously a million miles away. Most of the men were slouched in various positions, leaning against the side walls of the van, but Jenna had edged toward the back as if trying to separate herself from everyone. Only Isaac hadn't let her put any distance between him and her. He'd simply shifted in her direction every time she moved away.

"You okay, sweetheart?" Shadow asked in a gentle tone.

Jenna looked up with startled eyes, seemingly shocked that anyone had inquired as to her well-being. Did she think they were all pissed at her? Did she think anything about the way Isaac felt about her had changed? Fuck. As soon as they arrived at yet another of DSS's hidey-holes, they were going to have one serious come-to-Jesus meeting.

Her eyes watered, becoming shiny and luminous with tears, and Isaac clenched his jaw so tight it was a wonder he didn't crack his teeth.

"I'm sorry," she said brokenly, not answering Shadow's question. "I didn't mean this to happen. I'm so sorry I keep causing so much trouble. I didn't mean for you all to do this, to take this kind of risk. I didn't know what else to do. You've all already done so much and I just keep messing up."

She closed her eyes, turning her face completely away so no one could see her features. Shadow's expression was so black that it looked like he'd blow up at any moment.

"You're sorry you're not still with those bastards who planned to do God only knows what to you?" Shadow bit out. "Jesus Christ, Jenna, do you even realize what could have happened to you? All the ways they could have hurt you and made you suffer?

Did you expect us to just walk away and leave you to those bas-tards? Do you really believe you have so little worth?"

He sent a look of disgust Isaac's way as if believing Isaac hadn't convinced her just how much she meant, not only to him, but to Shadow. Isaac didn't pretend to know exactly what had happened in that moment when Jenna touched Shadow and healed him, but he knew a bond had been formed, just as an un-breakable bond had been formed the instant Jenna had touched him. She'd changed something in both men, had given them both something they'd never had and never knew they needed.

"I just don't want any of you to get hurt or die because of me," Jenna said, tears now leaking down her cheeks in damp trails. "I couldn't bear it."

"You don't think we feel the same way about you?" Isaac roared, causing Jenna to jump, her gaze shooting to him, fear sparking in her eyes for a moment. "Goddamn it, Jenna. Don't be afraid of me. Never be afraid of me. I'll never hurt you and so help me God, I'll take apart anyone who ever does."

Shadow seemed satisfied with Isaac's response, but he sent Jenna a stern look. It would likely scare most people, but it also held a glint of tenderness that was completely uncharacteristic of the secretive man.

"Promise me you'll never do something that foolish again," Shadow demanded, holding her gaze even as his features soft-ened at the sight of her tears. "We can't protect you if you won't let us."

He held up a hand when she started to open her mouth.

"I don't want to hear another goddamn word about protect-ing *us* or about you worrying about us," he said, staring her down even harder. "The only words I want out of your mouth right now are that you promise to do what I—we've—told you, and that's to let us do our job."

Jenna bit into her bottom lip and turned her face toward the window again, but not before Isaac—and the others—saw a fresh torrent of tears streaking down her pale cheeks.

Shadow sent Isaac a meaningful look. Hell, every single person in the van, including Brent, who was driving, gave him a stare that said he'd better handle the situation with Jenna and tell her whatever the fuck he had to in order to convince her to stop with her foolish notions of saving them all at the expense of her life. Dane looked like he was about to launch into his own lecture judging by the decidedly unhappy look on his face, but Isaac sent him a look that dared him to push any further. She'd gotten the damn message, or maybe she hadn't, but she would, because it wasn't the place of these men to get it through her head that she was the sum and entirety of Isaac's entire existence. It was his job, god damn it, and if she didn't get that yet, she'd get it before the night was over.

Isaac swallowed, his lips pressed into a tight line even though it was killing him to wait. But fuck if he was going to air his feelings for Jenna for anyone but her to hear, and fuck if he was going to tear into her in front of the others, make her even more upset and embarrassed than she already was. He merely sent everyone back a stare of his own that made it very clear he was marking his territory and for them to back the hell off.

Seemingly satisfied with the silent smack-down that had just occurred, the others turned their attention away from Isaac and Jenna and the rest of the trip was made in silence.

But Isaac could bear Jenna's distance no longer. Even if he was going to wait until they were alone to have a long talk with her, he wasn't about to allow her to think he was pissed at her. He was plenty pissed about a multitude of things, but he wasn't pissed at her.

He leaned across the distance to where Jenna was huddled as close to the double doors—and as far away from him—as possible, and he slid one arm behind her back and the other beneath her legs, lifting her and hauling her into his lap.

Her wide eyes found his and the way she stared up at him damn near broke his heart. Her gaze was so full of apprehension, as if she expected him to lash out at her. He wrapped both arms around her and crushed her to his chest, holding her so tightly he doubted she could breathe. Fair enough, since it felt as if he hadn't breathed from the moment he'd awakened to find her gone from his bed.

He buried his lips in her hair, pressing them tightly to the crown of her head, inhaling her sweet scent. He savored the feel of her in his arms, her precious weight finally setting his world to rights after hours of enduring hell.

"Never do that to me again, Jenna," he whispered. "God, baby, I can't breathe when you aren't with me. Swear you'll never leave me again."

She didn't respond, but she slowly relaxed, tension bleeding from her taut muscles, and her body melded to his like the missing half of a whole. He closed his eyes and sucked in deep breaths through his nose until all he could smell was her, until all he could feel was her. Never, *never* did he want to experience the agony of not knowing where she was, if she was hurt or afraid. Dear God, he wouldn't survive it.

How in the hell did Caleb and Beau endure what their wives went through at the price of their gifts? How had Zack survived over a decade of not knowing where Gracie was, torturing himself every hour of every day wondering what had happened to her, if she'd been hurt, if she needed him or if she was even alive?

And sweet Jesus, but how had Sterling not gone completely over the edge after seeing Eliza throw herself in front of him, taking the bullet that would have killed him when she'd spent days in a coma, so close to death that the doctor had given her only a five percent chance of surviving?

Seeing the woman you loved suffer the unimaginable marked a man in a way that was never truly forgotten, just shoved back, only to return in unguarded moments and in nightmares never shared for the sheer rawness of having to recount them.

Isaac shuddered at just how close he'd come to losing Jenna. Already she was so much a part of his every waking thought that he couldn't imagine his world without her in it. Sweat formed on his brow and he mentally shook away the lingering terror that still gripped tenaciously at his throat.

She was here. In his arms. He was holding her and she was unharmed.

Thank God.

They pulled into the underground parking garage of a thirty-story building that looked like any other downtown structure, complete with a directory of businesses listed by floor. Only there was just one actual business, and it was directly in the center of the building, fifteen stories up. That entire floor had been converted to a fortified sanctuary, complete with a full kitchen, a dining area, two large living rooms, half a dozen bedrooms and an entire armory that held every weapon in their arsenal, many of which the military didn't even have access to.

The building could withstand just about anything but a

direct hit by a missile. Isaac didn't even want to imagine the kind of money it had cost to fortify an entire skyscraper into an impenetrable fortress. In the past he'd made jokes with the best of them about the paranoia involved in creating such a massive safe zone, but right now he wasn't laughing, and he was damn grateful for Dane's meticulous, always-prepare-for-the-worst personality.

DSS's front man was a secretive man and there was likely only one person in DSS who even knew his story—Eliza. But Isaac doubted even she had the entirety of it. Dane came from obvious wealth but he didn't flaunt it and instead adopted a low-key appearance, quiet and very observant. He had connections most intelligence agents would orgasm over, but he never gave up his sources of intel—classified or not—and neither did he ever say how he got his hands on the high-tech weapons or intelligence he produced at extremely opportune moments.

His motto wasn't *prepare* for the worst. It was *expect* the worst and be damn ready to kick its fucking ass. Isaac would never crack another joke at Dane's expense again.

This building wasn't technically owned by DSS. It, and everything it contained, was brought to the table by Dane. Someone as wealthy and as well connected as Dane could easily be arrogant and attach strings or conditions to what he offered DSS and anyone working for him, but that wasn't who Dane was. He considered every single agent his family and he protected them as ferociously as a mother lion. Which was why he was slouched among the rest of the DSS men in the van. Because he was intimately involved in the majority of the missions, and perhaps what Isaac admired most about his leader was that he didn't insist on leading every time.

Isaac had seen how some of his other teammates had ben-
efited from Dane's vast stockpile, but he'd never considered how
important the extent of Dane's protection of those he considered
his own was until now, when it extended to Jenna. Dane already
had his absolute loyalty and dedication, but now he had his
deepest gratitude because he was protecting the most important
thing in the world to Isaac, and he'd never be able to repay that
kind of debt.

Instead of helping Jenna from the vehicle when they'd
parked, Isaac simply picked her up and cradled her in his arms,
as the others scrambled out to provide a protective circle around
them. They strode rapidly toward the secure elevator that would
take them to the fifteenth floor, while Dane made a quick call to
Caleb to assure him of their success in retrieving Jenna and made
sure that all was well at the secondary location where Caleb,
Beau, Zack and Sterling had stayed behind with their wives and
the youngest Devereaux sister, Tori.

Dane and Isaac both had lost their minds when not only
Beau and Zack but also Lizzie had insisted on going on the
retrieval mission. As far as Isaac was concerned, with so many
unknown variables, and the fact that they were all targets now,
the wives had to be protected at all costs.

The women had all endured far too much pain and suffering,
and the last thing Isaac wanted was for them to be dragged into
his fight. He and the rest of his teammates and Dane would provide more than adequate protection for Jenna without endanger-
ing any of the resilient women who possessed astonishing gifts.
Just like Jenna.

Isaac held it together, maintaining a tight grip on his composure as he carried Jenna to one of the far bedrooms. His teeth

ached from the force of his clenched jaw, but he wasn't about to say another goddamn word until he and Jenna were alone and assured of privacy.

Dane would want a full briefing and he'd want to plan and coordinate their efforts, but he could damn well wait until Isaac had the most important thing under control and decided. Making sure Jenna never tried to run from him again, even if in her mind she was doing it for all the right reasons.

Try as he might, he couldn't calm the turmoil swirling around in his belly like a bad case of food poisoning. With every passing second, it intensified, until it threatened to burst out of him regardless of whether they had privacy or not.

When he finally reached his destination, he kicked the bedroom door shut behind them and turned to lock it, using the hand underneath Jenna's thighs. He was reluctant to even let her down, but he knew he was about to explode and he didn't want to do it when she was this close to him.

He set her down on the bed and then took several steps back, his nostrils flaring as he inhaled several times in succession.

"Why are you so angry with me?" Jenna asked softly, looking up at him with troubled eyes.

He cupped the back of his head and blew out his breath. "I'm not angry with you, baby."

She sent him a disbelieving look. "Okay, then why are you angry?"

He sent her an incredulous look, then closed his eyes and shook his head, praying that he didn't completely lose it. He was literally shaking with fury. Fury that she thought so little of herself. Fury that he'd failed to protect her. Fury over the helplessness and uncertainty he felt over whether he would be able to ensure her absolute safety until every last one of the dirtbags who considered Jenna property—their property—were either ambushed and taken out when they came for Jenna again—and they would come—or were hunted down like the animals they were and a healthy dose of poetic justice was dispensed on their sorry asses. The latter was certainly Isaac's preference, but he couldn't leave Jenna. Not even for a second, because there were two distinct and very powerful entities after her and they both had eyes and ears everywhere.

"What the ever-loving fuck were you *thinking*, Jenna? You walked right into their goddamn hands, and there wasn't a fucking thing I could *do* about it. I didn't even know you were in danger, afraid, being hurt until it was too fucking late for me to act. You have *no* idea how that feels, baby. No. Fucking. Clue. Because if you did, you wouldn't be able to breathe, just like I haven't. You wouldn't be able to stand, sit or do anything without your knees feeling so weak you were about collapse, your hands shaking so bad that you couldn't hit a target at ten yards with a goddamn *grenade* launcher! I've never felt so helpless in my *life*!"

His skin was clammy with sweat as all the pent-up terror finally found its release. It was all he could do to remain standing and not fall to his knees right now, he was so damn weak with relief.

"God, you can't comprehend all I imagined could be happening to you and I was helpless to prevent it. Helpless, Jenna. Sweet mother of God, I never want to feel that kind of fear again. I can *taste* it. I don't think I'll ever be able to get rid of the taste of it. Six hours, baby. For *six hours* I lost you, and I didn't know if I would get you back or what shape you'd be in if I did. I thought the worst and when I say the worst, I mean *the worst*.

You can't possibly understand the horrific things I imagined and what that *did* to me."

He shuddered violently, nausea swirling in his stomach all over again.

"I'll never forget those six hours for as long as I live."

He prowled closer to her, trying to contain his rioting emotions, but he was fast losing that battle.

"As. Long. As. I. Live. Jenna. I'll never forget. I'll always remember waking up to find you gone and knowing in my gut that something was horribly wrong."

She had a faintly puzzled look in her eyes and her lips were turned down into a forlorn frown.

"I explained why I did it," she said quietly, glancing down as she knotted her fingers together, twisting them in agitation. "I did it to keep all of you safe. I'm not even *paying* you, Isaac, and you told me yourself this is your job—I mean it's what you do. You protect people. DSS is a company and companies have to make money. I may not know much about the real world and how it works, but I do know that much," she said, slight bitterness to her tone. "Not only was I a drain on your personnel and your business, but I was also putting every single one of you at risk of dying, because we all know they aren't going to kill me. At least not until they get what they want, and even then, why would they get rid of me when they could have use for me at any time? The rest of you are expendable. Killing you is nothing to them and only puts them one step closer to their objective. Me."

She cocked her head, sending him a look of pure confusion mixed with deep, unrelenting sadness. She looked so dejected that he wanted to howl because it seemed nothing he said got through, nothing he did made her happy or smile, and she was a woman meant for sunshine and laughter.

"I would think that every single one of you would be glad to see me go. Do you think Caleb, Beau, Zack or Wade want to lose their wives? Or that the Devereauxs want to lose their sister? Do you think any of your teammates want to die for a woman they don't even know who's giving them no incentive to take on the task of protecting her? You can't just stop everything and focus the full resources of your company on me."

"*The hell I can't!*" Isaac roared, making her jump. He stared at her, completely agape, unbelieving of all that had just come out of her mouth. "My God, woman, you just don't *get* it."

He tilted his head back, lifting his gaze to the ceiling. He roughly massaged his nape while wiping wearily at his eyes with his other hand.

"Jesus," he muttered, shaking his head. He was momentarily speechless, unsure of what the hell to say in response to the crap she'd just stated. Worse was the fact that she believed every word of it. This was the single most important battle of his life, and he was losing so fucking badly it wasn't even funny.

She stared at him in utter bewilderment. "What? What don't I get, Isaac? I don't understand any of this. I don't know the rules or much about anything in the real world. I'm doing the best I can, but I don't know what I'm supposed to do or think or feel!"

He closed the last few steps between them, pulling her into his arms and then sliding his hands up her body to frame her face so she was forced to look at him and unable to turn away. He put every bit of what he felt into his words, willing them to sink in, for her to understand and to accept what he had to say.

His expression was fierce, his actions were fierce, but he

poured every ounce of love he had for this woman into every word, every facet of his expression and in his gaze, willing her to finally see the heart of him, because God only knew he was standing in front of her naked and as vulnerable as a man could ever be. He was perilously close to dropping to his knees and *begging*.

He let it all go. He made no effort to temper his tone, his emotions, or even pretend to have a calm, rational conversation. He wanted to yell to the world that he loved her so damn much that it *defied* all rational thought or action. He didn't give one fuck if the entire floor heard his heated declaration just as long as the one person who mattered heard it. *Really* heard it. He wanted her to *feel* it.

"What you don't get is that I care about you, Jenna. I care so much it's killing me. The thought of being apart from you hurts. The idea that I can't protect you, that I've failed you, that destroys me!"

Her eyes were twin mirrors of shock and she went completely still in his hands.

"I'm in so deep that there's no way I'll ever dig my way out, and baby, I'm *right* where I want to be. So far inside you that you'll never be free of me. I want to make love to you with a desperation that's eating me alive and consumes my every waking thought. I want to take you bare, with nothing between us so we're skin to skin, as close as two people can ever be. I want to give you a baby. *My* baby. So you'll be bound to me forever with no way of ever escaping me. I love the image of you round and swollen with my child, of me loving you forever. Of building a family with you. I want to *keep* you pregnant all the time so you'll never even think about leaving me because you'll be wrapped up in me and all the babies I'm going to give you.

"I'll take such good care of you, honey," he said, caressing his hands over her cheeks, his words and expression pleading with her for understanding and acceptance. "*No one* will ever love you more than I will. There is nothing I won't do to keep you happy and safe every single day for the rest of our lives. I'll give you the moon if you ask me for it. I'll give you anything you ever wanted or dreamed of except . . ."

He dropped one hand from her face and dragged it raggedly through his hair, shame crowding his thoughts, but he'd long since lost any sense of shame or pride when it came to her.

"I won't let you go," he said in a voice clogged with emotion and worry as he waited for her to condemn him with a look. For fear or disappointment to fill her beautiful blue eyes and baby-fine features. He steeled himself for rejection, even as he barged forward, determined for her to have it all. Every single truth as he laid his soul bare.

"I can't give you that, baby. That's the only thing I'll ever deny you, because God help me, I'm a selfish bastard and it would kill me to ever let you walk away."

He sucked in a deep breath and then let her see exactly the kind of man he was. Selfish. Determined. And so fucking in love that she filled every empty void he'd hidden, refused to acknowledge and had accepted as a permanent, aching part of him.

"If I have to, I'll tie you to my bed every night so I never have to worry about you leaving me. I'll do *anything* to keep you. No matter what it takes or what lengths I have to go to. I'll give you the world, your heart's desire, and I just pray that your heart's desire is never to be free of me because that's the one thing I *can't* give you. Your freedom. I can't, Jenna. I wish I were a better man, but fuck it. If being a better man means just letting you walk away from me then I don't want to be that man.

"God, I'm such a bastard to even think that way, much less say it out loud, when you've been a prisoner for damn near your entire life, and yet here I am locking you up again and refusing to free you. But honey, it will be the sweetest of prisons. I swear on my life that I'll spoil you ridiculously and pamper and take care of you and love you so damn much that you never look at it for what it is—a prison—but instead you'll only see your forever home. And a man who loves you more than life."

He grew more serious, his eyes boring intently into hers. He knew this was everything. That nothing would ever be more important than this moment. No job, no mission would ever be this necessary for his survival.

"I'll protect you with my life. You and our children. I'll never let evil touch you again. I'll bust my ass every damn day we have together to give you everything you could possibly ever wish for, and the only reward I'll ever want or need is your smile and your happiness. For those things, I'll kill myself working to make it happen. Everything I ever do from this day forward is for you, baby. Only. Always. For you."

She looked overcome with emotion, hot tears running like rivers down her face, colliding with his hand, falling too fast for him to wipe them away.

"I'm sorry," she began, her voice breaking. "I never meant to hurt you. I didn't know . . . I didn't realize . . ."

Oh hell no. She wasn't apologizing. He silenced her with a kiss, molding his lips hotly to hers, licking at the seam of her mouth until she opened for him. He delved inward, stroking, tasting, savoring and absorbing the very essence of her. He pulled her close, so there was no space between them, his palm on the back of her head, holding her right where he wanted while he plundered her mouth in an endless kiss.

Nothing had ever felt—tasted—so sweet. Nothing had ever been so ... perfect ... as the feel of her in his arms, her small, soft body melting into his. He wanted a lifetime of these moments, holding her as tightly as possible and savoring their closeness. *God, please give me this.* He knew he'd sworn never to ask for more than for her to be safe, unharmed, and for him to get her back, but he had to make one last plea. For her to be his forever.

"Don't ever be sorry," he said fiercely, as he finally pulled away. He stroked her cheeks with his thumbs, soaking in every aspect of her delicate features and a beauty that shone so brightly from the inside out that it was blinding. "Don't ever look back. Never again. Only forward. Give me a chance to make you happy and to make you love me. I'll wait forever if that's what it takes, because in the end, hearing those words from you, no matter how long it takes, in that moment, it will all have been worth it."

"I already do love you," she choked out around the emotion clogging her throat. "I've loved you from the first moment I touched you. Show me your love, Isaac. Please. Show me how it's supposed to be. You've given me the words. Now give me the act itself."

EIGHTEEN

ISAAC froze, his hands that were still framing her beautiful face trembled as he soaked in the most beautiful words he'd ever heard in his life. He couldn't breathe. The knot in his throat was so huge, it was choking him and cutting off his ability to suck in air. His heart raced, pounding the inside of his chest like a jackhammer and his eyelids burned like they were on fire.

"Are you sure, my sweet angel?" he finally managed to rasp out, the words stuttering over numb lips. "Because just knowing you love me is enough. It will always be enough. If you aren't ready for me to make love to you then we'll wait. I'll wait. For as long as it takes until you're sure that this—that I'm—what you want. We have forever."

Jenna cupped her hands over his, then turned, sliding her mouth into the palm that had been cradling her cheek. She closed her eyes and pressed a tiny kiss into his large hand and simply held on to him, holding his hands in place against her face.

"You're the only thing I'm sure of, the only solid thing in my life. You're the only thing I've ever been certain of after so many years of fear, hopelessness and uncertainty. I may not have ever witnessed what love looks like, but I know what love *isn't*. I also know that I've never felt the way I feel right now about anyone else but you. So yes, Isaac, I'm ready. I've been waiting for you my entire life. Don't make me wait any longer," she pleaded as she nuzzled even further into his palm, peppering tiny kisses everywhere her lips touched.

Isaac was overcome and it took him a moment to regain his composure and to swallow back the wave of emotion that unsteadied him. He blinked away the tears that made his vision blurry. Then, still cupping her face, he lowered his mouth to hers, kissing her with tenderness he didn't even know he possessed.

"I'll go slow and I'll be gentle, baby," he whispered. "The last thing I want to do is hurt you but ..."

He was tormented by the fact that, regardless of how slow or easy he was with her, he would hurt her. She was untouched by any man, a virgin. If that wasn't enough, she was tiny and delicate and he was a large, hulking man who could so easily crush her without even realizing it.

His dick was rigid, swelling painfully against the confines of his pants, and he groaned. He was big *everywhere*. How the hell would she ever be able to take him? There was also the fact that he was on the verge of coming right now, and he wasn't even close to being inside her. He doubted he'd get much more than the head of his erection inside her before he came all over her. How was that supposed to be good for her? The last thing he wanted was for her introduction to making love to be over with in two seconds and wondering if that was all there was to it.

Christ, he had to get it together. And for now, he was leaving his damn pants on. He had to make this special for her. He wanted to make it good, wanted her to come screaming his name in pleasure.

He drew away, sliding his hands from her face down the length of her body until he got to the hem of her shirt. He slipped his fingers underneath but halted and stared into her eyes.

"I'm going to undress you, baby. I don't want you to be scared or embarrassed. You're the most beautiful woman I've ever seen in my life and I intend to show you just how beautiful I think you are. But if I ever go too fast, if I ever do anything that frightens you, let me know and I'll stop and take it down a notch and then we'll work up to it again until you feel comfortable enough to keep moving forward, okay?"

"Okay," she whispered, licking her lip nervously.

He regarded her seriously, making certain she was meeting his eyes with her gaze. "Promise me, sweet angel. We have all the time in the world. Promise me you'll tell me if you're afraid, if anything I do hurts you or if you just want to stop or take a break for a while."

She smiled back at him and it was as if the entire room was suddenly bathed in sunshine. He felt the warmth to his bones, felt it enter his bloodstream and quickly travel throughout his entire body.

"I promise," she said.

He began lifting her shirt, inching it upward, his eyes never leaving hers so he could be certain she was with him the whole way and that no panic ever entered her expression. When he had her shirt up over her breasts, he paused again.

"Lift your arms up," he said huskily.

Slowly she lifted them until they were above her head. He quickly pulled the shirt up her arms and over her head until it was free of her body. He tossed it aside and then slid his hands around her hips, tugging her toward him. She fell back, so she was flat on the bed, her hair spread out in a cascade of curls. He fumbled with the snap of her jeans and shakily unzipped the fly. As he began inching the denim down over her hips, he rose above her and leaned down, pressing his lips to her soft belly.

She flinched and what sounded like a moan escaped her lips. He nuzzled her navel, chuckling when she shivered uncontrollably and chill bumps erupted and danced across her skin. As he continued to kiss, lick and nip her belly, he pulled her pants further down. He broke away from her only long enough to impatiently disentangle the pants from her feet.

He nudged her legs apart, staring down at the sheer panties that covered the one part of her he was dying to taste. He wanted to make her come in his mouth. He wanted to show her how good he could make her feel so she would be completely limp and sated before he ever pushed into her.

He crawled up past her knees and then reached down and pressed one finger over her underwear, right between the puffy lips of her pussy. He groaned.

"You're so wet for me, baby. All that sweetness is just waiting for me to lap up."

Jenna blushed bright red, but her eyes were glazed with passion. She looked almost drunk with her swollen lips, tousled hair and hazy eyes. She stared back at him and then she surprised him.

"Yes, Isaac, it's all for you. Only you."

Oh hell. His dick jerked to the point of pain and he could feel moisture coating the inside of his underwear as he fought an epic battle not to come right then and there. He put one hand to his groin and squeezed hard, sucking in several steadying breaths.

Jenna cocked her head to the side, confusion evident in her expression.

"Why are you in pain?" she asked with a frown.

He let out an unconvincing laugh. "You have no idea, baby. I want you so damn much that just looking at you, you saying those words and me knowing I'm about to finally taste you has me about to come and I haven't even gotten my damn clothes off yet."

"Then take them off," she whispered, her eyes suddenly glowing with curiosity and desire.

He grunted. "Not yet, sweetheart. I'm not going to come all over you before I've had a chance to make you feel good. I'm only coming once I'm inside you."

She flushed again but smiled, her entire face lighting up as she continued to watch him.

He leaned down, pressing his nose and mouth to her damp panties and inhaled her intoxicating, feminine scent. It was heady, the sweetest ambrosia. He closed his eyes, feeling unsteady and drunk as he breathed in as much of her as possible.

"Isaac, please," she said, her voice strained as she fidgeted beneath him.

He glanced up her body to meet her eyes. "Tell me what you need, baby. You know I'll give you anything."

"I need . . . I want . . . please touch me," she said desperately. "Something is happening but I don't know what, but I know I need you to touch me to somehow make it better."

He didn't tease her or prolong her agony. He ripped her panties, tossing the remnants aside and then he got down lower, using his shoulders to spread her legs wider, until she was completely open to him.

"Hold on baby, because I'm going to devour you," he growled.

He slid his tongue between her folds and licked upward until he reached her clit and then he swirled the tip in a circular motion around the taut bud. Her entire body went rigid and she cried out sharply but she never asked him to stop.

He traveled lower again and traced the mouth of her tiny opening before finally sliding inside her, his tongue doing exactly what his dick wanted to be doing.

"Oh God, Isaac! What are you doing? What's happening to me?" she asked in bewilderment.

"*Shhh* sweetheart," he soothed. "Don't fight it. I'm here. All you have to do is let go and trust me. I'll always be here to catch you."

"But it feels like I'm going to splinter into a million parts!" she protested.

"I'm only going to make you feel very good," he said.

He returned to her sweet pussy, lapping and sucking greedily, not wanting to waste a single drop her body gave him. He wanted her to come all over his face, wanted her very first orgasm to be in his mouth. Her second orgasm would be around his dick.

He began tongue fucking her and her moans grew louder. Her legs were trembling and she began bucking almost as if it was more than she could bear. He slid a finger through her soft curls between the plump little lips to her clit and he began stroking it as he continued to have his tongue bathed in her honey.

"Isaac!" she cried, panic in her voice.

"Go with it, Jenna. Trust me. I'll never do anything that hurts you," he soothed. "Give it to me. Let it go. Give me what I want."

Her entire body went rigid and he increased his rhythm and pressure, knowing she was hovering right on the edge of her release. When the trembling increased to the point of frenzy and more liquid rushed onto his tongue, he clamped his mouth over her opening, not wanting to miss a single drop of nectar when she came.

Her back bowed, coming off the mattress, just as a cry echoed through the room. She screamed his name and suddenly she was flooding his mouth with the sweetest taste he'd ever experienced in his life. She flinched and jittered beneath him as he gently brought her down from her orgasm, licking and sucking her quivering flesh, but much more gently than before.

When he'd licked her clean of every single drop, he rose up and then slid over her body, kissing his way over her belly up to her breasts. Her expression was dazed, her eyes glowing with contentment as she lazily watched him worship her breasts. When he closed his mouth over one puckered nipple and sucked it strongly between his teeth, she arched off the bed, her mouth flying open and her eyes lost the dull, lazy satisfaction of just a moment ago.

"Have to get you right to the edge again, baby," he said in a gruff voice. "I want you right there, just about to come again before I get inside you. The first time, you came in my mouth. This time you're going to come all over my dick."

She licked her lips and hunger sparked in her eyes. As he bent to lavish attention on her breasts again, her fingers dug into his shoulders, her nails leaving their mark. He closed his eyes and groaned.

"God yes, baby. Mark me. Claim me just like I'm claiming you."

He turned his attention to her other breast, licking around the nipple and leaving a moist trail. The deliciously pink tip was pointed outward, rigid and straining as if begging for his mouth. He nipped lightly at it, coaxing it to even further rigidity and then he lightly grazed his teeth from bottom to top before sucking the entire bud into his mouth.

He suckled strongly, finding his rhythm and then switched back to the other one giving it the same treatment. She was writhing beneath him, her hands everywhere on him, leaving marks on his skin that made him want to beat his chest and roar like a Neanderthal.

He kissed and sucked at her tender skin in a path from her breasts to the tender skin of her neck and then up to her ear, sucking the tiny lobe as she shivered uncontrollably under his much larger body. He completely covered her. There wasn't a single inch of her that wasn't pressed against his skin. She was a part of him, an essential part of him. The very best part of him. She made him better. Made him want to be a better man. For her. And the children they'd one day have. Never had his future looked as good as it did now and it was all because of an angel's touch.

His mouth glided up her jaw until finally he captured her mouth again. He slid his tongue inside, sharing the taste of her nectar with her. His dick was screaming at him to take her. To slide so deep inside her that she'd never be free of him. It was swollen and rigid, straining upward so that it lay flat against his stomach.

When he lifted his body off her just a bit, she glanced down and her eyes widened in a mixture of fear and apprehension.

Then she glanced back at him, biting into her lip nervously. "Isaac, this will never work. How are you supposed to fit? You're so . . . big," she squeaked out.

Before she could work herself into a complete panic attack, he silenced her with another deep, languid kiss. When they were both breathless again, he released her lips and stared lovingly down into her eyes.

"You were made for me, Jenna. My own sweet angel. I'll fit. We'll fit. We will always fit. You're the other half of my soul, the missing half. And now I can't tell what part is me and what part is you because we fit so seamlessly. Don't be afraid, my love. Never be afraid of me. I'll never intentionally hurt you. It will be uncomfortable for you but only for a few moments and then it will pass and after that I'll take us both to heaven. Do you trust me?"

She nodded but he could still see the anxiety in her eyes.

He leaned down, kissing her as he slid one hand down between her legs and between her slick folds. She was drenched with need, even after he'd lapped up every bit of her moisture from earlier. He slipped one finger inside her as his mouth trailed back down to her breasts.

She tensed when his finger penetrated her just the tiniest bit but she also clenched around him, another surge of wetness soaking him each time he sucked her nipple further into his mouth.

"When I get between your legs, I want you to wrap them around my waist and hold on to my shoulders, okay, baby? Can you do that for me?" he asked tenderly.

She nodded, her eyes wide.

"You're ready for me, sweetheart. Your body is ready. You're so wet and hot, so very soft and silky," he murmured.

At his reassuring words, she relaxed, her body going limp against the bed.

He guided his erection between her legs and rubbed the tip up and down her satiny flesh until it was coated in her moisture. He pressed the head to her tiny opening, pushing in the tiniest amount just so the head was lodged there, freeing his hand to do other things.

He lowered his body onto hers, covering her as he propped himself on one forearm so he didn't smother her. He used his other hand to delve between them and he began to caress her clit, pressing against it and rolling it in a circular motion.

She curled her legs around his waist as he'd asked her to and she clamped down tightly each time he toyed with her clit. Her head was thrown back, her chest thrust upward and he'd never seen a more beautiful, erotic sight in his life.

"Hold on baby," he whispered. "I'll try to make this first part fast."

She opened her eyes, confused by his words.

"I love you," he said. "I'll always love you."

Then he thrust forward, hard and deep, rending the fragile barrier that proclaimed her innocence. She cried out, tears shimmering in her eyes as she gripped his shoulders. His heart damn near split in two when a tear trickled down the side of her face to disappear into her hair.

"I'm sorry, baby," he said, his chest aching as he lowered his mouth to kiss her. "I'm so damn sorry I hurt you. I wouldn't hurt you for anything in the world. Just stay still. I won't move until the pain goes away and then I'll make you feel good again. I swear it. Please forgive me," he pleaded.

She caressed his face with one hand and smiled tremulously up at him. "I know you didn't mean to hurt me, Isaac. It just took me by surprise, that's all. Will it be like that every time? I mean when you first get inside?"

She fidgeted with discomfort over asking such an intimate question and he had to kiss her again.

"No, baby, I promise. It'll never hurt like that again. You were a virgin and the first time with a man is often painful because I have to break through your hymen. But it's gone now and from now on, you'll feel nothing but pleasure."

Even as he reassured her, his fingers were on her clit, stroking and pressing. He could feel her body contracting and tightening around him and he could feel her bathe his dick with a flood of arousal.

She tentatively flexed around him, the walls of her pussy gripping him tightly. He groaned and closed his eyes, clamping his teeth together.

"Have mercy, baby," he said in a pained voice. "If you keep doing that, I'm going to come way too soon and it will be all over with."

She smiled and then arched upward, suddenly taking more of him inside her.

He swore and tried to withdraw but she clamped her legs tighter around his waist, preventing him from doing any such thing.

"It doesn't hurt as much," she said shyly. "I feel so . . . tingly. I need you to move. I want you to move."

With more restraint than he would have ever attributed to himself, he eased forward until just two inches of him remained outside of her opening. Then he pulled back, moaning as she rippled and fluttered tightly over his erection. When he was nearly all the way out, only the head remaining inside her, he pushed forward more forcefully, seating himself as deeply as he could.

Her eyes went wide at the sensation and her legs trembled violently around him, her heels digging into his back.

"Please," she begged. "I need . . . I don't know what I need," she said in frustration.

"I know what you need, baby," he said lovingly. "Hold on to me tight."

As soon as her legs and arms were around his body, he began to thrust harder and faster, planting himself deep before retreating only to do it all over again. He could no longer hold back, no longer measure his thrusts. He began moving faster and faster, his hips slapping against her ass as he reached maximum depth, every inch of his dick bathed in her heat.

Sweat broke out on his forehead and strain was evident in her expression.

"I need you to come for me," Isaac said through gritted teeth. "Let go, Jenna. Let it happen."

His thumb pressed more firmly against her clit and as he rolled it harder and faster, he lowered his head to suck her nipple into his mouth, using his teeth to add a tiny spark of pain.

It was all she needed. Her eyes shot to his and her mouth opened in a soundless cry. Her body tensed to the point she almost appeared as though she were in pain. Just when he knew he couldn't last even another stroke, he was surrounded by a sudden surge of hot, silken release.

He roared her name and then buried his face in her neck as he thrust himself as deeply into her body as possible. His release surged painfully, shooting from his dick into her warm, inviting haven. Never had he come so much in his life. He could feel it leaking from inside her, smeared on the inside of her thighs and the outside of his.

And never had he felt so damn satisfied—so *complete*—in his entire life. He'd found home. She was his home. Not a place, not a house. But her. His angel. Wherever she was, as long as he was with her, he was home.

NINETEEN

JENNA awoke sprawled across Isaac's body and she sleepily glanced up to see if he was awake. To her surprise, he was staring intently down at her and he slid his hand up her back in an intimate caress.

"We need to get up so I can feed you," he said, his eyes still glittering with heat.

She yawned sluggishly and wrapped her arm around his waist to hold him closer.

"I'm not hungry. Can't we just stay in bed?" she asked in a pouty tone.

He chuckled and kissed the top of her head. "Baby, we haven't left this room in three days. You have to be starving."

She lifted her head and stared at him aghast. "Three days?"

His grin grew bigger, a cocky lilt to his lips. "I'm not surprised you lost track of time—after all, I did keep you pretty busy. I was pretty hard on you," he said, his grin fading as concern touched his eyes.

She blushed self-consciously but sent him a dazzling smile. "I wouldn't call what you did being too hard on me. Besides, I think I likely wore you out as much as you wore me out."

He laughed and tweaked her nose affectionately. "You *definitely* won't hear me complaining, sweetheart. But you do need to shower and then eat, and I need to check in with the others before someone decides to check to see if we're still alive."

Panic seized her and she scrambled from the bed, searching desperately for her clothing. She'd die of mortification if anyone walked in on them naked in bed. But Isaac caught her hand and pulled her back down to him and kissed her long and hard, causing her to forget all about anyone else.

"I was teasing you, baby. They know damn well if they even tried to come in here, I'd cut their balls off. No one sees what's mine. No one will *ever* see what belongs to me from now on."

His words made her glow, her chest squeezing with absolute contentment and so much love that she couldn't even process the bombardment of emotions he made her feel.

"You really mean that, don't you?"

He frowned at her, his eyes searching her entire expression. "Clearly I didn't do a good enough job convincing you. Maybe I need another three days in bed with you until you see the light and fully understand that you are mine, Jenna. You belong to me and I belong to you. I don't joke about something like that. There's never been another woman I've even come close to saying those words to. Only you. It will always be only you."

"I'm going, I'm going!" she said, laughing. Then her tone turned rueful. "I'm not sure I'll be able to walk to the shower."

He gave her a look that suggested she was crazy for even

contemplating walking and then simply picked her up and carried her to the bathroom.

"Who said you'd be walking? After the scare you gave me I'm not going to want to let you out of my sight. Hell, I want you in touching distance at all times because I plan to do a lot of touching. I have no discipline when it comes to you," he muttered.

"You act as if that's a bad thing," she teased.

Her long, leisurely shower had her so hot and bothered that she wanted to haul him back to bed to satisfy the burning desire he'd built into an inferno. But he helped her from the shower and then dried her very thoroughly with a towel. He even brushed out the mass of tangled hair that was the result of their marathon of making love before he gave her a pat on the ass and told her to dress.

They finally left the room and headed for the kitchen, where Isaac deposited her on one of the stools at the island with instructions not to move while he made their breakfast. Jenna was self-conscious, knowing that the men were in the next room and knew full well what she and Isaac had spent the last three days doing.

She kept her head down, twisting her fingers together, and peeked in the direction of the living room several times from the corner of her eye.

Isaac placed a plate in front of her that was heaped with so much food that she had no hope of eating it all, but being allowed to have anything other than the vegetables she'd eaten for so long was a luxury she still savored.

"Relax, baby," Isaac said in a low voice. "No one will say a damn thing, and they'd never do anything to embarrass you."

She nodded, feeling stupid for being so worried. Isaac's teammates had been nothing but solicitous of her and not once had she gotten the impression that they'd ever do anything to make her feel uncomfortable.

She examined each offering on the plate in giddy delight. Never had she been offered so much food and so many delicious-smelling—and looking—kinds of food in her life. She realized she was smiling like an idiot when her cheeks actually began to ache, but she simply couldn't contain her delight at the new experience and the freedom to eat—or not eat—whatever she wanted.

When she'd fully examined every different food on her plate, she picked up her fork and for a moment paused, her brow furrowing as she stared down at the banquet he'd simply called a meal. Which one did she want to try first? Not one of them had an unappealing smell or appearance, though she had no clue what any of it was. Embarrassment flooded her and heat crept up her neck and into her cheeks. Even a child could identify the different dishes Isaac had prepared, surely. She suddenly wasn't as delighted by the new experience as she had been a few moments ago.

Feeling eyes watching her, she glanced up without lifting her head, instead peeking from underneath her lashes to see Isaac regarding her with so much sadness that her embarrassment made her faintly nauseous, and she suddenly lost any desire to eat.

Refusing to look up, she subtly pushed the plate forward and stared down at the fork she still held, wishing there were a hole that would just swallow her up.

"Baby, eat," Isaac said, his voice holding a gentle ache to it. As if he hurt for her.

She closed her eyes and just a second later, she felt Isaac slide onto the stool next to her, his heat enfolding her in its embrace.

"Honey, you have nothing to be embarrassed about," he said, sincerity echoing solidly in his tone, and when she got up the courage to glance up at him, she saw the same absolute sincerity etched in every line of his face.

"I wanted you to have the opportunity to try several new things," he explained. "It's why I made such a variety. You'll learn what you do and don't like, and that's information I need to know so that I don't ever serve you something that doesn't taste good to you."

She looked at him, appalled and confused at the same time. "You don't care if I don't like something you cooked for me? But it would be so rude for me to not appreciate something you put such an effort into."

She glanced nervously back at the plate. The idea of not liking something he'd cooked for her when he'd gone to such lengths to please her filled her with dread.

Isaac sighed and then curled his hand around her knee, swinging her around on the stool to face him. He tipped her chin up with his finger so that their eyes met.

"Baby, everyone has foods they love and foods they absolutely despise and wouldn't eat under any circumstances. It's called being human and being an individual. No two people like the exact same things. I want you to love what you eat every single time we sit down to have a meal and in order for that to happen, we have to experiment with foods until you have a good grasp of what you like, what you don't like and what you *love*, as in your absolute favorites. You'll learn I have my own share of foods I wouldn't touch with a ten-foot pole."

"Really?" she asked hopefully. "You won't be mad at me if I don't like something you cooked for me?"

"I will never—listen to me very closely, baby—I will *never* be angry at you for being honest with me. What I would be angry over is if you kept eating something you absolutely hated because you were afraid to tell me you didn't like it."

He grinned and tweaked her nose. "I already know not to serve you vegetables or I'll end up having to sleep on the couch."

She blinked in surprise and then realizing that he was teasing her, she laughed, relief spilling over into her amusement.

"Now, will you please eat whatever you want and leave whatever you don't want?"

Feeling more than a little bit silly after his explanation, she nodded and then eagerly reached for the plate, pulling it in front of her. She sampled each of the different items, taking a single bite with her fork from them all, taking in the tastes and textures, what tasted the best and what was the least appetizing to her.

She pointed in turn to each of the foods she'd sampled, giving Isaac her rating, her favorite being the fluffy, buttery biscuits. The scrambled eggs were an either/or for her, but bacon was absolutely decadent and she ate every single piece on her plate. She frowned at the grits as she rubbed the grainy mixture around her mouth, deciding she had no interest in ever eating it again. The pan-fried ham was delicious and the fresh fruit, she devoured, licking the juice from her fingers so as not to miss a single drop.

When she'd eaten her fill, she pushed her plate back with a heavy sigh of contentment. "I'm stuffed," she groaned. "And I need to make another trip to the bathroom."

Isaac took her plate and dropped a kiss on her upturned lips. "Hurry back to me."

She smiled and walked out of the kitchen toward the bedroom she and Isaac had occupied.

Isaac was rinsing the dishes when Shadow called to him from the doorway dividing the kitchen and living room.

"You need to see this, brother," he said in a low voice, sliding his eyes in the direction Jenna had disappeared in a silent message that it was something she didn't need to see.

But Jenna walked in at just the moment Shadow spoke and saw the look sent in her direction. Shadow's lips thinned, and it was obvious he was cursing under his breath. He sent Isaac a look of apology.

"What is it?" Jenna asked sharply, fear replacing her earlier sparkle and laughter.

Isaac cursed at the sudden change.

"You can't shield me from everything," Jenna said softly.

"The hell I can't!" he bellowed.

A look of defiance sparked in her eyes. "Whatever it is can't hurt me. We're here and they're somewhere else. Watching something on a television can't hurt anyone. Only people can hurt people and they have to be captured in order to be hurt. I get that I'm dumb and ignorant and hopelessly naïve, but how can I ever expect to learn the things I need to know if you are all determined to keep me locked away where I don't see anything disturbing? I need to know what's going on. The only time I'm afraid is when I don't know what's happening," she said in a pleading voice.

"You are *not* dumb and ignorant and you are *not* naïve, and I won't put up with you constantly putting yourself down or convincing yourself that you're less than everyone else. That you're nobody and nobody cares for you," he said fiercely.

"Damn it, Jenna, you've been isolated from the world since you were four years old. No one would expect you to learn everything in a few days, which is why we're protecting you and helping you gain the knowledge you need, but you have to be willing to let us do our job and listen when we tell you what you need to do in order to be able to protect yourself as well."

"We have a few minutes," Shadow said calmly. "There's a commercial break right now and when the newscast returns they're going with the lead story." He leveled his stare at Jenna, giving her a chin lift in respect. "It's your decision. Just make it quick."

Even though he knew Shadow was right and that Isaac couldn't continue to treat her like she would fall apart at any sign of adversity, it still pissed him off that he couldn't shield her from pain and anguish, and he knew it showed in his expression and tense body language.

Jenna's expression became troubled and she frowned. Her lips trembled and it was obvious she was fighting back tears. *Fuck*. He hadn't meant to upset her or hurt her feelings, but he was at a complete loss as to how to convince her that she was far from nothing. That she was important, and that she was *everything* to him. She was the reason he breathed, that he got up in the morning and for the first time since she'd stolen his heart and made it her own forever, didn't simply go through the motions of the day. Instead he savored every single moment with her, allowing himself something he'd never dreamed of being capable of having. Hope. Excitement for the future. Spending the rest of his life killing himself just so she'd keep smiling and be happy. For too long his life had been consumed by shadows and darkness, concealed places he didn't dare delve into for fear of unleashing painful memories and allowing all the mistakes he'd made to pour out. Because once he did, there was no going back. He would have had to walk away from everything he knew and the people who'd embraced him as family because he wouldn't have been able to look them in the eye and pretend that everything was all right. Perfect. Just another day like all the others.

It had taken him months to quit the bottle and sober up and then another year to work his body back into shape, eat the right foods or even eat at all. That had enabled him to do his job because he had become very adept at being aloof and unaffected, concealing his emotions and keeping any telling information from his face. But however good he'd gotten at fooling not just others but himself as well when he was on the job, the nights were an altogether different matter.

It was then, in unguarded, vulnerable moments, that the nightmares crept in, searching for the slightest crack in the barriers of his mind so they could pour insidiously into his dreams, smug and victorious, always making him feel like a shell of a person. A fraud, because he spent his days pretending and his nights reliving events that had broken him in a way that had taken him a very long time to recover from. And he still hadn't managed to piece himself back together completely. He knew because he still had nightmares that jerked him up in bed, sweat soaking his skin from head to toe and his heart pounding so furiously that at times he feared he was having a heart attack. They just weren't as frequent as they had been.

And yet with one touch, Jenna had healed not only the gaping wound in his chest that would have killed him in minutes, maybe seconds, but she had also done the impossible by filling his heart and soul with so much light, sunshine and sweetness that for a moment, he truly thought he *had* died and gone to heaven. Despite his past sins.

But most of all she'd given him a reprieve from years of constantly staggering beneath the unbearable weight of grief, blame and guilt that was never forgotten or forgiven. He hadn't *allowed* himself to be free, hadn't tried to forget or forgive because it was his penance, one he deserved. And in the place of all the pain and remorse he'd lived with for so long, Jenna had gifted him the most precious thing he'd ever been given, second only to her love, trust and her innocence. Absolution. Freedom from a lifetime of self-condemnation and self-hatred.

Somehow she'd removed every single one of the ugly, dark voids that he'd buried so deep in an effort to hide them from even himself so he could pretend they weren't there until they came roaring to the surface with a vengeance. She filled them with an angelic light so bright it could never be covered or disguised. It was simply so large a part of her that it spilled from her, encompassing and overtaking everything she focused her gift on. Natural and effervescent, just like her sparkling eyes and long blond hair that slid down her back in a mass of unruly curls. She'd done the impossible, sealing his gaping wounds on the inside so they would never be raw, painful or exposed again in a single moment of weakness and vulnerability.

She'd given him a miracle he was too ashamed to ask or pray for. Something he was desperate for, if only for a moment, even when he knew he didn't deserve it.

Peace.

The kind of peace that couldn't be wiped away in a moment of guilt when his past came back to haunt him. It was a permanent part of him now, every bit as much as she was a permanent part—the very best part—of everything he was. Even now he ached just remembering the beauty of that moment. As soon as she'd touched him there was no separation. Their hearts and souls had recognized one another and in that brief second when time seemed to stop, they'd been truly connected in a way Isaac had never been connected to another human being. Heart, soul and mind, closer than any two people could ever possibly be. He didn't believe for a moment that any other two people were capable of sharing something as inexplicable as the kind of bond that had instantly and irrevocably formed between him and Jenna.

And because she'd healed more than just the physical wounds he'd incurred and brought light back into a world that had been dark to him for so long, he hadn't had a single nightmare since finding her and bringing her home to him, knowing—and fully admitting to himself—that no other woman would ever own every single piece of his heart and soul like she did—and always would. If he ever lost her—fuck, it hurt to even entertain that thought—he'd never look at another woman again. She was his. Every inch of her body was his, and though she may have thought he was teasing, he'd been completely serious. He'd tie her to his bed in a heartbeat if he ever thought she'd try to leave him again.

Shadow cleared his throat in a not very subtle way and sent Isaac a pointed glare. "Daydream later when your attention isn't needed on the very serious matter we have on our hands."

Isaac glanced at Jenna, seeing trepidation in her eyes, but

most pronounced was the set of her jaw, how her lips were pressed together and the determined way she stared back at him unflinchingly.

"Fuck," he muttered. "I don't like this, baby. I swore on my life to love and protect you always, to never let evil touch you and to bust my ass every single day to make you happy. Whatever the fuck is about to come on the news completely negates every one of those promises because if it wasn't bad, and if it wasn't going to upset you, then Shadow wouldn't have indicated that you shouldn't be present."

She scowled in response. "Oh, let's see. Not letting me decide for myself whether I want to watch a news program is *not* going to make me happy. Me being here surrounded by men who make professional wrestlers look like wimps more than covers my safety and protection. And unless you plan to tell me you don't love me anymore because I didn't act like a good little girl and meekly walk into the other room, I fail to see how any of your promises are at risk unless you decide to go through with the first and fourth items on my list."

"Now you're just pissing me off," Isaac said in a near bellow. "Of course I love you, damn it. And of course you're safe here."

She lifted one eyebrow as she waited for him to address the first issue.

Dane strode into the kitchen. "We're out of time, so do what you're going to do but make it fast," he snapped.

Jenna narrowed her eyes as she marched past Isaac as if daring him to stop her. And he was tempted. He was so tempted to make good on his threat to tie her to his bed. It would certainly make keeping the rest of his promises a hell of a lot easier. His lips curled upward into a snarl, baring his teeth when Jenna followed Shadow into the living room and took a seat on the floor next to him, the two sitting cross-legged directly in front of the TV.

"What do you think it is?" she asked Shadow nervously. "What did they say before the break?" She struggled a moment, her lips pursed in concentration, clearly puzzled. "Commercial break. That's what you called it, wasn't it? What is that?"

Oh hell no. If she needed information, reassurance, someone to hold her if the newscast upset or frightened her, it sure as fuck wasn't going to be Shadow. Isaac moved pointedly between Jenna and Shadow, wedging his large body into the small space, unapologetically bumping into Shadow until Shadow gave him a disgusted look and moved over several inches.

"Let's just see what the news anchor says," Shadow said soothingly. "I'll explain a commercial break to you later."

Dane held up his hand for silence as the news anchor sat at her desk with a screen to the right of her shoulder showing images of flashing lights, dozens of ambulances, police vehicles and fire trucks.

As soon as the images began rolling, Jenna stiffened, her body going so rigid that the strain was evident in her face and eyes. Eyes that became haunted and so apprehensive that Isaac wanted to smash the fucking television to make it stop. The others cast Jenna worried glances and Shadow leaned forward, eyeing her sharply around Isaac.

It took everything Isaac had to focus on what the reporter was saying when all he wanted to do was shield Jenna from further distress, but the images meant something to Jenna, so they needed all the information the news could provide.

"We have a breaking development on a story we brought you

earlier. What was first believed to have been a mass suicide in a compound in an isolated area north of Houston by a previously unknown and highly secretive cult has now been determined to have been a gruesome mass homicide," the anchor said in a somber voice.

Isaac swore long and hard, and he wasn't the only one. Tensions skyrocketed in the room and everyone's eyes were glued to the television, where grisly details were being reported as calmly as if they were the weather report.

Jenna turned away from the TV, covering her entire face with her hands. She rocked back and forth, sounds of acute distress escaping her lips despite her having covered her mouth in an effort to prevent any sound from escaping. She shook uncontrollably and Isaac knew she was on the verge of shattering.

He exchanged helpless looks with Shadow and then glanced up at Dane, who was staring at Jenna with compassion and also fury over all she'd suffered. They all knew what this meant. What they didn't know is whether Jenna had put it together yet or if she was just reacting to the reminder of the horror her life had been for two decades.

"Give me a minute with Jenna," Isaac said in a low voice. "I'm going to take her into the bedroom and try to get her to rest." He gave Dane a meaningful look. "Do what needs to be done while I take care of her."

"There is a bottle of sedatives in the kitchen cabinet," Dane offered. "We keep all our safe houses stocked with stuff the women might need in case they ever have to go into hiding. The sedatives are Tori's. She still has anxiety attacks and she rarely sleeps worth a damn because her dreams frighten her."

He rubbed his hand over his face, his eyes stormy with rage.

"She has nightmares of the past and of all that bastard did to her and she has dreams of the future, of what is to be. Both are very hard on her and sometimes taking a sedative is the only way she's able to sleep."

Isaac nodded. "Thanks," he said quietly. Then he looked to Shadow. "Can you get me one of the pills while I take Jenna to the bedroom? Bring something for her to drink so she can take the medicine."

Shadow rose without hesitation and Isaac turned back to Jenna, who had shut out everything around her as she struggled with the many demons that haunted her. With all the tenderness he was capable of, he lifted Jenna's curled-up body and cradled her against his heart. He squeezed her to let her know she was safe, that he was with her and that he'd never leave her. Then he pressed a gentle kiss to her hair, nuzzling the silky tresses as he slowly walked to their bedroom.

He laid her down on the bed and immediately climbed in beside her, pulling her into his arms. She shoved her face in his neck, her body shaking. Her pulse was a frantic staccato, and heated moisture fell onto his neck and slithered downward to disappear beneath the collar of his shirt.

"Don't cry, baby. Not for them. They aren't worth your tears. I don't want you to ever have a reason to cry again."

She gripped him harder for a moment, pressing her face and lips more firmly against his neck before she released her hold on him and slowly eased her head back so she could look up at him.

She was prevented from speaking when a quiet knock sounded at the door and Isaac called for Shadow to come in. He carried a glass of water in one hand and his other was curled around something, trapping it in his grasp.

He handed the glass to Isaac and then opened his palm to reveal the small peach-colored pill. "I need you to take this, sweetheart. Can you do that for me?"

"What is it?" she asked cautiously.

Isaac caressed her cheek with his free hand. "It's just something to help you relax and it will ease the panic and anxiety. Most important, it will help you sleep, and you need to get some rest. I've kept you up the last three days and I'm sure you're exhausted."

She flushed, looking so adorable that Isaac wanted to spread her out and kiss and lick every inch of skin that was now a delectable shade of pink.

But then her expression became troubled and she lifted sorrow-filled eyes to both Isaac and Shadow. "But what about what happened? What does it all mean? Who would do something so horrible?"

"We'll talk about it after you wake up from your nap," Isaac said soothingly, stroking through her hair with his hand. "Right now I need you to rest. Will you do that for me? I won't withhold any information from you. I promise."

She eyed the pill Shadow was now holding just in front of her lips, waiting for her to open her mouth to take it, and hesitated.

"I'd never give you anything that would hurt you," Shadow said, sincerity ringing in his voice. "You have my word, Jenna. I'll protect you from anything or anyone harming you. I'm not the enemy."

She grimaced and looked ashamed. "I'm sorry, Shadow. I didn't mean for you to think I doubted you. I just feel as though

I have absolutely no control over any aspect of my life and I was afraid the medicine would make me feel even more helpless."

Shadow grinned. "Kinda hard to feel helpless when you're sound asleep, angel face. Now open up so Isaac can give you something to wash it down with."

She took the pill and immediately made a face, lunging for the glass in Isaac's hand. She swallowed hard and then shuddered. Then she sent Shadow an accusing look. "You *were* trying to kill me! That tasted awful!"

Shadow laughed and then gave Isaac a chin lift before ruffling Jenna's hair affectionately. Without another word, he left the room and Isaac gathered her in his arms once more, determined to stay with her until the medicine took effect and she fell into a deep and hopefully dreamless sleep.

"I wasn't upset that the elders were killed," Jenna said, suddenly interrupting the quiet that had fallen over the room. "I know it's wrong, but they're pure evil and they deserved what they got."

"What upset you then, baby?"

Tears glistened in her eyes. "They killed *everyone*. Even the children. And the women. Many of the cult members weren't evil. They were just misguided and brainwashed. They thought they were doing God's will. They didn't deserve to die just because they believed the wrong people."

Isaac nodded, tucking her head against his chest so he could rest his chin atop her head.

"I know it may not seem like it now, but honey, soon this will be all over and once it is, I'm making you mine legally, and then I'll go to work making you so happy that one day you'll look back at all that happened and it won't be so bright in your memory."

She yawned and snuggled closer to him, wrapping her legs around his. "You have no idea how much I want that, Isaac. But I'm afraid to dream. I'm afraid to hope. Before, I didn't have anything to look forward to, dream about or that gave me hope, so it didn't really matter what happened. But now there's so much I want, and I couldn't bear it if it was all taken away after I had the chance to experience it even for a short time."

"With love, miracles happen, and you were already a miracle, so I'm liking our odds. Don't count us out before we ever get to start on our journey together. I swear to you that if you'll trust me with your heart and your happiness, you'll enjoy every minute of the ride."

TWENTY

ISAAC eased himself from the bed, having waited until Jenna succumbed fully to the sedative, and he leaned down to press his lips to her brow, closing his eyes, his heart aching over what he knew lay ahead. She'd endured enough hurt and sorrow for a lifetime, and it frustrated him that he couldn't just make it all go away for her instantaneously. Before it was all over with, she would suffer still more emotional duress, but he'd give his life to prevent her from enduring more physical pain. He fervently prayed that violence never touched her again, though he knew he couldn't make that kind of guarantee. The only promise he could make was that he'd protect her as fiercely as he'd ever protected anyone and he knew his men would do the same. Their determination matched his own, and it was there to see in their eyes and their demeanor.

He quietly made his exit, softly closing the door behind him, and then strode to the living room, his mind already shifting gears to the next obstacle to keeping Jenna glued to his side for the rest of their lives.

"Sitrep," Isaac said, not wasting any time in getting to the heart of the matter.

Dane turned to him with a grim expression, his jaw tight and his eyes blazing with anger and worry. And that made Isaac that much more uneasy because Dane didn't get worried about much. Only when it came to the people closest to him, the men who worked under him, did he lose his characteristic unflappable calm.

It had been almost too painful to look at him when Lizzie had fallen off the radar and they'd learned she'd gone vigilante in order to spare the lives of the only people she cared deeply about: Dane and the men she worked with at DSS and the women, Tori, Ramie, Ari and Gracie. And when he'd knelt next to her while Sterling held her nearly lifeless body as blood ran like a river from the horrendous gunshot wound to her chest, it had been the first time Isaac had ever seen him in such an emotional state, battling tears and grief when the medics arrived and she'd flatlined.

Nearly losing Lizzie had changed him on a fundamental level. Though he was still cool and rarely rattled over any situation, he was more protective of all the people who worked under him and doubly so of the women who had such close ties to men who worked for DSS.

Where before he gave much latitude and adopted a hands-off approach when it came to missions he wasn't leading, now he kept his thumb on the pulse of every single mission that came DSS's way. He sat in on every meeting regardless of whether he was working that particular assignment and he checked in regularly with whoever was lead, always ensuring his men had every resource available to them possible.

And if he even thought there was any danger to any one of his teams, he didn't hesitate to insert himself and work side by side with every agent, but he didn't try to take over and assume leadership. Dane simply didn't have an ego, and it was one of the things Isaac liked most about working under him. His only priority was getting the job done quickly and efficiently without any DSS agent getting hurt or killed.

"I called Caleb, Beau and Zack first," Dane said tersely. "I explained what happened and that we're ninety-nine percent sure this was a calculated strike planned before Jenna even escaped. That after the prearranged exchange, the bastard buying her ordered every single person who had any knowledge of her existence to be terminated. It makes sense. Jenna's been with the cult nearly her entire life and no one outside the cult would have any way of knowing anything about her, so there would be no one to question her disappearance. The drug kingpin would have what he was desperate to possess with no fear of anyone ever causing an uproar over her vanishing. She simply wouldn't exist, much like she hasn't existed for the last two decades."

"But our interference changed everything and completely fucked up the asshole's plan," Knight growled. "Especially after we went in to retrieve Jenna and stole her back right under his nose. Now he has to contend with us and he knows that if he's ever successful in getting Jenna back, we'll hunt him relentlessly, and he can't afford to add another enemy to his long list of people who'd like to cut him into little pieces and make him fish food."

"Exactly," Dane said. "Which means he'll come at us with

everything he has and he'll move fast, because he can't take the chance of the knowledge of Jenna's existence going beyond our organization."

"Fuck," Isaac said, fury coiling and boiling through his veins. "God damn it. She's had enough! How much more does she have to suffer? How much longer does she have to live in constant fear? She's going to want to bolt the minute she realizes that we're that fucking drug dealer's next target and I've got to convince her that it wouldn't make a damn difference now. Whether she's gone or not, they're going to try to take every last one of us out because of what we know."

"Caleb, Beau and Zack are going to lock down the women and spread out to different locations so they don't present a single target. Tori will be with Caleb and Ramie. I'm going to call in a few favors because I don't want them alone, but we need every single DSS agent on Jenna's detail, so I'm going to arrange for protection for them," Dane said.

"What about Lizzie?" Isaac asked in concern.

"I've given Sterling the rundown and while Lizzie won't be happy she's in lockdown too, they're moving to an undisclosed location. Sterling has enough manpower to give them adequate protection."

Isaac exhaled in relief. He knew Lizzie was going to be pissed because she was a damn good agent and in any other circumstance, he'd be glad for her to have his back. But she still wasn't one hundred percent recovered from her brush with death. She'd been through her own hell and the last thing she needed was to be right back in the line of fire. Not that Sterling would ever allow it. Lizzie's husband was one of the few men who didn't back down from her and had no problem going toe to toe with her when it came to her safety. Her being at risk was never going to be an argument she won with Sterling. The man was every bit as hot-headed, stubborn and rigid as Lizzie could be, especially when it came to anything having to do with his wife being in harm's way. Sterling wasn't above cuffing her to his wrist, a chair or his bed, because he'd unapologetically done it before.

"So what do we do in the meantime?" Isaac asked, noting every one of his teammates come to attention and focus intently on Dane. They obviously wanted to know every bit as badly as he did. They all hated just sitting around with their thumbs up their asses, waiting for the enemy to come to them.

That wasn't who or what they were. It wasn't the way they operated. Ever. They took the fight to their opponent. They called the shots. They decided when, how and where and they always opted for the element of surprise. It had certainly served them well enough in the past.

"We keep Jenna safe. We watch our sixes at all times. I don't want anyone going anywhere alone. No easy targets. If they want us, they're going to have to take us all on," Dane said.

"So we sit tight, stay here and play house and pretend we aren't being hunted and that those bastards won't try to get their hands on Jenna again," Isaac said bitterly.

The others didn't look any happier with Dane's edict. Dane gripped his nape with one hand, rubbing and squeezing, his agitation evident.

"If you think I like this any more than any of you, you're fucking wrong," he snapped. "Our primary objective is to keep an innocent woman from the hands of a goddamn monster. A man who ordered the slaughter of over one hundred people, including babies, children and women. Staying here is the very best thing we can do for the time being, until we know more about them than they do about us. If we show ourselves in public then we betray Jenna, when we've sworn to her that we'll do anything we can to make sure she's never subjected to that butcher's brutality. Does it suck? Hell yeah. It turns my fucking stomach to stand down and hide like some fucking coward and send them the message that we're afraid of them."

Dane grew even more furious, his face reddening in rage.

"We aren't afraid of inept dickheads who get off on making an innocent woman suffer. What we are is smarter. While they're running out in broad daylight and in public, we're lying low and waiting for them to fuck up and make a mistake, and that's when we nail their asses to the wall. And you know what? Let them think we're afraid. It will only make them that much more confident and bolder and since they're already stupid as fuck, they'll screw up. We just have to be patient and not be the ones to fuck up first."

"Gotta say, boss man, that's twisted yet very righteous logic," Dex said.

Zeke nodded, and then one by the one the others did as well until only Shadow and Isaac remained still.

"You're right. It sucks," Isaac bit out. "But I won't risk Jenna in any way and if that means holing up here for however long it takes until they fuck up, then that's what I'll do."

Shadow merely nodded, remaining silent, though his eyes burned with anger and frustration.

"Who are you putting on the women?" Brent asked, speaking up for the first time. "They've been through enough fear, pain and horror. This doesn't need to touch them in any way." His eyes burned with the memories of all the women who'd come to mean so much to all of DSS, not just their husbands, who had suffered but survived. He was angry, and yet there was clear worry reflected in his expression.

"They're strong, no doubt," he continued. "But even the toughest nut will crack under repeated trauma. I don't like Caleb having both Ramie and Tori to look after. His attention absolutely can't be divided, and neither woman deserves to be the one who gets the short end of the stick. Tori wouldn't . . ." He inhaled sharply. "I don't think she'd survive it again," he said quietly.

Dane's face was a mask of cold fury, his entire body tense, his jaw bulging with the strain of clenching his teeth so tightly. "I'm taking over Tori's protection. I don't have a wife, no choice to be made if the worst happens. Isaac will take the lead here and all of you will remain for his backup and above all, Jenna's protection. When I said that Tori was with Caleb and Ramie, I meant, but didn't state at the time, that it was a temporary situation until I can get as much protection in place for Ramie, Ari and Gracie as possible. But Tori will be with me and Sterling has enough manpower that he can spare the muscle to add to my protection of Tori. No one knows where I'll be taking her. It's one of the few secrets I have from Caleb and Beau, but it wasn't meant to be a safe house until now. Given the fact that no one, not even a single DSS member, knows its location, it's the obvious choice. Sterling's men are going ahead to more heavily fortify the place and then they'll take position so they completely surround the facility, and should anyone make it past them, I have an impenetrable safe room with a meticulously stocked arsenal at my disposal. No one will get to Tori on my watch."

Isaac frowned. "If this place is impenetrable and so heavily fortified, then why not bring Jenna there?"

Shadow spoke up before Dane. "Because it would require moving Jenna and she would be easily recognized by Jaysus or any of his army of men. Plus they're expecting us to do just that. To move her to some badass safe house where all of us accompany her. It's exactly what they want because then they'll have the chance not only to take out the majority of our manpower, but also to grab Jenna at the same time. The very last thing we need to be right now is predictable. We have to be able to guess what they're expecting and then do the opposite."

It pissed Isaac off that he was so emotionally fucked in the head that he couldn't think straight and that Shadow had to explain something to him that he damn well knew. He wasn't some wet-behind-the-ears rookie, grasping at straws, but this wasn't just any mission. He wasn't protecting someone because he'd been hired to do it and could detach himself and objectively assess any potential threat. He was terrified out of his mind of losing Jenna. Of a sadistic drug lord getting his hands on Jenna and making her suffer things he couldn't even think about without losing the very thin grasp he had on his sanity and completely losing his shit.

Dane nodded. "That's precisely our objective. This place is stocked with enough food and supplies for six months. If this goes on too long, Jenna is going to go stir crazy and she's going to want her freedom. After being a prisoner her entire life, I don't blame her one bit, but you're all going to have to keep her busy and distracted no matter how you have to do it because we can't afford even one slip-up. Eyes are to be on her at all times in case she gets it in her head to sacrifice herself for all of us again," he growled, his displeasure obvious that she'd done it once already.

"How are you going to get out of here without compromising our location?" Knight asked Dane.

Dane's lips turned up into a faint smile. "I never use a safe house that doesn't have more than one exit. I won't be seen and I damn sure won't be tagged leaving the building. You just worry about your jobs and let me worry about getting Tori into protective custody without hitting anyone's radar."

Isaac stepped in front of Dane and stared him directly in the eye, not even attempting to hide the turmoil he knew to be present in his gaze.

"She's my life, Dane. I'll never be able to thank you—any of you—enough for this. She did more than heal a gunshot wound to my chest. She changed me. Brought me into the light when I was drowning in so much darkness, desolation and guilt from mistakes made what was seemingly a lifetime ago now."

"Then I have her to thank," Dane said, his tone gravely serious. "You have nothing to thank me for. I owe her for bringing you back."

"Does Tori know what's going on?" Capshaw asked quietly.

The four newest recruits were glancing between the more senior members of DSS, clear question and confusion in their eyes. They hadn't been working for DSS when Tori was kidnapped and brutalized. None of them had. DSS had been formed in the wake of her abduction. It was Caleb's vow never to leave his family insufficiently protected again. But those who'd hired on from the beginning, and then after Caleb damn near lost Ramie when he'd vowed to hire even more, and only the best, all knew the horrific ordeal that Tori had gone through. They also knew what Caleb had forced Ramie to suffer when he'd given her no choice but to use her psychic tracking abilities to find Tori before it was too late. As a result, they were all fiercely protective of the youngest Devereaux sibling and only sister.

Isaac sent the four men who'd hired on right before Lizzie had taken a leave of absence and gone rogue a quick look that said he'd explain it to the others later. They needed to know about Tori because they needed to treat her with extreme care and not inadvertently do anything to incite a panic attack.

Dane's expression hardened. "Tori will know only what she needs to know. There's no reason to cause her any more trauma than I have to. The dreams have been eating away at her night by night and right now she's operating on fumes and sheer will-power. I'm going to make damn sure she gets the rest she needs even if I have to sedate her. Caleb coddles her too much and is too quick to believe her when she says she's okay because he *wants* her to be okay. I know she's fucking out of gas and on the verge of collapse, and I'm not going to stand by and allow her to slowly kill herself."

His words were angry, but there was a slight shake to his voice that Isaac could remember hearing only one other time. When Gracie had burst into the DSS offices with a letter from Lizzie, who was supposed to be on vacation, that was a goodbye and admission of a suicide mission all in one. Dane had been so shaken that he hadn't been able to stand after reading the letter and had collapsed into his chair. He looked a lot like that now, except there was grim determination in his expression.

"I want to get back to Jenna," Isaac said. "I don't want her waking alone. She was deeply shaken by the news footage, and at some point I'm going to have to tell her why we're staying here and why everyone else is splitting up."

He dragged his hand through his hair, suddenly exhausted by the weight of his worry and fear for his angel.

"We'll rustle up something for dinner," Zeke said in a quiet tone. "We'll do our best to cheer her up and give her a good time. Maybe get her mind off all the shit being thrown at her just for a little while."

"Appreciate that," Isaac said sincerely. "We'll be out later when I know Jenna is up to facing a room full of people."

TWENTY-ONE

ISAAC eased into the bedroom, his eyes going to the bed where Jenna lay as he quietly closed the door behind him. Her back was turned to him and she was curled inward, her knees drawn slightly into her body. He wasn't going to wake her yet. She needed the rest and what he needed was simply to be close to her, touching her, holding her in his arms so he could immerse himself in her beauty and light and all the worry, stress and fear could fade away just for a little while.

This was a mission unlike any he'd ever faced before, and not just because he had such a personal stake in it. Always before, no matter how dire the circumstances, even at the lowest moments when one of the wives was in extreme danger and facing seemingly impossible odds, Isaac had approached the plan, the resolution and the rescue, with calm confidence, certain of their success. He'd never doubted for a moment that Ari would be found and that the extremist group who'd abducted her would be taken out in a coordinated, methodical fashion.

When Lizzie had gone missing while on Gracie's protection detail when Zack had abruptly left in what would later be revealed to be his mission to exact vengeance for the horrible wrong done to the woman he'd loved for half his life, Gracie had stepped up and enlisted the aid of Ramie and Ari, and though at the time, Isaac had nearly lost his damn mind when the women had showed up at the safe house where Gracie was being kept, he'd known then, as he'd known with Ari's rescue, that they'd find Lizzie in time to save her.

But now? This was bigger than anything he'd ever dealt with in his time with DSS. The threat of the cult had been removed, much to his relief, but Jaysus had a veritable army at his disposal and allies who owed him more favors than they could possibly repay. That was the way the drug lord operated. He collected favors and when he called them in, those who owed him didn't dare refuse to do whatever he demanded of them. He was ruthless and valued no life save his own. Every single one of his men were expendable. They gave him their absolute loyalty. He gave them absolutely nothing in return except the hope that he wouldn't one day turn on them for no other reason than to amuse himself or prove some point only he understood.

DSS was the best at what they did. Isaac would choose to work with any one of his teammates any day of the week. He trusted them implicitly and he'd give his life for them. But they were vastly outnumbered and outgunned. Jaysus had unlimited resources and while Dane was one wealthy, crafty son of a bitch who made sure DSS was better outfitted than any security agency in the entire country, for the first time they were facing someone with more power, influence, ability to intimidate, money and weaponry.

Now when it mattered most, when the success of the most important mission of Isaac's life was necessary to *his* survival, he couldn't conjure the same absolute confidence he'd felt in all the previous missions he'd taken part in.

He stood at the edge of the bed, staring at the mass of white-blond curls in disarray over the pillows, and felt the stirrings of something that horrified him and made him question everything about the man he thought he was. Panic.

He held up his hands, staring down at them in disbelief as they shook violently. Fear knotted his stomach and his throat until he wanted to throw up to alleviate the wretched anxiety paralyzing him.

A small movement caught his attention, diverting his focus from the savage assault of emotions systematically taking him apart and rendering him useless. He frowned and leaned closer, wondering if he'd imagined the slight tremor of Jenna's shoulders.

Fuck. He wasn't imagining a goddamn thing. He'd thought she was asleep the whole time he was having his epic meltdown when she was curled in a protective manner, faced away from the door, crying—something she was clearly trying to hide.

Instantly he crawled on the bed and curled one arm around her waist, turning her over so she faced him. Her eyes and nose were red and swollen. Her bottom lip was ravaged from chewing on it in agitation. There were dark shadows under her eyes, giving them a hollow, bruised look, and there was such despair in her eyes that the knot in his throat threatened to cut off his air supply entirely.

"Baby, why are you crying?" he asked desperately. "What's wrong? Are you hurting? Tell me what's wrong so I can fix it, please," he begged. "I can't bear to see you so unhappy. You're breaking my heart, honey. You have to know there is nothing I won't do to make you smile. To make you light up for me and to make you happy. Please talk to me so I understand."

He didn't care that he sounded like the most desperate of men. He could feel her slipping away from him and it was the most miserable, helpless, gut-wrenching sensation in the world. Never had he felt this kind of agony and the panic he'd felt just seconds ago about being unable to protect her was nothing compared to his terror of losing her over something he didn't know how to fight.

Jenna scooted as close to his body as she could and wrapped her arm around his waist, hugging and holding on to him tightly, the same desperation that was flooding through his veins reflected in her actions. She buried her face in his neck, her hot tears scalding his skin. Her body shuddered and her breath huffed out erratically as she seemed to try to get herself under control. She slid both hands between them and gripped handfuls of his shirt in her fingers, balling them into tight fists as if to reassure herself that he would never leave.

"You're scaring me, baby," he said, sounding completely unhinged. And that wasn't far off the mark because he was fast unraveling, panic destroying the last tenuous hold he had on his composure.

"*I'm* scared," she choked out. "Oh God, Isaac, what have I done? I know why they murdered every single member of the cult and I can't bear it. I'm so terrified and I feel so helpless and selfish and I've gotten you all in so deep that there's no way out. I don't know what to do."

Isaac took in a deep breath, knowing that she was on the

very edge of a complete breakdown and he had to be strong for her. He couldn't let her see how close *he* was to coming undone or it would push her that much closer to shattering.

He wrapped himself around her so that no part of her was untouched by him. He rubbed his hand up and down her back and pressed tiny kisses to the top of her head, her brow, her eyelids, her nose, her cheeks, her chin and finally her lips, inhaling her breaths like he was starved for oxygen. He willed himself to call upon the reserves that had served him so well in the past and focused on slowing his heart rate and stopping the shaking that had spread rapidly through his entire body until he'd felt too weak to stand even if he wanted to.

For several long moments he focused on pouring all the love he felt for her into every touch, caress and tender kiss while commanding his body to be stoic, steady and unwavering, her rock to lean on and depend on to make everything right in her world.

When he finally won the battle for control of his rioting emotions, he leaned back just enough so he could slide his fingers beneath her chin and nudge it upward till their gazes met. He nearly flinched at the raw pain and vulnerability in her eyes, but he forced himself not to react.

He rubbed his thumb lazily over her cheek, repeating the motion not only to soothe her but because he needed this contact. Needed to be touching her because as much as he'd sworn to be her rock, her anchor, she was his source of reassurance and calm.

"What's scaring you, honey? Talk to me. Get it out so we can deal with it and then put it away so you no longer dwell on it. You know I'll do anything to keep you from ever being in a situation you don't want to be in. From now on, you're in charge of your destiny and you're the one who'll make decisions for yourself. Not some fucking cult. Not some crazy fucking drug lord with a God complex and not me."

Her eyes filled with tears again and they slid hotly down her cheeks to collide with his thumb.

"Baby, talk to me," he pleaded. "It eats me up alive to see you so scared and unhappy. I know everyone in your life has let you down until now, but I swear to you, I will never be like those people. You are the single most important person in my life. My first and only priority. There is nothing you can't talk to me about."

"Oh, Isaac, isn't it obvious why they wiped out every man, woman and child in the cult?" She swallowed back a sob and lifted her hand to place over the hand he was cradling her cheek with, as if she needed to touch him every bit as much as he needed to touch her. "They are systematically getting rid of anyone who knew me or had knowledge of my existence."

Her eyes filled with pain unlike any he'd ever seen. Even having witnessed gravely injured people, his own teammates, the pain he'd seen in their eyes paled in comparison to what he saw when he looked into Jenna's. His gut clenched because it was killing him. He couldn't bear to see her in such agony when he was helpless to do a damn thing about it except listen to what she had to say. And he had a very bad feeling about the conclusion she'd reached. Dread filled his heart because he knew it was the exact same conclusion he and his teammates had.

"He'll come after you—all of you—next," she choked out. "He's crazy. He believes himself invincible and is convinced that if he has me he'll be immortal, that nothing can stop him. Death means nothing to him. God, Isaac, he inflicted terrible injuries on some of his own men and then forced me to watch. I was just a few feet away as they lay dying and they pleaded with me to save them, and yet I was powerless to do anything but watch because he wouldn't allow me to help them."

Isaac closed his eyes, knowing that he and Shadow had guessed precisely what the sadistic bastard had subjected Jenna to in the long hours of her captivity.

"He won't stop," she said in an aching whisper. "He'll never stop until he gets what he wants and he doesn't care how many people he has to kill to achieve his goal or even how long it takes. He'll always be out there, waiting and watching, and when we least expect it, he'll attack. Even if it takes multiple times and even if he has to wait years, he'll kill every single person who works at DSS and any family they have. You and I will never have a normal life together because every moment we'll be in fear of when he'll strike and I can't lose you, Isaac. I can't. You are the only person who has ever loved me, who has cared so deeply for me and who doesn't care at all about my ability to heal or try to use it and me to his advantage. When I'm with you, I'm not a freak who spent twenty years trapped inside the walls of a compound with no knowledge or understanding of the vast outside world. When I'm with you is the only time I feel normal. Like a real person and not some commodity to be used, traded or sold like I'm an inanimate object with no feelings, heart, soul or intelligence. I don't want you to ever leave me. I don't want you to *die!*" she cried, diving back into his embrace, pressing her face so tightly to the side of his neck that he wondered if she could even breathe.

He was overwhelmed by her impassioned words. His chest

was tight, not with panic now, but with emotion that swelled larger and larger until he felt the sting at his eyelids as tears formed. He blinked furiously, inhaling sharply as he sought to control the swell of love for her that threatened to completely overtake him.

"I will never leave you, baby," he vowed, barely able to choke out the words through the constriction in his throat.

He kissed her temple and ran his fingers through her tangled hair, wanting her to not just hear his words of love and his vow never to leave her. He wanted her to feel them. Wanted her to feel how awed and off balance he felt over the power of her declaration and what it meant to him. What *she* meant to him.

She lifted her face, which was raw and hid nothing of what she thought or felt. She scrubbed away at her tears as if annoyed that she'd allowed herself that momentary weakness. Yet he was in awe that she'd been able to keep it together so well for so long from the very beginning. Quite simply, he was in awe of everything she was and the unbreakable inner strength she retained even after twenty years of daily subjugation.

"I believe that you don't want to ever leave me," she said. "What I fear is that choice being taken from both of us and you being killed because of me. I could never live, knowing you sacrificed your life for me. I would have nothing to live for."

"Don't talk like that," he said fiercely, her sincere words nearly stopping his heart on the spot. "Never say that, Jenna. No matter what happens, I want you to promise me that you'll never stop fighting, that you'll never give up and that you'll go on, free and able to make your own choices about your life and do anything you've ever dreamed of doing. You have to swear it, baby, or

I won't even be able to function. I'll think of nothing else but the overwhelming fear of you giving up if something ever happened to me."

He gripped her shoulders and melded his lips to hers, taking her mouth hungrily, desperation beating at him, an incessant, unrelenting force.

Her eyes glistened with tears, but slowly she nodded and in a halting voice, hoarse from the strain of holding back so much emotion, she said, "I promise, Isaac. But only if you promise me the same."

His eyes narrowed as rage consumed him all over again. In no way, in no version of his life, would there ever not be a Jenna, but he'd forced the vow from her, even seeing the agony it caused her, so he could do no less than utter the same promise—even if he didn't mean a damn word of it. A life without Jenna was unthinkable. He'd be a mere shadow of his former self, a shell going about the motions like a robot programmed to perform specific functions, but his heart, and his soul, would forever be wherever she was.

He nodded, unable to give voice to the statement she'd barely managed herself.

"What are we going to do?" she asked, her eyes begging him for a miraculous solution, and God, he wished he could give her one. He wanted to give her everything her heart had ever desired, but this was out of his hands and there were no miracles, save those God chose to bestow on the worthy, and Isaac had proved his unworthiness long before Jenna had swept into his life and restored the faith he'd discarded along the way.

"We knew as soon as we saw the newscast why the cult was

eliminated, and in all honesty, the hit had most likely been ordered long before you escaped. It occurred mere days after the exchange was supposed to have happened. The cult still wanted access to you even after they turned you over to a drug kingpin and there was no way Jaysus would ever let anyone have use of his prized possession. If the exchange had taken place and you were now in his hands, the massacre would still have occurred because he didn't want to chance leaving anyone who had knowledge of your existence or your ability to heal alive. With no one left who knew you existed, no one would have ever asked questions about your disappearance and Jaysus would never have to worry about anyone but him knowing anything about your gift."

Her expression grew fearful once she realized how close she came to being swallowed up in a hole she could never escape from and having absolutely no one who would ever look for her.

"We have a plan that's already been put into action," he soothed. "Caleb, Beau and Zack took their wives to a safe house and they'll have heavy guard at all time. Tori is with Dane and he has money and connections, not to mention firepower, that likely will come damn close to matching Jaysus's own. Wade Sterling has taken Eliza to an undisclosed location not even known to us, and like Dane, he has not only a lot of money but a lot of power and an entire security team of trained professionals."

"And us?" she asked anxiously. "The rest of the men?"

"We're staying right here. It's heavily fortified, stocked with six months of provisions, not to mention a very impressive arsenal, courtesy of Dane. We're hiding in plain sight, and I don't think even Jaysus would think to look for us in a downtown high-rise building, and even if he did, we have a safe room that he'd need serious firepower, as in military-grade weaponry, to breach it, and there are multiple escape exits if we ever need to get the hell out fast."

"So we just stay here?" she asked hesitantly, biting into her bottom lip.

"That's exactly what we do," he said, injecting confidence and reassurance into his tone.

"But we can't just hide forever," she said doubtfully.

"No. We wait for him to come to us. He's desperate, and desperate men eventually fuck up. They always do. Eventually he'll grow tired of waiting for us to go out and he'll be furious that he's been thwarted, and he'll make a move to come after us. And we'll be watching and waiting and when he does rear his ugly head, we'll take him out."

Her breath hiccupped in a sigh of relief and she sagged against him, resting her cheek on his chest. "As long as I have you with me, it doesn't matter where we are," she said, sincerity audible in every word.

"You'll always have me, baby. I'm not going anywhere and neither are you. I need you, Jenna. I'm not ashamed to admit that I need you in order to breathe, in order not to lose the last vestiges of a soul you restored with your love and your light. Before you I existed in the shadows, never seeing the sun until the day you touched me and filled me with the most beautiful peace I've ever known."

"I don't know what to say, what to do when you say things

like that," she said, her eyes filled with bewilderment, her words laden with emotion.

"Just say you love me too and that you need me even a fraction as much as I need you," he said, knowing his expression, his eyes, his entire demeanor was as serious as could be. And truthful. It was all he needed from her. It was all he'd ever need from her. Just her love. She didn't even have to love him as deeply as he loved her, because he loved her enough for both of them.

"And promise me you'll never give up on me," he added, anxiety gripping him because he hadn't included this in his previous statement. "Never give up on us. I know it's not easy right now and at times I won't be easy to live with. I'm well aware of the disparity in what you offer me—how much more you offer me and can give me than what I can offer in return. I'll always be trying to catch up and while I know it isn't possible that I ever will, what I can offer is given with all my heart, my soul, my life. I belong and will always belong to you. I'm yours to command. Any wish you have, I'll move heaven and earth to make it come true. Just never give up on me, baby. Please. I can't even think about the possibility of a life without you in it because it makes me insane. It *hurts*."

He felt as though he'd just carved his heart out of his chest and laid the still beating organ in front of her as proof of just how utterly, completely, insanely in love with her he was. He'd just stripped himself of every defense, every shield that had become permanent fixtures over time. He'd never allowed anyone to see beyond those barriers and now he was completely vulnerable before her, his heart, his expression, his tense body begging her not to deny him and to trust him enough to give herself to him forever, even through the rough times.

Her eyes grew soft, her face suddenly glowing, and her smile chased away every doubt, fear and worry. She caressed his jaw, cradling it in her small palm, the very palm she held his heart in, and looked at him with such love that it caused a physical ache in his chest.

"Isaac, have you not been listening to anything I've been saying to you?" she teased, running her fingers over his lips and then back to his jaw. "I've been sick with worry over the thought, the very real possibility of losing you, of you dying because of me."

Her gaze went misty and she swallowed several times as if trying to collect herself.

"You don't ever have to ask for my promise not to give up on you or us or worry that at the first sign of adversity, I'll decide you aren't what I want or need and just walk away. You're my entire world, the very best part of my world," she whispered softly. "I believe with all my heart and soul that God sent you to me. To save me. To protect me. To love me. To be the man to give me all the things I've dreamed of having but never thought possible. I never thought I would be free, much less find freedom *and* a man who is everything I've ever imagined, when all I had were my hopes and fantasies of a life outside the walls of my prison. It's me who should be on my knees begging *you* not to ever give up on me or decide I'm not worth the trouble and anguish I've caused you and every single person you work with. You aren't getting the best deal," she said wryly.

"I'm ignorant of so many things that others take for granted. The world, what I've seen of it, still mystifies me and at times I feel utterly lost and like I'll never fit in. I don't know what's correct and what isn't. The city overwhelms me and makes me feel like I'll get swallowed up by it and never find my way out. People intimidate me and I'm painfully shy. I don't even understand why you would want someone like me, but I'm not questioning fate or the fact you love me and that I love you. I'll never give up on you, but please, don't ever give up on me either. I need your patience and understanding and for you to help me find my way in a vast, unfamiliar world that's suddenly been thrust upon me."

Isaac silenced her with his mouth, crushing his lips to hers. He couldn't bear to hear her disparage and doubt herself. He kissed her long and deep, fiercely at first, infusing all the passion, love and longing he felt for the woman who owned every single part of him.

Then he softened his movements and they became more gentle and tender, absorbing and savoring the sweetness of her taste, her smell, the way she felt in his arms. Finally, a long while later, Isaac drew back, sucking in great mouthfuls of air into his oxygen-starved lungs. Her face was flushed and glowing, her eyes were shining with wonder and her lips were swollen and a darker pink. She had the look of a woman who'd been thoroughly kissed. He loved that look on her, knowing that he'd been the one to mark her, the one to make her light up and to put the slightly dazed look of love and happiness in her eyes.

"Are we really okay here, Isaac?" she asked, placing her hand on his chest, right over his heart.

He slid his hand over hers to trap it there so she could feel the beat, that it beat only for her.

"We're safe, baby. We just have to be patient and wait for Jaysus to get *impatient* and start making mistakes. And he will. Men as obsessed and fixated as he is always fuck up and take stupid risks. And that's when we nail his ass to the wall."

TWENTY-TWO

JENNA sat in the corner of the L-shaped sectional amid a mound of pillows, pointing the remote control at the television as she slowly browsed the different channels. She'd driven the guys to the point of insanity within half an hour of surrendering the remote to her after she'd shyly asked if she could try it out.

Though why they were exasperated to the point of leaving the room, grumbling under their breaths, she had no idea. They all knew she'd never even seen a television until the day she'd reacted in horror when one had been turned on in the first safe house where she'd met Eliza and Wade.

She felt foolish about her reaction, and when she realized that she was still avoiding the TV—her only other encounter with it being when she'd seen the news footage of the horrible massacre of every single member of the cult—she'd been determined to stop spending so much time in the bedroom or the kitchen and actually see what television was all about.

Although her kitchen visits had been among the high points

of her enforced confinement. Not only did the guys spoil her ridiculously, taking turns preparing her their self-proclaimed specialty to the delight of her taste buds, but they also took turns teaching her to cook simple dishes. They were exceedingly patient and never seemed to get irritated when she pelted them with dozens of questions.

For the most part, she seemed to amuse them with her childlike enthusiasm. Even the men who hadn't drawn the short straw for cooking lessons that day usually gathered in the kitchen to watch, indulgent smiles on their faces when she beamed after a successful attempt.

Yet even Isaac, who never strayed far from her side, had abandoned the living room after being treated to her constant channel changing. But how could she decide on one before knowing what there was to see on every channel? What if she settled on one program and something more interesting and educational was just a few clicks away?

Admittedly the concept of television still confused her, especially the sheer number of channels and programs. What happened if two programs you really enjoyed came on at the same time? But she had found a practical use for it.

What she had discovered was that television was a good source of knowledge and information about the modern world. Some of the programs were fascinating, while others were downright horrifying. One night the guys had tried to get her to watch something they'd referred to as reality TV and explained how it differed from other television shows. Only a few minutes into something that was reportedly happening in real life and wasn't a fictitious program meant for the entertainment of others, Jenna had fled the living room, so appalled that she hadn't ventured near the television for the next three days.

But now she was in command of the remote. There was a certain sense of satisfaction in being able to push the button to change the channel as many times as she wanted. Now she understood why the guys fought over who got to control the remote for the night.

She snuggled deeper into her nest of pillows, sighing at how nice it was to do anything she wanted or nothing at all. Never had she enjoyed the freedoms most everyone else took for granted. For the first few years at the compound, she'd considered her life normal and it hadn't bothered her. It wasn't until she was around the age of nine or ten that a voice in the back of her mind started quietly nagging her. She began to really look around and more closely observe the other members of what they'd always referred to as a religious organization.

She hadn't known any better. It was what she'd been taught she belonged to. But when she started paying closer attention to the goings on, she realized how differently she was treated than the others.

While she couldn't say any woman in the cult was ever treated well, she could certainly state with assurance that the other women had been treated far better than her.

Jenna frowned, focusing back on the television, where she'd momentarily stopped on a channel while her thoughts had drifted. Angry for allowing herself to drift back to her life as a prisoner, she shoved aside the painful, humiliating memories and chastised herself for dwelling on events best left in the past.

She was about to change the channel again when she paused, recognizing the news show as the one that had aired the footage of the mass killing of the cult members. News changed from day to day. It would be interesting to tune in each day so she could follow current events. Then maybe she wouldn't feel quite so lost in the world she'd been so afraid of.

But when the lead-in for the next story began, Jenna went rigid with shock, her eyes glued to the screen. Frantically she turned up the volume, wanting to hear every single word because surely she'd misheard the reporter.

"Tonight, a mother's plea for information leading to the whereabouts of the daughter taken from her twenty years ago. We go live to the press conference, where Suzanne Wilder is speaking out after hearing the tragic story of the murders of what appears to be all the members of a mysterious cult that was located in a rural area north of Houston and apparently was there for the last twenty-five years."

A visibly distraught woman appeared on the television surrounded by several reporters, all holding microphones to catch her every word. Jenna shot up from the couch and stood directly in front of the monitor, not believing what she was hearing or seeing.

Jenna's mouth widened. She attempted to call out to Isaac, but no words would come from her tightly closed throat. She was inhaling rapidly through her nose and it felt as though the room was spinning around her, except the television remained fixed. She wanted to close her eyes and look away. Wanted to cover her ears so she couldn't hear. But she couldn't do either of those things. She was so numb that she felt paralyzed, a mixture of fear and hope roiling in her stomach, making her feel even sicker than she already did from the motion of the walls spinning.

The woman held a handkerchief delicately to her nose,

which was red and swollen as if she'd been crying. She stared into the cameras, her expression desperate and pleading.

"My name is Suzanne Wilder and twenty years ago, my daughter, Jenna Wilder, was violently taken from me. Her father tried desperately to save our daughter, but the kidnappers shot and killed him before running to a black van with Jenna in one of the kidnappers' arms. She was screaming and crying for me as they shut the door and drove away with my only child," the woman said, her voice breaking as a sob welled, and she pushed her fist into her mouth in a visible battle to control her emotions.

"I've searched for my daughter for the last twenty years, never giving up hope of her being returned to me. Despite the many investigators I hired and the investigation I launched myself, I never knew where the cult had established their compound, where they lived or were located," she said, stumbling over the words as though she wasn't sure what to call the place where Jenna had been a prisoner for nearly her entire life.

"It wasn't until I saw the news story last week that reported the mass killing of what was reported to be the entire cult at a compound north of Houston that I realized this is where my daughter had been held, where she'd been raised. I wondered if she even remembers me or knows who I am," she said tearfully.

"Two of the men identified and pictured on television I instantly recognized as the men who'd murdered my husband and kidnapped my precious daughter."

She bowed her head for a long moment, seemingly too emotional to continue.

Jenna stared in stunned silence, simply unable to comprehend what she was witnessing. A warm tear rolled down the side of her face, but she didn't lift her hand to wipe it away. Her breathing became even more rapid. It didn't make sense. What was she afraid of? The truth?

"I viewed each and every one of the bodies, hoping to find answers, something that would tell me if my Jenna was still alive or what might have happened to her. She wasn't among the dead, but I found a photo of her. It was my daughter! There is absolutely no doubt. I'm pleading with anyone who has information about her whereabouts or any information leading to the discovery of Jenna Wilder to please come forward. And Jenna, if you're out there, I have never given up hope of one day being reunited with you."

Jenna continued to stare blankly at the screen as suddenly her mind shifted to a long-ago event. The birthday cake and the four candles. Her father's proud, smiling face, filled with so much love. She reached farther back, closing her eyes as she strained to bring the memory into focus. A woman holding a gift-wrapped box, a strange smile on her face as she watched Jenna's father toss her into the air while she squealed with laughter.

"Mama?" Jenna said, her voice higher pitched, sounding more like the child twisting circles in Jenna's mind.

Her chest felt as though it was on fire and the rapid inhalations had halted for some reason. Why wasn't she breathing? The room blurred, moving in and out of focus as the press conference droned on and on, the only sound registering in Jenna's ears a loud, persistent buzzing.

TWENTY-THREE

"SHOULD we go rescue the remote before the batteries die and she beats the shit out of it because she doesn't know it takes batteries to operate?" Shadow asked Isaac in amusement.

Isaac chuckled. "I've been up in her grill twenty-four seven since . . . well, hell, basically since I pulled her out of my SUV she'd stolen and decided I was keeping her. I couldn't imagine any situation where I didn't want to be as close to her as possible, but she's like a kid with a new, obnoxiously loud, annoying toy who plays it over and over and over again."

Shadow cracked up while Knight and Dex, who'd entered the kitchen just as Shadow suggested mounting a rescue mission to retrieve the remote, both snickered. Then Dex stopped and turned one ear in the direction of the living room, standing silent for a moment.

"I dunno, it might be safe to go back in. The channel hasn't changed in the last minute or so—it's the same newscast I heard on my way to the kitchen," Dex said in a hopeful voice.

"I'll believe it when I see it," Shadow grumbled as he ambled toward the door leading into the living room.

He came to an abrupt halt, his body language putting Isaac on immediate alert. He was about to demand what the fuck Shadow was looking at when Shadow said, without turning around, "Isaac, you need to get in here fast."

The edge in Shadow's voice made Isaac's stomach plummet and he shoved by Dex and Knight, breaking into a run. He shoved Shadow so he'd move to the side, and then Isaac saw what Shadow meant.

Jenna stood as rigid and as ghastly white as a statue just a few feet in front of the television as it droned on. He could see even from where he stood that she was hyperventilating. As he started toward her, he heard a high-pitched, childish voice— Jenna, only not Jenna—and the only word that echoed softly through the room was, "Mama?"

Oh fuck. A dull roar began in Isaac's ears just as he noticed that she'd stopped hyperventilating. In fact she was so still that it didn't appear she was breathing at all. She wobbled precariously like a drunk in heels and he lunged for her, shouting for the others to help.

He caught her just as her legs gave out and she slid toward the floor. He gathered her in his arms, fear gripping him by the throat. What the hell had traumatized her to this degree?

He carried her to the couch, sitting her up and holding her when she began to list forward as though she was about to pitch right off the couch onto her face. He grasped her shoulders, turning her to face him, and he shook her lightly, just enough to gain her attention.

"Breathe, god damn it! Breathe, Jenna!"

Her eyelids fluttered, and for a moment she stared at him in blank confusion as if she didn't even recognize him.

"Jesus Christ," he whispered.

Shadow pushed in on one side, pressing a cold rag to the back of her neck while Knight slipped his fingers around her slender wrist to check her pulse rate. Dex was focused on her near nonexistent respiration rate while Isaac tried again to get her to snap out of it.

"Mama?" she asked again in a trembling voice.

"Oh honey," Isaac said, his heart breaking for her.

He did not have a good feeling about what had prompted her panic attack. Not a good feeling at all. He turned to Zeke, who'd rushed into the living room when he'd heard the shouting, and quickly snapped an order.

"Rewind the current program at least thirty minutes and pause it. Whatever Jenna saw on it fucked with her in a big way."

"Anything we can do to help?" Brent asked quietly as he stepped up beside Zeke, while Eric and Capshaw crowded in behind them.

"I need to know what the fuck she saw on the news that caused her to completely lose it and go into nuclear meltdown mode," Isaac bit out to no one in particular. "But do not play it back until I have her out of the room."

He refocused his attention on Jenna, who was now emitting sounds reminiscent of a fish gasping for air out of water. Her pupils were dilated, her eyes wide, her face completely devoid of any color or life. She had the look of someone who'd just lost everything that ever mattered the most, everything good, leaving her with nothing. The soulless eyes staring back at him were his complete undoing. He had to get her back from whatever hell she was in. He refused to let her stay there a moment longer. She was exhibiting signs of shock and that, combined with all the other factors in play, scared the holy fuck out of him.

He grasped her cold hands in his and rubbed them to infuse warmth into her fingers, all the while speaking to her in a calm, soothing voice about nothing in particular. After a moment, he ditched the nonsensical shit and leaned in so their noses were mere inches apart.

"Baby, come back to me," he pleaded, framing her face with his hands, pushing back the strands of hair from her cheeks to behind her ears. "I'm here. I'm with you. Whatever it is that's frightening you, you aren't alone. I need you to take some nice, deep, even breaths. In through your nose, out from your mouth. Like this."

He made certain he had her attention and then he demonstrated, inhaling and exhaling, taking his time, slowing his breathing down. Slowly she began to show signs of heightened awareness. She looked into his eyes and he knew the instant she'd come out of the worst of it because he saw recognition on her face, but it was the crushing relief that exploded in her eyes right before she threw herself into his arms and wrapped her arms as tightly as she could around his neck that rattled him to the core.

"I've got you, baby," he soothed, rocking her back and forth as she clung to him as though he was her only lifeline. "I'll never let you go, honey. Just breathe for me and try to relax. Focus on the most wonderful thing you can think of. The most beautiful dream you ever dreamed. See only that and nothing else and let me take care of you. I'll never let you fall. I'll always be here to catch you."

He knew he was babbling, but he was precariously close to succumbing to a panic attack of his own. When her breathing had regulated itself to a more even rhythm, she went limp against him, as though her strength had been completely sapped. He gently collected her into his arms and cradled her in his lap before rising from the couch, settling her more firmly against his chest.

He glanced Shadow's way. "Get another one of the pills we gave her last time. As badly as I want to know what in the fuck happened and what she saw that made her withdraw so sharply from reality, she's in no shape to relive it right now. She needs to rest and relax and when she wakes up, if she feels strong enough, we'll get into it then."

Shadow nodded and hurried to the kitchen while Isaac carried his precious bundle into the bedroom. He laid her down, pulling off her shoes, then her jeans and then the rest of her clothing, before rapidly getting one of his shirts that swallowed her much smaller frame and easing it over her head.

Though she was aware of her surroundings and was no longer lost in the hell she'd descended to briefly, she remained quiet, only her eyes moving as they followed his every movement. When Shadow entered with the medicine and a glass of water, she didn't even protest. She allowed Shadow to slip it onto her tongue, and then Isaac quickly held up the glass of water so she could swallow it down before the bitter taste filled her mouth.

She sank back onto the pillow, tears filling her eyes as she stared blankly at the ceiling, avoiding the gazes of both Isaac and Shadow. Shadow sent a look filled with deep concern Isaac's way.

Isaac stared bleakly back at him, having no idea what to do or say. He couldn't fix an unknown problem, couldn't fight an unknown enemy combatant.

"I'll leave you two alone," Shadow murmured, his gaze flickering back to Jenna, the look of worry growing deeper on his face. "I'll see what I can find out."

"Thanks," Isaac said hoarsely.

Jenna was already succumbing to the effects of the sedative. Her eyelids grew heavy and she blinked several times as if trying to fight going to sleep. Her eyes closed and remained closed and Isaac thought she'd drifted off, but as he was about to turn to go back into the living room, she sluggishly opened her eyes and they tracked sideways until they found him.

A tear trickled down her cheek, her paleness even starker than it had been before.

"I was loved," she whispered. "My father. He loved me."

Isaac's brow furrowed in confusion. "What do you mean, honey? Did you remember something?"

But her eyelids had fluttered closed after her cryptic statement, and this time she gave a little sigh and didn't reopen them. Soon her even breathing and the soft rise and fall of her chest registered the fact that she was sleeping peacefully.

Isaac sank down on the edge of the bed and buried his face in his hands for a long moment. What the hell had happened to her in there? Why the fuck had he left her alone? He hadn't left her by herself until today. And she'd paid dearly for his negligence, because she'd been left alone to deal with whatever ghost from her past that was now haunting her.

TWENTY-FOUR

WHEN Isaac strode back into the living room, his entire de-meanor demanded answers without him having to say a word. Brent looked up at him and Isaac didn't like what he saw in the other man's eyes.

"It's certainly understandable why she was in complete shock and meltdown," Brent said grimly. "She was flipping through the channels and enjoying new discoveries and was completely unsuspecting of the cement truck that got dropped right on top of her out of nowhere."

"What the fuck is that supposed to mean?" Isaac demanded.

"It would be a hell of a lot quicker and easier if you just watch it," Brent said. "I'm not even sure I can explain the shit storm that's currently brewing. The hell of it is, I don't know if it's a good thing or a bad thing. It could go either way."

"Or it could be a fucking setup," Zeke growled.

"God damn it, quit with the speculation and just play the fucking thing. While we sit here arguing, there's a woman in the other room who has so much hurt and confusion in her eyes that it puts knots in my stomach just to see it, and I can't do a damn thing until I know what the hell she saw that was so traumatic for her."

"It's not very long," Brent muttered. "I think you'll find it explains her reaction quite a lot."

Even having seen Jenna's complete breakdown and hearing the reactions from his men who'd watched it while he was taking care of her in the bedroom, he was utterly unprepared for the scene that unveiled on the television in front of him. Never would he have imagined this happening, and he had no idea what to think or how to feel about the woman's claims.

His mind went back to Jenna's childlike "Mama" as if she'd recognized the woman or had vague memories of her. Not much had been said about her mother in their brief conversation regarding her past. She'd had more concrete memories of her father, but she'd seemed to struggle when attempting to conjure up an image or a recollection of her mother.

Christ, no wonder she'd seemed so stunned, lost and bewildered. How she'd come to ever be in the cult was a question that had haunted her from the time she was old enough to question it. Had she been loved? Had her parents wanted her? Had she been taken from them or had they given her into the keeping of the cult, and were they even alive?

She'd had happy memories of her father, and now to find out that he'd been killed trying to prevent her abduction? It was little wonder she was so devastated, but even so, the knowledge that she had been loved seemed to give her a small measure of comfort. Her last words before she'd drifted to sleep were that she'd been loved.

He wanted to weep for her and at the same time he wanted answers for her. But where did the mother fit into the equation? His suspicious side considered the timing of her mother appearing on national television to plead for information regarding her daughter highly coincidental, given the fact that a powerful drug lord was desperate in his bid to own her like a prized possession.

But the mother's appearance and subsequent plea could very well have to do with the cult making national headlines when the tragedy was reported on local and national networks alike. On the surface her story seemed plausible enough, but fuck! What was he supposed to do? Forbid Jenna from being reunited with her mother because the timing was suspicious, since it was his goddamn job to be suspicious of anyone trying to get close to his woman?

Hell, he didn't even know Jenna's feelings on the subject. She'd received a shock she hadn't expected in a million years, and that had come on top of the other stressful events she'd endured in such short order. How much more could she take before she crumbled under the weight of the shit constantly being piled on her?

Frustration simmered and boiled in him, threatening to explode. He hated this feeling of helplessness. Of not knowing what to do to make everything better. To give her the kind of life she deserved, a family who loved her.

"This is heavy, man," Shadow muttered. "What the fuck are you going to do?"

Isaac sighed and ran his hands over his face. "It depends on what Jenna chooses to do with the bombshell just dropped on her. It's our job to make damn sure that everything checks out and she's protected at all costs.

"Before we get Jenna's hopes up or dashed, I think it would be a good idea if we did some discreet investigating on the mom and just see if she checks out. We can't be too careful until Jaysus is taken down for good, and we can't just waltz Jenna out in public for a reunion with her mother. It would end up being a fucking bloodbath."

"We'll get on it right away," Shadow said. "You just worry about Jenna and finding out how she's handling the news and figure out what she wants to do with it."

Isaac nodded, a curl of panic snaking through his stomach. He didn't like this one bit and especially the timing even if the timing was perfectly reasonable given the national attention the mass murder had been given.

He strode back into the bedroom, his chest tightening when he saw Jenna curled into the smallest ball possible. She huddled there on the bed, her eyes closed, but even in sleep, her thoughts were troubled and her dreams were haunted.

He slid into bed next to her with no hesitation and he wrapped his arms around her, pulling her against his chest so he surrounded her with his strength and warmth. She relaxed some, as if recognizing him in her sleep, and she let out a little sigh before burrowing her face into his neck and then she went limp as sleep once more claimed her.

For how long he lay there simply holding her, he didn't know, but he didn't sleep, instead staying awake to stand guard over his precious angel. He wouldn't close his eyes and succumb to sleep no matter how tired he was, because he couldn't risk her waking and him not knowing it.

After what seemed an eternity, she began to stir against him. She let out a soft murmur against his neck, one that sounded like "daddy." His heart broke for her. How much more loss could she endure when she'd already had everything in the world taken from her once?

She lifted her head, pulling away until she could look into his eyes. "Isaac?"

"Yes, baby," he said, caressing her cheek in a comforting gesture.

"Is it true? Is what I saw true?"

He blew out his breath, wishing he could give her definitive answers. "I don't know yet. We're checking on it right now and as soon as we know something you'll be the first one to hear."

"I don't remember much about her," Jenna said fretfully. "Will that anger her?"

"No, baby," he rushed to say. "You were just a child and you've endured so much trauma since then. No one could expect you to have clear memories of a life that was lost to you two decades ago."

She looked down a moment, her fingers fidgeting against his shirt.

"What is it, baby?"

She glanced back up at him, a sheen of moisture coating her eyes. Then she licked her lips, her uncertainty evident in her every movement.

"Should we contact her?" she asked hesitantly. "Should I meet with her?"

"That's a decision only you can make, sweetheart."

"Is it stupid that I'm scared to meet my own mother?"

"Of course not. Baby, I'd be more concerned if you weren't nervous over the prospect. But listen to me, okay? You don't have to make up your mind today. Or tomorrow. You take all the time in the world you want and when you feel you're ready then we'll set something up, but it has to be safe for you or it doesn't happen."

Jenna nodded and then swallowed visibly. "I want to see her. I have to see her. I have vague memories of a woman who looks so much like her. But most of my memories are of my father."

Tears filled her eyes and slid soundlessly down her cheeks.

"And now I know he's dead," she choked out. "For so many years, I held on to this thread of hope that maybe one day I'd get to see him again. That he'd remember me and that he missed me and that he'd want me to come home. But they killed him. God, and I saved those monsters' lives time and time again. I'm glad they're dead," she hissed, her jaw clenched tightly. "I only wish they'd suffered more."

Isaac pulled her into his arms again and rubbed his hand up and down her back, not saying anything, just doing what he could to comfort her when she was hurting so badly.

"If you want to have a meeting with your mother, we can arrange it, Jenna. But only if that's what you want and only after we do some checking to make sure she is who she says she is."

Jenna nodded. "I understand. I think it's something I have to do even if it's just to finally know if there were ever people out there who loved me. A family. Someone who grieved for me after I was taken. I've always felt so alone in the world, as if I had no one."

"You have me," he said fiercely. "You'll always have me. Never again will you be alone. Never, Jenna. Do you understand what I'm saying?"

She gave him a wavering smile, but she nodded and then leaned in to brush her lips across his. "I do know," she whispered. "And thank you. That means more to me than you'll ever know."

"Are you sure this is what you want?" he asked.

Slowly she nodded her head. "It's what I need to do whether I want to or not. I have to make peace with that part of my life if I'm ever going to be truly free."

He kissed her, soft and warm, lightly so as not to overwhelm her when she was so vulnerable, but just so she remembered that he was here, that he'd always be here, and that he loved her with everything he had.

"I'll tell the others then," he said after he'd pulled away. "Provided everything checks out, we'll set it up as soon as we come up with a plan that provides the least danger to you."

"Will you be with me?" she asked tentatively. "I don't want to meet her alone."

He cupped her cheek with his palm and stared directly into her eyes. "Honey, listen to me. Where you go, I go. Always. And that's a fact. There will never be a time where you go anywhere without me right by your side. I'm never letting you out of my sight if I can help it."

She relaxed visibly, some of the worry and strain lessening in her face. "Thank you," she whispered. "I'm afraid to meet her and I don't know why. I'm so nervous I feel like I could throw up. But my heart tells me I have to do this, and as long as you're with me, I can do anything, Isaac."

TWENTY-FIVE

TORI Devereaux woke with a gasp, tears streaming down her cheeks from the horror of the dream that had played in real time as if she'd been there, standing just feet away as the event had occurred.

Familiar arms wrapped around her and she found herself against Dane's chest as he ran his hand down her hair to soothe her. She blinked in confusion even as the tears continued to seep from her eyes. How had he known? Why was he in her bedroom?

Dane gently pulled her away as he reached with one hand to turn on her bedside lamp. The implacable lines of his face were immediately illuminated and for a moment she thought he was angry with her. But then his eyes softened as they filled with concern. For her?

They'd certainly butted heads in the past, but he'd also been there when she'd dreamed of Caleb with blood all over him and was certain she'd seen his death, and Dane had comforted her then as well. He seemed to run hot and cold with her, though for the most part he treated her with indifference and kept his distance. That was why she'd been so shocked when he'd taken over her protection when all the women were locked down because of the possible threat to the entire organization.

Some of her confusion must have been evident in her expression, because he gently wiped away her tears and said in a soothing tone, as if he were trying to calm a wild animal, "You screamed during your dream."

At the stark reminder of the dream still raw in her memory, her face became a mask of sorrow.

"Was it a nightmare?" he asked quietly.

"Nightmare" was a code name for the lingering horror of her time in the hands of a madman who'd tortured and raped her and would have killed her if Ramie hadn't been able to give Caleb information on where she was being held. As a result she'd been rescued, but not before her soul had been destroyed by a monster.

She lowered her head and shook it, tightly squeezing her eyes shut. "I saw someone murdered in cold blood."

"Who?" Dane demanded urgently.

"Not one of ours," she whispered. "I don't know who it was." She beat her hand on the mattress, anger mixed with helplessness sharpening her fury and frustration. "I've never seen her before in my life! Why have a dream of some poor unfortunate woman who will soon die if I can't do anything to stop it?" she said in a shrill voice. "I hate it, Dane. I hate this stupid ability. It helps no one, but it tortures *me* because I know what is to come and there's not a damn thing I can do about it!"

Dane carefully pulled her into his arms again and rubbed his hand up and down her back as she beat her fist against his shoulder in frustration and grief.

"I know, baby. I know. I'm so sorry you have to endure this on top of so much else," he murmured against her ear. "I wish I could make it go away. But you need to know this, if you don't understand anything else. What happened to you before will never happen again. I—we—will protect you. Always."

She sighed. "I know, Dane. I believe you. I know my brothers blame themselves and it hurts me to see them shoulder that blame. It wasn't their fault and I've never blamed them for what happened. I wish they could see that for themselves. They still look at me with pain and guilt in their eyes. They've become overprotective as a result and they hover constantly. I feel so terrible, like I'd sound ungrateful or heartless, for wanting to ask them how I can forget and get past what happened when they can't."

"Then you should tell them exactly that," Dane said against her hair. "This isn't about them, Tori. You should say and do exactly what makes you feel better and what will make you heal. You aren't responsible for their sense of guilt. They love you and worry about you. We all do. But you should just be honest with them. You're all hurting, but no one will talk about it and avoiding it isn't the answer."

She sighed again. "How did you get to be so wise, Dane?"

He stiffened in surprise and then laughed, though there was no amusement in his voice. "I'm far from wise, little one. In fact I've done some pretty stupid things in my life."

She knew better than to pry. Dane was one of the most private people she knew, and she was surprised he'd opened up this much. She wasn't about to do anything to push him away. Nor would she ever admit her true feelings regarding him. Humiliating herself wasn't very high on her priority list and she thought Dane saw her as a spoiled, ungrateful little rich girl. He'd probably pat her on the head and be amused by her "little crush" on him.

"Let me get you one of your pills to help you get back to sleep," Dane said, pulling away from her. "It's only one in the morning and you need more sleep, Tori. You're running on fumes and if you don't start taking better care of yourself, you're going to collapse."

She opened her mouth to tell him no, that she didn't want another damn pill, but he held up his hand and silenced her with a look. Then he took the bottle from her nightstand, shook one of the pills into his hand and offered it to her with some water.

She blew out her breath in frustration but didn't argue—what was the point? He didn't understand. He'd never understand. She hated to sleep because it was the only time she felt truly vulnerable. When she was either plagued by nightmares of the very real events of the past or haunted by things yet to come that she was helpless to change or stop.

To her shock, it was as if she'd spoken her thoughts aloud, because he cupped her chin after she'd swallowed back the pill and their eyes met.

"If you'd take the medicine as you're supposed to, then the dreams wouldn't be as frequent and you wouldn't be so exhausted all the time."

When Dane turned to leave, Tori swore she saw more than just normal worry or concern in his eyes, but it—and he—was gone before she could decipher exactly what it was she had seen in his gaze.

At her doorway, he paused and without looking back said in a gruff voice, "I'll be back to check on you periodically. I don't want you to worry, Tori. Nothing will happen to you while you're in my care. I won't let it."

TWENTY-SIX

"ZACK and Gracie just went in," Shadow's report sounded in Isaac's concealed earpiece. "Caleb and Ramie and Beau and Ari are already in position. The others are at the bar having a drink and doing the guys' day-out routine, watching the game on television, acting like a normal group of friends without causing too much disruption. The table where you, Jenna and her mother will be is surrounded and we have eyes on all the entrances and exits. Wait two minutes and then take Jenna in and seat her at the arranged table. I'm watching the front and will alert you when I see her mom arrive."

"Got it," Isaac responded quietly.

He glanced over at Jenna sitting in the passenger seat, who was clearly in an agitated state. He reached over to take her hand and he squeezed it reassuringly.

"You ready to go in, baby?"

Fear and uncertainty swirled in her blue eyes and she bit her bottom lip in nervousness.

"I'm afraid," she admitted. "I don't know what to say to her or what to even ask her."

"Then let her do the talking," he advised. "You'll know what to say or how to handle it when the time comes. And if at any time you want the meeting to come to an end, we get up and leave. Okay?"

She nodded, then reached up to slide her hand down the side of his jaw. "I love you, Isaac. It means the world that you arranged this for me."

"Anything for you, angel. I'd give you anything in the world. And I love you too. So damn much."

She smiled, seeming to relax as the anxiety lessened in her eyes. Then she sucked in a deep breath. "I'm ready."

"We're coming in," Isaac said to Shadow.

He got out and then walked around to Jenna's side, his eyes rapidly scanning the area, carefully looking for any potential threat. He opened her door and helped her from the vehicle and then pulled her close against his side, wrapping his arm around her body.

Moments later they were seated at the prearranged table and as Isaac had instructed her, Jenna didn't acknowledge or look in the direction of the other couples.

Jenna flipped through the menu, not even dwelling on the excitement of her first time eating in an actual restaurant or being able to choose any of the delicious-sounding entrees. It felt as if a thousand butterflies were swarming around in her belly.

Her gaze flew to the doorway every time someone new came in, her pulse leaping, wondering when or if her mother would arrive. Their telephone call had been brief. Both women had been overcome with emotion and Jenna hadn't been able to stop crying long enough to go into any detail about her ordeal. Her mother had just repeated over and over that she had prayed for this reunion every single day since Jenna had been taken from her.

Now that the day had come, Jenna had no idea what to say. The fact that she had family, someone who loved her and who'd grieved for her for so long, should hearten her. She was... scared. Not just afraid, but utterly terrified.

Isaac's gaze was constantly on her, worry for her reflected in his eyes. Then he straightened in his seat and reached down to enfold her hand in his. He held it tightly, not letting up.

"She's coming in now," Isaac murmured.

Jenna's pulse was like a hammer pounding at her temples, her heart racing so fast she felt light-headed.

"I'll be right here the whole time, baby," Isaac said, pulling her hand into his lap.

Jenna's gaze locked onto the front entrance as a blond woman, the same woman Jenna recognized from the news program, walked in, her gaze eagerly scanning the occupants of the restaurant. The hostess smiled at her and after the two exchanged a few words, gestured toward the table where Jenna and Isaac sat and escorted her to the seat just across from Jenna.

Her mother stopped, staring at Jenna, seemingly in shock. She should greet her mother, surely. Should she hug her? Say hello?

Jenna rose on shaking legs and met her mother halfway around the table and was immediately enfolded in a tight hug as her mother gathered her in her arms.

"Oh my darling baby girl," her mother said, her voice choked with tears. "You have no idea how long I've prayed for this day. I never gave up hope of finding you. I've missed you so much."

"Mama," Jenna whispered, closing her eyes as she clung to the older woman.

When the two finally drew away, one of the buttons on her mother's coat caught on Jenna's wrist and scratched her bare skin.

"Oh I'm so sorry," her mother fretted, wiping at the light scratch evident on Jenna's skin. "That button is forever catching on stuff. I really do need to have it mended."

"It's all right," Jenna said softly. "It's nothing. Really."

"Ladies, please have a seat and we'll order something to eat. Jenna's been so nervous over getting to see you again that I couldn't get her to eat breakfast," Isaac said.

"You must be Isaac," Jenna's mother said, beaming at him.

"Oh, I'm being terribly rude," Jenna said, a flush burning her face. "Yes, this is Isaac. He's . . ." She glanced at Isaac standing so protectively beside her and a flood of love washed over her, her heart aching with the ferocity of the emotions she felt for him.

"He's the man you're in love with," her mother said with a laugh. "Oh darling, that much is very obvious, just as it's obvious he loves you very much as well."

"That I do, ma'am, and it's a pleasure to meet you," Isaac said, leaning to kiss her on the cheek.

Tears were bright in her mother's eyes when she took the seat across from Jenna and Isaac. "I'm so glad she has you, that someone has been here for her when I couldn't be," she said to Isaac. "You look at her the way Jenna's father used to look at me. I was devastated when I lost him and my sweet baby daughter on the same day. I've missed them both every single day of my life."

Jenna tensed, and Isaac rubbed his hand up and down her leg as he quietly gave the waitress their order.

"I remember him," Jenna said tearfully.

Her mother looked at her sharply. "You do? What do you remember?"

She smiled sadly at her mother. "My birthday party. It was my fourth, I think. It's the last memory I have of him. He was swinging me around and there was a cake with lots of pink flowers and icing."

Her mother's expression changed to one of anger. "Yes, it was your fourth birthday. And the next day he was killed and you were taken from me."

Jenna lowered her head, staring down at the hand clasped in Isaac's. Her stomach knotted. She was suddenly besieged by nausea and she fought back the urge to throw up.

"Are you all right?" Isaac asked, bending his head so he could look into her eyes.

She nodded, not wanting to worry him even more. "I just need to eat," she said. "I'm feeling hungry. Missing breakfast wasn't such a good idea after all."

"I don't like you missing any meals," he replied with a growl. "I don't like anything that causes you so much upset or worry that you can't eat."

His expression eased into one of relief when the waiter arrived with their food. Jenna had never eaten shrimp, and on the commercials she'd seen for various restaurants as well as on the menu she'd absentmindedly perused, it had looked delicious. After Isaac had patiently answered all of the hundred questions she had about the foods she saw on television, she'd wanted to try the seafood the first opportunity she had. And so she was having a delectable-looking pasta dish with shrimp sautéed in butter and Cajun seasoning.

Isaac and her mother had both chosen succulent-looking steaks, and Isaac cut a piece and offered it to Jenna to try. As they ate, the turmoil in her stomach only grew, but she distracted herself by listening and responding to her mother's excited chatter.

Isaac and the others had expressed the need for Jenna not to disclose any of what had happened after her escape from the cult and certainly not that a dangerous threat existed. The only story Jenna could relate was that she had made her escape days before the unfortunate murder of the rest of the cult and that Isaac had found her and stepped in to protect her, and they'd fallen in love in the process.

Jenna's mother seemed to think the story was wildly romantic, though her expression hardened at any mention of the cult. Her only remarks were that the bastards had deserved exactly what they'd gotten.

"But certainly no threat exists to her now," her mother said to Isaac, prompting him to tense.

"I'm protecting Jenna from anyone whose intention is to hurt or exploit her in any way."

"I'm glad she has you, then," her mother responded.

Then her mother's sharp glance honed in on Jenna and her expression became one of concern. "Is something wrong, darling?"

Isaac immediately turned, and Jenna wished her mother hadn't called attention to her. But the truth was, her stomach was about to revolt despite her huge effort to get through lunch without causing a fuss.

"What's wrong, baby? You're pale and you've hardly eaten anything."

"I feel sick," she admitted. "I'm not sure the shrimp agreed with me at all."

"I'll take you to the bathroom," her mother offered, rising swiftly from her chair.

"She goes nowhere without me," Isaac said in a steely voice.

Her mother smiled. "Of course not. But you can't go into the ladies' room with her, so I'll go in and make sure she's okay and you can stand at the door and make sure no one else comes in."

Jenna could tell Isaac was about to argue that he'd damn well go into the bathroom with her and no one would stop him, so she laid her hand on his arm and looked pleadingly at him.

"Please just wait for us at the door. I'll just be on the other side of it. I really do think I'm going to be sick."

As she spoke, perspiration broke out on her forehead and her stomach lurched. Even her hands felt clammy and the room was starring to blur around her.

She heard Isaac curse, and then his arm slipped around her and he guided her toward the bathroom. Once there, he opened the door and quickly did a scan, ensuring no one else was in it. It was a single-occupant bathroom, a fact that obviously eased some of Isaac's worry, and he quickly motioned Jenna and her mother in.

"You come get me if she needs me," Isaac told her mother tersely.

"Of course I will," she said in a soothing voice.

Jenna was just grateful to be inside the bathroom and out of view of customers inside the restaurant. She felt faint, but most of all the contents of her stomach felt as though they were trying to claw their way up her throat.

She rushed to the toilet and violently heaved. She put one

hand down on the toilet seat to brace herself and wrapped her other arm around her waist in an effort to calm her rioting stomach.

She continued to heave until there was nothing left to come up. She felt so weak that she knew she'd never be able to walk back without Isaac's help. And right now she wanted Isaac. Wanted his strong arms around her because he'd never let her fall.

She tried to right herself but lacked the strength. Her mother's surprisingly strong grip helped her get to her feet and then Jenna murmured, shocked at how weak she felt and the slurring of her words, "Please get Isaac for me."

To her ultimate shock, she saw a gun appear in her mother's hand and then felt the cold metal of the barrel press bruisingly hard into her side.

"It's not Isaac you'll be going to see, Jenna, dear," her mother said coldly. "There's someone right outside that window who wants very much to see you."

Jenna stared in shock at her mother, unable to comprehend what was going on.

"You can't fight me," she said dispassionately. "The button I scratched you with? I drugged you. You're as weak as a kitten and if you don't move fast, not only will I shoot you, but I'll shoot your precious Isaac too, so if you don't want him to die, then you're coming with me through that window and you're going to do it fast before he gets worried and barges in. Because if that happens? I kill him, Jenna. So get moving."

She shoved Jenna toward the blind-covered window even as she shouted loud enough for Isaac to hear, "She's okay, Isaac! Just getting cleaned up now. We'll be out in a minute. She just needs to wash her face and get her bearings back."

"Are you all right, Jenna?" Isaac called back, concern evident in his tone.

"Answer him," her mother hissed. "And you'd better be convincing or he's dead."

Fear nearly made speech impossible. Her mind was cluttered with a million things, memories, brief snippets and fragments of long-ago events all coalescing into place.

"I'm okay, Isaac. We'll be out in a minute."

Her mother made quick work of the blinds and getting the window open and then she shoved Jenna out, following behind her. Jenna stumbled when her feet made contact with the ground, the drug making her unsteady and dizzy.

"*You* killed him," she whispered. She lifted her stare and looked right into the eyes of evil. "You killed my father and you were the one who sold me to the cult," she said hysterically.

TWENTY-SEVEN

DANE was standing in front of the television, holding a cup of coffee in his hand, as he replayed the interview that had Jenna's mother pleading for information about her long lost daughter. He didn't know why he was so bothered by it. They'd checked her out, dug up every nonexistent skeleton from her past, and all they'd found was a woman who'd lost everything shortly after her daughter, Jenna, had turned four.

It wasn't personal. It never was. Suspects were suspects until they weren't. People were investigated and either found to be a source of use or not. So why did this woman stick in Dane's craw so badly? What was it about her eyes that bothered him so damn much?

He was about to turn the television off when he heard Tori enter the room. But one look at Tori's mask of horror, the fact that she'd gone rigid and her face had leached entirely of color, momentarily froze him.

"Who is she?" Tori demanded hysterically. "Who is the woman on the television?"

She ran to Dane, fighting him for the remote, kicking and hitting. Never had he seen her react this way to anything. He let go, letting her do what she wanted so desperately as she hit the button to turn the volume way up. But he walked up behind her and enclosed her in his arms, afraid she'd only become more violent and hurt herself.

"Tori, honey, it's me, Dane. Talk to me. Talk to me right now. Tell me what's going on. Who is this woman to you? You don't understand how important this is. If you know something, you have to tell me right now."

She whirled around, her eyes wild with so much fear that he hurt for her. "Who is she?" she screamed.

"Who is she to you?" Dane demanded, still holding her by the shoulders so she wouldn't do anything crazy like run out of the safe house where he was keeping her completely hidden from the public—or private—eye.

"She's the woman in my dream," she said hoarsely. "Don't you understand, Dane? She's the woman I saw being shot to death but she wasn't wearing that. God, if we can find out who she is, then we might actually be able to save her!"

Dale felt the blood drain from his own face as he stared back at Tori in horror. "Are you sure about this, Tori? You have no idea how important this is. That woman is Jenna's mother, or the woman claiming to be her. Isaac took Jenna to meet her today. The footage you're seeing is from several days ago when she made a public plea for help locating her missing daughter, and Jenna saw it."

Tori's mouth gaped open. "Oh my God, Dane. You have to tell them what I saw. You have to tell them now!"

Dane yanked out his phone, and as he was pressing buttons for the secure line so Isaac would know to answer it regardless of the situation he might be in, he glanced up at Tori again.

"What was she wearing when she was shot? You said that wasn't what she was wearing on the television program. *Think*, Tori. I need this information."

"Designer blue jeans, spike-heeled boots, long-sleeved white turtleneck sweater. It's why the blood was so vivid in the dream," she whispered. "All the red on her white shirt. So much blood."

Dane wrapped one arm around her, pulling her into his side, and she turned her face into his body, overwhelmed by having to describe the event that had already played over and over in her mind. He hated making her relive it, but now he realized the impact this could have on . . . everything.

"Tori, this time there is something you can do about it—I can do about it—we just have to hope to hell we aren't too late."

Tori stared at him with wide frightened eyes. "I didn't see Jenna or Isaac. No one from DSS. Why did I only see her mother? What could have happened to her—I mean will happen if it hasn't already?"

"I can't answer that, honey. I just have to try to warn them before it's too late."

TWENTY-EIGHT

JENNA was forced upward as she was dragged to her feet and then pushed forward, the gun never far from a vital part of her body. She was violently shaken from the sudden surge of memories and the ugliness revealed in her mother. Jenna recoiled from something so evil, wondering how her mother could have passed off acting with so much sincerity. She'd fooled them all, but Jenna most of all.

"It's not often I get the chance to sell my brat daughter for a fortune not once in my life but twice," her mother sneered. "When Eduardo annihilated the compound, he tracked me down and asked me to help him find you. For a price of course," she added with a chuckle.

"Ah, here he is now," her mother said as she shoved her toward a group of men who'd materialized from the nearby stand of trees that divided the commercial strip from a residential area.

The man she called Eduardo, Jenna only knew as Jesus, or "Jaysus" as Isaac and the other DSS men called him in order to deflate the egotism he'd wrapped himself in by comparing himself to the son of God.

Before anything else could be done or said, Jaysus pulled out a gun and quickly fired off two, silent shots at her mother, hitting her first in the chest and then right through her head. She crumbled to the ground, her white top now crimson with all the blood erupting from the enormous wound in her chest. Jenna slid to her knees, covering her ears and shutting her eyes as her silent screams echoed through her mind over and over. She wasn't a healer with a beautiful, miraculous gift to save life. She was dirty, tarnished, a bringer of blood and death, disguised by something that appeared to be good. She should have never left the compound. Every single innocent person who'd made the mistake of protecting her and being kind had been marked for death. She was nothing more than a death sentence and she was to blame. This was her penance for daring to dream of a better life and for wanting so many of the things that had been denied her.

"Get up," Jaysus ordered, grabbing Jenna's arm and hauling her to her feet. "You've cost me far too much time and delay as it is. All you've done is earn the deaths of every single person who came to your aid."

"Hands up, Jesus! Back away from the woman or you and every one of your men will die."

Jenna heard Isaac's voice in the distance, but she was too in shock to register how close he was. All she could think was that her own mother had betrayed her not once but *twice*. Her mother had killed her father, the one person who'd loved her when she was a child. And now she had put Jenna in the position of losing the only person who loved the woman she'd become. She was going to lose everything and be sentenced to hell *again*.

Jenna found herself roughly hauled up against the muscled body of Jesus, whose stench reeked of death. To her horror, he seemed to be looking for someone among the DSS agents who'd given pursuit. Then she saw the look of triumph spark in his eyes as he held up his gun, and Jenna began screaming and kicking and fighting as hard as she could.

Jesus merely knocked her away, instructing his men to handle her while he took careful aim and shot.

A cry of pain rose from the distance and a roar of rage and grief bellowed from Beau.

Oh no. Oh no! Jenna turned, scrambling against her captor's hold as she watched a barrier being formed around Ari, but it was too late. She was lying on the ground in a pool of blood.

Beau's gaze found Jenna's through the chaotic turmoil, his eyes begging her. "She's pregnant," he said, his voice cracking. "We only just found out. Please help her. You have to save her and our baby."

Jenna fought against the drugs that had slowed time and the entire world around her. It all seemed like something straight out of a nightmare, and for a moment she closed her eyes, praying she'd wake up in Isaac's arms, being soothed while he told her it was just a dream. That she was safe. But when she reopened her eyes, she knew it was only too real. And she had to act fast if she was going to save Ari.

Isaac motioned desperately for his men to get into the best position to take out Jesus and his men the moment they got a clear shot. He could see Jenna struggling against the effects of whatever drug her bitch of a mother had given her at the restaurant. This was all his goddamn fault. None of it had seemed right from the very first, and worse, he'd allowed Jenna out of his sight, believing that nothing could happen to her in the small confines of the bathroom with him standing right outside. Damn him for not being more observant. For not insisting on taking care of Jenna himself. He'd let her and every single member of his team down and he'd never forgive himself.

The bastard had done his homework on DSS and he'd taken out the biggest long-distance threat to him at the very first opportunity. Ari.

Isaac watched, even as his men grimly reported in that no clear shot was available and they couldn't simply start picking off Jesus's men, because then Jenna would die.

Jenna straightened in Jesus's hold and shot him a look of pure hatred. It was a look that told Isaac she was about to act and he silently pleaded with her not to incite the man's anger even more. They just needed to buy more time. Just one slip-up and they'd take the son of a bitch out and lay waste to every single one of his men.

"Let me heal her," Jenna said coldly.

Jesus laughed. "You're in no position to be making demands. I'll kill every last one of them and not give a shit."

"Then you'll lose what you most want. Me," she said, shrugging indifferently, as if she didn't care one way or another.

He actually looked confused for a moment and then laughed again, though this time it sounded nervous and not at all confident.

"I don't lose. Ever," he said, grabbing her arm and shaking

her like a rag doll. "Especially when I've had to work this hard to get what I want."

Both Zeke and Dex had to hold Isaac back when he went crazy, trying to get to Jenna.

"You'll get her killed," Dex hissed. "Hold it together until we are able to make our play."

Isaac hated that they were right, but he hated even more having to see that bastard's hands on her.

Jenna stared coldly at Jesus until his eyes narrowed in question. Her voice was soft but full of promise as she spoke loudly and clearly so that everyone could hear.

"Nothing you'll ever do to me will make me perform for you. I'll let every single person you bring me to heal die, and that includes you," she spat.

"You say that now, but you'll be singing a different tune when I'm finished with you," he said menacingly.

She didn't react to his threat and continued to stare at him unflinchingly, her voice and demeanor calm.

"The beatings, the torture, the brainwashing, every single thing they did to me while I was their prisoner worked because I didn't know any different. I had no knowledge of the outside world, and I knew I *had* to endure and play their game until I could one day escape.

"If Ari and her baby, Isaac and all the others die, then I have nothing to live for anyway. You'll have taken every single thing that matters most—the *only* things that matter to me in this screwed-up world—so it doesn't matter what you do to me. I'll never give in," she vowed, her voice so cold and defiant that the drug lord seemed genuinely flustered.

And it froze Isaac to the bones, because he knew she meant

every single word of her threat. He knew she would defy Jesus until her very last breath. Never in his life had he been this terrified. So unsure of himself and utterly helpless to save the woman he adored beyond measure.

"Then what do you propose?" Jesus asked, arching one eyebrow at Jenna.

"An exchange," she said softly. "You let me heal Ari and you let everyone go without further incident. In exchange, I'll go with you and do whatever you want. You'll always have leverage over me because I'll do *anything* to keep them alive, to keep Isaac alive."

"God damn it, no, Jenna!" Isaac shouted hoarsely. "You aren't going anywhere with that son of a bitch!"

Her gaze found Isaac across the distance and instantly her eyes filled with love, so much love. "It's my choice to make, and I choose to save Ari and her baby and the rest of you. You are all the very best part of my life, and knowing that you're all alive and well will be all I ever need. I can survive *anything* as long as I know you're all safe."

Then her gaze turned back to the drug lord and her eyes narrowed in warning. "Don't ever think of double-crossing me, because if at any time I even think you've broken your word, I'll let you or anyone else die without a single regret, even if it means my own death."

There was grudging respect in the drug lord's eyes but also a smugness, as if he believed he still held the upper hand. He was a fool. Jenna was being absolutely honest in that she felt she had nothing to lose if everything was taken from her. Isaac knew because if he lost her, no force on earth would ever stop him from seeking vengeance, even if it cost him his own life.

Because without her, he had no life. No reason for living. None of the reasons he'd worked and been so passionate about his job at DSS would sustain him if he lost the one person who mattered most to him. Just as Beau, who was kneeling brokenly over Ari, would never survive the loss of his wife and child. As much as he hated Jenna bargaining with the devil over being able to heal Ari and give her and her child a chance, he knew that in Beau's place he would beg, give anything, make any promise even to the devil himself to ensure that his wife and child survived.

Finally the drug lord nodded his head. "All right. We have an agreement. You may heal the woman, but not fully," he said, his tone a warning. "I'll not have her well enough to use her powers against me, and I'm well aware of her abilities, so don't try to fool me by downplaying them."

Isaac glanced at Caleb, shooting him a warning stare. It was obvious Jesus had studied up on DSS and knew of Ari's power, but he hadn't even looked in Ramie's direction or mentioned her name. As their gazes locked, Caleb nodded his understanding and pushed Ramie back, obscuring her from view as he slowly retreated while attentions were focused on Jenna and Ari.

Yes, Ari was likely the most powerful weapon in their arsenal, but only as it pertained to brute force. Ramie was every bit as powerful and every bit as valuable a weapon and if, God forbid, this went like Jenna wanted and they weren't able to stop Jesus from taking Jenna with him and escaping, they'd need Ramie to locate her.

Jenna looked in Gracie's direction to where she was solidly behind Zack, who acted as a barrier between her and danger, risking his body for hers.

"Gracie," Jenna called out loud enough to silence the others, who now looked at her with even more curiosity.

Some of Jesus's men shook their heads and muttered that Jenna was loco. That she was of the devil and would bring death upon them all. This angered Jesus and he barked an order for them to shut up.

But his men were right—only it wouldn't be Jenna who brought death and the bowels of hell down on their heads. Isaac and his men would be the ones to carry out that mission, and it would be the most satisfying mission of his life.

"Does he tell the truth?" Jenna asked Gracie in a solemn voice.

Gracie peered around Zack's back much to his protests and then stepped out to the side, nearly causing Zack to lose his mind. But Gracie had decided that if Jenna had risked so much in order to save Ari, she wouldn't be the only one to do so.

Gracie reluctantly nodded, staring at the drug lord with a mixture of fear and disgust. "He speaks the truth."

Jesus was visibly confused as he yanked his gaze between the two women. Then he frowned, his brow crinkling as he stared at Gracie, as if finally realizing her ability.

"If you think to change the deal in any way, I'd advise against it," Jenna said, steel in her voice. "If you don't keep your word, then neither do I."

"Then how do I know *you're* telling the truth?" he said mockingly to Jenna.

She nodded her head in Gracie's direction. "Ask her," she said defiantly.

Jesus snorted. "Oh, I'm supposed to believe she *really* reads minds."

Gracie's expression became one of disgust, and then she began to recite in great detail precisely what the drug lord was currently thinking. Like how a bunch of uppity women who hadn't ever had to deal with a real man and who'd been allowed to get away with far too much, especially when it came to disrespecting the men who had power over them, should all be firmly put in their place by a real man like himself. She looked like she wanted to throw up when she added that there was nothing more that he wanted than to be able to fuck the truth into them all so that by the time he was finished with them, they'd know who their lord and master was.

His eyes widened, but he seemed amused and not at all regretful of the broadcasting of his thoughts. He smirked in her direction, as if to tell Gracie she was certainly included in his lascivious fantasy. Then he raised his hand. "Okay, okay, then tell me, is *Jenna* telling the truth? If I honor my end of the bargain by allowing her to heal the woman and allow the rest of you to go free and unharmed, then she'll go with me without fighting and do every single thing I demand of her?"

Gracie's eyes filled with tears, which should have been answer enough, but again she nodded and then choked out, "Yes, she will never break her word as long as you don't give her cause to do so by breaking yours."

"Very good," Jesus said with smug satisfaction.

He shoved Jenna forward in Ari's direction, his and his men's guns trained on her and all the others as tensions rocketed in the area.

"Make it quick," he barked.

Jenna stumbled past her mother's body, her face whitening. She closed her eyes and continued on, squaring her shoulders even as pain burned brightly in her eyes. Pain and so much betrayal that it sickened Isaac. Betrayal he was part of, because he'd failed to keep his promise to Jenna.

"Everyone away from the woman except Jenna," Jesus barked. "Anyone make a single move not to my liking, then I open fire and I'll kill every last one of you fuckers."

Jenna found Isaac standing in the distance, and her eyes filled with tears. "I love you," she mouthed.

Before he could respond, she turned and found Beau, who was being forced to leave Ari's side by his own men and was putting up one hell of a fight.

"Beau," Jenna called softly.

Beau stopped immediately and turned to face Jenna, his eyes bright with tears, his face a picture of complete devastation.

"I'll save her and your child. Please trust me. I'll do just enough that if you get them both to the hospital, I vow on my life, they'll be okay."

"I'm trusting you with all that I am and all that I have or will ever have," Beau said in an aching voice. "Please save her, Jenna. You'll never know what your sacrifice means to me. Never. I owe you a debt that can never be repaid. But know that I will do everything I can to try."

Jenna knelt beside Ari and gathered her hands in hers, and spoke gently to the woman to ascertain whether she was conscious or not. Ari's eyelids weakly fluttered open and she looked up at Jenna with pain-filled eyes, tears pooling in a swirl of arresting colors.

"You have to save my baby," Ari whispered. "He shot me in the stomach. I'm so afraid my baby is lost."

"Never give up hope," Jenna said. "I need you to lie still and try to believe. Have faith and don't give up, Ari. You can't give up. I need you to help me by doing that."

Without further delay, Jenna placed both hands directly over the abdominal wound, blood covering her fingers and palms, and she closed her eyes, calling on the gift that at times had seemed more like a curse. But right now she embraced it for what it was. A miracle. God's sweet mercy and grace. She sent light radiating into Ari's shattered womb and gently cradled the tiny life in her palm, encasing her in the most radiant, warm, glowing light Jenna had ever called forth.

Isaac and the others watched, stunned as light illuminated Jenna until she appeared every bit the angel he'd dubbed her the very first time she'd used her shining goodness and light to heal him. Even Jesus looked upon the healing in astonishment, as if he truly hadn't been certain that Jenna was all she'd been purported to be.

Ari's entire body was bathed in the golden light and was lifted from the ground, where she hovered in midair six inches from where she'd lay a few moments ago.

Jenna began to sing a soft lullaby and it was obvious she was holding the infant's life-form to her, refusing to let her go. The notes of the song lifted hauntingly in the air and flowed through the distance until not a single person present was unaffected by the amazing event occurring right in front of them.

"Be strong, sweet baby," Jenna crooned. "God is with you. You are his child and he will forever grant you mercy and grace. You must fight as your mother fights and cling to the light in her womb. Never move away from that light until the time comes when you are called away. You are his chosen," she whispered, after which she continued to hum the sweet lullaby.

Then she closed her eyes and leaned over Ari, who'd slowly been lowered back to lie on the ground, and finally it was evident that she was finished but so exhausted by the session that she continued to lie over Ari's body as if protecting her, still too drained to move.

Beau ran forward just as Ari opened her eyes. "Ari?" he asked tentatively.

Ari's eyes filled with tears. "I don't know how she did it, but she saved us both and I felt the presence of our child. It was so powerful. It was the most beautiful thing I've ever felt in my life. In that moment I knew everything would be all right. Please, Beau, you must see to her now. You can't let that monster take her. I couldn't bear it if she traded her life for me and my child."

Jenna roused long enough to lift her head, though it was obvious she barely had the strength to do so.

"You must get her to the hospital to be monitored at once," Jenna said weakly. "I did what I could to satisfy Jesus's demand, but your child is fine and so too will Ari be. I swear it on my life."

"Thank you," Beau choked out.

Jenna looked up at the others, tears slipping down her cheeks. "I'm sorry," she whispered. Then her gaze found Isaac's and he nearly fell to his knees, because her expression was one of goodbye. "I'll always love you," she said in a low voice. "Be the *reason* I can endure anything. Stay alive."

Then Jesus appeared above her and Isaac wanted to bring down hell on him and every last minion in his devil's army, but they were in a losing proposition and they knew it. The only ace in the hole they had was Ramie and if they did anything to fuck that up now, Jenna would die, they'd all die, and it would have been for nothing.

"Touching. I think I may have felt a tear," Jesus sneered. "Now get the fuck away," he said, waving his gun as his men gathered to reinforce the threat.

Isaac and the others had no choice but to back down as Beau cradled Ari in his arms and ran for the waiting ambulance.

"I believe I kept my end of the bargain," Jesus sneered at Jenna.

She nodded tiredly. "Yes, and now I will honor mine."

As he turned, his men still facing down Isaac and the rest of DSS, he threw Jenna over his shoulder and strode rapidly into the distance, where a helicopter waited to fly him—and Jenna—away.

Isaac turned as Jesus's men began melting away and making their escape, looking desperately for Ramie.

"Ramie!" he screamed. "God—please, Ramie, you have to help me. Can you touch something of hers so we know where to look for her? I have the light sweater she brought with her to the restaurant but left on the chair when she went to the bathroom."

Caleb didn't even argue. He knew that they all owed Jenna a price they could never repay. He looked anxiously to his wife for answers, but her expression was devastated as tears sliced down her cheeks.

She looked up at Isaac with so much regret that Isaac felt dead to his soul.

"I can't use my powers yet," she said urgently, as if trying to make him understand. "All I ever know is what's happening right here and now, and we *know* where they are now. They're in a helicopter. I can't tell the future and if I did attempt to use my powers now, I'd be too drained to use them again later, when they'd actually do us good and I could then tell you where they have her."

Isaac completely lost it. His men tried to hold him back, tried to calm him, but he was adrift, with no anchor and no way to find the woman who meant more to him than life itself. Having to wait for God only knew how long, while Jenna endured hell just so they could locate her and then start to mount a rescue that might be too late, was more than he could bear.

TWENTY-NINE

EVERY DSS agent, as well as Tori, Ramie and Gracie, gathered in Dane's private impenetrable fortress, where he'd taken Tori for her protection. Beau and Ari were heavily guarded by Ari's father, Gavin Rochester, a very powerful, wealthy man with a shadowy past and vast connections. He had offered his services to Beau for the rescue mission that would be mounted as soon as Ramie was able to pinpoint Jenna's location.

Dane was busy on the phone as well, calling in every marker he'd meticulously collected during his long years in security— and the man had an astonishing number of people that shocked the hell out of Isaac.

Then there was Wade Sterling, Eliza's husband, who before marrying Eliza was just as steeped in gray and questionable business practices as Gavin Rochester used to be. He unapologetically offered the full power of his resources, uncaring if DSS knew or found out about them. He kept nothing from his wife, and while she wasn't happy to have her husband's dirty laundry aired in front of her coworkers, she wasn't about to interfere when Jenna's life was at stake.

Not after she'd done so much to save every single one of the people Eliza cared about so much and had once been willing to sacrifice everything for. She recognized a kindred spirit in Jenna and remembered well the horrific choice she'd been forced to make when she believed her teammates'—her family's—lives were on the line.

Tempers were edgy and emotions were running high, and an argument immediately broke out when Eliza told Dane and Wade in no uncertain terms that she was not being left out of the mission to save Jenna. Especially since Wade was going with a contingent of his best men. She'd stubbornly set her foot down and while Isaac would have normally sided with Dane and Wade when it came to Eliza's safety, given that she still wasn't back on full duty with DSS, at this point he was grateful to have her support. There was no one else he'd rather have at his back than this tenacious, extremely loyal woman.

He was humbled and grateful at the outpouring of unconditional help from so many different areas when many otherwise wouldn't be so forthcoming about exposing their connections or the gray areas of their past. But for Jenna, not a single person stood on pride, and they opened their lives to the scrutiny and knowledge of the others.

There was trust involved in those offers, and Isaac knew that he could ask for no better men or women to support him in getting back the woman he loved with every piece of his heart and soul.

He checked his watch, swearing in frustration. Though it had seemed a lifetime since Jesus had taken off with Isaac's entire life in that damn helicopter, it had in fact been only a few hours. Every DSS agent and those connected with the DSS family had pooled their resources in a record amount of time and Dane was still on the phone arranging what sounded like a full-scale military operation from a highly secretive special ops group, though which branch of the armed services they served under was a mystery to Isaac. That was if they even officially existed.

From providing highly classified stealth prototype aircrafts in the past to the partnering and coordinating with a badass black ops military team, Dane always managed to pull off the impossible and pull it right out of his ass. One of these days, Isaac was going to ask Dane exactly who the hell he was and what he did before agreeing to head up DSS for the Devereauxs, because this was not indicative of a regular civilian, coordinating a civilian operation with a civilian security service specializing in personal protection and kicking asses for a living.

Dane had more secrets than the rest of the DSS recruits put together, and that was saying a hell of a lot given the men—and women—who'd signed on as Dane had continued to put together the best of the best to work under him at an agency that didn't even belong to him. And that begged the question. Why did Dane work for someone else when it was so obvious he didn't need Caleb or Beau's backing, support or business name to operate under?

But despite the fact that everyone knew the secret that wasn't a secret, that Dane's word was law when it came to DSS and Caleb and Beau were mere figureheads who deferred to him as having the final say in every situation, Dane didn't act as though he wielded that kind of power or influence. Yes, he wanted to be kept apprised of all his men's comings and goings, but he was never on a power trip, and he didn't insist on taking charge and inserting himself into every situation. Only the ones he had a personal stake in. Like Lizzie's going rogue and vigilante without her teammates, and most importantly her partner and the person she was closest to at DSS—Dane.

Even then, to Dane's frustration, he hadn't been able to take the lead and had to defer to Wade Sterling, whom Dane had himself called in and unleashed on Lizzie when he knew she wasn't being completely forthcoming with him. But for Lizzie, and what he knew to be best for her, he allowed Wade to dictate the plan of action, and Dane and the rest of DSS acted in a support capacity, something that likely still ate at Dane to this day.

Isaac waited impatiently. With every minute that passed, he died a little more as he imagined what his angel was enduring right now. What was that cocky, victorious little bastard doing to show her what he thought of her having the audacity to bargain with him and not back down in the face of his threats? Hell, she threw his threats right back in his face like she didn't give two fucks what he did to her, and that was what made Isaac break out into a cold sweat and panic eat holes in his gut. Because he knew the kind of man Jesus was and he knew he'd make Jenna pay for every one of those insults.

He glanced helplessly at Ramie, who was pale and looked as though she was going to be sick. Caleb was hovering over her, holding her, kissing her, trying his best to comfort her in any way. As if feeling Isaac's gaze, Ramie looked up, raw regret terrible in her eyes. He pleaded silently with her, knowing he was baring himself to anyone and everyone in the room in a way that a month ago would have made him crawl out of his skin in discomfort. Hell, never would he have allowed anyone to see anything but the stony stoicism he always brought to the job. But that was before Jenna. He had no pride when it came to her. There was nothing he wouldn't do or say to have her back in his arms, safe and loved. He'd vowed not to ever ask God for another thing, but wasn't this merely a continuation of that same prayer? That he'd never ask for more than for her to be back in his arms so he could spend the rest of his life loving her so damn much that she never had another dark cloud so much as pass over her.

Caleb looked at Isaac, sympathy bright in his eyes. "It's not me holding her back. It's not even Ramie. She's ready to go as soon as she gets the go-ahead. But there's little point in having Ramie give us information we can't act on. We have to have every man, every source of firepower we can pull in, be ready to go the minute Ramie gives us what we need. If we wait even a little while after she's found Jenna, she could end up giving us faulty intel, because the bastard could move her again before we make our move and then not only are we fucked, but we tip our hand, and then we stand zero chance of having the element of surprise on our side."

Isaac swallowed back the knot that threatened to choke him. He wanted to scream that he knew. God damn it, he knew! But just because he knew the right way to handle the mission—any mission—it didn't make it any fucking easier to sit here on his ass while the reason for him to live was out there, terrified, hurting, wondering if she'd ever be safe again.

Everyone looked up when the door opened to admit Ari and a haggard-looking Beau along with Ari's parents, Gavin and Ginger Rochester. Thankfully, Ari showed no signs that she'd ever been shot, and she smiled at the greetings and relieved hugs she received.

Gavin's sharp glance, however, immediately found Isaac in the throng of DSS agents, and he strode directly to where Isaac was leaning against a wall, his heart sick and every nerve, muscle and instinct ready for action. Anything but this terrible waiting game where every minute that passed meant another minute Jenna was in the hands of a twisted, sick maniac who had no qualms about making her life hell.

"Mr. Washington, I don't know if you remember me, but I'm Gavin Rochester, Ari's father."

"Of course I remember you, sir," Isaac said politely.

"I never got to thank you personally for taking part in the mission to retrieve my precious daughter and save her from the monsters who killed her birth parents."

"I was doing my job," Isaac said from behind clenched teeth.

"I'll also never be able to thank your woman, Jenna, for the sacrifice she made today to save my daughter and my grandchild. Son, there is only one other person in this world who means more to me than my only daughter and the grandchild she carries, and that's my wife. My wife and I would be mourning both their deaths were it not for the bravest damn thing I've ever heard of in my life. She saved not only Ari, who may or may not have survived the wound to her abdomen, but Jenna snatched my grandchild back from the jaws of death. She fought evil for that innocent child and she kicked its ass. I wasn't present to witness the miracle, but I've been told about everything that happened in exacting detail, as well as having my daughter tell me that she'd never felt anything as beautiful as Jenna's healing light and the way she coaxed her baby to not let go and to cling to the light Jenna provided until it was that child's time to enter the world."

The imposing older man looked as if his entire world had been rocked, and emotion shone brightly in his eyes. His words cracked under the weight of the love he felt for his daughter and the relief he felt for the safety of his daughter and grandchild.

"I have dedicated all that I have, all that I own, to the mission to get back that woman, but my debt doesn't end there. There is never anything I can do to repay the debt to the woman you love, but I vow on my life, and on the lives of my daughter and my grandchild, that if there is ever anything I can do for you or for Jenna Wilder, you've only to name it. You'll never have to ask. You name it and I'll do all that is in my considerable power and influence to ensure you have it."

Isaac swallowed back the tears that threatened to completely unhinge him and crack the iron grip he was holding on his composure.

"All I want, all I will ever want, is to have her back," Isaac whispered hoarsely. "I love her more than anything and there's nothing I won't do to have her back where she belongs and I swear to God, as long as I live, I will never let her go again."

Gavin put a comforting hand on Isaac's shoulder and squeezed. "We'll get her back, son. I've been through what you're going through. I thought I'd lose my wife and my daughter and was helpless to do a damn thing to prevent it. But you and your men changed that. You and your teammates gave me back my family and as God is my witness, I'll get you back the missing piece of your soul just as I was once missing that same piece of my soul and had it returned to me. With the resources we have at our fingertips? Look around you, son. No one stands a fucking chance against the full power of our connections and more importantly, the iron will of every single DSS agent in this room. You aren't alone in this. There's not a single person in this room who won't die to get that young woman back after all she's done for those the people in this room hold dearest to their hearts."

"Thank you, sir. I appreciate that more than you'll ever know."

"Be thinking about your wedding and where you want to go afterward," Gavin said, in an abrupt change of subject, one that had Isaac reeling as he imagined the beauty of the day when he'd make Jenna his under the eyes of God and the law. "If you're anything like me, all you'll want to do is marry her as fast as humanly possible and then leave for a very extended, very isolated honeymoon where the only concern you'll have is seeing to your new wife's every need."

Isaac nodded, unable to speak for fear of breaking down.

"I can make that happen. You just say the word. Security will be taken care of. No one will get within a mile of you and Jenna and your every need or wish will be catered to."

"Thanks for the offer," Isaac finally managed to choke out. "I may have to take you up on that. But first, I just want her back."

"Listen up," Dane called from across the room.

Isaac surged forward. Thank fuck the man was finally off the goddamn phone. Dane made eye contact with Isaac as Isaac pushed his way through so he was standing closest to Dane. Dane nodded at him, his expression tight and his eyes hard and utterly focused.

"We're going to get her back, Isaac," Dane said quietly. "Fucking Jaysus will never know what hit him."

Then he glanced across the room to Caleb and nodded. "It's time," he said grimly.

Isaac's pulse sped up and he had to swallow back the urge to vomit as his nerves assaulted him.

"As soon as Ramie can give us information identifying the location where she's being held, then we move out," Dane announced. "They no longer outnumber us nor do they have not one, but two black ops groups who about came in their fatigues when I offered up Jaysus on a silver platter and all they had to do was go in with us and kick some fucking ass."

A chorus of "hell yeahs" and cheers echoed through the room until Isaac's ears rang with them. But this wasn't over. Not by a long shot. They still had no idea where Jenna was. What if Ramie wasn't able to see? Her gift wasn't infallible. But she was their only chance. Because it didn't matter how much firepower and muscle they had behind them or that every single man and woman involved in the mission had vowed to bring Jenna back at all costs. If they couldn't find her, then all the might and resolve in the world was utterly useless.

THIRTY

WITH half a dozen groups of men, including two military black ops groups, waiting nearby for the command to move out once Jenna's location had been ascertained, the mood inside had gone silent and tense as all focus was directed on Ramie.

Knowing well how devastating the process was on her and how vulnerable she was during and in the aftermath, Caleb quietly conveyed his wishes to Dane that only he, Isaac and Dane be present during Ramie's ordeal.

"I understand, Caleb, and normally you know I'd agree to keep the people around Ramie to a minimum, but in this case, I think we should include Gavin and Wade Sterling, as both men are familiar with the underworld where Jesus operates and it's possible they would clue in on things Ramie says better than we would. I also think Eliza should be present in support of Ramie," he concluded quietly.

Caleb nodded, closing his eyes. "I understand. I hate it but I get it. And Ramie will understand as well. Hell, she wouldn't care if the whole room was present. It's me who's so protective of her and tries to shield her from as much scrutiny as possible when she's at her most vulnerable."

"Let's get to it," Dane said. "We don't have any more time to waste if we're going to get to Jenna in time."

Everyone except those mentioned by Dane left the room to prepare to leave at a moment's notice. The tension could be felt throughout the room and every single agent was armed to the teeth, determination etched into their expressions. Tonight, only Caleb and Beau would remain in Dane's fortress to watch over Ari, Tori, Gracie and Ramie. The women had argued vehemently in favor of going but were shut down on all sides so forcefully, they'd had no choice but to give up the argument.

But after the showdown between Eliza and Wade, no one dared suggest she too remain behind. She would have had the balls of every single man who suggested it. In the end, it had been Gracie who'd gotten Eliza to agree to remain behind by telling her with complete sincerity that she would feel much safer if Eliza was here to help Beau and Caleb should anyone breach the safe house.

Wade had shot Gracie a look filled with gratitude and relief, but he'd made sure his wife hadn't seen his silent thank you.

Ramie sank down on one of the now vacant couches and immediately locked eyes with Isaac. "I won't stop until I have what we need to find her. I swear it." Then she turned to her husband, whose face was a mask of agony. "Promise me you won't stop me, that you won't bring me back until we have what we need. Swear it, Caleb." Her expression was identically tortured and her fear of not being able to provide the information they so desperately needed was tangible in the air.

Caleb merely nodded tersely and then positioned himself beside his wife. Isaac sat on her other side, while the remaining people gave her appropriate space, but remained close enough to hear and witness anything she said or experienced.

The rest of the room fell away, and there was only Isaac and Ramie and the quiet vow he read in her eyes as he tentatively held out the sweater Jenna had been wearing earlier that day. Ramie sucked in a deep breath, staring down at it for a moment before finally taking it and wrapping her hands in the material.

Isaac immediately moved back to give her space while Caleb closed in, hovering anxiously over his wife. Ramie's eyes glowed brightly for a moment before she closed them and slumped forward, Caleb catching her and easing her to the floor, where she lay in a fetal position.

Isaac stared, unable to look away, studying every nuance of Ramie's demeanor, seeking some sign she'd connected to Jenna. Then Ramie hunched inward, grunting in pain, her arms instantly surrounding her stomach. Tears burned Isaac's eyes as helpless fury began to eat away at his very soul.

"You think you can so easily make a fool of me in front of my men and all those people you claim are so precious to you."

It was a gruff voice that sounded eerily just like Jaysus. Coming from Ramie's mouth, it was even stranger that it held nothing of her soft, feminine tone. It was as if she was channeling the very devil himself in that moment.

Then her head snapped back and a bruising handprint appeared on her face.

"What the fuck?" Isaac yelled.

He tried to lunge for Ramie, attempting in some way to protect both her and Jenna, who was miles away from the abuse being heaped upon them both. It took the combined strength of Dane, Sterling and Gavin to wrestle him away and pin him down, but he never moved his gaze from the horror that stared back at him from the floor.

"You're a fool to even think I'd keep my promise, especially if you don't do exactly as I tell you at all times," Jaysus continued, taunting Jenna through the medium of Ramie.

"You're the idiot," Jenna gritted out, pain evident in her voice.

Oh God. Isaac choked, unable to form the words he wanted to scream. *Don't anger him. Give him no reason to continue hurting you, baby. I'm coming for you. I swear to God, I'll never give up until I have you back. Please stay alive and safe for me.*

"Do you honestly believe in your overinflated arrogance that you could ever just waltz back in and kill all those people?" Jenna said in a flat tone, devoid of emotion. "You got lucky and managed to manipulate a woman who already despised me into doing your dirty work for you. You would have never gotten within a mile of me otherwise. You'll never be able to get to them, much less kill a single one of them. So maybe you should consider whether I'll keep my promises, you bastard, because pissing me off isn't the way to go about doing it."

"That a girl," Dane whispered.

Eliza's expression was fierce with pride over Jenna's statement, and it was echoed by her husband as well as Gavin Rochester.

"You have yourself one hell of a woman," Gavin whispered to Isaac while still maintaining his tight hold on him to keep him from completely losing his shit.

Isaac just closed his eyes as tears leaked from the corners.

"Do what you want if it makes you feel more like a man," Jenna said in a weary, pain-filled voice. "But remember this when someone shoots your ass off and you come wag it at me to heal it. I might decide to say 'fuck you' and let you die a long, slow, painful death."

Isaac's eyes shot open and went wide in shock. He'd never heard Jenna speak that way, but then he'd never really seen her angry, certainly not as furious as she appeared to be right now. He'd seen her confused by the world around her and desperately trying to take it all in. Maybe he'd even viewed her as weak and in need of constant protection, but in this moment, he was seeing a side of Jenna that made him so fucking proud that she was his yet at the same time worried out of his mind that she'd pay for every single one of her taunts.

Ramie was actually knocked from Caleb's grasp and went sprawling on the floor several feet away, and Isaac growled, his fists swinging as he tried to hit something, anything.

"You won't kill me, Jesus. You're too chickenshit," she taunted again, in a much weaker voice that scared the hell out of Isaac. How much more could she endure? "You need me, because the one thing you fear above all else is death. Your death. It's why you went on this crazy pursuit for immortality and when you realized you were indeed as batshit crazy as everyone labeled you, then you settled for the next best thing. Some poor, naïve, easily manipulated girl who'd been abducted by a cult when she was four and spent the last twenty years as their prisoner. A woman who happened to possess the ability to heal. Did you think I would be grateful to you for taking me away from the cult?" she egged him on. "Did you imagine me falling at your feet, thanking you over and over and vowing to do your bidding forever in my gratitude? It seems to me you got one crappy bargain."

"Shut up!" Jaysus screamed, his high-pitched voice sending chills up the spine of every person assembled. "I may not kill you, but by God, you'll wish I had when I'm done with you."

"For God's sake, Caleb," Isaac pleaded. "Do we have their location? Can we put an end to this?"

Caleb was faring no better and he shook his head. "God damn it, Ramie hasn't said anything that identifies their location. We've gotten nothing from her at all! Only what she relays from Jenna and that goddamn son of a bitch who is abusing them both."

Ramie flinched, but it didn't appear that she, or rather Jenna, had been struck again. Instead, Ramie was suddenly dragged along the floor by invisible hands and made to sit upright against the wall.

"Why did you shoot him?" Jenna asked hysterically. "Are you insane? Why would you shoot one of your own men? Do you think the others are going to continue to give you such blind loyalty when they see that this is their reward? For God's sake, let me heal him before it's too late."

"You aren't to touch him," Jesus said coldly. "*You* did this to him. *You* killed him, you stupid bitch. And now you get to sit there and watch him die when you could have saved him."

"You're out of your mind," Jenna said, raising her voice, anger vibrating from Ramie's entire body. "I didn't kill this man. *You* shot him. And by not allowing me to do what you seemed so desperate to abduct me and have me do, his blood is on your hands. Not *mine*," she spat. "Or do you only intend to keep my healing ability for yourself? I think you've sold your men a line of crap by making them *feel* invincible by telling them you have a miracle worker, that no matter what happens to them, I can fix them, but in reality, you don't give a shit about them or if they die. You merely want the unwavering, unquestioning loyalty and the *attitude* of invincibility so they'll carry out your commands, no matter that they're as insane as *you* are."

Ramie flinched again and then clapped her hands over her ears and began rocking back and forth, her eyes wide open, fixed and unblinking.

"Fuck," Dane said, rubbing both hands over his face in supreme agitation. "Jesus fuck, he just shot someone else and he's going to torture her by making her watch him die when he damn well knows she can heal him and it's her nature to want to heal even when the person is undeserving. She doesn't judge."

"She doesn't feel it's her right," Isaac said, sorrow heavy in his voice. "She believes her gift is from God, no matter that the cult leaders tried to make her rebuke that belief her entire life. They tried to brainwash her into believing she was Satan's instrument and that only God decided life or death and that she was evil, her gift was evil. They even beat her until she spoke the words they wanted to hear, but they never broke her spirit or her belief that her gift was bestowed upon her by a merciful and loving God, and so she doesn't feel she has a choice in whether she uses it or not, nor is she qualified to pass judgment on someone or deem them worthy or unworthy of being saved."

"This isn't good," Wade muttered. "This isn't good at all. He's physically and psychologically torturing her, for fuck's sake. We need a fucking location!"

"I hope someone shoots you," Jenna said, devastation in her voice. "I vow on my life I won't lift a single hand to save you. Kill me, torture me. I don't care. I got what I wanted and you? You're a monster who got nothing in the end but the promise of a very short life."

"Oh no. No no no, Jenna!" Isaac bellowed. "Oh God, baby. Don't give him any reason to believe you won't heal him, god damn it!"

Once again, Ramie went flying across the floor, and spittle flew from her mouth as Jaysus's words spilled out.

"Take that back!" he screamed. "Take it back or I swear I'll make you pray for death with every breath."

"This is fucking enough!" Isaac roared. "We need a goddamn location and we need it now!"

Caleb, no longer able to withstand watching the horror his wife was being subjected to, bent over her and immediately began the process of trying to bring her back as Isaac prayed with every part of his being that it had been enough. That Ramie had been in Jaysus's mind long enough to be able to tell them where to find Jenna.

"Ramie, please, come back to me," Caleb pleaded, as he alternately rocked and shook her in an effort to bring her back from the dark, evil place she seemed to be drowning in.

After five long minutes, Ramie gasped and jerked upright, her eyes clear and no longer lost in another time and place. She yanked her head around as if confused by her surroundings. Then she locked onto Isaac and frantically began begging him to hurry.

Isaac knelt by Ramie and eased his hand over hers, squeezing to give her as much comfort as he was capable of when he was eaten alive by grief and terror for Jenna's life.

"Hurry where, Ramie? Tell us where. Do you know where he has her?"

Ramie nodded even as tears welled in her eyes. "You have to hurry or there'll be no hope. He took her to a place a few hours away because his pride was hurt and he got sloppy, thank God. He wanted the chance to discipline her and reprimand her, to bend her to his will before he disappears into the heart of the cartel-controlled district of Mexico. Once he's there, you'll never be able to find her, much less get her back."

"Then where is he now, Ramie?" Dane asked her urgently. "How much time do we have left before he moves her?"

"You have four hours, and the place he's holding her is three hours away," she said in defeat.

"Fuck that!" Dane said, fury blasting from every nuance of his body. He was trembling with anger and clenching and un-clenching his fists with so much agitation that he looked precariously close to losing *his* shit.

Isaac was right there beside him.

"We'll get there in two hours and not a minute later," Dane vowed. "On my fucking life! Now let's get the fuck out of here. Go, go, go, god damn it!"

THIRTY-ONE

THE two black ops groups met with Dane and the DSS agents as Wade's and Gavin's men took position at the only other two entry points, while they waited for the report from Shadow's stealthy recon on where Jenna was located in the building and exactly what they were up against. Mere minutes after Shadow had disappeared, he reappeared to give the results of his surveillance.

"Jesus, this is going to be like taking candy from a baby," Zeke snorted as he listened to Shadow's unimpressive rundown of the security he'd evaluated. "The bastard's ego is a hell of a lot bigger than the size of his army or his strength. We should be in and out in twenty minutes tops."

Enraged, Isaac curled his fingers into the Kevlar vest Zeke was wearing and slammed him against a tree just behind him. "Shut the fuck up," he snarled. "When your entire world is being held by a torturing, abusive sick fuck, then let me hear *you* stand here and brag about taking candy from a baby. Until that day comes, shut your fucking mouth and keep it shut and follow goddamn orders. When I need or want your commentary, I'll damn well ask for it."

Not a single man called Isaac down or even attempted to get between him and Zeke. They knew Zeke was way out of line and they didn't appear to be any happier about it than Isaac was.

Zeke closed his eyes. "I'm sorry, man. That was a shitty thing for me to say. My only defense is that this *has* to be just any other mission for me or I lose perspective and I don't do the job I need to do because it becomes personal. My dumb-as-shit remarks were stupid and uncalled for, but it's what I'd say in any other situation where such a brainless fuck has left himself virtually undefended. Hell, he's taken out a good portion of his men just so he can force Jenna to watch them die, and from what Shadow is reporting, the rest of his oh-so-loyal followers are having some serious second thoughts, and some are even now sneaking away and abandoning ship before they become his next casualty."

Isaac let Zeke go and blew out his breath. "I get it. I *do*. But I don't *have* any fucking perspective and as long as Jenna is in there and not here in my arms where I know she's finally fucking safe, then I'm not *going* to have any damn perspective."

"Wouldn't expect you to, brother," Shadow murmured, throwing a black look Zeke's way.

Dane was conferring rapidly with the two leaders of the military groups, and then he turned back to his own men. "The black ops groups are going to make their way in, clear a path as quietly and as undetected as possible. This is what they do. What they're best at. We need to stand down and let them do their job. When they give me the go signal, then everyone goes at once from all sides. Isaac, from Shadow's report, Jenna is still in the east wing with Jaysus present. Our objective is to clear any other possible obstacle or threat until we get to where he's holding her. You'll go in with Black Ops One while the second black ops group falls back to give support and to make sure no one crawls up our sixes unannounced. Shadow and I will have your six, and everyone else will fall back in a seek-and-protect role."

Isaac nodded, impatience burning a hole in his gut. At least Dane hadn't kept him out of the action altogether, especially after his eloquent speech about not having any fucking perspective. Any other time that would get his ass benched faster than he could blink, but they all likely knew the consequences if they even tried it now. Isaac would take on the enemy himself and he'd tear the motherfuckers apart with his bare hands, just as he would destroy any other obstacle between him and his reaching Jenna and getting her to safety.

"We're a go," Dane said as the first group moved out, the second falling in behind.

"Fuck, I hate waiting," Isaac growled.

"We all do," Dane said in a surly voice Isaac wasn't used to. "Chaps my ass to have had to call in every marker ever owed to me because we couldn't get the fucking job done ourselves. That shit's going to change. If we don't have the manpower to protect our *own women*, then something is really wrong. I don't give a flying fuck what it costs—we're expanding operations and adding to our numbers, and that means we hire more of the best and *only* the best. If I have to steal some of the baddest asses from the military, I'll do it, and if I have to pay for it myself then so be it. It's bullshit that our women have had to suffer because we got caught with our fucking pants down and outnumbered to boot."

"You won't have to pay for it," Beau growled, surprising

everyone with his arrival. "Caleb and I will be more than happy to foot the bill. Our old man had more money than God and he was probably an even bigger asshole than Jaysus, so it's only fitting that his money be used for something good for a change."

"What the fuck are you doing here, Beau?" Dane asked in a low, dangerous voice.

"Look, I'm not any happier about it than you, although being stuck on the sidelines while letting the rest of you risk everything for the woman who saved everything precious in my life is also bullshit. But it was either me or Ari, and so I think you see why I'm here and she's not. The women were pissed that they were being babysat and being kept out of the action. For fuck's sake, the stubborn woman just got shot and nearly lost our child and I nearly lost them both, and she's pissed because she wanted in to exact her own brand of revenge for that asshole daring to fuck with her child."

"Can't see that I can find much fault in that," Zeke admitted.

"Righteous," was Dex's one-word response.

"Ari sent a message for you, Dane, since she knew you'd have a kitten there was one less person to protect the women. Caleb is there, but my brother is hardly a match for Ari's powers, so if any protecting is to be done, it will be done by Ari and Eliza. Trust me, she's pissed. Only my threat to rat her out to her father got her to stand down, although as we speak, she's plotting retribution with her mother, so I'm fucked either way. She said to tell you that the women are just fine, thank you very much, and that if you spent as much time focusing on your mission to rescue the woman who needs it as you do worrying about the rest of them, Jenna will be just fine and home before the sun rises. I'll only add here that someone would be a damn fool to take on Ari *and* Eliza both."

There was a series of muffled coughs and suppression of laughter as Dane blew out his breath in disgust and shook his head. "Jesus, Beau. Can't you control your woman at all?"

Beau just lifted his middle finger to Dane in response. "Just wait until you go down, Mr. Smooth. Then we'll see who controls his woman and who doesn't. I don't even know who she is yet, but my money is on her controlling you, hands down."

"Jesus, I'm glad Lizzie wasn't here to hear that particular remark, Dane, or you'd be ball-less and singing soprano right now. Lucky for you, Gracie sweet-talked her into staying behind," Brent said, warily looking around as if worried Lizzie would be the next surprise arrival and *had* heard the remarks.

Dane scowled at Brent and then threw a Kevlar vest at Beau, smacking him right in the chest. "If you're going to show up on an op then damn well come prepared. You could have been shot coming in and Jenna would have never made it in time to save your sorry ass."

"Someone needs a reminder about who signs the fucking checks around here," Beau muttered even as he suited up.

"Fuck you *and* your checks," Dane said sourly.

"Righteous," Dex repeated, and Isaac merely nodded his agreement.

Isaac had had enough of the chitchat and was growing more impatient by the minute. He knew it had been a few minutes at most since the black ops groups had breached the building, but it seemed like an eternity. He stood there, dying a little more with each breath, as he tensed, waiting with dread to hear the first sound of combat. But the silence stretched on until it felt as though his sanity was slipping away, piece by shattered piece.

He closed his eyes and focused on Jenna's smile. Her beautiful, unusual eyes, her angelic features, most notably the pale, almost white hair that spilled down her back in unmanageable curls. He loved her hair, the wildness of it, how it never could be tamed and how it suited her.

I'm coming for you, baby. Please, I'm begging you. Hold on for me. Don't leave me alone in this world without you. I'll never survive. I don't want *to survive without you to wake up to every single day for the rest of our lives.*

Suddenly Dane straightened, his hand going to his earpiece, his gaze sharpening as he concentrated on the report he was receiving. A split second later, he grabbed his assault rifle in the ready-for-shit-to-get-real position and said, "Time to lock and load. They've cleared the bottom floor and are holding on the stairs for Isaac. Jenna hasn't moved from the east wing and neither has Jaysus."

He turned back as everyone fell into position, and then he issued another order to Wade and Gavin to have their men take out everything in the west wing and secure it and then make damn sure no one slipped through the cracks.

Isaac's muscles twitched with nervous energy and the readiness to finally take out the son of a bitch who'd made hunting Jenna down and owning her like some prized possession his obsession. And he was obsessed. With the idea of immortality. Jenna had nailed it right on the head when she'd taunted him with his quest for immortality, as if he were a complete moron to believe any such thing existed and that when he'd gotten wind of her abilities, he'd convinced himself that Jenna could simply keep him alive for eternity. The faulty point in his reasoning, proving what a stupid, unstable fuck he was? The fact that *Jenna* wouldn't live forever and when she was gone, the miserable bastard would blessedly have left the earth as well.

No, Jenna wouldn't live forever, but she sure as damn well was going to live for a very long time, because Isaac was going to make it *his* life's obsession to keep her safe, protected, happy and well. If he had to put her in a bulletproof bubble to ensure her protection, then he'd damn well climb into it with her and stay there with her forever.

He swallowed back his sudden insecurity, because Jesus fuck, he was as crazy and obsessed and over the top as Jaysus, only Isaac's obsession was with making her laugh, smile, giving her every single thing, no matter how large or small, her heart desired from now until the end of their time on earth together. And then he'd simply follow her into the afterlife, where he'd continue driving her every bit as crazy as he knew he'd likely drive her in this lifetime, and he felt not one iota of remorse, nor would he ever apologize, for *his* brand of obsession.

He didn't give two fucks what anyone thought or that people would most assuredly think he'd lost his damn mind when it came to Jenna. Some might even draw comparisons between him and Jaysus, the only difference being the motivation behind their obsession with the same woman. All he cared about was what *she* thought and that *she* was happy and that *she* loved him enough to put up with his suffocating, overprotective manner of showering her with all the love he felt for her.

Those thoughts carried him through the entryway to the not very well fortified or defended compound, and finally to the staircase leading up to the east wing where the two military teams had held up. The leader of Team One nodded to Isaac and issued a small salute of respect, then motioned for him to fall in behind his men as they started up the stairs. As Dane had stated, he and Shadow took Isaac's six while the others fanned out to ensure no one got up those stairs behind them, trapping them between whatever manpower Jaysus had remaining with him and whoever would be coming up the stairs to box them in.

Isaac had absolute confidence not only in his own teammates, whom he knew would give their lives for one another without hesitation, but also in the two black ops groups Dane had managed to pull out of his ass and also the men Wade and Gavin had brought to the table. Having been acquainted with both Wade and Gavin for a while now, he had total respect for the power they wielded and the fact that they put the protection of their loved ones above all else. And now they were extending that protection to Jenna. They spoke of debt they would never be able to repay, but it was Isaac who would be buried under a mountain of debt to so many people that he'd never be able to dig himself out to repay them even if called upon to do so.

They were literally saving his entire life, his entire *world*.

At the closed door where Shadow had reported Jenna being held by an obviously completely-over-the-edge Jaysus, the leader of Black Ops One held up his hand for the others to hold up. He pressed a device to the door and then put his ear to it and listened closely. Then he frowned.

He held up his hand and gave his men a quick signal.

"He says it's way too fucking quiet for his liking," the man standing closest to Isaac said.

Isaac's heart damn nearly exploded on the spot. Oh dear God, what did that mean? Were they too late? Had he killed her?

The leader mouthed "on my count," and then quickly attached an explosive device to the door and motioned everyone to take several steps back.

"No mercy," the leader murmured. "Go in fast and low and take out anyone who isn't Jenna Wilder. We don't pull this off just right and he has a chance to kill her. Understand?"

Jesus, did Isaac understand. Sweat made his hands clammy and his chest was about to explode under the force of his heartbeat.

Then the leader did something unexpected. He lifted one eyebrow, and then a look of amusement twisted his lips. *What the fuck?*

"I tend to forget that not everyone locks the door," he murmured. "No need to blast our way in and take the risk of getting Jenna killed if we can simply ease the door open and opt for a sneak attack. This idiot has already proved he's not the smartest tool in the woodshed."

He motioned everyone into position, pointing at each of the men and ordering them to take a different part of the room so that everything would be covered simultaneously. Then he held up his fingers and signaled "three, two, one," before he soundlessly eased the door open, cracking it the slightest amount.

They all froze as the door was opened wider in preparation

for them to rush the room when they finally heard the heavy silence broken.

"You don't want to do this."

Isaac's brow furrowed and he exchanged "what the fuck" looks with Dane and Shadow. It was Jaysus, a very nervous, scared-shitless Jaysus, sounding as if he were about to piss himself. What the hell was going on?

They froze yet again in the act of moving through the door, only this time, it was Jenna's voice they heard loud and clear, and so devoid of emotion that it scared Isaac shitless.

"That's where you're wrong," she said in a voice Isaac didn't even recognize. "You have no *idea* what I want, you worthless piece of a human being."

"What do you want then?" he asked, stammering and sounding extremely flustered. Then he began begging, and that's when Isaac knew shit was about to get real. "Please. I'll give you whatever you want. Anything. Money. Power. You name it and it's yours."

"Jesus H. Christ. The man is crying," the black ops leader said in disgust.

Then they heard the sound of a gun being cocked.

Oh God no. Isaac's panic flared. They had to get in there *now*.

"What I want is for you to die," Jenna said, her voice weak and trembling, but full of conviction. There wasn't a single man outside that room who didn't believe her.

"Go, go, go!" the team leader whispered harshly.

They burst into the room and Jaysus whirled around, and oddly, he looked relieved. Did the stupid fuck think they were there to save him?

And then Isaac's gaze finally found Jenna and his stomach

bottomed out. She was bruised, battered and bloody. There were over half a dozen bodies strewn around the room, blood covering the floor in a macabre scene. And she was standing, her entire body rigid, leaning against the wall for support, and she was holding a gun pointed directly at Jaysus's head.

Isaac rushed forward, leaving the others to take care of any potential remaining threat.

"Jenna, don't, honey! Jenna, it's me, Isaac. I'm here, baby. Don't do this. Please, this isn't what I want for you," he said softly. "You don't have to kill him. Let us take care of him, but more importantly, let me take care of *you*. Let me take you away from here. You'll never have to worry about this son of a bitch again," Isaac vowed.

Jenna's eyes were grief stricken and tears spilled over the rims as she turned slightly to acknowledge Isaac's presence.

"You have *no* idea what he's done," she hissed. "He has to die. He *deserves* to die."

"I do know, baby. I was here with you through it all, and there's not a single person who'd dispute that he deserves to die," Isaac said sorrowfully. "I'm so sorry I let you down. But please, honey. Just drop the gun and come with me now and let me take you away from all of this forever. You don't have to be the one to serve justice."

"Justice is mine to dispense," she whispered.

Jaysus, obviously believing he was well and truly fucked, proceeded to do the dumbest—and last—thing he'd ever do. He drew a weapon from a concealed holster on the inside of his thigh while Jenna was momentarily distracted and he turned it on Isaac, his clear intention to shoot him. Or maybe he was just going to attempt to bargain with Jenna. Either way, it was the wrong thing to do when the woman he'd tormented for hours was hell-bent on delivering her own brand of justice.

Before any of the men could take Jaysus out with one of the many guns pointed directly at him, Jenna pulled the trigger and shot him right in the temple. He went down like a domino and Jenna curled her lips in disgust and hatred, giving him one last look of contempt, before she slid down the wall, her legs no longer able to hold her up. She carefully placed the gun to the side and buried her face in her hands, heartbreaking sobs shaking her entire body.

Isaac slid down beside her and simply wrapped his arms around her, pulling her into his lap, anchoring her to his chest as he rocked her back and forth, tears stinging his own eyelids while Jenna wept as if her heart was broken.

"Baby, you have to stop crying," Isaac choked out. "I can't bear it. I can't stand to see you cry. It makes me crazy. You have to know that I'm utterly helpless against your tears. I'll do anything to make it right again, baby. God, I love you so much. You have no idea how fucking scared I've been since the moment you disappeared from the bathroom. My heart stopped, baby. And it hasn't beat worth a damn until . . . now. Right here and right now with you in my arms, I can finally breathe again. I can live again. Please look at me, baby. Tell me you're all right. Tell me what to do for you."

He was begging and pleading and didn't give one damn who saw. He ignored the others as they surveyed the carnage of Jaysus's earlier rage.

Jenna finally lifted eyes filled with so much grief and devastation to Isaac that he wanted to die right on the spot.

"He k-killed them," she wept, gesturing at the bodies that were still fresh, rigor not having set in yet. "And he wouldn't let me heal them. He wanted me to see them die and all I wanted was to see *him* die," she whispered as if confessing a great sin.

Isaac cradled her gently in his arms and then shakily stood to his feet, determined to get her out of this room of horrors. The stench of blood and so much death clung to his nostrils, and he wanted nothing more than for both of them to be cleaned of the whole experience.

Shadow waited until they were outside the door, and then he stopped Isaac and tucked his hand beneath Jenna's cheek. "Look at me, angel face," he said gently.

When she reluctantly lifted her gaze to his, he leaned forward and brushed a kiss across her forehead. "Not a single person blames you for wanting to see him die or for being the one to kill him. He drew and would have shot Isaac. You saved Isaac's life as well as your own. Don't know how the hell you managed to get the upper hand, little bit—hell, you didn't even need us—but I'd sure as hell love to hear the story sometime when you're up to it."

She offered him a shaky smile. "Maybe one day. Right now I just want to go home." She glanced up at Isaac, a pleading look in her eyes. "Can you just take me home now? To our home? Please?"

If he hadn't been holding her in his arms, his knees would have given out in that moment and he would have face-planted on the floor in relief. After failing her time and time again, all she'd asked was for him to take her home. To *their* home.

"Baby, you don't even have to ask me for a damn thing that's in my power to give you," Isaac vowed. "There's nothing I'd love more than to take you home so you can rest in my arms for as long as you need. Always whatever you need. I'll give everything I own to make you happy, my angel."

THIRTY-TWO

ISAAC carried Jenna into his bedroom, in his house, marveling that he could finally bring her home—to *their* home—instead of having to move her from safe house to safe house because of the constant source of threats she was forced to live under.

She was already sound asleep in his arms, having succumbed to exhaustion halfway into the ride home. He gently laid her down and very carefully removed the clothing that still had blood on it, anger building all over again as he examined the bruises on her small body from the repeated blows Jaysus had given her.

Her poor little face was swollen on one side and a dark bruise covered one cheek. He bent to kiss it, unable to control himself. In the morning, he'd draw a bath and wash away every last memory of this night and of the bastard who'd terrorized her, and he would wait on her hand and foot every single day until he was satisfied she was fully recovered.

Stepping back, he stripped off his own clothing and after

hesitating to leave her even for the briefest of moments, he ducked into the bathroom to take the world's fastest shower, because he wouldn't taint their bed or her with so much as a drop of the blood on his clothes and skin.

He strode back into the bedroom in the act of toweling himself dry and then dropped the towel and rushed to the bedside, sliding beneath the covers to wrap his arms around her when he heard her pained whimpers that whispered past her lips in her dreams.

He held her tightly, running his hands up and down her body, kissing her hair, her face, whispering his love for her, telling her he'd always love her and protect her with his last breath.

After a moment, she quieted and he relaxed, curling himself completely around her so that no part of her wasn't surrounded by him. He had nearly drifted off in the heaven of her body when the nightmares began again, and this time she began weeping softly in her sleep.

His heart breaking, he kissed away every tear as soon as it slid from her eyes. Then he began talking to her, telling her all over again of his love for her and that he'd never allow her to hurt again.

Each time he soothed her, she immediately settled, but it wasn't long before she became lost in the throes of another nightmare, convinced she was still in hell. She called out his name, over and over, and he was in agony that nothing he seemed to do could rouse her from the horrible things happening to her in her dreams. He finally broke down and cried with her, because it tore his heart apart to think she was so desperately calling for him and thought he wasn't there or that he wasn't coming for her.

"Please, baby, come back to me. Wake up and see me. I will

never let you go again. I'll love you more than any woman has ever been loved before. I'll never let anyone or anything hurt you again. I'll wrap you in the finest cotton and never let you so much as stub your toe without going insane. Just imagine, angel, you could already be carrying my baby," he whispered. "And I'm going to love you both so much that I'll spend every day taking such good care of you and all our children, that you'll never want for anything."

Once more, she settled, burrowing more tightly into his embrace, clutching at him even in her sleep as if she'd never let go. He'd never *allow* her to let him go, he vowed with such fierceness that he shook.

He didn't sleep the rest of the night, instead keeping watch over his sleeping angel, soothing her when she began to whimper and become agitated as dreams held her in their tenacious grip. He kept swearing his love for her and making her every promise under the moon, until he was nearly hoarse from the constant reassurance he offered.

When the first faint rays of dawn entered the room, lending their soft light and warmth to the couple so tightly entwined in the bed, Jenna stirred, and at first, Isaac assumed that she was once more in the grip of the terrible dreams that had preyed upon her all night. He was so immersed in the urgency to silence the demons attacking her that he didn't realize that her eyes had lazily fluttered open until he saw her staring back at him, her expression so very warm with love that it took his breath away.

"Isaac, I don't need you to promise me the sun, the moon, the stars and the world," she said, her lips curving upward into a soft, inviting smile. "All I'll ever want or need is *you*. Your love. It's all I'll ever ask of you."

"First, you *never* have to *ask* me for something that is already yours, will always be yours and has always *been* yours since the day you fought death for me and healed more than just my physical body," he said, his tone utterly serious. "And secondly, I'll spoil you ridiculously as is my right, and there's not a damn thing you can say or do that will ever change my mind, so if you won't ask me for anything you want or need, then it's my duty to provide for you as I see fit."

Her delighted laughter warmed him all the way through, melting away the regions of ice and darkness that had re-formed in the time she'd been taken from him.

"We're getting married as soon as possible," he said with utter gravity, staring into her eyes so there was no possible way she could misunderstand his intention.

She arched one eyebrow and stared challengingly at him. "Granted I may be ignorant of how things work in a world I was denied nearly my entire life, but I'm pretty sure that you're supposed to *ask* me to marry you."

She pursed her lips as if in great thought and pretended to ponder the matter further.

"And I'm also fairly certain there's something about you being on one knee, and I *definitely* know a gorgeous ring is involved."

She sniffed and glanced around. "Funny, but I don't see any of that. Do you?"

Isaac narrowed his eyes and then groaned, knowing he'd been had. "You've been talking to the other wives," he muttered.

She grinned back at him, even as her hand cupped his face in the gentlest of caresses. "Of course I have! How else am I going to know when you're not doing things the correct way and taking advantage of my lack of knowledge? They all showed me their rings, and wow. And *then* they told me about how romantic their proposals were and I have to admit, I totally cried over Gracie's story." She emitted a sniffle, her eyes glistening in remembrance. "Such a beautiful love story," she said with a deep sigh.

He echoed her sigh and then leaned forward and kissed her, unable to resist those perfect, pouty lips. God, but this woman had the ability to twist him into absolute knots. This didn't bode well for his future, not that he minded one damn bit. And God, if their daughters were anything like their mother? He was *so* fucked. He needed to have a conversation with God. One last request to give him sons. *Lots* of sons. Well, and then lots of daughters, but he needed sons first so he'd have plenty of help protecting his beautiful daughters, not to mention needing to teach his sons all about the snot-nosed teenage boys they needed to ensure never came around their precious baby sisters.

"I'll show you gorgeous and romantic," he murmured into her mouth.

"Oh good, because I've decided I really do love those parts the best," she said impishly.

He couldn't help but be affected by her happiness and amazed at how she could rebound so quickly, seeming to have put aside all the torment she'd been subjected to the other night and focus only on their future. Together.

Then, realizing she was likely distracting *him* from the terror he'd endured, which would be so typical of her generous, loving soul, he just as quickly decided he was having none of that, and if any distracting was going to be done, it would be done by him, and he would give her the most romantic proposal and the most gorgeous ring she'd ever seen in her life.

He *may* have studied the other wives' rings long and hard so he could ensure his bride would have bragging rights where engagement rings were concerned. But wait, they were getting fucking engaged? Oh *hell* no. There'd be none of this waiting shit. He'd give her the ring and then he'd haul her before a preacher before it could ever be considered an engagement ring.

With an exaggerated sigh, he slid out of the bed and took her hands in his to pull her into an upright sitting position, and then he picked her up and placed her very carefully on the edge, ensuring she wasn't dizzy or suffering any ill effects from the injuries she'd sustained.

Then he reached under the pillow where he'd placed the ring last night when he'd crawled into bed with her so that it would be right there when the moment was right, and well, he hadn't had any intention of letting her out of bed until the moment *was* right.

He dropped to one knee and took her hands again, after having laid the box on the floor out of her sight, and he entwined her fingers in his.

"Jenna Wilder, I fell in love with you the moment you touched me and filled me with so much love and light and warmth that I was absolutely overcome. You not only healed the physical wounds I'd sustained just moments before, but you healed wounds that were buried so deep that they hadn't seen the sun in more years than I can count.

"You are my very own miracle, when I stopped believing in miracles when I was just a child. You brought me back to life and back into the light. You gave me back my belief in a higher power, but the thing you gave me that irrevocably changed me from the man I used to be and gave me hope and the image of the man I wanted to be was ... peace. You gave me *peace*, my angel," he whispered. "No one and nothing has ever been able to give me what you did with a single touch, and I knew right there that my life had just been changed forever in the best possible way. I knew that you were the only woman I'd ever love in my life, the only woman I've *ever* loved. And I also knew that I'd do anything to keep you with me, no matter what I had to do to make that happen. I just thank God, every single day, that you love me back, that you want a life with me as much as I want a life with you. So I'm not asking you to marry me, my angel love. I'm *begging* you to marry me and make my life whole, to spend the rest of your life at my side, allowing me to make you happy every single day. To give you so many children that you're utterly consumed by our life together and the products of our love."

He reached down with one hand, refusing to let go of her entirely because his hands were shaking and only her grasp was keeping him from completely embarrassing himself. He fumbled with the box, managing to open it with trembling fingers, and after only dropping it once, he finally lifted the box, turning it toward her so she could see the huge diamond nestled in the velvet material.

Tears gathered in her eyes, but this time he didn't panic or demand to know what he needed to do in order to make her stop crying, because she looked so utterly ecstatic, so beautifully happy, that she glistened from head to toe. There was an honest-to-goodness glow that emanated from her body and surrounded her like a halo, golden with purity, radiating from her like the rays of the sun, just like his angel *should* look.

For a moment, she stared at him, her eyes shining to rival

the brightest star, her face soft with answering love, and then she lifted her hands to his face, ignoring the ring, and placed them on either side of his jaw. She dragged him toward her, their lips meeting in a hot, sweet rush. Her tongue lapped lovingly against the seam of his mouth until he sighed, opening to her just as she'd opened to him so many times before. Then she slid inward, exploring his mouth, tasting him while spreading her own sweet nectar on his tongue.

"Yes," she whispered into his mouth. "Oh yes, Isaac. All I ever want is to be yours. Always. Forever. Until the end of time."

He dragged one of her hands down to her lap while still kissing her hungrily, feasting on her mouth like a man starving. He took only a quick look down to make sure he was sliding her ring on the right finger before resuming their passionate kiss. Their first kiss with his ring on her finger and her promise to marry him fresh from her lips.

Finally she glanced down at her hand and held it out, inspecting the ring in awe as she stared and stared some more. "Oh my God, Isaac. It's huge! I've never seen a ring so beautiful in my life!"

"You like it?" he asked gruffly.

She threw her arms around him, squeezing until he laughingly begged for mercy.

"I *love* it," she vowed. "I'll *never* take it off."

"Damn straight you won't. Now that we've got the romantic proposal and the ring all taken care of, I'm taking you shopping for the wedding dress of your dreams, because honey, I don't know what you know about marriage and engagements, but all you *need* to know is that I don't do long engagements. In fact, I don't do engagements at all. What that means is that the minute we find the dress you want to be married in, we're calling every person at DSS—our *family*—and telling them to get their asses down to the church so they can see the most beautiful bride who ever existed and watch us get married."

Jenna laughed joyfully, and then her expression became somber as she gazed deeply into Isaac's eyes. "I love you and I never want to be without you. I know in my heart that God sent me to you, that you are who he intended for me, and I'll be eternally grateful to him for that."

His expression turned even more grave than hers. "You're wrong about that, my angel. God gave you to *me* and *you* saved me, and for that *I* will always be grateful. Not a single day will go by that I won't be thankful for the most precious gift—the only gift—I've ever been given in my life. I was lost until you walked into my life and I've never been more grateful for someone trying to steal my vehicle, because if not for that, I'd still be lost in a world so bleak and hopeless that nothing would have ever been able to break through the darkness and fill my heart and soul with sunshine. Except you, angel girl.

"Only you brought the most beautiful, hope-filled light to permanently erase the dark stains I thought had become permanent scars in places I never allowed *anyone* to see. You made me whole again, and because of you, I can look back on my past with a sense of peace and forgiveness instead of the overwhelming pain and sorrow that had dug so deeply into my memories that I didn't think they'd ever let go or that I'd ever be free of them."

He gathered her tightly in his arms, holding her left hand up so the ring caught the light in a blinding myriad of sparkles.

"You truly are an angel. *My* angel. And there's not a single shadow or shameful and painful memory, or constant torment forced on me by guilt, that could ever survive the shining, golden, pure light that radiates from an angel only as beautiful as you."

JENNA watched in amusement as Isaac gingerly held their three-month-old in his huge hands, which even at her size and weight now completely dwarfed her, and rocked her in the over-sized rocker they'd had to specially order to accommodate him. Even as he cooed utter nonsense, it didn't escape Jenna's notice how careful he was in his every movement. He was forever terri-fied that he'd hurt little Evangeline by simply crushing her with his "clumsy, giant hands," as he referred to them. Jenna merely rolled her eyes and shook her head, which always instantly gar-nered a wounded, "What?" from her husband.

The man treated his firstborn like she was spun from the most fragile, delicate glass ever manufactured, but his grip was always sure and steady. It was then Jenna reminded him, as she always did, that *she* was more likely to drop their daughter than he ever was. Of course, in Isaac's eyes, his wife was perfect, and he took immediate exception to her even thinking such a thing about herself.

He didn't just keep his opinions regarding his wife and daughter to himself either. He proudly proclaimed that Jenna was the most perfect mother a husband could ever ask for and that Evangeline, or little Evie, as she'd been dubbed by Jenna, though she was often trumped by Isaac, who'd insisted that she should be called Angel, since she'd certainly descended from one, was the most beautiful baby girl who ever lived.

Thankfully, Ari and Beau had been blessed with a little boy, because if not, the arguments between the two proud fathers would have gotten ugly and physical. Now they could both claim to have the cleverest, most intelligent, most beautiful baby of their respective sexes. As for Ari and Jenna, they merely tolerated their husbands' nonsense by shaking their heads and leaving the room so the men could indulge in all the baby-talk nonsense they liked while the two women could actually have an adult conversation.

Usually Jenna was content to watch her husband dote on Evangeline for hours, but today was their one-year anniversary, and she had plans for her husband that didn't include him spending the entire afternoon speaking the language of "goo" and "gah." True to Isaac's word, he had knocked her up as fast as humanly possible, which was why they were celebrating their first year together with a three-month-old child.

He was inordinately proud of that fact, and that too was something he smugly let her know on a regular basis. But Jenna just smiled her secret smile as if she somehow endured, when in fact she was living the most wonderful dream she'd ever imagined in her life.

"Is she ready to go down for her nap yet?" Jenna asked softly as she approached the rocker, where she'd noticed that Isaac had grown quiet.

Isaac nodded and whispered in a hushed tone, "She's got a full belly, a clean diaper and Daddy just rocked her to sleep. I'd say we're good for a couple of hours at least."

"Good, because I have plans for you, mister," she said in her most threatening tone.

He arched an eyebrow but she saw the instant gleam that entered his eyes. That predatory gleam that never failed to make her shiver all the way to her toes.

"Depending on how fast you get her down in her crib and get back to the bedroom, you might get to see me undressing. Of course, if you take too long, alas, the deed will already be done and you'll have to find me underneath all those covers."

The look on Isaac's face was priceless. "What plans exactly are you talking about?" he asked hoarsely.

She narrowed her eyes. "The kind of plans a wife tends to make on the one-year anniversary of her marriage to her husband. But . . . if you're not interested, I'm sure I can find something else to do."

Isaac scrambled up as quickly as he could manage without jostling and waking Evie. Fortunately for them, she was a sound sleeper once you got her to that stage.

"The hell I'm not interested," Isaac burst out, wincing when he realized how loudly he'd bellowed and immediately lowering his voice. "I'll be there in thirty seconds, and I will not be pleased to find you already undressed, Mrs. Washington."

"Then I suggest you get a move on, Mr. Washington," she teased.

He very nearly tripped on his shoes as he hurried into the next room to deposit Evie into her crib. Jenna giggled and then mentally counted to five before she moved to the side of the bed and ever so slowly began removing the clothing from her body.

At first, Jenna had been very self-conscious of the changes in her body wrought by her pregnancy—changes that hadn't exactly gone away after her delivery. The fact that her behind had become a little wider and a little fuller, her belly just a little softer and her breasts, dear Lord—she'd gained two cup sizes during her pregnancy and it would appear she was stuck with them.

Isaac had had an absolute fit when she'd hesitantly asked him whether he was turned off by the seemingly permanent changes in her body. He'd looked at her like she'd lost her damn mind and then proceeded to show—not tell—her precisely what he thought of every (in his words) delectable, delicious curve. He especially showed her newfound upgrade in cleavage his profound appreciation, and then tenderly gathered her in his arms and told her with utter sincerity that there was nothing that would ever make him stop loving her and worshipping her body every damn chance he got. That she was the most beautiful woman in his world, the only woman in his world. He'd been so sincere that his words had brought tears to her eyes, and then he'd kissed them away and made love to her all over again, showing her twice as much appreciation in the end.

She'd only managed to slide her—or rather his—shirt down her shoulders when he came barreling into the doorway of their bedroom, his heated gaze immediately finding her. She loved wearing nothing but one of his button-down shirts as it dwarfed her much smaller frame, and he loved her wearing nothing but his shirts, his hands finding their way up the inside of her leg a dozen times a day when she wore one, to see if she was wearing any underwear.

On the days she wasn't? Well, suffice it to say, wherever they were when he made his discovery was where he impatiently made love to her, barely managing to get his pants unzipped before he was on her and inside her so deep that she felt him against her womb.

He stalked purposefully over to her, his eyes glittering with desire that hadn't waned even a little in the year they'd been married. If anything, their passion grew crazier, needier and more desperate by the day.

"God, please tell me you aren't wearing any underwear under my shirt," he said in a growl.

"I might be," she teased. "Or I might not. I believe it'll be up to you to find out," she said, knowing that if he investigated and found her bare, his favorite way for her to be, she'd get the rough loving she craved when he was intensely and painfully aroused.

He closed his eyes and swore, surprising her because that wasn't his typical response in a situation like this. He pressed his mouth to hers in a hungry kiss. "Stay right here. Don't move," he said, before slipping into the bathroom.

He returned holding something in his fist and he stopped in front of her, his expression suddenly serious. Then he opened his palm and she looked down to see a pregnancy test resting there. She glanced back up, staring at him in obvious confusion.

"I think you should take this, baby," he said gently.

"What?" she asked, her confusion only growing.

"Surely you didn't think I was teasing you about keeping you knocked up so much that you'd never even think of ever leaving me," he said, looking down at her with a smug grin on his face.

"But Isaac, I'm not pregnant! I'm still breastfeeding, for Pete's sake, and Evie is only three months old! I know you want to have a lot of children, but even you have to give nature time to take its course."

He leaned in and nipped her bottom lip. "Babe, I know your body better than mine and I can count. You had one period after you had Evie, and while I am aware that not all women have periods until they stop breastfeeding and that breastfeeding is sometimes an act of birth control itself, as I said, I know your body, honey. I know it very, very intimately," he said, his voice dropping to a husky whisper. "Go take the test. For me? I need to know because you looking like you do right now and looking at me the way you were when you told me you had plans for me? I'm as hard as a fucking stone and if you're pregnant then I need to be more careful with you, especially since you haven't fully recovered from having Evie."

Jenna's mouth dropped open as she stared silently up at her husband. "Is this a joke? Are you playing a prank on me for our anniversary? Do you really think I'm pregnant? And why would you know but I wouldn't? Do you know how insane that sounds for the husband to know before the wife does?"

"Not when it comes to you, angel," he whispered against her mouth as he took it again. "I know every inch of your beautiful body and I paid attention to every single detail of it when you were pregnant with our little Angel. Your smell is even different and your taste. Oh God," he groaned. "You haven't noticed the fact that I've been going down on you for the past few weeks like a man being given his last meal before his execution?"

Jenna flushed to the roots of her hair, her cheeks so hot she was sure she had to be bright red. He patted her gently on the ass and coaxed her toward the bathroom.

"Do it for my peace of mind before I fuck you so hard that

you're going to feel me for an entire week," he pleaded. "For my anniversary present, I either get to fuck you hard and long every possible chance I get—and trust me, babe, I'll make those chances happen—or you're going to once again make me the happiest man in the world by telling me you're going to have my baby again."

Then he lowered his mouth to whisper in her ear. "I know I said I wanted lots of boys first, but I wouldn't trade our little angel for anything in the world, and I have to admit, I'm kind of hoping for another one just like her."

"Oh God, you are serious," Jenna said, flabbergasted. Then she shook her head even as she headed in the direction of the master bathroom. "You'd better be glad I'm so on board with all these babies you've promised me, and that I want as many as you can give me, or you'd be in a world of trouble right about now."

He pulled her into his arms when they were inside the bathroom and then he unwrapped the test and placed it reverently in her hand.

"You have to know that if at any time you ever changed your mind and wanted to stop, even at the one—or, well, the two it's possible we already have—I would never love you or our girls any less. I only want you to be happy, my love. And I'll spend the rest of my life busting my ass to make you happy every damn day."

"Well, let's see how happy you make me today," she said, a soft glow lighting up her face as she stared at the early pregnancy test in her hand.

Exactly five minutes later, with Jenna standing at the counter with Isaac's arms fully wrapped around her, his hands resting on her belly, their eyes met in the mirror.

"Time to look down," he whispered, almost as if afraid of ruining the moment.

"Let's look together," she whispered back. "On three."

After the count of three they both looked eagerly down at the test, and Jenna's vision became watery with tears as she saw the clear, undeniable evidence that once again she was pregnant.

Isaac swung her around to face him, and she was shocked to see the glimmer of tears in his own eyes. "You have no idea how happy you've made me, angel girl. And you have no idea how much I'm going to love you for the rest of our lives."

"Happy anniversary, darling," Jenna said, "though I will say, this wasn't the present I had planned for you."

His expression became calculating. "Oh yes, I know exactly what my present was going to be, and I plan to collect on it right now."

With that he swung her up into his arms and carried her to bed, laying her down before blanketing her with his body as he began to make slow, sweet love to the absolute love of his life.

S BY #1 *NEW YORK TIMES*
TSELLER MAYA BANKS

JUST ONE TOUCH
A Slow Burn Novel

Raised in a strict religious cult, Jenna has no connection to the outside world. Years held captive, she is biding her time, waiting for the perfect moment to escape. When a terrified young woman tries to steal the SUV of Devereaux Security's toughest recruit, Isaac's anger quickly turns into a strange sort of protectiveness for the beautiful, bruised stranger. As he tries to bring Jenna to safety, Isaac vows to do whatever it takes to gain her trust…and her heart.

WITH EVERY BREATH
A Slow Burn Novel

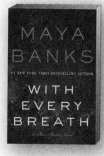

terling never allows anyone close enough to see the man behind penetrable mask—but one woman threatens his carefully leashed trol. She was under his skin and nothing he did rid himself of the an with the courage of a warrior and who thinks nothing of putting her life before others.

SAFE AT LAST
A Slow Burn Novel

They say young love doesn't last, but a girl from the wrong side of the tracks with unique abilities and the hometown golden boy were determined to defy the odds. Until one night forever alters the course of their future, when a devastated Gracie disappears, leaving Zack to agonize over what happened to the girl he loved.

IN HIS KEEPING
A Slow Burn Novel

Arial's only link to her past lies in the one thing that sets her apart—telekinetic powers. Protected by her adoptive parents and hidden from the public, Ari is raised in the lap of luxury, and isolation. That is, until someone begins threatening her life.

KEEP ME SAFE
A Slow Burn Novel

When Caleb Devereaux's younger sister is kidnapped, the scion of a powerful and wealthy family turns to an unlikely source for help: a beautiful and sensitive woman with a gift for finding answers others cannot. But while Ramie can connect to victims and locate them by feeling their pain, her ability comes with a price.